2

# WHEN NIGHT FELL

# WHEN NIGHT FELL

*An Anthology of
Holocaust
Short Stories*

*Edited by
Linda Schermer Raphael
and
Marc Lee Raphael*

*Rutgers University Press*
New Brunswick, New Jersey and London

**Library of Congress Cataloging-in-Publication Data**

When night fell : an anthology of Holocaust short stories / edited by Linda Schermer Raphael
and Marc Lee Raphael.
    p.   cm.
    Includes bibliographical references.
    ISBN 0-8135-2662-0 (cloth : alk. paper). — ISBN 0-8135-2663-9 (paper : alk. paper)
    1. Holocaust, Jewish (1939–1945)—Fiction.   2. Short stories, Jewish—Translations into
English.   I. Raphael, Linda Schermer, 1943–   .   II. Raphael, Marc Lee.
PN6071.H713W54    1999
808.3'108358—dc21                                   98-52808
                                                       CIP

British Cataloging-in-Publication data for this book is available from the British Library

# Contents

# Preface

This anthology has its origin in repeated visits to the Education Resource Center at the United States Holocaust Memorial Museum in Washington, D. C. Among its large numbers of document collections are hundreds of syllabi of Holocaust courses taught in high schools, colleges, and universities in the most far-flung areas of the United States. Anyone seeking to teach this subject is confronted with an overwhelming mass of literature, making it almost impossible for a single individual to keep up with the printed material in every genre and field of inquiry.

Remarkable about many of the syllabi we studied is the wealth of individual short stories, usually photocopied from a journal or a book which were included for courses in history, religion, philosophy, or literature, or even as part of high school curricula. But we did not find a single anthology of short stories nor a book collection suitable for the courses we were teaching. Several anthologies of poetry or of poetry and literature do exist, but no anthology exclusively dedicated to the short story ever seems to have been published.

"Holocaust short stories" has many possible definitions, ranging from stories written by victims of Nazi persecution to stories written after the war by writers who either lived through the events or experienced the beginning of the Nazi regime but managed to flee in time, and still others whose authors imaginatively reflect on those events without having experienced them directly.

This anthology thus represents stories from a wide range of sources. Some were written by those who lived through the ghettos, *l'univers concentrationnaire,* the concentrationary universe, and the death camps. Others are by writers who were refugees from Nazi oppression. And still others are by writers who were born after the war or who had never lived in Nazi Europe, but who are now increasingly contributing to shaping the memory of the Holocaust as well.

Each story is preceded by a brief biographical sketch of the author. The biographical information available about individual authors varies, for some hardly any information could be found at all, leaving the field open to future research about these individuals and their works. Colleagues and friends, too numerous to mention all by name here, have contributed to this volume by sharing their own list of favorite stories. We have tried to incorporate most of the stories that were suggested, and regret that for two or three we would have liked to include, we were unable to obtain rights to publish.

# Introduction

Holocaust survivors and artists who may have been there in imagination only agree that it is impossible to tell exactly what happened as the Nazi Final Solution was put into effect and that this is precisely why they must tell and retell what happened.[1] Speaking for the survivors, Elie Wiesel has said, "What we really wish to say, what we feel we must say cannot be said."[2] And speaking for writers of fiction, D. M. Thomas has said, "The living [cannot] speak for the dead" and those who were not there have "no right to imagine" the events.[3] These are two of many commentators who insist that what was done to the Jews during World War II defies artistic representation and interpretation. In the words of the film critic Ilan Avisar, it is "unrepresentable, unimaginable, incomprehensible."[4] Or, as one survivor said in Claude Lanzmann's film *Shoah,* "No one can describe it. No one can re-create what happened here."[5] Whether everyday language is simply inadequate to express the horrors of places like Auschwitz or whether artistic vision simply falls short of evoking the world of concentration camps, ghettos, and death camps, Lawrence Langer and George Steiner have insisted that it is the normal use of language that is now inadequate to express the horrors of places such as Auschwitz that artistic vision cannot adequately imagine the concentration camps. They thus agree with many others that trying "to speak or write intelligently, interpretatively, about Auschwitz is to misconceive totally the nature of that event and to misconstrue totally the necessary constraints of humanity within language."[6] Langer and Steiner join their voices to many who have affirmed what Theodor Adorno first declared in the early 1950s, "Nach Auschwitz noch Lyrik zu schreiben, ist barbarisch" (to write poetry after Auschwitz is barbaric).[7]

And yet, no survivor has written more fiction than Elie Wiesel. Nor did his hesitancy prevent D. M. Thomas from crafting *The White Hotel.* As Aharon Appelfeld, reflecting on Adorno's admonition, put it, "We must agree with it with all our being . . . but what can we do?" Thus talking about the Holocaust in spite of, or perhaps because of, the fact that they must not, presents writers with a terrible dilemma. For some, like Wiesel, the only narrative that can be told is that of the impossibility of narrative.[8]

Writers who nevertheless feel compelled to write face the struggle of finding a form of expression that has, in Langer's words, the "appropriate tone and point of view, a suitable angle of vision and convincing center of consciousness through which to filter" the Shoah.[9] Sometimes the answer lies in irony. For example, the title of Chaver Paver's story "The Boxing Match" gives no hint of its setting, a death camp, and the story itself is told with almost complete emotional detachment. Explaining that the commandant had been promoted to head the death camp for responsible conduct, the narrator observes, "But here in the death camp, the poor man was bored by the monotonous daily routine of exterminating people and the 'boxing matches' were life-savers for him. Without them, God forbid, he would have gone crazy." In other instances, the descriptions, such as the one of the Commandant's robe as a "swastika besprinkled silken robe," are a mélange of the ordinary, the grotesque and bizarre, and the honorable.

In a manner different from the detached ironic tone of Paver's story, the raconteur narrator in Giorgio Bassani's "A Plaque on Via Mazzini" relates the pretentious, illusory views of the people of Ferrara, among them some Jews, about the way the Jews were treated during and after the war. An ironic moment occurs when Geo, the only survivor of 183 Ferrarese Jews sent to Buchenwald,[10] appears as the city is about to erect a monument to the Jews who had been deported in 1943. His return elicits mixed, frequently paradoxical, responses. Some citizens do not recognize Geo at all, while others believe that his corpulence proves that he could not have been in a camp, or that the treatment in the camps could not have been all that bad. To all of the town's people, he is the incarnation of Jewish duplicity in which they need to believe.

While Langer urges writers to find a suitable narrative form for representing the Shoah, other writers question the appropriateness of aesthetic forms in general. The self-contained universe of Nazi concentration camps generated its own vocabulary and usage, infusing ordinary language with euphemistic meanings so that writers of the Holocaust face the added dilemma of having to use language and terms coined by the Nazis.[11] Some solve this problem by inventing new terms: Arthur A. Cohen calls the death camps "the tremendum," and Alan L. Berger, following Wiesel, speaks of "the Event."[12] The traditional words for describing calamities fail to comprehend the Shoah.[13] Sara Nomberg-Przytyk's story "Old Words—New Meanings" addresses precisely this issue of investing common language with new, sinister meanings. Neutral nouns like "gas" and "selection" take on horrifying meanings in the context of Auschwitz; a positive verb like "to organize" gains ambivalence in connection with morally ambiguous struggles for personal survival.

Other writers, especially poets, use "a language and imagery of silence to overcome the silence imposed by the incomprehensibility and horror of the Holocaust experience."[14] In the words of Aharon Appelfeld: "You have to appreciate the silence that lies between one word and another."[15] Story writers must ask themselves Langer's question:"Can artistic vision as a technique ever adequately convey the experiences of the dead and the survivors?"[16] Appelfeld's fiction is silent about the Holocaust, except for certain veiled clues that hint at the underlying subject of his narratives. In the story "Bertha," the Holocaust is implied only within the context of liberation. What one critic has referred to as the "partial suspension of the realistic element" becomes in Appelfeld's fiction a particular angle of vision that takes the reader deep into the consciousness of characters for whom language and meaning have become troubled partners.[17] In the mysterious, almost surreal landscape of "Bertha," Max, a survivor, who carries with him a dark secret without a name, merges his identity with that of the disabled child/woman Bertha. The narrator reveals his fears of exposure and vulnerability:"Sometimes your cunning leaves you and you are left naked and ashamed . . . vulnerable as a bare neck at the change of seasons." However, Max is unable to express his anguish and seeks refuge from the world in the cinema. In the visual and vocal representations of film, he attempts to find the self and the secret he cannot name.

In another Appelfeld story, "Kitty," an eleven-year-old Jewish girl is hidden in a convent. Her dilemma is expressed in a French lesson when, the narrator relates, "the words hit the stone and returned to her, chilled." Silence envelops her as she is cut off from her roots, unable to make sense of her present condition, which however, in the end, she comes to understand better than the other characters, or even the narrator. Hidden underground as German soldiers encroach on the convent, she develops a relationship with the fermenting beets stored in the cellar. Her inner turmoil subsides and yields to a profound quiescence as the story draws to its wondrous end.

Agnon uses symbolic and fantastic images that draw the reader into the narrator's confusion about what is real and what is not. Long repressed memories emerge in dreamlike displacements and condensations. "There are guests who come no matter how tightly one's door is shut, as they are the thoughts surrounding our actions," Agnon's narrator concludes. For the Holocaust survivor the story is never-ending.

At a time when literary critics seem to have erased the word "truth" from their vocabulary, few short story writers give expression to what "really" happened. Historians of the Holocaust focus on events of a specific time (mostly 1939–1944) and place (mostly Nazi-occupied Europe); imaginative writers are concerned with these events and imagined ones, what Hayden White calls "the fictions of factual representation."[18] The stories selected for this anthology meet the test of correspondence; each represents the human experience of the Shoah and upholds a rigid standard of "truth."[19] Fiction may never be more successful in evoking a sense of life in the ghettos and the camps than eyewitness testimonies, but we join Hayden White in the hope that "the discourse of the

historian and that of the imaginative writer [will] overlap, resemble, or correspond with each other."[20]

Of course, the reader may not always separate fiction from reality, but this
is acceptable since the best fiction weaves the documentary and the imagined
into a seamless whole. The Library of Congress categorizes Ida Fink's stories
as "fiction," notes Sara R. Horowitz, even though Fink insists that the events
"really happened." Art Spiegelman has criticized the *New York Times* for plac-
ing his cartoon books on its fiction bestseller list; they are, he insists, "factual."
If anything they are, he says, on the borderline between fiction and nonfiction. At the other end of the continuum from Agnon and Appelfeld are stories
that read like memoirs or factual accounts. The above-mentioned story by Sara
Nomberg-Przytyk, "Old Words—New Meanings," in particular, resembles a
factual account. Henryk Grynberg's "Uncle Aron" relates the narrator's uncle's
recollections of past family history as well as his reflections on the present (of
the story) in memoir style. However, like Hans Peter Richter in "The Teacher,"
which recounts a teacher's first encounter with antisemitism, Grynberg's use
of extensive dialogue gives the effect of a work of fiction. For literary artists
the question is not whether their work is true or factual, but how well their
art illuminates previously hidden truths.[21]

Whether a story was written by Nazi victims or is a story about those
victims, it is a representation and a representation is, of course, never perfect. The fragility of human memory limits what is being recalled. In addition, there is often a reluctance to narrate, based on the feeling that once
narrated or represented the horror is no longer the horror that it was.
The Nazis sought to eliminate the physical presence of all Jews, to erase
their memory from literature, art, and life. Omer Bartov is certainly
right to insist that the post–Holocaust world "can never suffer from too
much memory."[22]

The relationship between history and art, and how they become memory, is complex. There are cultural memories, collective memories, public
memories, individual memories, deep memories, and common memories.[23]
Memory alone, of course, guarantees nothing; it depends on what type of memory is evoked. As James E. Young, in his book about Holocaust memorials,
reminds us, public memories are constructed and our "understanding" of events
depends on memory's construction. Stories about the Holocaust are not so
much about the actual events as they are about how the events are remembered, how they are imagined. Indeed, the Holocaust did not enter everyday
American consciousness until the late 1960s; recovery of the history of the
Holocaust was a long arduous process of remembrance, retrieval, and representation. And in the course of moving from what we know (historical facts)
to how we remember, in the interplay of event and word, short story writers have played a pivotal role.[24]

In a particularly complex and remarkable story of remembering, "My Father's Deaths," Yehuda Amichai's narrator seeks to understand himself by remembering certain milestones in his father's life, particularly as they relate to war. The father had fought for the German side in World War I. When the Nazis came to power he was forced to flee with his family from Germany, his native land. Through a child's narrative perspective as filtered through the narrator's later contemplative self, the reader identifies with both the voice of the adult, who knows the later significance of events, and the vision of the child who experiences the events close-up with great emotional intensity, but comprehends them on a different level. The narrative effect is similar to Agnon's "The Night." However, in Amichai's narrative the twilight is not a place where the real and the unreal meet, but one where pure feeling is rendered in the symbolic language of a fully mature articulation.

The story begins with the narrator remembering the back of his father's neck as he saw it in synagogue on Yom Kippur, the Jewish Day of Atonement as a child. Because the neck "is always fixed and unchanging," unlike the face which is constantly transfiguring itself, this childhood vision adumbrates the themes of the story: the desire for permanence, the reality of continual flux in the world, and the need to atone. While memory does not provide a simple intuition into the reality we all share, such as death, it offers the possibility of bringing together aspects of reality, human desire, and atonement for the world's cruelty.

The father's deaths occurred on various occasions: at the Yom Kippur service, when he is "dressed in his white winding-sheet"; during the four years of trench warfare in World War I (the narrator thinks that he and his father might have killed one another had World War I and II occurred simultaneously, since he fought in the latter war against Germany—a significant testament not only to the changing world, but the killing of one's brethren); when the family left Germany for Palestine; and the time of his actual death. His father's death "when they came to arrest him because of the Nazi armband which I had found and thrown into the garbage-can" marks the end of the narrator's childhood: the moment when he realizes that the Nazis could burst into the house against the father's wishes—no doubt a common experience for Jewish children living under Nazi terror. In lyrical, metaphoric language, the story reflects on the infinite regression of terror and death, symbolized by the powerlessness of the father to protect the child against violence.

Some critics and writers believe that the human imagination can create (and re-create) nuanced, multilayered worlds in which historical facts and fantasy correspond but little. The worlds of Amichai, Agnon, and Appelfeld reflect not so much their authors' impressions of the Holocaust as their ideas about it. Rachmil Bryks, on the other hand, once argued that writers who want to proclaim what happened in Europe should tell the world what the Germans, aided by their creatures in other nations, did to the Jews and to others; they should write "concisely, compressed, without embellishment, without adornment." In other words, their aim should not be to "create art."[25] Only then will their work will be genuine, not an artifice.

Bryks's stories adhere to his dictum. The settings are unambiguously Eastern Europe at the time of the Nazi occupation. They are filled with scenes familiar to him from the Lodz ghetto and a journey in a cattle car to what was to be the final destination for many.[26] In "The Last Journey," the passengers bemoan the greed and selfishness of the ghetto inhabitants in their dealings with one another and blame themselves for excessive acquiescence to the Germans. In the course of the conversation, the central character, Blaustein, comes to reconsider his attitude toward his fellow Jews as well as his view of religion. Concern with the nature of God also informs Bryks's story "Children of the Lodz Ghetto."[27] It begins with Tobtche, a much-loved young woman who is both a teacher and playmate to the children of the ghetto. She teaches through a popular rhyme: "Alef, bet gimel / There is a God in himel (heaven);/ Daled, hay, vov" which continues with praises of God. Another rhyme the children chant is about Rumkowsky, the "Elder of the Jews," who, according to Bryks's story "Berele in the Ghetto," "unctuously, personally, possessively regarded everything in the ghetto, even its inhabitants, as 'his.'"[28]

"Bread" is a dialogue between Blaustein and Zeide, who both refuse to submit to Rumkowsky's abuse of power and treachery. Their rage is directed against his "stooges," as they try to preserve their own "integrity." "Artists in the Ghetto" raises the possibility of psychological resistance through art, even if the infrequent creations and responses provided only a sporadic, temporary uplift for both artists and spectators.[29]

In keeping with Bryks's counsel to writers to make their accounts of the Holocaust experience as straightforward as possible, Rachel Korn, in "The Road of No Return," depicts the dilemma of a Jewish family in Galicia faced with having to choose a member to go with the Nazis. There are scenes of the family's everyday life: women preparing food, children scuffling while playing. Yet the mother's "bottled up fear and dread of the unavoidable future now found its way through some obscure channel inside her" when she looks at her fourteen-year-old daughter. The father, on the other hand, reacts to his son "as if he himself were guilty for...having taken a wife and for having brought children into the world." The theme of logical behavior in a situation that defies all reason, and especially all notions of humanity, is realized as the story reaches its dramatic denouement.

Our earlier discussion of the problem of "truth" has already shown the very thin line that separates fact from fiction. In the same vein, Robert Alter has observed that many stories "break down the divisions between vision and factual experience."[30] Most writers who have written about the Holocaust, explicitly or obliquely, have themselves experienced the places and events they describe in their fiction. Fiction complements our knowledge of "historical" facts, but even the "facts" of the Holocaust need interpreters; they can come to life only through interpretation. The stories in this anthology contain more "life" than historical "fact," for they exist independent of their interpreters. The short story, therefore, represents an important vehicle for understanding history and links the receptive reader to the events of the past. Art, of course, implies artifice and readers must be aware of the difference between fictional representation and the Holocaust universe as it existed in reality.

True, one cannot separate the tale from the telling, what a story is about is a question of how it is told. But, unlike Elie Wiesel, we do not believe that "only those who lived. . .[through Auschwitz] in their flesh and in their minds can possibly transform their experiences into knowledge" and that all others "can never do so." Wiesel, in fact, has often demanded "silence from whoever was not there," while Appelfeld has argued that "good literature on the Holocaust comes only from those who were Holocaust children." Others, he says, "have written memoirs, but not good literature."[31]

A subgenre that has grown out of Holocaust literature is the story of children caught in the Holocaust. Jerzy Zawieyski's "Conrad in the Ghetto" is in part the story of a child who serves as a messenger between two Jewish intellectuals, separated by ghetto restrictions. As the title suggests, the narrative's intellectual power derives from reflections on the writer Joseph Conrad, among other writers, but it gains its emotional intensity from the fate of the child. Arnôst Lustig's collection, *Children of the Holocaust,* is specifically dedicated to telling the stories of young victims. As in Amichai's "My Father's Deaths," an adolescent boy's anxiety over the loss of his father is the focus of "The Lemon." While the father lies dead in the family's ghetto home, the boy, Ervin, desperately attempts to find food for his mother, whom he remembers as once beautiful, and his sister, who is close to death. Along the way he finds that even for his friends among the gentiles, the Jews are the scapegoats. By contrast, "Stephen and Anne" is a story of beauty and innocence, found in the passion that develops between two young people in the ghetto. The language of tenderness and desire contrasts sharply with the surrounding brutality and lends the narrative extraordinary power.

Leonard Tushnet and Sandi Wisenberg, two American writers who never lived in Europe, nonetheless have written fiction about the Holocaust. Tushnet's "The Ban" takes place in the immediate postwar period. Two brothers are reunited outside the now-barricaded gates of Auschwitz. They exchange tragic stories of the deaths of neighbors and friends, but soon the conversation turns to God who "shamed [the Jews] before the nations" by leaving them "unjustly . . . cut off." Both find recourse in a belief in justice and brotherly love. Simple on the surface, this narrative is a complex examination of the survivors' psyche. The attitudes toward God and personal relationships in the aftermath of the death camps is also the theme of Chaim Grade's "My Quarrel with Hersh Rasseyner." Grade's story may be more polished in style and content, but Tushnet lends a fresh perspective to questions of the relationship of an all-powerful, benevolent God to his people in light of the events of the Holocaust.

Like many writers and critics, among them those discussed above, S. L. Wisenberg is preoccupied with the question of how, if at all, the Holocaust can be represented artistically. The narrator of her story "Liberator" is concerned with the effect of the Holocaust on later generations. The story centers on an American soldier who was among the liberators of Mauthausen, as told by his daughter, and the effects of the Holocaust on contemporary American Jews. "My father and his buddies," says the daughter, "opened the doors . . . and liberated the people who might have been us, the people we used to be."

In "My Mother's War," Wisenberg takes up the problem of artistic representation of the Holocaust and its impact on contemporary life from the perspective of an American Jewish woman whose mother was an artist. Though the narrator's mother had not been in Europe during World War II, nor were any of her known relatives among the victims, her final artistic effort, interpreted and assembled posthumously by an artist appointed by the daughter, is an environmental piece intended to replicate for the viewer/participant the experience of someone entering a camp. Both stories illustrate the paradox that the people we used to be and the people we now are have not been liberated from the subject of the Holocaust. Rather, "we," like many of our contemporaries, are increasingly bound by the imperative of seeking to understand an event beyond comprehension and to remember what most of us did not personally experience.

The narrator's reaction to the Nazi atrocities and the writer's own attitude toward her Jewish origins give voice to several profound questions concerning the Holocaust and Judaism, as well as the effect of the events on the life of an American Jew who seemingly had no direct connection with them. Just as Sholem Asch, a Russian Jew who emigrated to America before the Holocaust, raises the question in his story "Heil, Hitler" of whether a German Jew living in New York after the war should hate Germany, so Wisenberg gives resonance to responses to the Holocaust in a time and place removed from the actual events and from her own direct experience.

Artists like Wisenberg confirm our view that even if they were not there, it is still possible for them to imagine what it was like at Auschwitz and that representation should not be left to survivors alone. For Saul Friedländer, the "voices of the contemporaries of the second generation are as powerful as the best work produced by contemporaries of the Nazi epoch." To Arthur A. Cohen, the Holocaust is accessible to all because "all Jews are survivors and the children of survivors." And Abba Kovner, himself a survivor of the Vilna ghetto, insists that "the Holocaust is ... not something peculiar to those who experienced the horrors themselves, but ... is part of the historical consciousness of every Jewish generation everywhere." Yael Feldman has noted that in Israel most Shoah literature, from its very inception, has been the work of writers who never experienced the terrors of the Holocaust firsthand, and this is becoming truer of young writers every year.[32] This collection permits the reader to compare the works of writers who lived in Nazi-occupied Europe with those who lived far from Europe or were not yet born, as they all struggle with the moral and artistic problems of writing about the Holocaust.

## ◆ Notes

1. Jean-François Lyotard, *Heidegger and "the jews."* (Minneapolis: University of Minnesota Press, 1990).

2. Elie Wiesel, "Does the Holocaust Lie Beyond the Reach of Art?" *New York Times* (17 April 1983).

3. D. M. Thomas, *The White Hotel* (New York: Viking Press, 1981), 251.

4. Quoted in *Thinking About the Holocaust: After a Half Century,* ed. Alvin Rosenfeld (Bloomington: University of Indiana Press, 1997), 51. See also Isaac Deutscher, *The Non-Jewish Jew and Other Essays* (New York: Oxford University Press, 1968), 163.

5. *Shoah: The Complete Text of the Film by Claude Lanzmann* (New York: Pantheon Books, 1985), 6.

6. George Steiner, "The Long Life of a Metaphor: An Approach to the 'Shoah' " in *Writing and the Holocaust,* ed. Berel Lang (New York: Holmes & Meier, 1988), 156. See also Lawrence L. Langer, *Holocaust Testimonies: The Ruins of Memory* (New Haven, Conn.: Yale University Press, 1991) and *The Holocaust and the Literary Imagination* (New Haven, Conn.: Yale University Press, 1975).

7. "Engagement" in *Lyrik nach Auschwitz: Adorno und die Dichter,* ed. Philip Kiedaisch (Stuttgart, Germany: Reclam, 1995), 53. See also Adorno's famous similar statement: "Nach Auschwitz ein Gedicht zu schreiben, ist barbarisch" (to write a poem after Auschwitz is barbaric), the header to "Kulturkritik und Gesellschaft" in *Lyrik nach Auschwitz,* ed. Rolf Tiedemann, 27, and in *Gesammelte Schriften,* vol. 10 (Frankfurt/Main, Germany: Suhrkamp Verlag, 1974), 30.

8. Aharon Appelfeld, "After the Holocaust," in Lang, ed., *Writing and the Holocaust,* 83.

9. Lawrence L. Langer, *Admitting the Holocaust: Collected Essays* (New York: Oxford University Press, 1995), 99.

10. There were in fact seven hundred to nine hundred Jews in Ferrara in 1943, eighty-seven of whom were deported by the Nazis. Four or five returned. See Marilyn Schneider, *Vengeance of the Victims: History and Symbol in Giorgio Bassani's Fiction* (Minneapolis: University of Minnesota Press, 1986), 57.

11. Henry Friedlander, *The Origins of Nazi Genocide: From Euthanasia to the Final Solution* (Chapel Hill: University of North Carolina Press, 1995); Sidrah D. Ezrahi, *By Words Alone: The Holocaust in Literature* (Chicago: University of Chicago Press, 1980).

12. Arthur A. Cohen, *The Tremendum: A Theological Interpretation of the Holocaust* (New York: Crossroad, 1981), 19; Alan L. Berger, "The Holocaust Forty Years After: Too Much or Not Enough Attention" in *Holocaust Studies Annual* III (1985):1–20.

13. See also Langer, *Admitting the Holocaust* and Nachman Blumenthal, "On the Nazi Vocabulary" *Yad Vashem Studies* VI (1967): 69–82.

14. David H. Hirsch, "Deconstructing the Holocaust" *Holocaust and Genocide Studies* 9, 1 (spring 1995): 138.

15. "On Being Hidden: Silence and the Creative Process—A Conversation with Aharon Appelfeld" *Dimensions* 6, 3 (1992):16.

16. See Langer, *Holocaust and Literary Imagination*.

17. "Whose Story Is It Anyway? Ideology and Psychology in the Representation of the Shoah in Israeli Literature" in *Probing the Limits of Representation: Nazism and the "Final Solution,"* Saul Friedländer ed. (Cambridge, Mass.: Harvard University Press, 1992), 227.

18. Hayden White, *Tropics of Discourse: Essays in Cultural Criticism* (Baltimore, Md.: Johns Hopkins University Press, 1978), 121–134.

19. Alvin Rosenfeld, *A Double Dying: Reflections on Holocaust Literature* (Bloomington: Indiana University Press, 1980).

20. White, *Tropics of Discourse,* 121. This is in contrast to Langer, who sees a "conflict" between "historical fact" and "imaginative truth." See Langer, *Holocaust and Literary Imagination*.

21. For a discussion of the relationship between history and fiction, history and art, see the opening pages of Sara R. Horowitz, *Voicing the Void: Muteness and Memory in Holocaust Fiction* (Albany: State University of New York Press, 1997).

22. Omer Bartov, *Murder in Our Midst: The Holocaust, Industrial Killing, and Representation* (New York: Oxford University Press, 1996), 130.

23. On cultural and collective memories, see *Holocaust Remembrance: The Shapes of Memory,* Geoffrey Hartman ed. (Cambridge, Mass.: Blackwell, 1994), 19–20. On public memory, see James E. Young, *The Texture of Memory: Holocaust Memorials and Meaning* (New Haven, Conn.: Yale University Press, 1993). On individual and collective memories, see Dan Diner, "Memory and Method: Variance in Holocaust Narrations" in *Studies in Contemporary Jewry: An Annual* XIII (1997): 84–99. On deep and common memories, see Charlotte Delbo, *La Mémoire et les jours* (Paris: Berg International, 1985), 13.

24. Young, *Texture of Memory,* 15. Also, Judith Miller, *One, by One, by One: Facing the Holocaust* (New York: Simon and Schuster, 1990), 9.

25. Tony Kushner, *The Holocaust and the Liberal Imagination: A Social and Cultural History* (Cambridge, Mass.: Blackwell, 1994), 249 and 276.

26. Rachmil Bryks, "How to Write Churban Literature" in *Hebrew Literature in the Wake of the Holocaust,* Leon I. Yudkin ed. (Rutherford, N. J.: Fairleigh Dickinson University Press, 1993), 487.

27. See *Lodz Ghetto: Inside a Community under Siege,* Alan Adelson and Robert Lapides eds. (New York: Viking, 1989).

28. The Germans set up a council of elders in Lodz and made Rumkowsky the Elder of the Jews. When the Lodz ghetto was established in late winter 1940, he became its virtual ruler.

29. In *The Chronicle of the Lodz Ghetto 1941–1944,* L. Dobroszycki ed. (New Haven, Conn.: Yale University Press, 1984), 30. One entry notes: "Yesterday at the House of Culture, there was a symphony concert conducted by [David] Benjamin and organized for the women workers of the rubber coat factories."

30. *Modern Hebrew Literature,* Robert Alter ed. (New York: Behrman House, 1975), 315.

31. *Point of View: An Anthology of Short Stories,* James M. Moffet and Kenneth R. McElheny eds. (New York: New American Library, 1956, 1966), 567; Elie Wiesel, *From the Kingdom of Memory* (New York: Summit Books, 1940), 166. The Wiesel phrase comes from Feldman, *Probing the Limits,* 228. Wiesel has made this statement frequently; for example, "Only those men and women who lived through the experience know what it was, and others ... will never know." *Comprehending the Holocaust,* 12. Also, Wiesel, "On Being Hidden," 16.

32. Friedländer, "Trauma, Memory, and Transference," in *Holocaust Remembrance,* 263; see also *Judaism in the Modern World,* Alan L. Berger ed. (New York: New York University Press, 1994); "From Generation to Generation" in *Holocaust and Genocide Studies* 8, 1 (spring 1994): 107; Feldman, "Whose Story Is It Anyway?", 228; see, among many, Melvin Judes Bukiet, *Stories of an Imaginary Childhood* (Evanston, Ill.: Northwestern University Press, 1992), *While the Messiah Tarries* (New York: Harcourt Brace and Company, 1995), and *After* (1996); Thane Rosenbaum, *Elijah Visible: Stories* (Evanston, Ill.: Northwestern University Press, 1996); Harvey Grossinger, *The Quarry: Stories* (Athens: University of Georgia Press, 1997).

# WHEN NIGHT FELL

*S. Y. Agnon 1888–1970*   Agnon, whose birth name was Shmuel Yosef Haleski Czaczkes, was born in Buczacz, Galicia, which was then part of Austria-Hungary, and moved to Palestine in 1907 or 1908. He returned to Europe in 1913 and lived mostly in Germany until 1924 when he returned permanently to Palestine, except for a period of three years (1929–1932) when he traveled through the Jewish communities of Poland and Galicia. He subsequently shaped these experiences into a historical novel, *A Guest for the Night* (Hebrew 1938/39; English 1968). The recipient of the Bialik Prize in 1934 and 1954 as well as the Israel Prize for Literature in 1954 and 1958, Agnon was awarded the Nobel Prize for Literature in 1966.

According to Agnon, his parents combined two worlds; his father was qualified for the rabbinate and versed in Jewish philosophy, while his mother read widely in classical German literature. He too combined two worlds; Judaic tradition, or a vocabulary from classical Jewish literature (Bible, Mishnah, Midrash, liturgy), and a deep embracing of European literature in stories and novels ranging from simple folk tales to complex, expressionistic narratives. His style changed with the rise of Hitler and the Nazis; the light rhythm and simple narrative structure came to compete with nightmarish images of madness, violence, disintegration, spiritual decay, disorientation, alienation, disillusionment, and loss.

## THE NIGHT

When night fell I went home; that is, I went to the hotel room I had taken for my wife and myself. I was hurrying, as I knew that my wife was tired out by all the travel and wanted to sleep, and I had no intention of disturbing her.

There was a multitude of people in the streets, mainly new immigrants, who were arriving here from all over the world. For many years they had wasted away in the death camps, or wandered aimlessly over hill and valley, and through forests, all this time without seeing so much as the flicker of a candle, and now that they'd stepped from the dark into this sudden brightness, they seemed puzzled and somewhat suspicious, not being able to grasp whether all the lights had been left burning by an oversight, or whether it was part of some scheme of the authorities.

An old man came toward me, wearing a greenish coat that came down to his knees, exactly like the coat Mr. Halbfried, the bookseller in our town, used to wear for as long as I remember. The coat had lost most of its color, but had kept its original shape. Short coats are better at keeping their shape than long ones, because long coats sweep the ground and get frayed, whereas short coats flutter in the air, and the ground cannot harm them in any way. Even though their appearance might have changed, their hems remain as the tailor finished them and seem to have retained their perfection.

While I was wondering whether this was really Mr. Halbfried, he ran his weary eyes over me and said:"From the day that I arrived here I've been looking for you, and now that we've met I'm happy twice over, once because I've found someone from my home town, and twice because that someone happens to be you."The old man was so excited that he forgot to greet me properly, instead of which he straightway reeled off a string of names, people he'd asked about me, and after each name he'd express his amazement that so-and-so didn't know me, and had he himself failed to recognize me the moment he saw me, he could have passed me as if we were not fellow townsmen. Having come around to mentioning our town, he began talking about the past, the time when we were neighbors, and his bookstore was filled with books that united all the learned people of the town, who were passing in and out of the shop all day, and having heated discussions about what was going on in the world, and about the future, and coming to the conclusion that the world was evolving into a better place, and there was I, a small boy, fingering the books, climbing the ladder, standing at the top reading, not realizing that I was endangering myself; for had someone blundered into the ladder by mistake, I could very easily have fallen off. But as if the large stock of books which he kept were not sufficient for me, I had asked him to get me *The Poem of Jerusalem Liberated.* However, he couldn't remember any more whether he'd placed the order before I emigrated to the Land of Israel, or whether I did so before he'd placed the order.

Another thing he was reminded of, said Mr. Halbfried, was the time they showed my first poems to that old mystic who had written two interpretations of the prayer book, and the old man had looked at them and murmured, *"Kehadin kamtza dilevushe mine uve"* ["like the snail whose garb is a part of it"], and the learned listeners tried hard to understand the meaning of these words, and did not succeed. He, Mr. Halbfried continued, was still puzzled that they never took the trouble to look them up in a dictionary, and that he himself did not do so, although he had a number of dictionaries in stock, and could have done so quite easily, yet somehow never did.

He broke off his story and asked me was I angry with his brother?—Why? His brother had just passed us and greeted me, and I made as if I didn't see him.

Mr. Halbfried's last words shocked and saddened me. I had not noticed anyone greeting me; as for the man who had passed us, I was under the impression that it was Mr. Halbfried himself. As I didn't wish him to think that I would turn my eyes away from people who greet me, I said to him: "I swear I didn't notice your brother; had I noticed him, I would have been the first to greet him." So Mr. Halbfried began talking once more of the good old days, of his bookshop and the people who came to it. Every time Mr. Halbfried mentioned a name, he did so with great warmth, the way we used to talk about good friends in those long-lost days before the war.

After a while, Mr. Halbfried stopped and said: "I shall leave you now, as I do not want you to keep a man waiting who wishes to see you." With that he shook my hand and went away.

The man Mr. Halbfried had mentioned was not known to me, nor did he seem to be waiting for me; however, Mr. Halbfried's mistake came in handy, as it enabled me to shake the old man off politely, and so avoid disturbing my wife's sleep.

But Mr. Halbfried had not been mistaken; after I'd gotten rid of him, this man barred my way, then poked his stick into the ground and leaned on it with both hands, while looking at me. Then he lifted his hand in greeting, lifted it to his cap, a round cap of sheepskin leather, and while he was doing so, he said: "Don't you know me?" I said to myself: Why tell him I don't know him? So I gave him a warm look and said: "Certainly I know you, you're none other than—" He interrupted me and said: "I was sure you'd know me, if not for my own sake, then for the sake of my son. What do you think of his poems?" From this I realized that he was the father of someone or other who had sent me his book of poems. I said to myself: Why tell him that I haven't looked at them yet? So I gave him a warm look and said whatever it is one says on these occasions. Yet he didn't seem satisfied with it. So I said to myself: Why not add a few nice words? So I added a few compliments; but he was still unsatisfied, and began singing his son's praises himself, and I kept nodding my head in agreement, so that an onlooker would have thought that the praise came from my mouth.

Having done, he said: "No doubt you wish to make my son's acquaintance, so go to the concert hall, that's where you'll find him. My son is a well-loved man, all the doors are open to him, not only the doors of music but the doors of all the important houses in town. Why, if my son desired, let's say, to ride on a mouse, why, the animal would rush up to him with its tail between its legs and beg him to take a ride. Truly, I myself would love to go to that concert, all the best members of our intelligentsia will be there, the trouble is they won't let you in if you haven't got a ticket." Saying this, he rubbed two fingers together and made a noise with his lips, as if to say, you need real coins for that.

I kept quiet and did not say a word. It was some years now that I hadn't gone to a concert. I could never understand how a crowd of people could assemble at a fixed date and hour, in a special hall, just to hear some singing. Nor could I understand how it was that the singers were ready to lift up their voices in song at the exact hour the ticket holders were filling the hall, ready to listen.

I'm just a small-town boy; I can grasp that someone is singing because his heart is full; but this singing in front of an audience rich enough to buy tickets, because some impresario organized it all, was beyond me. So when I saw how much this man wanted to go to the concert, I asked myself whether I should help him, and decided to buy him a ticket. He saw what I was thinking, and said, "I won't go without you." I asked myself whether to go with him, and then I said, "All right, I'll buy two tickets, and we'll go together." He started feeling the air, as if it were full of tickets. Again he rubbed two fingers together, and made a popping noise, like a cork coming out of a bottle.

So we walked together, and he kept praising the concert hall, where there was so much music one could almost drown in it. Then he told me about this violinist whose violin was so precious that even the case he carried it in was worth more than the instruments of other violinists. Then he returned to his son, to whom poetical rhymes came for the sole purpose of the matching of words. Then he returned to the subject of the tickets, out of respect for which the doors used to open themselves. Suddenly he began worrying, as it occurred to him that he could be wasting his time, for, although I seemed willing enough to buy him a ticket, what if every seat was sold out, or supposing there was only one single ticket left—wouldn't I buy it for myself, and leave him standing outside. Thus we came to my hotel.

I said to him: "Wait here, I'm going in to change, and then we're off to the concert." He poked his stick into the ground, leaned on it with both hands, and stood there.

I left him outside and told the doorman I wanted two tickets for the concert. The doorman said: "I have two good tickets, which were ordered by the Duke of Ilivio, but he left them with me, as he cannot come since he has been called to the Emperor." Here the doorman whispered to me that the Emperor had arrived secretly in town, with most of his retinue, dukes, lords, and officers, and that some of them were actually staying at our hotel.

I took the tickets and went up to my room, leaving the door open so that I could change by the light in the corridor, and not have to turn on the light in the room, which would have awakened my wife. I walked in on tiptoe, noiselessly, and to my surprise and distress I found a strange man in the room. Who was that who dared to enter my room in the dark of the night? Should the earth refuse to open at his feet and swallow him, then I would be forced to throw him out myself, and not too politely, either.

As I approached him, I saw that it was Moshele, a relative of mine. This Moshele and I had grown up together, and we went through difficult times together, until one day he was called up into the army, where he stayed until he was wounded and dismissed. We thought that he had been burned in the gas chambers of Auschwitz, but here be stood, alive, in my room.

I said, "What brought you here?" He said, "My troubles brought me here. I have been shuffling from one mound of refuse to another without a roof over my head, and when I heard you were here I came running, for I was sure that you would put me up."

I said to him: "Do I have a home that you should ask to sleep here? As you can see, I'm myself but a guest for the night."

He said: "All I'm asking is a place on the floor."

I began laughing. A hotel where dukes and lords live, and he wants to sleep on the floor.

I don't know if his brain succeeded in grasping what I meant and if his heart accepted my words. In any case, he got up and left.

I went to the window to watch him go, and I saw him in the street, cowering as he was hit by the whips of the coachmen who drove the coaches of the nobility. I called to him, but he didn't answer me; I called to him again and he didn't answer, probably being too busy trying to evade the whips to hear my voice. I decided to call louder, but then I remembered that my wife was sleeping, so I didn't. And it is probably just as well, for had I shouted, all the other coachmen would have seen him too, and joined in beating him.

I looked after Moshele until he disappeared from view. Then I went to the wardrobe to change.

Two small children came in and started walking around me in circles. As I opened the door of the wardrobe to take some clothes, one of them jumped in, and his brother jumped after him, and they shut the wardrobe door behind them. I was somewhat perplexed; as they were probably the sons of a duke or a lord, I couldn't very well be rude to them. On the other hand, I couldn't let them go on playing, as they were liable to wake my wife.

Their governess came and helped me out of this trouble. She said to them: "If I may be so bold as to say, it behooves not the princes to enter the room of a strange person."

I apologized to the governess for having left the door of my room open and caused the two king's sons to enter my room. I added that I was going to the concert and had only come to dress.

The governess examined my clothes with her eyes and said: "You can't show yourself in that collar you're wearing." I said to her: "Yes, you're quite right."

She said: "Surely, you can find another collar." "Probably," I said. She said: "Go on, put it on." I said to her: "I am afraid that when the king's son did me the honor of jumping into my wardrobe, he trampled on my collars, and they got soiled." She said: "In that case, I'll tie your tie. Your gracious highnesses, would you be so kind as to leave the room until I finish tying the tie of this gentleman, who is the brother of your teacher." The little boys stood there and looked very surprised that this creature, which had been created to serve them, should now wish to serve a simple mortal.

The graciousness of the young lady and the envy of the king's sons put me into a much better mood. I stuttered somewhat and said: "It is not my custom to go to concerts, but what is a custom worth if you're not ready to disregard it for the sake of another person." The young lady didn't pay much attention to my words; she was too busy tying and then untying every knot she tied, saying "It wasn't such a knot I meant to tie, now I shall tie one that is much handsomer." Finally, she stroked my arm and said: "Look in the mirror and see how beautifully tied your tie is." I said to her: "I cannot look in the mirror." "Why?" "Because the mirror is screwed onto the inside of the wardrobe door, and if I opened it wide it would squeak and wake my wife." "Your wife?" screamed the young lady in a rage. "And here you were talking to me as if we were alone in the room. If your wife is here, then go and be happy with her." With that the young lady went away.

"Who were you talking to," asked my wife. I said to her: "No one." She said: "I must have been dreaming." I said to her: "Dream or not, I'm going out for a walk, and won't be back till after midnight."

I went looking for the man who was waiting for me in front of the hotel, but he was nowhere to be seen. I asked the doorman about him; he answered: "Some time ago I did see a person loitering in front of the hotel. Had I known he was a friend of yours, sir, I would have looked at him more carefully." I said to the doorman: "Where could he be now?" "Where? I really don't know." "Which way did he go?" "Well," said the doorman, "I seem to remember that he turned right, or maybe it was left, people like these have round shoulders and one never knows quite which way they turn." I gave him a tip. He bowed low and said: "If your excellency would care to listen to my advice, he would visit the servants' quarters in the hotel, as the serfs of the nobles have brought a Jewish clown with them, and it is quite possible that the man your excellency is looking for has gone there to see the fun."

I went to the servants' quarters of the hotel, and saw the serfs sitting like masters, their bellies shaking with laughter, and a small man, shrunken and beautiful, standing on the big stage doing tricks, and talking all the while. When the tricks were funny, his voice was sad, and when they were sad, his voice was funny. I wondered whether he did it on purpose. It seemed to me to be great art, being funny in a sad voice, and being sad in a funny voice. I looked around and found the man I was searching for. I waved the two tickets at him, but he pretended not to see me, and left. It seemed as if his leaving were only temporary, because of me, that is, and he was likely to return as soon as I had gone.

Another man came up to me; he had a long face and a cheerful beard. He stroked his beard and said: "Who are you looking for?" I told him. He said: "I could manage to go with you to the concert." I threw a look at him and shouted in amazement: "What! You?" He shook his beard and said: "Why not?" I repeated what I had said before, only with a great deal of sarcasm: "What! You?" He disappeared, and so did his beard. "What do we do now?" I thought to myself. I waved the tickets in the air, but nothing happened. The man I was waving at didn't show up. So I said to myself: Not only can't I give him the pleasure of a concert, I'm even preventing him from the pleasure of seeing the clown, as he won't show his face in the audience as long as I'm here. I got up and left.

As this man didn't wish to come, I gave up the idea of going to the concert; but, having told my wife that I wouldn't be in before midnight, not until the singer had finished his recital, I had time to take a walk. I began thinking about what had happened, about these incidents which seemed to grow each out of the other, and yet there was no connection between them. I started from the beginning, from the ladder in the bookstore, *The Poem of Jerusalem Liberated,* and that small creature whose garb is a part of him.

After skipping over some matters, I got to thinking of Moshele, my own flesh and blood, who had escaped the fires of cremation and now was shuffling from one mound of refuse to another. As the concert had not yet come to an end and it was not yet time for me to return to my room, I was able to think a great many thoughts. As I strolled along I thought: If only I could find Moshele now that I am just strolling and have nothing else to do, I would talk to him and let him tell me all his troubles; I would appease him and bring him to the inn, give him food and drink and order a soft, warm bed, and we would part from each other with a hearty goodnight. As I was strolling and thinking such thoughts, it suddenly dawned on me that there could be nothing finer. But favors do not come at all times, or to anyone. Moshele had been saved from cremation, and as an added favor it had been given him to find his own flesh and blood. Whereas I, who was his flesh and blood—no favors at all were granted to me, and I couldn't find Moshele again.

Finally, the singer ended his song and the audience went home. I too returned to the room at the hotel and closed the door behind me carefully, as an open door calls to uninvited guests. But there are guests who come no matter how tightly one's door is shut, as they are the thoughts surrounding our actions. So many guests came that the air in the room got fouler and fouler, and I was afraid I was going to choke. I then untied the knot which the young lady had made in my tie, and that helped a little. Now there was more air to breathe, and the guests brought some more guests, and very soon I was choking again.

## Yehuda Amichai 1924 –

Amichai and his family left his native town of Würzburg in Germany for Palestine when he was twelve years old. Rejecting the orthodoxy of his parents, he continued his education in Jerusalem, joined socialist youth movements, fought with the Palestine brigade of the British army in the Middle East during World War II and, after finishing high school in 1942, served as a commando in the Hagganah underground during the Israeli War of Independence of 1948.

Amichai was a secondary school teacher of Bible and Hebrew literature in Jerusalem for many years. He rose to sudden prominence in Israel in 1955 with a book of Hebrew poems (*Now and in the Other Days*) and soon established an international reputation not only as a poet but also as a novelist with *Not of This Time, Not of This Place* (Hebrew 1963; English 1968), one of the earliest Hebrew novels about the Holocaust. He has been the recipient of the Bialik Prize and the Israel Prize for Literature (1981). English translations of his Hebrew poems (especially of love, such as *Love Poems* and of Jerusalem, *Songs of Jerusalem and Myself*) are found in every major bookstore in North America. Amichai regularly lectures and reads his poems in many parts of the world.

Amichai once said of himself, "I am the result and very contents of the twentieth century." America's poet laureate Robert Pinsky has described Amichai's poetic virtues as "directness of approach linked with a lively and mischievous imagination, and the power of memory balanced by a trenchant sense of what is immediate." These words apply equally well to his short stories.

# My Father's Deaths

It was Yom Kippur, and Papa was standing in front of me in the synagogue. I climbed on a chair in order to see him better from the back. It is so much easier for me to remember his back than his face. The back of his head never changed. His face was so mobile. When he spoke his mouth was like a dark and cavernous entrance or like a waving flag. His eyes were like butterflies, or like stamps on a letter which is always sent to a faraway place. Or his ears, which were like ships about to cast off over the oceans of his God. His face was either red or white as his hair. The wrinkly waves of big forehead were but a tiny beach-head fronting a universal sea.

All I saw then was the back of his neck. A deep furrow swept over its width, almost like a split. Although at that time I was still faraway from this country, I then saw for the first time a dry wadi, dry and deep. Perhaps Papa, too, began with such a wadi, for the rains had not yet descended and intense heat prevailed in this land, which on that Yom Kippur was not yet mine.

I now see his face on a photograph in the closet. He looks like a man who had begun to eat what looked like a delightful dish and who has just become aware of something noisome in its flavor, and now feels disappointed. The corners of his mouth, which turn downward at its edges, testify to this. The wrinkle in his nose testifies to this; the crow's-feet at his eyes express this in sadness. I see the testimony of so many details in his face. And I see this testimony not for the sake of judging him, but rather for the sake of judging myself.

On that Yom Kippur he stood before me, oh so busy with his grown-up God. How white he was in his shroud. Beside him the whole world looked like an abandoned picnic-ground all blackened by campfire soot. As if the dancers had left and the musicians, too, and all that remained was blackened rock. Thus Papa remained, dressed in his white shroud. This then was the first death I remember.

And when they came to recite the Adoration, he kneeled altogether, touching the floor with his forehead. It seemed to me as if he were drinking with his forehead. I thought that perhaps his God was flowing between the legs of the table. Before he kneeled, he spread the wings of his *tallith* in order not to soil his knees. But he did not seem concerned about soiling his forehead—

and then he was resurrected. He rose without separating one foot from the other. He rose and the colors of his face changed several times and again he lived, again he was mine and I climbed on a chair to see the back of his neck and the furrow on it. He was the resurrected flesh and blood. Why do they call people flesh and blood? Flesh and blood you only see when someone is wounded or when someone is injured or dead. When people are alive all you see are other combinations: skin and eyes, a smile and a dark entrance, hands and a mouth.

I went up to the women's gallery. I just had to tell Mamma about the miracle of Papa's resurrection. They had apples there with cloves stuck in them, for smelling so that the women would not faint while fasting. I am jealous of the women. I always wanted to faint, but I couldn't manage it, to be wiped from the blackboard, to step back from it all without having to be told what to do and without having to face opposition. The spiced apples were in the women's hands as was I, as is the whole ball of the earth. They kept me opposite the big clock as if to balance the time against me. They eyed me with a smoldering light yet to burn, burning up the whole *shul*.

From up there I saw how they undressed the Torah scrolls, how they took the white shirts off, pulled on the shoulder-straps and pulled the dress off and the poor Torah was naked. It must have felt cold.

Papa was again resurrected in the evening after the "closing" prayer. The year made a big wheel, enclosing within its walls days and seasons. What a strange game! To me sins and atonements were as yet doubled up and had one and the same face. In the evening, a moon made its rounds about the town like a shiny atonement rooster.

◆

Papa has been dying many times. He still keeps on dying from time to time. Sometimes I am present, at other times I am not. Sometimes his dying is quite close to my table, when I work or when I write nice words on the blackboard or when I look at the multicolored countries in the atlas. There are times when I am far away when he dies, just as it was when he fought in the First World War. It is a good thing that children don't see their fathers in the war. It is a good thing that I did not have to fight in that war, otherwise we might have killed one another. He wore the uniform of Kaiser Wilhelm and I that of King George, and God put between us a distance of twenty-five years. I put his medals in the same box as my own decorations from the Second World War. There is no other place to put them. On one of his medals there are a lion and crossed swords, as if two invisible warriors were fencing in a duel. I guess that the images of wild and ferocious animals take a place of honor on emblems: lions, eagles, bulls that fight, and all sorts of other beautiful and destructive beasts. In the synagogue, too, two lions have to hold the tablets over the Holy Ark. Even our laws need wild beasts to guard and strengthen them.

One time, it was a long time ago in Germany and many years had passed since the war. Papa got dressed in a black dinner jacket on which he hung all his medals; he also put on a sparkling top hat to go to the unveiling of a war monument. All the names of the brave soldiers who had died in the war were inscribed there in alphabetical order. Where was that monument? Oh yes, now I remember: it was in the public park right next to the playground, right next to the swings and the sand-boxes. I can't remember what the monument looked like. The chances are it had soldiers raising rifles of stone under a flag of stone, with stony mothers bewailing the death of stony sons. Surely, there also were all sorts of animals of prey to remind one of the greatness of man and of generals and of emperors.

Papa died for about four years in the war. Oh, how many trenches he dug. Some people say that sweat saves blood and the blood of soldiers saves the sweat of generals, and the sweat of generals saves the sweat and the blood of factory-owners and of emperors and so it goes endlessly. All of it is an effort to save lives. Papa dug many trenches; he dug many graves for himself. Only once did he get wounded. All the other bullets and shrapnel missed their aim. But, when Papa really died many years after that, then all those bullets and missiles which had missed him united and tore his heart all at once. Neither did he ever leave that last trench of his which others dug for him. He lived through many wars and many a time he was among those statistically dead in these wars, among the dead of the statistics of conquest. His blood shone in him like elevator buttons. I guess this was so that death should be able to see and illuminate his body with his blood. But death didn't really press the elevator buttons of his blood and Papa didn't really die. The God in whom he believed hung over him like a white conductor and saved him, higher even than the wings of a Pegasus. He didn't mix his God into matters of war. He left Him among the laws of nature and the stars. He left Him floating above him, like a light foam upon the dark and heavy waters of his life.

Sometimes, as his duties in the service increased, Papa's body became like a tree which had cast off its leaves. Only the nerve branches remained but his whole life had wilted away. So many letters did he send. In the beginning he sent single letters, but in the course of the four years of war the letters accumulated first into small and then into bigger bundles. These bundles became as hard as stone. Where do letters really end up? In the beginning they float lightly and white like the wings of a dove, then they get harder and all the letters turn into stone. Then the letters are transferred from one hiding-place to another, from one box to another, from the closet to the top of the closet and from there to the attic and to some place under the rafters. When Papa really died, he went in one jump much higher than all his letters which were kept in the attic, and when the true resurrection of the dead will take place, he will have to open up all those bundles and read his letters, for man gives off in his letters his life, blood, sweat, excrement, and poetry.

One time, he told us in a letter about some French prisoners of war who asked him for water in their language: "de l'eau." He gave them the last of the water in his canteen. From then on I could never rid myself of the memory of their call for water. At times they even come to me and ask me for water. Maybe Papa told them about me. It is difficult to say that he did because it was before I was born. But a war, doesn't it mix up people and lands and turn everything upside down making those who are lying down pictures on the wall? Anything is possible.

◆

Once—it happened before Hitler came, just before Hitler came—that his friends invited Papa to a reunion. They wrote him a very nice letter. On top of that letter they had printed a single military symbol—a hunter's cap, the antlers of a deer, and crossed rifles. And why was this so? Because it was a battalion of fusiliers. It was a battalion which had a great and honorable tradition, an aristocratic battalion. At first they hunted rabbits and deer, and they hunted people in wartime. They didn't really hunt them; they killed them. Not because they wanted to eat them like people eat rabbits, but because they had to kill them and to break them open, so that all the flesh and blood should be seen and not hair and smiles and arms or any other pleasing combination.

Papa didn't answer the invitation. This, too, was a death, for they loved him a great deal and called him David. It was on Yom Kippur during the war that they gave him part of their rations, so that he should be able to fast afterwards, and they gathered little stars for his prayers, brief moments of quiet for his quiet supplications, and Papa in his turn strengthened their spirit with his faith and his funny stories.

He kept on dying at more frequent intervals. He died when they came to arrest him because of the Nazi armband which I had found and thrown into the garbage-can. Black they were when they came to the door. These black ones broke the door open. How heavy their steps were! How frightening it was for me to see that my Papa wasn't able to protect our house and stand up against this enemy storming in. This was the end of my childhood. How was it possible for them to come in and enter our home against the will of my Papa? Perhaps if I had been bigger, I would have been able to cover Papa just as he covered me as he stepped back.

He died when they placed pickets before his store with signs reading *"Arier! kauft nicht beim Juden."* He died when we left Germany in order to come to Israel. All the past years died at that moment, and when our train passed the Jewish Home for the Aged, of which Papa was one of the supporters, all the old people were leaning out and waving their white bed sheets from porches and windows. Not as a sign of surrender but to wave good-by to him. What is the difference between good-by and surrender? In either case flags or white handkerchiefs or even sheets are waved.

Yes, he died many times. He was made from all different kinds of material. Sometimes he was like iron, sometimes he was like white bread, sometimes he was like precious old wood, and all these had to die. Sometimes I saw him when his hands were like a garment covering his face, so that I might not see his face in all its nakedness. Sometimes his thoughts were heavier than his small body and he walked stooped under their weight, under their burden. At times he was as strong as telephone poles and his amazing thoughts flashed like messages through the wires. Sometimes songbirds came down to rest on them.

◆

When Papa truly died, God didn't know whether he had died in earnest. He was used to his being resurrected again, but this time he wasn't. Several weeks before he had a heart attack. Funny, people say "heart attack." Who attacks whom? Does the heart attack the body or does the body attack the heart? Or perhaps the world attacks both of them?

One day I came to visit him when he was lying beside a huge oxygen tank. His eyes were like broken slivers of glass at a wedding. When I came closer I heard the whisper of that huge oxygen bomb. There used to be a time when angels stood next to sickbeds and now there are bombs full of oxygen which whisper. Men in submarines and airplane pilots get oxygen. Where is Papa going? Will he go under the water or will he be lifted up? One thing is sure; he is about to leave us. He motioned to me and I stepped close to him saying: "Papa don't talk; it'll strain you." And he said: "The cat is howling on our neighbor's roof. Perhaps it has been locked in and wants to get out." And I went over to our neighbor's and freed the cat. After that, again we heard nothing but the whisper of the oxygen. On top of the oxygen tank there was a clock measuring the pressure. All the time Papa has left is the time that there is oxygen in the tank. My mother was standing at the door. If she had been able to, she too would have stayed like the oxygen bottle, right next to his bed and given him strength from her own life.

After that Papa got slightly better. Day by day the colors returned to his face. It was as if all the colors had fled and dispersed at the time of his heart attack; now the colors came sneaking back like refugees after a bombing. The oxygen tank was kept outside on the porch.

On the day preceding the evening of his death, they made a cardiogram. A doctor came, opened a sort of radio and connected all sorts of electric wires to Papa. If someone truly loves you, he doesn't need such a complicated instrument to examine your heart. But it isn't like this when a person is sick.

The needle zigzagged on paper like a seismograph registering earthquakes, and Papa looked like a radio station, surrounded by wires and antennas. That was the day of his last broadcast and I heard it.

The doctor however said: "Oh, we are okay!" As if someone had asked whether he was okay. He took his machinery apart and showed us the zigzag. It was quite okay for a zigzag. That evening my wife and I went to see a film. After the distorted faces on the screen stopped laughing or crying, we went out into the street. My wife bought some flowers from a vendor right next to an artists' café. Young poets with sad faces forever scanning the distant horizons come there, as well as people with all sorts of medals from various wars. Some of them walk with a limp because of a war injury, and they limp because it is considered aristocratic to limp; and mustachioed people come and those who love war, who do not wear uniforms, and those who love peace who do wear uniforms, and girls who just love to be with all of them. We bought red roses. Perhaps in order to encourage the color on Papa's cheeks.

We went in and sat down near Papa. My wife put the flowers into a vase so that they would be able to breathe better. We moved our chairs right next to his bed and Papa began to talk—about the man who came to Israel after he had jumped off a train and been hidden by kind *goyim*. Papa's eyes filled with tears when he told about the good people who hid this hunted man. His eyes were filled with tears and his mouth was filled with a strange gasp. His speech was cut off like a ripped film in a movie, like a radio jammed by another station. Which station had interfered with Papa's broadcast? And then both stations were silent—his and the jamming one. His mouth remained open, as if it were about to tell many more stories about good people, all pushing through this opening and as if Papa's mouth were unable to express them all at the same time.

I jumped up, ran to his bed, embraced him and kissed him on his cold forehead. Perhaps it was then that I remembered how this forehead used to touch the ground on Yom Kippur. Perhaps I thought that I could bring back his spirit, like Elisha. Mother came out of the bathtub. My wife called the doctor and the doctor came and pronounced a decision on things that had already been decided. A kind neighbor came and made all sorts of arrangements. A rabbi came, one of Papa's acquaintances, and he set up what had to be set up. Furniture was moved from its place, windows were closed and opened. Oh, he knew his way about the dead! They placed a candle on the floor, much like a danger-signal on a road which is being repaired. And then the rabbi opened the book and began to whisper and at his whisper the oxygen bottle did not need to whisper anymore.

In the morning, they washed Papa in the house. Furniture was moved about and torrents of water were spilled and then they tied him up with many linen tapes. After the funeral, relatives and friends arrived, even Aunt Susannah came in from her village. Oh, how glad she was to leave her hundreds of chickens and meet with friends whom she hadn't seen for a long time!

There were many opportunities for great and sorrowful weeping, of which we somehow didn't avail ourselves. Perhaps it was because he died in the middle of a story, or because all the radio stations were shut down, or because his heart needed a wider mouthpiece and his wasn't wide enough. But it was quite possible to mourn along with the wailing of the train-whistle between the narrow and embattled mountains on the road to Jerusalem. Or even in the silence like a window which has not been closed and is moving back and forth in silence.

◆

How few gestures and expressions we have! We have pain, we have fear— we have a smile, and just a few more expressions. But it's just like the manikins in the display-windows of clothing stores. Fate sets our expressions as the window-decorator sets the expressions of these manikins. At times he will lift their hands, at times he will turn their heads one way or another, and so they will remain all the time, and so do we. I grew a mourning beard. In the beginning it was hard and then it softened, and sometimes as I lie down I hear either shots or a tractor backfiring in one of the valleys. Papa was like one of the quarries. He gave up all his stones, and then remained empty. And now that he is dead and I am built up, he remains open and forsaken. And the woods grow around the quarry. At times when I travel down into the valley, I see these forsaken quarries by the side of the road and they are lonely. Quarries, gravestones. I ordered a gravestone. The evening before I ordered it, I saw a girl standing next to a gravestone, tying up a shoelace that had opened. When I came closer, she fled between two big houses. I ordered a wide gravestone with a stony pillow at its head, and the stoneman asked me for dimensions, just as a tailor asks for measurements.

The graveyard is close to the border. In days of political unrest the dead remain lonely. Only soldiers are seen there from time to time. Next to Papa, a German doctor is buried but they didn't get a chance to set a gravestone for him. All they left him is a small tin tablet. Near the town one can see a tower. Such towers won't help us anymore. Only silos and water towers. They have to be big in order to fill all the houses with water, and God who is so big and so high filled my Papa altogether. Too bad I was filled with other things and not always from tall towers either. At times the pressure is low and I am only half-filled with thoughts and dreams. A few days ago I went to the cemetery and over the grave there is a name and a quotation. The burial place of Moses isn't known to us, but his living place is known to us and even until this very day we know all about his life. Everything is topsy-turvy. Now only the burial places are known to us; the living places are neither distinct nor known.

We move about, we change and we become different, but only our burial places are fixed.

As I am alone now, I continue to walk on my way and I'm developing all sorts of traits which belong to Papa, and some of the lines of his face and of his nose. Some of them I develop and some of them I leave out.

But, as I told you at the beginning, Papa still continues to die. He came into my dream; I was worried about him and I said to him: "Take your coat, walk slowly, don't talk. I don't want you to be upset. Rest up from this awful war." But, I, I cannot rest, I keep going. I go on without praying. I take the *t'fillin*, but I do not put them on my arm and my forehead, but into their little bag which I never open again.

Once I was walking along the ancient Via Appia in Rome. I was carrying Papa on my shoulders. Suddenly his head fell off and I was afraid that he might die. So I laid him down on the side of the road and I put a stone underneath his neck and went to call a taxi. At one time they used to call God to help and now they call a taxi. I couldn't find any and walked far away from where Papa was lying. After every few steps I turned to look at him and then ran again past the traffic. And so I saw him lying by the side of the road. Just his head was turning towards me, holding me back. I saw him through the ancient Arch of San Sebastian. People were passing him; they turned to him and then continued to walk on. I found a taxi but it was too narrow and looked like a snake. I came to another taxi and the driver said: "Oh, we know him. He just makes believe that he is dead." And I turned back and I saw that he was still lying there, that it was still my Papa lying there by the side of the road and his white face was turned toward me, but I didn't know whether he was alive or not. I turned once more, and then I saw him like something very, very distant, on the other side of the gate of the ancient Arch of San Sebastian.

# *Aharon Appelfeld 1932—*

Born into a highly assimilated German-speaking family ("for my generation, assimilation was no longer a goal, but it had become a way of life") in Czernowitz, Bukovina, which was then in Romania. Appelfeld was eight when the Nazis murdered his mother in the streets of his hometown and he and his father were interned, though separately, in the Trans-Dniestria labor camp. He escaped within a year, and then spent several years hiding in Nazi-occupied Ukraine. He wandered through several countries and lived in refugee camps, until he arrived in Palestine in 1947 at the age of fourteen.

Although Appelfeld knew German as well as some Yiddish and Russian, he had virtually no formal education before he began to study Hebrew. He fought in the Israeli War of Independence, studied at the Hebrew University, and published his first collection of short stories (*Smoke*), in Hebrew, in 1962. Appelfeld denies that he writes "Holocaust literature," declaring that he "had come from the camps and from the forests [and] from . . . the absurd" and just tells austerely understated, richly symbolic, Kafka-like stories about Jews. Yet nearly all his fiction translated into English centers around Central European Jewry in Nazi-occupied locales on the eve of and during World War II.

In 1960 Appelfeld was reunited with his father when he chanced to see his name on a list of new immigrants arriving in Israel. In 1983 he won the Israel Prize for Literature. By the 1980s, the emotionally neutral and even distant fabulistic stories and novels of this "displaced writer of displaced fiction" had won him national and international acclaim.

# BERTHA

In winter, he would return. Perspiring, a knapsack on his back, he would bring with him the fresh scent of worlds unknown here. His comings and goings were quiet. You never knew whether he was happy to leave or happy to return.

Inside, in the small room, life remained unchanged. Bertha would sit on the floor, knitting. It seemed as if the passing of years did not touch her. She remained just as he had left her in summer, small, dwarfish even, and quite unaltered.

"Maxie," she would exclaim, as a crack of light came through the door. Throughout the long months she had waited for this light. As the door opened her gaze would fall on him, helplessly.

Very slowly, with studied caution, he would unpack the knapsack. There were clothes and household articles that he had brought with him from his travels. At the sight of them, tears of joy welled up in Bertha's eyes. "That's for you, for you," Max would say, stroking her hair.

The first days after his return were delightful. Bertha sat beside Max, talking. She told him the various details that had accumulated in her memory, trivial experiences, which in this dark room became objects of childlike admiration. Max also talked. He had little to say; what had happened had frozen somewhere on the way. Of course, it was not possible to tell her everything. During the long summer months, on the floor among the skeins of wool, the gaps which he had left between the stories provided her with food for fantasy with which to amuse herself.

Bertha would light the stove, and Max, like a weary traveler, would sink into a long slumber which lasted through the winter. Only in early spring would he stretch himself saying, "Well, Bertha, it's time I was on my way."

Between naps he would try, half maliciously, half affectionately, to discuss his plans for her. The conversations were full of tears and laughter, and in the end everything remained as before. Max would leave on his travels and Bertha remained behind. And so, the seasons changed, one year followed another, a sprinkling of white appeared at Max's temples, stomach pains began to trouble him, dysentery, a harsh cough, but Bertha remained as she was, small and dwarfish, these qualities becoming more pronounced, perfected as it were.

At first, he had tried, firmly enough, to put her into an institution for girls. He had even had a few preliminary meetings with the headmistress of the institution, who had turned out to be a strong woman with piercing eyes whom he couldn't stand from the very first meeting. The plan, of course, came to nothing. For several days she roamed the streets, until they found her desolate, and brought her back. No amount of persuasion on his part did any good, he did not have the courage to force her to go, and so she stayed on. There had been one other serious attempt to find her what might be called a suitable living arrangement. This was with a woman, an old woman whose children wanted to find her a companion. Bertha returned the next day, her eyes full of tears, and the matter was closed.

Soon afterwards, he began to travel.

Max left, hoping that within a year people would make some arrangement for her, or that she herself would find some way out, but when after a year, upon returning to his room, he found her sitting on the floor among the skeins of wool, half knitting, half playing, he simply couldn't be angry with her.

Several years passed—five years, or more. The passage of time became blurred, especially since there were no innovations. Life went on its lazy routine, devouring time. The coming of winter left a stale taste, something like the sourness of a cigarette. Little by little he began to take the fact of her being there for granted. Even when he made far-reaching plans for her, he made them good-humoredly, for he knew with growing certainty that he would never be able to get rid of her.

Between naps he would sit and watch her, as if he were observing his own life.

Sometimes, he went haunted by the old question of his purpose in life. What was he to do with her, or what was she going to do? It was her duty to think of it—she must not be a perpetual burden on him.

Bertha would stand up, looking at him helplessly with her big eyes, unable to understand. When he nagged her, she would burst into tears. This weeping was deep and bitter. It wasn't she that wept; some sleeping animal wept inside her. Sometimes it was a high-pitched wail. After words of reconciliation, everything returned to normal. Bertha would go back to her knitting and Max would cover his head with the blanket.

Sometimes he teased her with riddles. "Don't you ever feel any change; don't things weigh upon you?" Or, in another direction, "What would you like to be someday?" The questions were venomous, aimed at her most vulnerable feelings, but she did not react. Closed, encased in a hard shell, she dragged after him like a dead weight, and sometimes like a mirror wherein his life was reflected.

She was stubbornly loyal, another quality which was not quite human. All summer long she would sit and knit fantastic patterns in strange colors. "I'm knitting for Maxie," she would say. They were not sweaters. A dumb smile would appear on her face at the sight of the patterns. In the end she would unravel them and then the same wool would appear again on the needles, year after year. The tape measure he brought her was no help, since she did not seem to understand what it was for.

But sometimes she, too, asked questions.

They were not the sort of questions that one person asks another, but a sort of eruption, not entirely irrational, that would claim his complete attention. These questions drove him out of his mind; at those moments he was ready to throw her out, to hand her over to the welfare authorities, to denounce her, even to beat her, something which he, incidentally, never did. At these moments, he felt the whole weight of this human burden which had been thrust upon him.

Sometimes he would let her ask her questions and she would sit and drift along with them, like a ship tossing in the wind. Then came the time when he reconciled himself to his fate. Now he knew that he would not leave Bertha, and Bertha knew that she was to stay with him.

Bertha would remain with him . . . some day she might change . . . medical care might cure her . . . she was a girl like all other girls. They were great thoughts, and they surged up within him. At those times everything seemed pleasantly near. "I'll wind up my affairs, Bertha, and I'll come." The feeling was powerful, leaving no room for doubts. "Isn't it so, Bertha?" he would ask suddenly.

At the moment she was that same Bertha who had been handed to him during the big escape when the others couldn't take her, when the only thing they could do was to give her to him. He hadn't been able to carry her either, but he couldn't throw her into the snow.

At the same moment, he conjured up the snow, those thick flakes falling from the sides, soft as a caress, but sometimes swooping down on you, hard, like the beating of hooves.

From the day that they had reached this country, oblivion had overcome her. Her memory froze at a certain point. You couldn't make her disclose anything from the past, nor was she capable of absorbing anything new. "Some pipe is stopped up." This feeling, oversimplified as it might be, remained a sort of certainty which he could not doubt, feeling as he did that something was clogged up in him, too. This had been so several years ago, but perhaps now as well.

When spring came he didn't go out to work. He took Bertha with him to the Valley of the Crucifixion, opposite the monastery. At that moment they were close to each other as they had never been before.

"The sun is good," said Bertha.

"It's a beautiful spring," said Max.

And there was a feeling that the pipe had become unstopped; there was communication, they weren't suspicious of one another any more, they had left their experiences behind them. Now the words, half-syllables groped towards their hearts. Something was happening to her as well.

The future became misty and sweet. The way it had been in the first day of the liberation. Open roads and many wagons full of refugees, and an inexplicable desire to walk, to take Bertha and to walk with her to the end of the world, just the two of them, and to swallow up the beautiful distances.

"Isn't it beautiful today . . . " he tried.

"Beautiful," she said.

"Isn't it beautiful today . . . " he tried again.

"Beautiful," she said.

Exposed to the spring, to the good sun, the thoughts welled up in him until he could almost feel their physical movement. He was only slightly annoyed with Bertha for not feeling the change.

He bought food; as long as he had enough money, no one could force him to go out travelling. It was a moment of sweet abandonment which would sooner or later bring some sort of whiplash in its wake. Soon he would have to go back to work, but in the meantime, there was something festive about this walk, in the glittering olive trees, the comfortable warmth, the light playing on his shirt.

This sweet indolence lasted a few days. Not many. A letter arrived reminding him that he must be on his way. The letter was brief and unequivocal, with a sufficiently firm conclusion and certain threatening overtones.

Now he didn't know how these months of his vacation had gone by— or perhaps they had never existed at all. The cars, the refrigerator, the workers, the whole atmosphere of busy commerce suddenly came to life and seemed so near that you could smell them. The signboards flashed vividly before his eyes.

His pity was aroused, pity for himself, for the room, for Bertha, for his belongings and for a small body which made him too bend his head a bit, surrender, and also love a little.

The parting was difficult for Bertha this time; promises did no good. She begged him to take her with him. The next day he saw her packing her belongings.

"Where are you going, Bertha?"

"With you."

In the evening he managed to get away. At the station, when he turned his head, he saw the flickering of lights on the road. A car was being towed to the garage. The trip was slow, as if they wanted to delay him, to prolong that which cannot be prolonged, perhaps even to bring him back. He saw that he was mean, so mean, that he felt the heaviness of his shoes, even the dirt at the roots of his hair, the sweat in his armpits. "It's not the first time I've left her, but I have always found her again—I left her enough to live on." Thus he stifled his thoughts.

That night, when he arrived at work, Frost greeted him warmly. "Well, how was the vacation, Max?" He was glad that he could go out with the first truck, unloading the cold drinks all over the city, feeling the cases on his back, full of good foaming beer. For some reason, he didn't feel like any now. He felt fresh and vigorous, ready for any load.

Late that night, after two whole rounds, he was still as fresh as he had been at the beginning. Only his thoughts pounded inside him, as if they had disengaged themselves from him, leaving him incapable of directing them. He didn't really grasp what they demanded of him, he only felt them revolving in his head.

"You've left Bertha again"—he heard this clearly; the voice resounded like the ceaseless ringing of a bell.

Then came the time which seemed ordained to bring this feeling to a head; a decision had to be taken. His fellow workers saw the need to interfere. Max needed a wife. It started, as these things usually do, as a joke. Later they fixed up a date for him—with a typist at the plant.

He didn't have much to offer her. They didn't speak about Bertha. But with her feminine intuition she discovered it in a roundabout way.

He could have said that she was retarded, that she would soon be put in an institution. This was an accepted way of speaking, even to Mitzi. But he couldn't put it that way; something stopped him from saying the words. Sometimes your cunning betrays you, and you are suddenly left naked and ashamed. At those moments you are as vulnerable as a bare neck at the change of the seasons. Mitzi delved deeply into the matter; she too, had been hurt enough in her life.

Max was called upon to clarify matters, so that, for the time being her own affairs were pushed aside.

"This Bertha," she said, "I don't understand why she hasn't been put into an institution by now."

What could he answer? Her questions were direct, going straight, to the heart of the matter; they showed up all the contradictions, and even contained an element of mild reproach.

"She didn't want to." Max tried to shake off his embarrassment.

"What do you mean, she didn't want to?"

They met every evening; It was as if she were trying to exhaust the matter completely. In order to ease the confession, she invited him to her room.

The problem was not dismissed in her room. It kept floating up to the surface like a buoy.

"It's only a question of making the arrangements," he tried to defend himself.

"Then why has it been going on for so long?"

One day he felt that something had happened to him, something physical—something which had to do with the way he handled the crates. He moved differently, and once he even dropped a crate of bottles. "Take it easy there!" cried the foreman, who liked him.

His thoughts fumbled, as though he were tipsy. Late at night he felt the fire burning in his head.

He tried to clarify the matter to himself logically, drawing the thread of Mitzi's questions to himself. In his dreams, the stark mystery took hold of him—Bertha's knitting needles, toys, hell and paradise, a strange combination of rudimentary symbols and objects.

"Does Bertha dream of me, too?"—Now he did not doubt it.

If she knew how to read, he would write her a letter. He would clarify, explain, enumerate all the reasons, one by one. Distance made it easier to hide one's facial expression. One day during the noon break, between loading, he tried to write, but in the end, when he was about to fold the letter, he realized how idiotic it was.

Mitzi asked him no further questions, as if waiting to see the impact of her words. The silence was hard for him since he knew that it would only lead to new questions.

The cinema became his most comfortable refuge.

But the secret weighed on him. Was it still a secret? He had told everything. He thought he had exhausted the matter. That is how it seemed to him as they sat in a small café once, after the cinema.

Late at night, during the second shift when the storehouse was empty, he suddenly felt that he was still carrying the secret within him. If only he could give it a name, he would feel easier; but the name eluded him.

The days were as flat as the cement floor of the storehouse. He felt that the light which protected him was being taken away. Sometimes a feeling of nakedness overcame him. He tried in vain to glean something from Mitzi's eyes; they were watery eyes, the color seemed to melt in them; something was melting in him, too, but he didn't know what it was.

If there were a starting point, it would make things a great deal easier—to say, I will begin from here, to take a day off and go up to Jerusalem, to Bertha, even to bring Mitzi, to show her. How complicated the possibilities seemed, and in the meantime all he saw were the bottles; in the darkness of the warehouse the alcohol was fermenting. He had to make a decision; Mitzi's moderate tone demanded it.

"When was Bertha entrusted to me?" The question arose from some dark depth. "Fifteen years ago." The event seemed so near to him, as if it had taken place during his last vacation.

Mitzi did not tell him what to do. She wanted to see what he would do himself. Only once did she say to him in passing, as she always did: "Maybe she's yours: you can tell me, I won't blame you; things like that happened during the war." She had thought it all out beforehand.

Now he had to act, to prove to Bertha if not to himself, to finish once and for all, to get rid of the nuisance. How close he felt at that moment to Mitzi.

He asked for his quarterly vacation. "To take care of something," he said to Frost.

He wore his good suit, and in the evening he came to Mitzi. "Very nice, very nice," said Mitzi, like a merchant who leaves the way open for negotiations, not over-eager but never refusing an offer.

"Aren't you pleased I'm going to finish it?"

"Of course, of course."

For some reason he was reminded of the headmistress of the institution with whom he had negotiated—the long corridor, girls dressed in blue.

"The institutions here in this country are fine," he said.

"Of course."

"Maybe you'll come with me."

"Better not . . ." she said, as if shaking off some unpleasantness.

The next day he got up early. It was a nice day, mild after the first rains. There was an air of simple festivity on this weekday, little traffic. He thought he would get there quickly by taxi, but meanwhile he was attracted by the shop windows. He never came empty-handed, and he was angry with himself for leaving her so little cash.

First he bought her a short winter coat, then a woolen blouse. In the next shop he bought shoes; the colors matched, colors that he liked. Then he was drawn to the central shops. A sudden fit of spending took hold of him. He ended up with two large packages. In the taxi he started a conversation with a man, telling him that he worked for Frost, and the man in the blue suit said that he also knew Frost.

Suddenly he felt the cool mountain air in his shirt.

"On vacation?" asked the man.

"Have to arrange something," said Max.

It wasn't clear to him what he would do. The certainty started to fall apart. The chill wrapped itself around his neck. He was exposed to the cutting air. He just wanted the journey to go on, to take as long as possible.

"Aren't you afraid of catching cold?" asked the man.

Jerusalem was as beautiful as on the day he had first arrived with Bertha. Lights glittered in the city. For some reason he was slow in his movements. It turned out that the man who had traveled with him was still standing next to him. "I've come to arrange something," apologized Max. They parted.

His head was empty of all thoughts. He wasn't sure for what he had come. His feet drew him to the slope. He caught a glimpse of Bertha's head. Simple indifference was written on her face. She was sitting outside, knitting.

"Bertha," he said. It was the biggest word that he could cut out of his heart; it seemed that only once had he called her that way, once at a Gentile woman's in Zivorka, after the big hunt when he was forced to leave her. It was the same head with the same tangled hair. A small, warm body which needed nothing, which was beyond patience, beyond any change that might come. It asked for nothing except to be left here, among these skeins of wool, to sit and knit thus, like a spider, like a bee, you couldn't call it stupidity, idiocy or any similar names called to mind by that strangeness. It was something different, something which a man like Max couldn't give a name to, but could feel.

"Max!" she said. Not a muscle moved in her face.

"I came early this time." He too was unable to utter another word.

He got down on his knees. "This coat," he said, starting to take apart the package, "this coat will suit you. It's warm, at this time of the year you have to be careful."

Bertha put down the knitting needles without saying a word. Supreme indifference froze her face. Now he had no doubt she knew everything. But he could not detect any signs of anger in her. She was a princess, a devil, a gypsy, something that could not be contained in any human measure. She was not a girl to whom he could say "I couldn't, I was forced, I never loved Mitzi, it was only a blind incident." But again he repeated: "Bertha"—as if trying to suggest everything in this one word.

He tried to explain to her in the vocabulary that he had carried with him all these years, that had ripened within him.

"Max!" said Bertha, as if cutting short his confession. A deep flush suffused her face.

At that moment, he could not guess how near the solution was. Sometimes catastrophe wears festive garb.

Bertha wanted to put on her new clothes and go to town. She had matured during these months, or perhaps she had just acquired some of the gestures of a woman. She was different.

"Let's go!" she said. This was a new tone which was unfamiliar to him.

They passed by the institution. In the corridor there was confusion. Girls in blue were running around and the headmistress appeared in the entrance. It was an old Arab house which was disproportionately tall. No one noticed them.

Again he didn't know how he had got here; Bertha's cheeks were burning and they were already in the center of town. The traffic was very heavy.

Max suddenly realized why he had come and he said, "You must understand, Bertha, you're already grown up; one must marry, set up a household. You too, you too!"

Bertha turned her head and looked at him.

He wanted to say something else, but the noise in the street prevented it. Afterwards, when they came to the quiet side streets, to Ibn Gabirol Street and Rambam Boulevard, it was too quiet for them to speak.

Their walk continued for some time. It was as solemn as a ceremony, as a farewell, as a simple never-to-be-forgotten occasion. You are not in control of yourself, other powers dominate you, lead you as in a procession. Oaths are broken, but another oath, greater than all, takes their place. Your eyes glisten with tears. The lights begin to dance.

Now he was already in the realm of mystery.

A smile lit up Bertha's face, and there was something sharp in her eyes like an inanimate object unexpectedly changing its form. Darkness rose up from the streets, and above them was light. Among the trees there were dark shadows.

When they returned home, her face was very flushed—a fire burned in her. Her eyes were open, but you could see nothing in them. Towards morning she began to shiver.

In the morning, the ambulance came.

She was as light and small as on the day when he had received her; the years had added no weight. He asked permission to go along with her.

The casualty ward in the hospital was full, but they made room for her. A man wheeled her carefully through the corridor on a low bed, as if trying to smooth her passage, as if he did not want to break the silence.

They told him that he must leave. The gate closed behind him. At that moment he could remember nothing. His eyes saw, his heart fumbled, the tips of his fingers were tingling. Inside the cavity of his skull, something floated as in a heavy fluid.

"Now, my load is lighter," he said naively, failing to understand the situation.

The cars crept slowly down the slope, the traffic was heavy, everything flowed as through blocked pipes. He remembered nothing. The sky was clear without a trace of cloud, like glass that had been well polished in order to see through to its depths. Each object was unique: the traffic signs, the posters and the two people coming towards him.

"Can't I remember anything at all? My memory is gone."

The landscape was bathed in bright sunshine, as if it wanted to exhibit every detail to him slightly more enlarged than usual and brought closer to the eye.

"But I must remember," he said to himself. "Forgetting won't release me."

There was no connection between one thought and another. It was as if they had frozen in one of his arteries. His body was working properly and you could hear the gentle pulse within it.

The neighborhood began to empty as if it wanted to hide the traffic from him, to illustrate the paralysis of the inanimate landscape.

"I must choose a starting point; from now on I will try to reconstruct. One detail will bring another in its wake, and in this way I can reconstruct all the events to myself."

Nothing came to him, not a single detail that would lead him on or connect anything. His eyes saw, and he could make out everything, still enlarged, as it had seemed to him before. But he couldn't remember a thing.

If some sort of guilt erupted within him, it would make him feel easier. But no feeling of this sort existed in him at that moment. Everything was just more enlarged than usual, everything seemed so close that it made him dizzy.

He turned towards the slope, trying to thaw the solidity, and suddenly he began to feel a current of warmth in his knees. He was still in the grounds of the hospital; a bluish light flickered at the windows, something like the light in Frost's warehouses.

He felt lighter in weight; only something outside him made his walk heavy. Thus he walked round and round the hospital, unable to tear himself away from the circle.

Slowly, like a sharp stimulus, memory started ebbing back, around the thin tubes of his temples. He clutched his head, afraid that it would burst.

A slight chill met him at the entrance to the yard, and he drew his short coat closer around his body. There was a warm light in the streets. Low pinkish clouds stretched across the skies. The copper-colored rooftops glistened in the light. The street was long and exposed; one could see the remarkably straight rows of trees and the white, almost transparent, traffic signs. Then the redness descended, intertwining itself with the roads, and Max tried to submerge his eyes in it.

The street gradually filled with rich colors. The shadows, dumb and cautious, passed across. Dark circles whirled at its end. When he turned his head back, he saw the thick redness strangled by damp powerful arms.

The street emptied and you could see how the mist was being absorbed by the tree-trunks.

His vacation permit was in his pocket.

A pain, a kind of stimulus, stabbed him in the ankles, pricking his toes. He remembered that from here he used to leave for work, a long journey which always began with an attack of nausea.

Now, he was already in the realm of forms. Reality, as it were, shed its skin; all he felt was a kind of familiarity, as if he were being drawn—he did not know towards what; to the blue color, to the trees or to the stray dog who chanced to be there. He did not see Bertha. She had become something that could no longer be called Bertha.

He entered the hospital. The nurse told him that the girl had amazed the ward. That was all she said, and the other nurses said nothing.

He became a regular visitor there; the attendants soon recognized him, and let him in as if he belonged there. Most of the day he would sit on the bench, looking at the tiled walls. If they had let him remain at night, he would have stayed. The dream became full of ceremonies. Sometimes she was handed over to him and sometimes a delegation came to claim her from him; sometimes it was in a forest and sometimes in Frost's warehouse.

Was it Bertha, or only a vision? Again details rose up, denying it. The shoes, the beads, the knitting needles, the blue wool—was this Bertha?

Again you went out to search for her the way you searched for her in the forest, the way you searched for yourself in the street. You just found details; you couldn't see her, just as you couldn't see yourself.

The nurse came out again. She kept her distance as if he were a stranger, she didn't trust him. Nurses trailed behind her.

The doctor came over to him, ready to start a conversation.

"Yours?" asked the doctor.

"Mine," he said.

The next day they didn't let him enter. The walls grew higher and the gate was locked. A blue light twinkled in the windows, that familiar blue, the color of a bruise.

Silence descended; it touched his body, slithered through the hair on his head, and was still.

Opposite, there were girls dressed in blue on the pavement, near the side entrance to the institution.

The evening light rested on his shoulders.

Suddenly he saw that Bertha's clothes lay in his hands. He didn't dare to open them—or perhaps these were no longer his hand, but iron rings . . .

# KITTY

She was expected to read slowly and to memorize the sentences. She felt how the words hit the stone and returned to her, chilled. They called her name, which rustled within her as in the starched linen dresses which made her shudder. The windows shimmered in the sharp yellowness, kindling the floor with little flames. Sometimes she felt the full impact of the air gripping the back of her neck, stifling the syllables in her mouth. But at other times the flow increased, the good words remained within her, like a warm secret which planted itself slowly, spreading its roots.

Once a day Maria would come in. They would speak for a while. The words, for some reason, took on different proportions in the large hall, as if it were someone other than the nun who spoke them. They seemed to flow from space. She was taught French, arithmetic, and a few passages from the New Testament, a sort of catechism for beginners. In her present, limited state only repetition was of any use.

Maria would sit and read with her, and Kitty tried to repeat words after her with the same inflection. Sometimes it seemed as if they really communicated, but at other times, when the child tried to overcome the difficulties of language, she would stammer in syllables, sounds which hardly seemed to come from her.

Afterward they would walk in the garden. Maria would say the names of the birds and Kitty would repeat them after her. Sometimes it would be plants.

The landscape opened into the distance and when you looked out, you felt the height.

Steps led to this place, but the child did not know this yet, since she was living those days with the impressions of a first encounter. A tree, a stone, a bedraggled bush, a trickling puddle, all these were the extension of the images from within, from the hall. But outside, the universe was slacker. Outside she could take longer steps, she could stretch out her hand to touch a tree.

When she came back from her walks, the hall looked more beautiful to her. It was always toward evening. The light here was concentrated, its tones were fuller. It was a room full of flying angels, embellished inscriptions which she didn't understand, but which fit into the flight of the angels, creating a flowing movement. Sometimes the sound of the organ accompanied the dance.

She would return to her copybooks, intoning the conjugations, and then, in accordance with Maria's instructions, repeating the passages from the New Testament. She had still not learned to say the vespers; in the evening they would kneel together by the bed, momentarily silent.

In the meantime they found out that the abbess was about to pay a visit. A different atmosphere now animated the courtyard. In the rooms one could hear the creaking of closets being moved, the sounds of scrubbing, and other noises which seemed to indicate that some chained being lurked behind the heavy furniture, and whenever one tried to move it, it screamed. Maria tried to soothe her in vain. Kitty was affected by the uneasiness in the air; for even within these halls, screened off as they were by dividing walls, some contact, existed which bound people together. Perhaps here of all places you could sometimes even hear the silence talking.

One morning the abbess arrived. Her steps reminded Kitty, somehow, of other sounds. Where were they from? She didn't know. The convent filled her entire life, imbuing her with its solid being, pushing out memory.

At noon she was brought before the abbess. It was in the refectory, which was different from the other halls. Waiting in the doorway for a sign, she had the opportunity to scrutinize the walls. They were in a different style. Later she found out that the treasures of the convent were stored in this hall: ancient paintings, gold crowns, silver lamps, and other objects unsuitable for everyday use.

The abbess was sitting on a chair. There was an air of vitality about her. She stretched out her hands, beckoning the girl. Kitty came near and stood before her.

"Is this the girl?" asked the abbess.

The nuns nodded.

"Has she been given any instruction?"

"The New Testament, and some French," said Maria.

"Can you already feel God in your heart?" asked the abbess.

The nuns, in a body, turned their heads. Kitty looked at them, then turned her head back to the abbess, and said "God."

They spoke in French and Kitty did not understand. Father, Mother, Son, were the only words she knew. A few days before she had recited them together with Maria. Then she was led out of the hall. Before she left, the abbess tried to ask her something, but, seeing her confusion, she did not pursue the question.

Once again there were quiet days. No closet was moved, no picture was taken down. Everything was wrapped in that serene silence which is found in deep wells. She recited the words and the conjugations. And in the afternoons

Maria would come in and read with her. Memory was inaccessible. It had sunk to the darkest recesses.

Thus, in her eleventh year, she made her first ardent contact with life.

Slowly, as her vocabulary grew, her wonder blossomed. Her face took on the paleness which was common to all those who had lived here for many years, even the plants. Every month some new line, gesture, facial expression was added; this development filled Maria's heart with rejoicing and anxiety. This human creature must have other qualities.

What Maria did not reveal to Kitty, the walls would relate to her. The air in the room, the little statue—everything surged here, flowing and expanding:"Who are you?" "We are the *angels.*" "And who are you?" Only now was *he* revealed to her. It was the face of a man. The rivulets of blood flowed as far as the angels' feet, and from there to the windows. This was the first contact. He came to her from the concealed part of the picture. Neither old nor young, but suffering.

The next day Kitty was sunk in deep contemplation. Curiosity died in her, and when she touched the copybook, the crude letters spoke to her. She passed her hand over them, trying to calm them.

With Maria she spoke little. Her poor vocabulary made communication impossible. But Maria sensed that in spite of the rapid progress which she had made, the child was slipping away from her. She therefore decided to improve her speech, to enable her to converse with her and thus penetrate to her inner life. For the girl was like a dumb being, weaving a life of her own in the inmost depths of her soul. Maria did note that the concepts of the Father, the Mother, and the Son were not unknown to her, and that when she uttered their names in broken syllables, a tremor of joy lighted up her eyes. Her life, however, was dumb and expressionless. It found no outlet in exclamations, questions, or anger.

Once in a while, Maria would find her engrossed in a game. She played with the small square stones which she had removed from the crumbling mosaic at the entrance to the hall. For a moment she looked like a child, but when she raised her eyes, they held a strange look.

The abbess did not come. She left the convent to itself. The nuns worked as usual, and in the garden, the creepers, the roses, and the lawn came to life. Every murmur proclaimed growth. It seemed as if even the shade encouraged it. The windows were adorned with different colors. And when Maria said: "Spring has come," her voice rang with festivity.

Maria's efforts were unrewarded. Kitty did recite the verses, reading and rereading with stubborn dedication, but her own words remained unsaid. Maria would say:"Speak." And Kitty would respond. Between utterances, the silence loomed large, a solid barrier.

Summer came, and with it the change. Suddenly, like the transition from budding to blossoming, speech burst forth. It surged in her, colorful and wild, crystallizing into French words which fluttered in her like caged birds trying to escape. They emerged only with the greatest effort, twittering syllables which took on meaning only by virtue of the voice, the fluency, and the intonation. You couldn't call them words. They didn't seem to come from the speech center. It was her whole being which spoke.

The defect was now apparent. Maria had, in fact, suspected that there was something wrong with the child, but she had not said so specifically. Now the defect was prominent. Something in the child's movements, even more than in her voice, made it obvious that lack of words was not her only obstacle.

Sometimes Maria asked herself whether she should not take the matter up with the abbess as was customary in such cases. But this procedure, simple as it seemed, awakened doubts within her, which made her postpone the decision. The first thing they would do would surely be to take the girl from her and put her in the charge of one of the older nuns. Old nuns were not very particular about their methods; convinced that sin stubbornly assails the young, they sometimes rebuked them in an effort to stimulate the positive forces.

She decided to make the girl's life her own. She no longer sat beside her like a stranger, but observed her as if observing her own life. And thus, after many years of being a nun, she began to regard her life as one connected sequence, in which every detail stood out, testifying clearly to growth and development.

The days which followed brought no decisive changes. Maria felt that in her, too, something was dawning. It was a sort of compassion by virtue of which she wanted to bring the girl near to her, to make her happy, to tell her about herself. How attentive Kitty's eyes sometimes seemed. A slender body, a reluctant gesture, and sadness—one could not make her speak. The child spoke to herself, inventing phrases which did not exist in the language. Only daydreams and secret desires give rise to such meaningless combinations. Sometimes a sound escaped her, as if rent from the innermost recesses.

The girl's closed being bared something in Maria. She contemplated her own life. Sometimes it seemed to her that until now her own life had been moving in evasive superficiality, barely making contact. Finally, in a moment of weakness, it had anchored and closed up, but without any essential change taking place. The years as a nun had brought no turning point The vain desires of life died within her, but grace did not shine on her. Now, as a result of her meetings with the girl, she began to become aware of the deep hollowness within her. Her thoughts, even the most beautiful of them, seemed to float over the surface never becoming part of her. Such feeling had recurred to her ever since childhood, and with successive consistency ran through her life like a chain whose links were well forged.

Now, with the distance of years, her youth took shape within her with remarkable concreteness. The street, the inn, the tavern. An impoverished family; the sons sent off to the army; the daughters dispersed over many cities; and she, the youngest of them, finding herself in a convent. These were the bare facts, like the scaffolding of the building. The rest were just details, arising from circumstance. One cannot sever oneself from one's thoughts, from the first sights seen, from oneself, from one's family, from one's sisters who had taken up a dubious profession. Gradually she had realized that she was linked to them, that even in her solitude, or perhaps because she was here, she was linked to them, as a kind of delegate who must render account. Sometimes she thought of her father, his stubbornness, that movement of his hand whose abrupt motion she began to discern in her own manner. But not always. Sometimes her thoughts lay dormant and she worked industriously and devotedly, taking on that frozen expression which one assumes here. But in the hall, with the girl, her thoughts surged up in her as if suddenly set free from some focal point to which they were bound.

There was a crabapple tree in the garden and Kitty sometimes sat underneath it. The scene was like a reproduction of one of the big paintings on the wall. "Sister Maria," the girl would call, and Maria felt as if the holy infant itself were calling her.

But gradually the secret came between them. The more questions Kitty asked, the larger it loomed. "And my parents?" Kitty once asked.

"We have no parents, God is our father."

She had kept this sentence in her heart for many days, and only now did she utter it. She too wanted to be the child of God, like the girl, with no thoughts, with no defiled past. But when she tried to dismiss her thoughts, their full weight bore down upon her.

But she wanted to protect the child in the good shade of prayer and holy studies, to have her become a nun, not because of external motives; to plant her in the realm of eternal silence.

She began to be strict with Kitty.

The war again stood at the gates of the convent. The soldiers set up a camp. Shots filled the night with terror. The walks stopped. Kitty remained in the hall, her entire world restricted to the confines of its stained-glass windows. Only once a day, in the twilight, was she permitted to look out beyond the walls. Half-naked soldiers walked around, near the huts. Gradually this scene, different in color, merged with the scenes inside, until the contrast became blurred. She was filled with a peaceful sense of unity. Maria's presence filled her with warm intimacy. The abbess was forgotten. Saint Matthew, Saint Nicholas, and above all the Holy Virgin, became her friends; she could appeal to them even with the smallest requests.

Then, Kitty had other feelings. At first they were physical sensations, not unpleasant; then a hardening in her breasts. She realized that something was stirring inside her; it seemed to be a sign for whose revelation she must wait patiently. How lovely it was to nestle under the blanket, pulling it over her head, and to feel the body's pulse, to listen to the sweet murmurs.

She wanted to tell Maria about it, but something stopped her. The sweet secret to which she had loved to listen turned into heavy burden, which between dreams took on the form of a nightmare.

She would sit at the back of the garden, under the apple tree, watching the reddening fruit. Indoors, they were making preparations for the visit of the abbess. Again, the familiar squeaks were heard. Closets were moved from their usual places, pictures were removed from the walls. On the lawn a plaster bust, a lamp, and a shaky table were heaped together as if to embody a new combination of the sacred and the profane. Buxom maids were brought from the villages. Carrying brooms and brushes, they looked as if they were in charge of the place. Maria and Sister Katherine, who was older than she, took off their nun's habits and joined their efforts. Maria did not say much about the abbess, but what she said was so full of unadulterated praise that it aroused in Kitty a feeling of uneasiness which was mingled with awe and even anxiety. Imprisoned as she was by her secret, the abbess's forthcoming visit filled her with foreboding.

One day, during the noon recess, Kitty chanced to speak with one of the maids. She was a big-boned, rather masculine-looking woman who had apparently had a difficult life. Her husband had first wanted to be a priest. But after becoming involved in a murder had fled to Germany and enlisted in the army. She spoke fluently, in a peasant dialect, often accompanied by gesticulations in which revulsion and joy alternated swiftly as in a game full of unpredictable changes. But she did not only tell about herself. She tried, with that peasant cunning which knows how to employ flattery when necessary, to find out about the girl. A girl in a convent, thought the peasants, was a phenomenon worth noting, for she had certainly not arrived by chance.

Kitty told her that her parents had died in the war. This was the logical thing to say, for she could not tell her anything else; and besides, her new sensations seemed to point to this explanation. Sometimes she thought about it. Sometimes she saw herself as a child who had been left at the gate of a convent. But sometimes, near the sacred pictures, she would imagine that she was the child of God. Memory was of no help to her.

Often this certainty filled her with satisfaction. "Not everyone is lucky enough to be God's daughter, protected under His wing," she repeated to herself. Of course, the visit with the abbess and her meeting with her belied the fact that she occupied an honored position. Nevertheless, she did not lose the feeling of superiority which she kept secret in her heart.

Now, in the presence of the maid, in the face of this uninhibited confession, she had a feeling of sin, but also of seductive sweetness.

"Where did I come from?" Maria's explanations seemed like a fairy tale which was real and even believable, but at the same time there was now a presence which required another explanation. It was a moment of transition which only children experience, at times. It was, as it were, a realm of two truths each with its own rights.

Maria was busy with the housework and let the girl wander among the rubble, left to her own reflections. She realized only vaguely, if at all, that the girl was becoming wholly lost in them.

The meetings with the maid were marvelous; her speech was spiced with invective; her body was buxom. As she swept the floor, Kitty felt the lightness and the nonchalance with which she walked around in the hall which had previously been dominated by silence.

Usually their conversations took a rather practical turn. Peppi would speak, and when Kitty admitted that she felt a hardening in her breasts, she had the feeling that she was only acknowledging something that Peppi herself had mentioned. The maid burst into a raucous, splattering laugh as if her vocal cords had burst. From then on the conversation deteriorated. Peppi described the Germans encamped in the village without trying to hide her connections with them, and she spoke about other things which Kitty probably did not understand. But she felt a sort of strange sweetness which penetrated her gradually, destroying something of her own.

The next day everything was as usual. The maids were sent away and when Kitty woke up, the familiar silence was firmly established. The pictures hung in the hall. The smell of kerosene pervaded every corner. But it was not the same hall. Something had been taken away from it, from the corners, from the pictures. Her eyes looked at them, but all they saw were the drawings themselves.

Maria was tired and did not notice the change. She was taken up with preparations for the visit of the abbess. What she did notice was a rebellious turn of the shoulder which Kitty was unable to control.

The next day the signs of maturity burst forth. Kitty was full of shame. She tried to avoid Maria and at night she fell on the bed as tears scalded her face. In her dream Peppi appeared; in her torn dress she looked like a creature dragged out of a murky river. The next day, the dream remained alive within her. During the late hours of the morning, as she sat over her copybooks, she said to Maria: "I am a good girl," and Maria confirmed the fact with a caress.

Later, Maria left the convent suddenly. It turned out that the abbess had sent for her. Maria packed her belongings, and while she stood for a moment, gazing at the shining lamps, she looked unusually thin. She turned her head and Kitty noticed a sudden motion reflected in the bronze. The parting was very hasty, and as the gate creaked behind her, Kitty suddenly felt that something had been taken away from her.

Complete silence reigned as always in the noon hours. A dozing goat, a water basin and picture frames were scattered around like creatures obliged to bear the weight of the heat, each in its own corner. The objects were familiar to

her, but nevertheless a certain strangeness emanated from them. She had to
become reacquainted with them. Left to herself, she wandered around the building, looking for an entrance to the small rooms which were hidden from view,
living their lives for many years without anyone entering them. All the doors
were locked, and through the bars nothing could be seen. Finally she found
Katrina sitting on the threshold. Thin, dressed in festive clothes, she seemed
to be frozen in reflection. "Katrina," called Kitty in embarrassment.

Katrina was Maria's cousin. Steeped together as they were in faith, they had
not become intimate according to the laws of love. The enmity which they
had brought with them from home only deepened, and each day underscored
their past. Here they had met; the hand of fate pursued them and had brought
them together. When the matter had become known to the abbess, she had
not been willing to separate them. She had ordered them to remain together.

Kitty's heart was filled with compassion. She came near to Katrina, trying to find a suitable expression. Katrina rose slightly. She folded her dress around
her and sat withdrawn in the corner of the step.

"Maria's gone." said Kitty.

Aside from a few words about practical matters, Katrina said nothing. She
could not hide her uneasiness in Kitty's presence. Finally, when there was nothing left to say, she went away with the excuse that she must go to prayers. This
was a hint to Kitty that she, too, should be more pious. Kitty remained fixed
in her place.

She had bad dreams that night. She felt the heavy bell pressing down on
her shoulders, and when the bell chimed three it was as if the bell tongue swung
inside her. She rose and prayed, trying to break out of the wall that closed in
on her. Only toward morning did she discern a spark of reconciliation in the
eyes of the Crucified One.

Peppi appeared in the morning like a good messenger from another
world. With her torn dress and merry eyes she was the embodiment of total
abandon. She told Kitty that the front line was advancing, that soldiers were
being concentrated in the neighborhood, their number increasing from day
to day. It was obvious that she enjoyed the military preparations; the motions
of her arms, wide apart as if in an embrace, indicated as much.

"Maria won't return; she won't be able to. The roads are blocked. The soldiers will break into the convent; there aren't enough sleeping quarters in the
neighborhood. The abbess is worried; that's why she called her. They won't touch
Katrina. Her being a nun and her anger have dried her up"—that was the way
Peppi spoke. A confusion of facts and desires.

"And what about me?" asked Kitty.

"Don't you be afraid of them. Tell them you belong to me. You belong to
Peppi. They all know Peppi. I'll work for them in the canteen. Maybe you want

to work there too? Together, Kitty? This war is going to finish us. We're going to die without having a bit of fun. We must take the golden lamps out of here. They'll be yours, mine."

"No," said Kitty, taken aback.

"No," repeated Peppi, drawling the word. "No, you say. I have something to say to you also. You're a dirty Jew. They threw you into the convent, but I know. I saw. Tomorrow they'll come and take you. You won't get away; you won't get away."

"You won't get away, you won't get away"—these were not words; they were sounds escaping from a furious existence, like barks, until the gate closed them out with a bang.

The gate was an iron gate crowned with barbed wire and Kitty's eyes made out the two locks which were upon it.

Kitty stood for a moment, turning her head away. Down in the valley the soldiers were encamped. They encircled the mountain without leaving a gap. Half naked, in the radiant sunlight, they looked like moving masses of flesh. On the parade field, soldiers marched to military tunes. It was like the scene depicted in the big picture hanging in the hall. Leaning against the wall, Maria had once told her about the Crusades which had gone on for many years until the crusaders had finally succeeded in redeeming the tomb of the Son. It was the same scene. Even the colors were similar.

She was still agitated over the encounter with Peppi. "Was she angry with me, or maybe she was just joking." But her heart told her otherwise—Katrina's room was locked. She did not dare to knock. She stood on the steps touching the white marble. Gradually the pattern began to emerge, at first only meaningless details. Only later, as if aided by other sensations, it emerged and took shape. In the evening, when Katrina came in and told her that from now on she must remain in the cellar, she accepted the news calmly, as one who knows what is in store for her.

Outside, the dusk was fading. The sky was redder than usual. A sharp, moldy smell greeted them. Jars of beets covered with white kerchiefs stood in a row on the shelves. They looked like frozen creatures in whom life was still stirring.

"They're looking for me. Katrina is hiding me"—there was no longer any doubt of it. Now she visualized how they would find her. The door would open, light would blaze in, first on the jars, then on her. She came nearer to the jars. The bubbling of fermentation could be heard.

Groping, she acquainted herself with the objects around her, picture frames, broken statues, sacks of apples. She stretched out her hand and touched an apple. Its juice filled her.

After a while, Katrina came down and told her that from now on she must remain here, and Kitty said she knew that it was written in the Holy

Scriptures that the children of God must suffer until the light shines for them. But Katrina answered in a voice that sounded angry that she must not pride herself on this belief. "Am I a hairy Jew?" said Kitty, Peppi's voice echoing in her ears. No answer was forthcoming. Katrina was already behind the door. Her steps echoed for a while and then were silent.

Now all doubts vanished. Certainty formed the pattern. She stroked her skin and said, "Yes, I am hairy." Now she remembered that, even in the past, Peppi used to call her "little Jewess" as she pinched her cheek. Katrina too, as she stood before the abbess, had said something of the kind.

For many hours she sat behind the bars, waiting for the light. Nothing was heard. The silence of the convent deepened. She felt the hair growing from within her, spreading around her neck and under her arms.

"Yes, I am hairy," she said, as if acknowledging a fact that there was no point in denying anymore. "Who are you, jars?"

"We are jars of beets," the voice answered, "our color got lost in the dark. Can't you hear the song of fermentation?"

"I hear," said Kitty. "Am I hairy?"

"You are not hairy. You are our sister. God is hiding us."

Afterward she curled up on a pile of hay and fell asleep.

Katrina came down to her and Kitty told her that she felt well.

She had many friends here. The beets were fermenting in the jars, the Vishniac gave off an aroma of sanctity. Katrina said that the soldiers were encircling the mountain. They were encamped near the walls. Maria was on the way, but could not get there. In the convent nothing had changed. Kitty stretched out her hand, touching the starched dress. A tremor went through her. Now she knew that soon she would move to another place. Katrina spoke of other worlds, and Kitty asked for details, thinking it was the thing to do.

The war was drawing to an end. A final ceremony was still needed. The convent almost begged to be broken into. Katrina said that it was not she who had hidden Kitty. At this, the soldiers burst out laughing. They no longer had any urge to kill. Now it was the game which intrigued them.

Kitty had grown taller in the cellar and when she was brought out into the light, dressed in her white nightgown, she looked even taller. The gown trailed behind her.

She was led along narrow paths behind the fence. How marvelous it all seemed—like floating in space. Now all the people were gone. Angels embraced her arms and when the shot was heard, she stood for a moment marveling at the miracle revealed.

*Sholem Asch 1880–1957*  Asch was born and raised in Kutno, Poland, where he received a traditional Jewish education. At the age of eighteen, he moved to Warsaw where he met the great Yiddish story writer Isaac Leib Peretz who persuaded him to write in Yiddish for the masses rather than in Hebrew for the elite. After moving to New York in 1914, he gained prominence as a Yiddish writer. By 1924 his stories, novellas, novels, plays, and poems were so numerous that the Yiddish edition published in Warsaw amounted to eighteen volumes. He also wrote in English and his *Three Cities: A Trilogy* became a bestseller in 1933. Among his most popular English novels are *Kiddush Ha-Shem: An Epic of 1648* (1926), *The Nazarene* (1939), *The Apostle* (1943), and *Mary* (1949)—the latter three, very ecumenical, Yiddish novels about Jesus and his world estranged him from many Yiddish readers. In 1946, he published the novel *East River*. Many of his nearly two dozen Yiddish plays were performed not only in Yiddish theaters in Europe and America but also on the Polish and Russian stages and in Max Reinhardt's Deutsches Theater in Berlin. *God of Vengeance* (Yiddish 1907; English 1918), produced in Berlin in 1910 and banned in Russia, was closed by the police in New York in 1922 after 133 performances because of its setting in a brothel and its theme of lesbianism. However, this did little harm to Asch's popularity; he remained the most popular and prolific Yiddish writer in Europe and America for many years.

# "HEIL, HITLER!"

I had, of course, heard much about the professor; I had also dipped into his books. His fame traveled before him; not always, to be sure, "like a precious ointment," for there were people who accused him of undermining the moral sense in man. Still, it was a name to conjure with. His books were the first to be flung into the flames in Berlin—a tribute to the world conquest which his new ideas had achieved. Men who became famous always send out before them a false impression of themselves. I, at least, must confess that the picture I had formed of the professor was altogether wide of the mark. I probably expected his presence to have about it something as sensational as his reputation. I was utterly amazed by the unaffected simplicity and modesty of the man and by the strange touch of resignation in his bearing.

What struck me most, however, was the fact it was impossible to detect in him the faintest manifestation of hatred; not a single harsh expression escaped him when he spoke of the enemy. Yet I knew only too well, as did hundreds of thousands of others, what he had passed through in the last few months. Not only had they destroyed the work of a lifetime, scattering to the wind in one day what it had taken him decades to build up; not only had they stripped him of his fortune and his books; they had subjected him to the foulest tortures of which the Nazi prison cell and concentration camp have ever been the witnesses. His friends and admirers abroad had given up hope of getting him out alive, and it was only by a miraculous combination of influence and bribery that they finally obtained his release. Now he stood before me, an elderly man, bent and graying. But the gray had come on him suddenly; it had attacked him as a bandit attacks an unsuspecting wayfarer in a forest. His stoop, too, was not that of age, but of pain recently endured. Only the face was serene, completely serene, almost transfigured, one would have said. It radiated spiritual peace and made a space of silence about itself. It made one think of the silence in which a man wanders when he has lost his way in the desert. This man, too, had lost his way in his latter years; he could not tell where he would be on the morrow and to what place he would give the fleeting name of home. But never a word of bitterness from him. When we spoke of Germany, he said, with a resignation which suggested confession:

"Yes, we've sinned a lot; our post-war generation has a lot to answer for."

It happened that shortly before I was introduced to the professor, I had met again, after a long interval, an old acquaintance of mine, a New York financier, of German Jewish origin. His English still betrayed a German accent which even Hitlerism had not been able to obliterate. This man, I happened to know, had had a hand in the refinancing of post-war Germany; together with many other American bankers he had helped to put that country once more on its feet. His first words to me were:

"I've learned to hate!"

"Whom?" I asked.

He answered, in an excited voice which brought out more sharply his German accent:

"Whom do you think? The Boches, of course."

When I told the professor this story, having first explained what role the financier had played in the post-war history of Germany, he smiled. It was a thoughtful gentle smile, which rested for an instant on the childlike lips under the overhanging moustache.

"Yes, he can permit himself to hate."

"How so?"

"Only his pocket was affected."

"Pardon me, professor, if I suggest that with this man it wasn't a question of financial loss. I think his hatred springs from something else entirely; he feels himself outraged and insulted, as all of us do. He suffered as a Jew. To be quite frank with you, professor, I am a little astonished."

I hesitated, and the professor broke in. For the first time he betrayed a faint excitement.

"What do you mean, 'suffered as a Jew?'" he asked. "He personally didn't suffer anything, did he?"

And I, in turn: "How can you say he didn't suffer personally? Each one of us feels these sufferings personally."

"Just words," said the professor. "'Insulted,' 'outraged,' 'humiliated.' Certainly these words call out resistance, a desire for revenge. By 'personally' I mean physically."

I must have turned pale, for I felt as if the blood were standing still in my veins. I suddenly wanted to sit down.

"Why are you so startled?" asked the professor, and smiled again. "Here is what I mean. For more than a thousand years we Jews have been living in Germany, and our lives were woven into the life of that country with a thousand threads. Take my own family. Our records go back more than three hundred years. For the last three generations we've been doctors. And here a man comes along, and in the course of a brief, catastrophic period, wants to obliterate our thousand-year-old history, wipe it off the record, make it as if it hadn't been. And we let him do it! For that is what it amounts to, if we permit him to infect us with hatred of Germany. If I let myself be overcome by hatred, I am implying that Hitler is right, that we have never been part and parcel of the country, that we never really belonged to it, that we were always strangers, clinging to the land as long as circumstances were favorable to us. . . . That is what I mean by 'personal.' You, the Jews outside Germany, can permit yourselves to feel insulted and outraged by Germany, to hate and talk of revenge. But we German Jews, for whom Germany, with all her faults, was our homeland, and must remain our homeland, we German Jews can't permit ourselves to hate. No humiliations, no outrages, can sever the threads which bind us to the country, and have bound it to us for a thousand years. We have had bad times in Germany, we have had good times. This is a bad time; a good time will follow. That, too, is what I meant by 'personal.' "

What had at first been only a faint touch of excitement in the professor had grown, to my astonishment and distress, into a violent agitation; and though he undoubtedly meant, in all honesty, what he was saying, there was evident—at least to me—in the curious over-emphasis, in the staccato utterance, an attempt to overcome the suspicion which had been aroused by the word "physical."

As a matter of fact, I would have liked to drop the subject at this point; I was glad that the professor had lifted the conversation to the level of generalities, thereby evading the painful impression which his use of the word "physical" had created. But my curiosity and my obstinacy were stronger than myself, and before I knew it I had plunged back.

"Excuse me, professor," I said, "all these considerations which you raise, as to why you should not hate Germany, are themselves generalities; they are not personal factors. However pertinent they may be for German Jewry as such, they don't explain why an abstract concept like history can affect you, the person, the individual; because you, the person, the individual, surely can't help crying out for liberation and revenge. What are the arguments based on generalities and logical considerations which can quiet the feelings aroused by the physical sufferings—yes, let me use that word, 'physical'—by the physical sufferings through which you have passed?"

This time it was the professor who paled. His lips trembled. His eyes fell, and it seemed to me that his voice had become unsteady.

"Yes, that's just it . . . the physical torment. Does physical torment always and inevitably evoke hatred and the desire for revenge? Don't we often get just the contrary effect?"

I shrank from the suggestion, but offered no comment. The professor continued eagerly:

"What I mean is quite simple. Yes, easy to die once; but how hard it is to die over and over again! You know that wonderful legend of Tolstoi's, of the man who is clinging to a twig above an abyss and yet feels not the slightest trace of the death-horror. Man is condemned to live in whatever situation he finds himself; no matter how imminent the danger, he looks for something, he risks everything, if only it offers the prospect of survival."

"No," I said, at last. "I don't quite understand you, Professor. I would be grateful if you'd make it simpler."

"Very well. Let's take, as our instance, a certain prominent political figure, and try to explain his course of action. We all know the man. He is thoroughly honest, thoroughly decent. His life has been devoted to the progress of mankind; he has been consistently faithful to his ideal of human liberty.

His hands are clean. Then the disaster comes, and this man shares the fate of the rest of his party. He's thrown into a concentration camp. And suddenly, a few months later, we hear from him; he has recanted everything he believed in; he has made public utterances which falsify everything he has fought for. Well, you can't convince me that this man has been bribed, or that he doesn't mean what he now says. No, there are deeper factors at play here, deeper human elements, which we don't want to consider, which we don't want to face. We, who stand outside of events, and who want to think of them as things that happened in a book, want to believe in strong characters, consistent heroes. We would have liked to impose on this man the role of a martyr. He is tortured in a concentration camp! What a marvelous figure he will cut in history! And no doubt if the man were given the opportunity to die for his cause, he would be able to summon up the little bit of courage which is needed for the right exit. But they didn't give him that little opportunity to die heroically, according to the pattern we've made for him. What they did give him, was the opportunity to live, that is to say, the opportunity to die over and over again. And for that sort of thing his nerves lacked the requisite strength."

"Very well, then. I listen to this man, making his shameful public retractions; and I must confess that they impress me as his honest conviction; he has discovered that throughout his life he has been following a false ideal: Hitler, and Hitler alone, is right! And I must accept one of two conclusions, it seems: either the man has been a dupe all his life, and was not honest with himself, or else he is lying now."

"But as a matter of fact the dilemma doesn't exist. He was honest before, and he's honest now; however dreadful and improbable it may sound, he is thoroughly convinced that Hitler is right. That's why I've tried to make it clear that a man can't go on living without some sort of ground under his feet; and if that ground doesn't exist, he invents it in his own mind. . . . For instance, let's look into the following situation. The majority of men are quite courageous, combative, even heroic, on one side of their bodies: that is, when they face the enemy and do their fighting frontward. But the vast majority of men would be utter cowards if they had to fight an enemy whom they did not face, but to whom they had their backs. The backbone is an extremely delicate and nervous organ. It has much less power of resistance than a man's front—his face, for instance. It therefore often happens that a man who is capable of the highest heroism and endurance when his enemy is in front of him, collapses and sells out when he has to protect his rear."

"Am I to understand that figuratively, Professor?"

"By no means. You must take it quite literally. There are certain sicknesses which manifest themselves in an exaggerated sensitivity. The chief symptom is that the patient won't permit his back to be touched. When he gets into a crowd, or when he has to stand in a queue, he becomes frightfully nervous. He is afraid that someone will touch his back. And if someone actually does it, he leaps round like a wild beast—as if someone had thrust a hand into an open wound. A man like that is capable of any amount of heroism frontward, or faceward. But suppose he happens to be taken to a concentration camp, where they discover his particular weakness—as they discover similar weaknesses in others. What do they do with such a man? Well, they strip the clothes from him, and they make him stand with his face to a wall, and his hands in the air. And they tell him to shout 'Heil, Hitler!' The man doesn't know, of course, what's going on behind his back, and what they're going to do to his back; whether they're going to touch it with a red-hot iron, or whether they're going to turn a stream of ice-cold water on it, or bring down on it a lash loaded with leaden weights; or whether—and this is the most horrible of all— they're going to touch it with their fingernails. His entire backbone is tensed like a harpstring—one touch, and it will snap. . . . Now let's assume that this man is by nature honest, that he has deep-seated convictions, for which he's prepared to suffer, even to offer up his life. He isn't a young man, who could begin life anew. Most of his life is behind him, the future affords little prospect. He's a conscientious man; he knows that if he endures these tortures without yielding, his life will retain its significance; whereas if—God forbid—he fails himself, he has denied and destroyed his own past. It is clear to him, then, that there is only one course for him to follow; and that is, to die, and with his death to place an honest seal on his own life. And he's ready to do it—if only they'd give him a chance to do it frontward, faceward. With his front he could endure anything. He would throw himself, frontward, into a boiling caldron, or leap into a blazing furnace; and the last word on his lips would be one of defiance and affirmation, just as it was with the martyrs of old. But don't you see, they withhold just that opportunity from him; they won't let him die a heroic death. They've discovered his weakness, his back; and they've stripped, and put him with his face to the wall. And now there's only one thought in his mind. *They mustn't touch his back.* Not with a hot iron, and not with ice-cold water, and least of all with their fingernails, their naked fingernails. Everything in him concentrates on that one frightful idea—all his thoughts have this one hideous fear—no, he has no thoughts; he has only open wounds in his brains, and the wounds are like mouths screaming this one demand. *Don't touch my back!* Honor, honesty, consistency, faith, decency— all these things have become a single, squirming confusion; shuddering waves of sensitivity pass up and down his spine, yes, with some sort of sexual overtone in them. But it always amounts to that one thing: *They mustn't touch his back.* And the only protection that he has is: 'Heil, Hitler!' 'Heil, Hitler!' His voice is the only shield which he can interpose between his back and the poised horror. And so his voice becomes clearer, louder, more and more sincere; it takes on faith and conviction. 'Heil, Hitler!' Yes, 'Heil, Hitler!' 'Hitler, the savior, the Messiah!' *'Jude, verrecke!'* And 'When Jewish blood flows from the knife!' 'Heil, Hitler! Heil, Hitler! Heil, Hitler!'"

"Professor! In God's name!"

His face had become an ashen blue. A thin line of foam came out on his lips. He continued to shout, in ever louder tones: "Heil, Hitler! Heil, Hitler!" And then suddenly he collapsed in my arms, in a dead faint. I put him down in an armchair and ran for a glass of water. In a little while he came to. He even mustered a faint smile.

"Yes," he murmured, "If only you don't have to fight with your back, you can manage."

"Professor, we won't talk about it any more."

"It doesn't make any difference now," he said. "I only wanted to make it clear that a man who's been shouting 'Heil, Hitler!' day after day, week after week, whether he does it willingly, or against his will, has no right to hate."

"But what?"

"I don't know. I haven't a word for it. But it's quite different from hate, quite different."

We were both silent.

*Giorgio Bassani 1916–*     Born in Bologna into a prosperous
middle-class Jewish family, Bassani was reared in
Ferrara, the place of much of his fiction, in the years
before and during World War II. He studied literature at the University of Bologna (1934–1939) and,
while holding a series of minor journalistic and edit-
ing jobs in the 1950s, began issuing the stories collected in 1956 in the book *Cinque storie ferraresi*
(issued in England by Faber in 1962 as *A Prospect
of Ferrara* and in the United States by Harcourt in
1971 as *Five Stories of Ferrara*). Bassani gained international fame when he won the Premio Viareggio
for *The Garden of the Finzi-Continis* in 1962, which
was translated into English (1965) and many other
languages. Vittorio de Sica made it into a highly
acclaimed film in 1970.

Bassani became politically active at the beginning
of World War II when he joined the Action Party
(Partito d'Azione). This time also marks the begin-
ning of his literary career with the publication of
*A City of the Lowlands* under the pseudonym Giacomo
March. In 1943 he was arrested for participation in
the resistance movement. He remained in jail until
the collapse of the fascist regime later that year.
Many of his relatives from Ferrara were deported to
Buchenwald, where most perished.

# A Plaque on Via Mazzini

◆ *I*

In August 1945, when Geo Josz reappeared in Ferrara, sole survivor of the
hundred and eighty-three members of the Jewish Community whom the Germans had deported in the autumn of '43 and whom most people, not without reason, considered long since exterminated in the gas chambers, at first
nobody in the city recognized him.

They didn't remember who he was, to tell the truth. Unless, some added in a dubious tone, unless lie could be a son of that Angelo Josz, well-known cloth wholesaler, who though exempted for patriotic reasons (these were the terms of the decree of '39; and after all it had been only human, on the part of the late Constil Bolognesi, at that time already the Fascist Party Secretary of Ferrara and always a good friend of old Josz, to adopt, in memory of their common enterprises with the Fascist squads of their youth, a language that was so generic) had been unable, despite this distinction, to keep himself and his family out of the great roundup of Jews in '43.

Yes, one of those withdrawn young people, they began to recall, pursing their lips and frowning, no more than ten in all, who after '38 had perforce broken off all relations with their former schoolmates and had also, in consequence, stopped visiting their homes, and had been seen about only rarely, growing up with strange faces, frightened, wild, contemptuous, so that when people saw them every now and then, rushing off, bent over the handlebars of a bicycle, speeding along Corso Giovecca or Corso Roma, they became upset and preferred to forget about them.

But apart from that: in this man of indefinable age, so fat he seemed swollen, with an old lambskin hat on his shaven head, wearing a kind of sampler of all the known and unknown uniforms of the time, who could have recognized the frail boy of seven years ago, or the nervous, thin, shy adolescent of four years later? And if a Geo Josz had ever been born and had existed, if he too, as he asserted, had belonged to that band of a hundred and eighty-three shadows devoured by Buchenwald, Auschwitz, Mauthausen, Dachau, etc.; was it possible that he, only he, should come back from there now, and present himself, oddly dressed, true, but very much alive, to tell about himself and about the others who hadn't come back and would never, surely, come back again? After all this time, after so much suffering which all had more or less shared, without distinction of political belief, social position, religion or race, what did he want, Geo, at this moment? Even Signor Cohen the engineer, the President of the Jewish Community, who had insisted on dedicating, the moment he got back from Switzerland, in memory of the victims, a large marble plaque which now stood out, rigid, enormous, brand-new, on the red brick façade of the Temple (and then the plaque had to be done over, naturally, to the satisfaction of those who had reproached Signor Cohen for his commemorative haste, since dirty linen—as love of Fatherland teaches us—can always be washed without causing scandal), even he, at first, had raised a host of objections; in short, he wanted nothing to do with it.

But we must proceed in an orderly fashion; and before going any further, we must linger for a moment on the episode of the plaque set in the façade of the Temple thanks to Signor Cohen's rash initiative: an episode which is, properly speaking, the beginning of the story of Geo Josz's return to Ferrara.

To tell it now, the scene might appear scarcely credible. And, to doubt it, you have only to picture it taking place against the background—so normal, so familiar to us—of Via Mazzini (not even the war touched the street: as if to signify that nothing, ever, can happen there!): the street, that is, which from Piazza delle Erbe, flanking the old ghetto—with the Oratorio of San Maurelio at the beginning, the narrow fissure of Via Vittoria at the halfway point, the red brick façade of the Temple a bit farther on, and the double line of its hundred warehouses and shops, each harboring, in the semidarkness steeped in odors, a cautious little soul, imbued with mercantile skepticism and irony—connects the winding, decrepit little streets of Ferrara's medieval core with the splendid Renaissance avenues, so damaged by bombardments, and the modern section of the city.

Immersed in the glare and silence of the August afternoon, a silence interrupted at long intervals by the echoes of distant shooting, Via Mazzini lay empty, deserted, intact. And so it had appeared also to the young workman wearing a paper hat, who at half past one, climbing onto a little scaffold, had started working on the marble slab that they had given him to put in place, six feet from the ground, against the dusty bricks of the synagogue. His presence there, a peasant forced to the city by the war and obliged to turn himself into a mason (he was slowly filled by the sense of his own solitude and by a vague fear, because this was a commemorative plaque, surely; but he had taken good care not to read what was written on it!), had been erased from the beginning by the light, and he was unable to cancel the deserted quality of the place and the hour. Nor had it been canceled, this emptiness, by the little group of passers-by who, gathering later, apparently without his being aware of them, had come gradually to cover, in their various attitudes and colors, a good part of the cobbled pavement behind his back.

The first to stop were two youths: two bearded, bespectacled partisans, with knee-length shorts, red kerchiefs tied around their throats, automatic rifles slung over their shoulders: students, young gentlemen of the city, the young mason-peasant had thought, hearing them speak and turning slightly just to glance at them. A little later they were joined by a priest, unperturbed despite the heat, wearing his black cassock, but with its sleeves rolled up—he had a strange, battle-like manner, as if defiant—over his hairy white forearms. And then, afterward, a civilian, a man of sixty with a grizzled beard, an excited manner, his shirt open over his scrawny chest and his bobbing Adam's apple: this man, after beginning to read in a low voice what was presumably written on the plaque (and this was names and names; but not all Italian, or so it seemed), had broken off at a certain point to cry, emphatically: "A hundred and eighty-three out of four hundred!" as if he too, Aristide Podetti of Bosco Mesola, by chance in Ferrara, where he had no intention of staying longer than strictly necessary, a man who stuck to his work and nothing else, could be stirred by those names and those numbers to unknown memories, as if they aroused unknown emotions in him. What did it matter, to him, whose names those were and why they had been carved in marble? The remarks of the people who had instead been attracted precisely by them, and who were becoming more and more numerous, made a tiresome buzzing in the mason's ears. Jews, yes, all right, a hundred and eighty-three out of four hundred. A hundred and eighty-three out of the four hundred who lived in Ferrara before the war. But what were they, after all, these Jews? What did they mean, they and the *others*, the Fascists, by that word? Ah, the Fascists! From his very village, in the Po plain, which in the winter of '44 they had made a kind of headquarters, they had sown terror through the countryside for months and months. The people called them *tupin*, mice, because of the color of their shirts; and exactly like mice, when the time had come for settling scores, they quickly found holes to hide in. They stayed hidden, now. But who could guarantee they wouldn't come back? Who could swear they weren't still walking around the streets, also wearing red kerchiefs at their throats, waiting for the moment of revenge? At the right moment, as quickly as they had hidden, they would jump out again with their black shirts, their death's-heads; and then, the less a man knew, the better off he was.

And he, the poor boy, was so determined not to know anything, because all he needed was work, nothing else interested him; so unaware and distrustful of everything and everybody, as, locked in his rough dialect of the Po delta, he turned his stubborn back to the sun, that when, all of a sudden, he felt a light touch on his ankle ("Geo Josz?" a mocking voice said at the same time) he wheeled around promptly with a nasty look.

A short, square man, with a strange fur hat on his head, stood before him. Raising his arm, the man pointed to the plaque behind the boy's shoulders. How fat he was! He seemed swollen with water, like a drowned man. And there was nothing to be afraid of because he was laughing, surely to make himself agreeable.

"Geo Josz?" the man repeated, still pointing to the plaque, but now serious.

He laughed again. But at once, as if repentant, and dotting his words frequently with "please" like the Germans (he spoke with the polish of a gifted salon conversationalist; and Aristide Podetti, since he was the one being addressed, listened open-mouthed), he declared that he was sorry, "believe me," to spoil everything with his interruption, which, as he was ready to admit, bore all the earmarks of a *faux pas*. Ah, yes, he sighed, the plaque would have to be done over again, since that Geo Josz, to whom it was partly dedicated, was none other than himself, in person. Unless (and, saying this, his pale blue eyes looked around, as if to seize an image of the Via Mazzini from which the little crowd, surrounding him, holding its breath, was excluded; not a head, meanwhile, had peered out of the many shops nearby), unless the Committee which sponsored the commemoration, accepting this event as a hint from fate, were to give up entirely the idea of the memorial plaque: which, he sneered, though it offered the unquestionable advantage of being set in that place where there was so much traffic that it had to be read almost perforce ("You aren't bearing in mind the dust, however, my dear friend; in a few years no one will notice it any more!"), had also the serious defect of unsuitably altering the straightforward, homely façade of "our dear old Temple": one of the few things, including also Via Mazzini—which the war, thank God, had spared completely, and which had remained exactly as "before"—the few things on which (". . . yes, dear friend, I mean this for you also, though I imagine you are not Jewish . . .") one could still count.

"It's a bit as if you—for example—were obliged with that face, with those hands, to put on a dinner jacket."

And, at the same time, he displayed his own hands, calloused beyond all belief, but with white backs where a registration number, tattooed a bit above the right wrist in the skin so flabby it seemed boiled, could be read distinctly, all five numbers, preceded by the letter *J*.

◆ *II*

And so, with a look that was not menacing but rather ironic and amused (his eyes, a watery blue, peered up coldly from below, as if he were emerging, pale and swollen as he was, from the depths of the sea), Geo Josz reappeared in Ferrara, among us.

He came from afar, from much farther than the place he actually had come from! And to find himself again suddenly here, in the city where he had been born . . .

Things had gone more or less like this:

The military truck, on which he had been able to travel in a few hours from the Brenner Pass to the Po Valley, after driving off the ferry at Pontelagoscuro had slowly climbed up the right bank of the river. And then, having reached the top, after a final, almost reluctant jolt, it offered to his gaze the immense, forgotten plain of his childhood and adolescence. Down there, a bit to the left, should lie Ferrara. But was Ferrara, he had asked himself, and had asked, also, the driver sitting at his side—was Ferrara that dark polygon of dusty stone, reduced, except for the Castle's four towers which rose airy and unreal in the center, to a kind of lugubrious flatiron which weighed, heavy, on the fields? Where were the green, luminous, ancient trees that once rose along the crest of the maimed walls? The truck was rapidly approaching the city, as if, gradually accelerating along the intact asphalt of the straight highway, it were going to plunge on Ferrara from above; and through the wide breaches here and there in the bastions, he could already see the streets, once so familiar, now made unrecognizable by the bombings. Less than two years had gone by since he was taken away. But they were two years that counted for twenty, or two hundred.

He had come back when no one expected him any longer. What did he want, now?

To answer calmly a question like this—with the calm necessary to understand and sympathize with what, at first, had probably been only a simple, if unexpressed, desire to live—perhaps other times, perhaps another city was required.

It required, in any case, people a bit less frightened by those certain gentlemen who set the norm, again as always, for the city's public opinion (there were, in that group, along with some big merchants and landowners, several of the most authoritative professional men of Ferrara: the sinew, in short, of what had been, before the war, our so-called leading class): the people who, having been forced to "support," more or less in a body, the defunct Fascist Social Republic, and who couldn't resign themselves to step down even for a short while, now saw traps, enemies, and even political rivals on all sides. They had accepted Party cards, the infamous card, true. But out of pure civic duty. And, in any case, not before that fatal December 15th of 1943, when fully eleven fellow citizens had been shot at once, the date which had marked the beginning, in Italy, of the never sufficiently deplored "fratricidal struggle." Riddled with bullets across the street from the portico of the Caffè della Borsa, they had lain for a whole day, guarded by troops with guns at the ready; and the others had seen them, with their own eyes, the bodies of those "poor wretches," flung in the filthy snow like so many bundles! And so, continuing in this tone, all caught up as they were in their effort to convince others and themselves that, though they may have erred, they had erred more from generosity than fear (for this reason, having removed all other badges, they began to appear with every possible military decoration stuck in the buttonhole of their jacket), they surely couldn't be considered the ideal sort to recognize in others that simplicity and normality of intention, that famous "purity" of action and ideas which, in themselves, they were unable to give up. As for the specific case of the man in the old fur hat: even assuming he was Geo Josz—and they weren't entirely convinced of that, however—assuming he was, he still could not be trusted. That fat of his, all that fat made them suspicious. Oh yes, starvation edema! But who besides Geo could have started such a story circulating, in a clumsy attempt to justify a corpulence in singular contradiction to what was said about German concentration camps? Starvation edema didn't exist, it was an outright invention. And Geo's fat meant two things: either in those *Lager* one didn't suffer the great hunger that propaganda insisted on, or else Geo had enjoyed conditions of special favor there. One thing was sure: under that fur hat, behind that lip curled in a perpetual smile, there was room, they would have sworn, only for hostile thoughts and plans.

And what of the others—a minority, to tell the truth—who remained shut up in their houses, ears alert to the slightest noise from outside, the very image of fear and hate?

Among the latter there was the man who had offered to preside, a tricolor-sash across his chest, at the public auction of the Jewish Community's confiscated possessions, including the silver chandeliers of the Temple and the ancient vellum Scriptures; and those who, pulling black caps with the Brigade's death's-head over their white hair, had been members of the special tribunal responsible for various executions: almost always respectable people, for that matter, who perhaps before then had never shown any sign of being interested in politics, and who, in the majority of cases, had led a largely retired life, devoted to the family, to their profession, their studies. . . . But they feared greatly for themselves, these people; they had, on their own account, such a fear of dying that even if Geo Josz had wanted only to live (and this was the least, really, that he could want) well, even in such a simple and elementary request, they would have found some personal threat. The thought that one of them, any night of the week, could be seized quietly by the "reds" and carried off to be slaughtered in some unknown place in the country: this terrifying thought returned, constantly, to drive them mad with anxiety. To live, to stay alive, no matter how! It was a violent demand, exclusive, desperate.

If at least that man in the fur hat, "that wreck," would make up his mind to leave Ferrara!

Unconcerned that the partisans, having taken over the command post of the Black Brigade, were using the house on Via Campofranco, his father's property, as their barracks and prison, he was clearly content, on the other hand, to carry around that obsessive, ill-omened face of his: surely to add new fuel to the wrath of those who would make it their business to avenge him and all his people. The greatest scandal, in any case, was that the new authorities put up with such a state of things. It was no good appealing to the Prefect, Doctor Herzen, installed in office just after the "so-called" Liberation, by the same National Committee of Liberation of which, after the events of December '43, he had been the underground President, if it was true, and it was, that they compiled black lists every evening in his office, in the Castle. Ah yes, they knew him, well, they did, that character who in '39 had allowed his property to be confiscated, almost smiling at the loss of the big shoe factory he owned at the gates of the city, and whose possession now, if Allied bombers hadn't reduced it to rubble, he would surely demand again! A man of about forty, bald, tortoise-shell spectacles, he had the typically peaceful and inoffensive look (except for the "Jewish" name, Herzen, and the stiff, inflexible back which seemed fastened to the seat of his inseparable bicycle) of all those who are seriously to be feared. What about the Archbishopric? And the English military government? Was it, unfortunately, a sign of the times that even from these offices no better answer came than a sigh of desolate solidarity or, worse, a mocking grin?

There's no reasoning with fear and hate. For if they had wanted, getting back to Geo Josz himself, to understand something of what was really going on in his spirit, they had only to begin, after all, with his extraordinary reappearance in Ferrara; and specially with the sequel of that singular scene which, just by the entrance to the Temple on Via Mazzini, at a certain point had led him to extend his hands, not without sarcasm, to a young mason's stunned examination.

Perhaps the man of sixty, with the sparse grizzled beard, will recall it, he who was among the first to stop before the marble slab, the memorial plaque desired by Signor Cohen, the man who at a given moment had raised his shrill voice ("A hundred and eighty-three out of four hundred!" he had shouted proudly) to remark on its content.

Well, after silently following with the others what happened in the next minutes, when he pushed his way awkwardly through the little crowd and fell on the neck of the man in the fur hat, kissing him noisily on the cheeks and showing that, first of all, he had recognized in him Geo Josz, the latter, his hands still outstretched, remarked coldly: "With that ridiculous beard, dear Uncle Daniele, I hardly knew you"—a remark that was truly revealing, not only of the kinship between him and one of the city's surviving representatives of the Josz family (a brother of his father's, to be precise, who having miraculously eluded the great roundup of November '43 had returned to the city the end of last April), but also of the deep, sharp intolerance that he, Geo, felt for any sign that spoke to him, in Ferrara, of the passage of time and of the changes, even the tiny ones, that it had wrought in things.

And so he asked: "Why the beard?"

"Do you think perhaps that beard is becoming?"

It honestly seemed he could think of nothing but observing, with critical eye, all the beards of various form and shape that the war, and the notorious forged papers, had caused to become common usage; and this was his way, since he could hardly be called a talkative type, of expressing his disagreement.

In what had been before the war the Josz house, where uncle and nephew appeared that same afternoon, there were, naturally, plenty of beards; and the little, low, red-stone building surmounted by a slender Ghibelline tower, so long that it covered almost a whole side of the brief and secluded Via Campofranco, assumed a military, feudal air, perhaps suitable for evoking the ancient lords of the palace, the Marquesses Del Sale, from whom Angelo Josz had bought it in 1910 for a few thousand lire, but it hardly evoked Angelo, the Jewish cloth wholesaler who had vanished with his wife and children in the ovens of Buchenwald.

The main door was wide open. Outside, seated on the steps of the entrance with guns between their bare legs, or lying on the seats of a jeep pulled up by the high wall that, opposite, separated Via Campofranco from a vast private garden, about a dozen partisans were loafing. But others, in greater numbers, some with voluminous files under their arms, and all with faces marked by energy and resolution, came and went constantly despite the sultry air of the late afternoon. And so, between the street half in shadow and half in the sun and the breached door of the old aristocratic palazzo, there was an intense bustle, lively, gay, in perfect harmony with the cries of the swallows that dipped low, grazing the cobbles, and with the typewriters' clicking that came steadily through the enormous seventeenth-century grilles of the ground floor.

The strange couple—one tall, thin, perky, the other fat, slow, sweating—came in the door then, and immediately attracted the attention of those present: mostly armed men, generally with long hair and flowing beards, sitting, waiting on the rough benches set along the walls. They gathered around; and Daniele Josz, who evidently wanted to demonstrate to his nephew his own familiarity with this environment, was already willingly answering their questions, for himself and for his companion.

But he, Geo, examined, one by one, those tanned, flushed faces that pressed around him, as if through the beards he wanted to investigate some secret, some hidden corruption.

Ah, you can't fool me! his smile said.

He seemed reassured only for a moment, discovering that beyond the gate of the portico, right in the center of the bare little garden that stretched beyond, there still shone, dark and flourishing, a large magnolia. But not sufficiently reassured to prevent him, a little later, upstairs, in the office of the young Provincial Secretary of the Partisans Association (the same man who two years later was to become the most brilliant Communist member of the Italian Parliament, so polite, reserved, and reassuring that he made not a few of our most worthy *mères de famille* sigh with regret, since he also belonged to one of the finest middle-class families of Ferrara, the Bottecchiaris, and, what's more, was a bachelor) from repeating his now time-worn remark:

"That beard isn't at all becoming to you, do you know that?"

So, in the frozen embarrassment that fell immediately on what until then, thanks entirely to Uncle Daniele, had been a fairly cordial conversation, in the course of which the future Deputy had acted as if he didn't notice the formal *Lei* which Geo on his part had maintained, while the other man insisted on the affectionate *tu* used among those of the same age and the same Party, it was suddenly clear what Geo Josz really wanted, the reason why he was there (and if only those who, on the contrary, were so afraid of him could have been present!). That house where *they*, like the others, the blacks, had made their headquarters before them, was his, didn't they remember that? By what right had they taken possession of it? He looked threateningly at the typist, who jumped and suddenly left off striking the keys, as if he meant to tell even her, especially her, that he wouldn't be at all satisfied with a single room, even if it were this one, so handsome and sunny—once a salon for receiving, of course, even if the parquet had been torn from the floor probably for firewood—which was nice and comfortable, wasn't it, from dawn to dusk, and perhaps even after dusk, working with the young partisan commander who seemed so determined, out of the goodness of his heart, to remake the world.

Down in the street they were singing:

> The wind is whistling, the tempest screams,
> Our shoes have holes, and yet we must march on . . .

And the song, impetuous and absurd, came through the window, open to the sky, which was a tender, very gentle pink.

But the house was his, they should have no illusions. Sooner or later he would take it back, all of it.

◆ *III*

This was to happen, in fact, though obviously not at once.

For the moment, Geo seemed to be satisfied with only one room—and it wasn't, of course, the office of Nino Bottecchiari! Instead, it was a kind of attic at the very top of the tower that dominated the house, and to reach it he had to climb at least a hundred steps, then, at the end, some worm-eaten little wooden stairs which led directly from a space below once used as a storeroom. It was Geo himself, in the disgusted tone of one resigned to the worst, who first spoke of this "makeshift." As to the storeroom below, that too, he added, would be rather useful, since he could put, as he meant to, his Uncle Daniele there. . . .

But it was soon clear that Geo could follow from that height, through a wide glass window, whatever happened in the garden, on one side, and in Via Campofranco, on the other. And since he hardly ever left the house, presumably spending a great part of his day looking at the vast landscape of dark tiles, gardens, and green countryside that stretched out below him (an immense view, now that the leafy trees of the city wall were no longer there to cut it off!), for the occupants of the lower floors, his constant presence soon became a troublesome, nagging thought. The cellars of the Josz house, which all opened onto the garden, since the time of the Black Brigade had been transformed into secret prisons, about which many sinister stories had been told in the city even after the Liberation. But now, subjected to the probable, untrustworthy control of the guest in the tower, they no longer served, naturally, those purposes of summary and clandestine justice for which they had been set up. Now, with Geo Josz installed in that sort of observatory, there was no being sure even for a moment, since the kerosene lamp he kept burning all night long—and you could see its faint glow through the panes, up there, until dawn—led everyone to suppose he was always alert, he never slept. It must have been two or three in the morning after the evening Geo first appeared on Via Campofranco, when Nino Bottecchiari, who had stayed working in his office until that hour and was finally about to allow himself some rest, stepping out into the street, happened to raise his eyes to the tower. "Watch yourself" Geo's lamp warned, suspended in the starry sky. And the young future Deputy was bitterly reproaching himself for guilty carelessness and his acquiescence—but at the same time, as a good politician, preparing to take the new circumstances into account—as he decided, with a sigh, to climb into the jeep.

But it was also possible for him to turn up at any hour of the day, as he soon began to do, from one moment to the next, on the stairs or down in the entrance: passing before the eyes of the partisans permanently gathered there, dressed in his impeccable civilian suit of olive gabardine which had almost immediately replaced the fur hat, the leather jacket, and the tight trousers of his arrival in Ferrara. He walked among the mute partisans without greeting anyone, elegant, perfectly shaven, with the brim of his brown felt turned down at one side of his brow, over a cold, icy eye; and in the vague uneasiness that followed each of his apparitions, he was from the beginning the authoritative landlord of the house: too polite to quarrel, but strong in his right, he needs only to show himself to the vandal tenant in arrears, who has to leave. The tenant grumbles, pretends not to notice the silent, insistent protest of the owner of the building, who for the present is saying nothing, though, at the right moment, will surely ask for an accounting of the ruined floors, the stained walls; so, from month to month, the situation worsens, becomes more and more embarrassing and precarious. It was late, after the elections of '48, when so many things in Ferrara had by then changed, or rather had gone back to their prewar state (but meanwhile young Bottecchiari's candidacy for Parliament had had time to be crowned with the most complete success), it was then that the Partisans Association decided to move its headquarters elsewhere, specifically to three rooms in the former Casa del Fascio on Viale Cavour, where in 1945 the Provincial Labor Council had established its offices. It is true, all the same, that the silent, implacable action of Geo Josz made that move seem long overdue.

He hardly ever left the house, then, as if he wanted them not to forget him there, not even for a moment. But this didn't prevent him from showing up every so often on Via Mazzini, where in September he had arranged for his father's storehouse, in which the Community had collected all it could recover of the possessions confiscated from the Jews during the period of the Fascist Republic, to be cleared out in view of the "more than necessary"—as he said to Signor Cohen in person—"work of restoration and reopening of the business"; or, more rarely, along Corso Giovecca, with the uncertain tread of one advancing in prohibited territory, his spirit torn between the fear of unpleasant encounters and the sharp, conflicting desire for them, joining the evening promenade that had already begun once more, animated and lively as always; or at the apéritif hour, sitting abruptly at a little table—because he arrived each time breathless, dripping sweat—at the Caffè della Borsa on Corso Roma, which had remained the political center of the city. Nor did the ironic, contemptuous attitude habitual with him, which had persuaded even the expansive Uncle Daniele, so electrified by the early postwar atmosphere, to renounce quickly all conversation through the trapdoor above his head show any signs of being disarmed by the show of cordial welcome, the affectionate cries of "Good to have you back!" which now, after the uncertainty of the first moment, began to be addressed to him from every direction.

People came from the shops near the one that had been his father's and was now his, with the outstretched hand of those offering help and advice or even promising, in a hyperbole of generosity, honest competition forever; or they crossed the Giovecca on purpose, broad as it was, with excessive enthusiasm, made even more hysterical by the fact that, as a rule, they knew him only by name, and they flung their arms around his neck; or else they left the counter of the bar, still immersed in that turbulent darkness where, in the past, every day at 1 P.M. the radio's announcements of defeat had come (announcements that could just reach, as it passed, the fleeting bicycle of the young Geo), to come and sit beside him, under the yellow awning that offered such slight protection from the blinding sun and the dust of the rubble. He had been in Buchenwald and had come back from there, the only one, after having undergone God only knows what physical and moral torments, after having witnessed unknown horrors. And they were there, at his disposal, all ears, ready to listen. He should tell them; and they would never grow tired, prepared to sacrifice, for him, even the dinner to which the Castle clock, with two strokes, was already summoning them. In general these seemed so many pathetic apologies for having delayed recognizing him, for having tried to reject him, to exclude him once again. It was as if, in chorus, they said: "You've changed, you know? A full-grown man, by God, and then, you've put on so much weight! But, you see, we've changed too, time's gone by for us as well . . ."; and as if to testify to their sincerity, supporting the development, they displayed their trousers of rough canvas, their rolled-up sleeves, the military bush jackets, the collars without ties, the sandals without socks, as well as, naturally, their beards, since nobody was without one now. . . . And they were sincere in submitting themselves, each time, to Geo's examination and judgment, and sincere, afterward, in lamenting his inflexible repulsion: just as, in their way, just about everybody in the city after April of '45—including those who had most to fear from the present and to distrust the future—was sincere in the conviction that, for better or worse, a new period was about to begin, better in any event than the other, which, like a long slumber filled with atrocious nightmares, was ending in bloodshed.

As for Uncle Daniele, who for three months had been living hand-to-mouth and without a fixed address, the stifling storeroom in the tower had immediately appeared, in his incurable optimism, a marvelous acquisition, and nobody was more convinced than he that, with the end of the war, the happy age of democracy and of universal brotherhood had begun.

"At last we can breathe freely!"—he had ventured to say, the first night he had taken possession of his stairwell—and he spoke, lying supine on his straw mattress, his hands clasped behind his head.

"Aah, at last we can breathe freely," he repeated, in a louder voice. And then:

"Don't you feel, too, Geo, that the air in the city is different from what it was before? Things have changed, believe me: inside, in people's bones, not just on the outside. These are the miracles of liberty. For myself, I am profoundly convinced . . ."

What had profoundly convinced Daniele Josz must have seemed of quite dubious interest to Geo, since the only reply he ever let fall from the aperture toward which the wooden ladder and his uncle's impassioned exclamations rose was an occasional "Hmm!" or a "Really?" which didn't encourage the other man to continue. What can he be doing? the old man would ask himself then, falling silent, as his eyes went to the ceiling, scraped back and forth by a pair of tireless slippers; and he didn't know what to think.

To him, it seemed impossible that Geo didn't share his enthusiasm.

After fleeing Ferrara in the days of the armistice, he had spent almost two years as the guest of some peasants, hidden in a remote village of the Tuscan-Emilian Apennines. And up there, after the death of his wife, who, poor thing, devout as she was, had to be buried under a false name in consecrated ground, he had joined a partisan brigade as political commissar. He had been among the first, tanned and bearded on top of a truck, to enter liberated Ferrara. What unforgettable days! To find the city half destroyed, true, almost unrecognizable, but completely clear of Fascists, of those from *before* and the last-ditch Salò ones— all those faces, in short, many of which Geo should also recall: this, for him, had been such a complete, such an extraordinary joy! To sit calmly at the Caffè della Borsa, which, as soon as he returned, he immediately made the base of his operations in his old, modest activity as an insurance agent, where no frowning eye ordered him to leave but, on the contrary, where he felt the center of universal affection; now, after the fulfillment of such a wish, he was ready even to die. But Geo? Was it possible Geo felt none of all this? Was it possible that, after having descended into hell, and having miraculously risen from it, there was no impulse in him except the desire to evoke the static past, as was demonstrated somehow by the ghastly array of photographs of his dead family (poor Angelo, poor Luce, and little Pietruccio born ten years after Geo, when nobody in the family was expecting him, born to know only violence and anguish and to end at Buchenwald!): the photographs which, one day when he had secretly climbed into the room above, his nephew's room, he had found papering all four walls? Was it possible, finally, that the only beard in the whole city to which Geo had raised no objection was the beard of that old Fascist Geremia Tabet, poor Angelo's brother-in-law, who even after 1938, despite the racial laws and the consequent ostracism imposed against Jews everywhere, had still been able to frequent the Merchants Club for the afternoon bridge, though not officially? The very evening of Geo's return, he, Daniele Josz, had had reluctantly to accompany his nephew to the Tabet house on Via Rover-sella, where he had never set foot since his return to the city. Well, wasn't it inconceivable, the former political commissar kept repeating to himself, the sixty-year-old ex-partisan, as his nephew, in the room above, never stopped pacing heavily up and down—wasn't it inconceivable that, the minute the Fascist uncle peered out of a second-floor window, Geo should let out a shrill cry, ridiculously, hysterically passionate, almost savage? Why that shout? What did it mean? Did it mean perhaps that the boy, despite Buchenwald and the massacre of all his family, had grown up like his father Angelo, who in his ingen-uousness had been to the last, perhaps even to the door of the gas chamber, a "patriot," as he had heard Angelo proclaim himself so many times with fool-ish pride?

"Who is it?" a worried voice asked, from above.

"It's me, Uncle Geremia; it's Geo!"

They were down below, outside the closed front door of the Tabet house. It was ten o'clock by then, and at the end of the narrow street you couldn't see more than a foot ahead. Geo's cry, Daniele Josz recalled, had made him start with surprise. It had been a kind of strange howl, choked by the most violent and inexplicable emotion. Surprise and embarrassment: impossible to say any-thing. In silence, bumping into each other, stumbling over the steps, they had groped their way, in the most total darkness, up two steep flights of stairs.

Finally, at the top of the stairs, half in and half out of the door, the lawyer Geremia Tabet, wearing his pajamas, had appeared, in person. In his right hand he was holding a little dish, with a candle erect in it, whose wavering light cast vague, greenish glints over the natural pallor of his face, framed by the beard which hadn't even become very gray. As soon as he saw him, he, Daniele Josz, stopped short. It was the first time he had seen him since the end of the war; and if he was there now, on the point of visiting him, he had been induced into it only to please Geo, who, on the contrary, after his examination of the house on Via Campofranco a few hours earlier, seemed to have thoughts only for "Uncle Geremia." Setting the candle on the floor, Lawyer Tabet clasped his nephew to his bosom, in a long embrace; and this sufficed to make the out-sider, who had remained on the lower landing to observe the scene, forgotten down there like a stranger, feel once more the poor relation that all of them—his brother Angelo agreeing, in this, with the Tabets—had always avoided and scorned for his "subversive" ideas. He should go away. Go away without a word of good-by. Never set foot in that house again. What a pity he had resisted that temptation! Actually, he had been stopped by a hope, an absurd hope. After all, he had thought, poor Luce, Geo's mother, was a Tabet, Geremia's sister. Perhaps it was only his mother's memory which, at first, kept Geo from behaving toward his maternal uncle with the coldness the old Fascist deserved. . . .

But he had been mistaken, unfortunately, and for the rest of the evening, indeed until late in the night, as Geo seemed never to make up his mind to leave, Daniele had to sit in a corner of the dining room and witness displays of affection and intimacy which were little short of disgusting.

It was as if a kind of instinctive understanding had been established between the two, and with equally immediate promptness the other members of the family had fallen in with it: Tania Tabet, so aged and worn, and hanging always, with those dazed eyes, from her husband's lips; and also the three children, Alda, Gilberta, and Romano, though, like their mother, they soon went off to bed. The pact was this: Geo would not refer, not even indirectly, to his uncle's political past, and his uncle, for his part, would avoid asking his nephew to tell about what he had seen and undergone in Germany, where he too, for that matter—and this should have been recalled also by those who wanted to throw some of his little youthful errors in his face, some only human mistakes in political choices—had lost a sister, a brother-in-law, and a nephew whom he loved very much. What a misfortune, to be sure, what a calamity! But a sense of proportion and discretion (the past was past, no use digging it up again!) should now prevail over every other impulse. It was better to look ahead, to the future. And in fact, while they were on the subject of the future, what Geremia Tabet asked at one point, assuming the serious but kindly tones of the head of the family, who looks ahead and can deal with many things—what were Geo's plans? He was surely thinking of reopening his father's shop: a very noble ambition, which his uncle could only approve, since the storehouse, *at least,* was still there. But to make a success of it, he would need money, a lot of money; he would have to have the backing of some bank. Could he help him, in this last matter? He hoped he could, he really did. But if, in the meanwhile, in any case, seeing that the Via Campofranco house had been occupied by "the reds," he would like to come and live temporarily with them, a cot, if not a proper bed, could always be found!

It was exactly at this point, Daniele Josz recalled, that he, looking up with more lively attention, had tried once more, though in vain, to understand.

Sweating profusely, even in his pajamas, old Tabet sat with his elbows propped on the great black "refectory" table in the center of which the candle was gutter-ing, about to die; and at the same time, puzzled, Geremia twisted with his finger-tips the little gray beard, the classical Fascist goatee which, alone among the old Fascists of Ferrara, he had had the courage, or the effrontery, or—who knows?—perhaps the cleverness not to cut off. As for Geo, while he shook his head and, smiling, declined the invitation, that now-graying goatee and the pudgy hand toying with it were the object of his attention, from the other side of the table, as his pale-blue eyes looked at them with a stubborn, fanatical stare.

◆ *IV*

The autumn ended. Winter came, the long, cold winter of our region. Then spring returned. And slowly, with the spring, but still as if only Geo's examining gaze were evoking it, the past also returned.

Strange, isn't it? And yet time was arranging things in such a way that between Geo and Ferrara—between Geo and us—you might say a kind of secret dynamic relationship seemed to exist. It's hard, I know, to explain clearly. On the one hand, there was the progressive reabsorption by Geo's body of those unhealthy humors, that fat which, at his first appearance on Via Mazzini in August of the previous year, had given rise to so much argument and perplexity. On the other hand, there was the simultaneous reappearance, first timid, then more and more evident and determined, of an image of Ferrara and of ourselves, moral and physical, which no one, in his heart, had ever wanted, at a certain point, to forget. Slowly Geo grew thinner, as the months went by; he regained, except for his sparse hair prematurely gray at the temples, a face whose glabrous cheeks made it even more youthful. But also the city, after the highest piles of rubble were removed, and an initial rage for superficial changes had died down, also the city was slowly settling into its sleepy, decrepit lines, which centuries of clerical decadence, suddenly at history's malicious decree, following the remote and ferocious and glorious times of the Ghibelline Seigniory, had by now fixed for any possible future in an unchangeable mask. Everything in Geo spoke of his desire, or rather of his determination, to be a boy again, the boy he had been, yes, but also, plunged as he was into the timeless hell of Buchenwald, the boy he had never been able to be. And so we too, his fellow citizens, who had been the witnesses of his childhood and adolescence, and yet recalled him as a boy only vaguely (but he recalled us, to be sure, so different from what we were today!), we became what we had once been, our prewar selves, our selves of forever. Why resist? If *he* wanted us like that, and if, especially, that's how we were, why not satisfy him? We thought with sudden indulgence and weariness. But our will, one could feel clearly, had little or nothing to do with it. We had the impression that we were all involved, Geo Josz on one side and the rest of us on the other, in a vast, slow, fatal motion, which it was impossible to evade. A motion so slow-synchronized, like that of little connected wheels, gears operated by a single, invisible pivot—that only the growing of the little plane trees replanted along the city's bastions as early as the summer of '45, or the gradual accumulation of dust on the big commemorative plaque on Via Mazzini, could have furnished an adequate measurement of it.

We came to May.

So that was the reason! we said to ourselves, smiling. So it was only in order that an absurd nostalgia wouldn't seem so absurd, so that *his* illusion could be perfect, that, at the beginning of the month, along the Via Mazzini, their bicycles' handlebars spilling wild flowers, flocks of pretty girls, their arms enlaced, came pedaling by, returning from excursions to the nearby countryside and heading for the center of the city. And it was, moreover, for the same reason that, at the same time, coming from God knows what hiding place and resting his back against the marble shaft that for centuries had supported one of the three gates of the ghetto, there appeared again down at the corner, unchanged, like a little stone idol, a symbol for all of us, without exception, of the truly blissful *entre deux guerres,* the enigmatic little figure of the notorious Count Scocca. ("Look, the old madman's back again!" people muttered, spontaneously, as soon as they recognized in the distance the unmistakable yellowish boater tilted over one ear, the toothpick clenched between thin lips, the fat sensual nose raised to sniff the odor of the hemp-macerating vats that the little evening breeze carried with it.)

And since, in the meanwhile, Ferrara's latest generation of beautiful girls, inspiring open exclamations of praise from the narrow sidewalks, and more secret glances of admiration from the darkness of the shops beyond, had almost finished, one of those evenings, their lazy ride back down Via Mazzini and, indeed, was about to debouch in Piazza delle Erbe and go by, laughing: thus, facing the spectacle of life eternally renewing itself, and yet always the same, and indifferent to the problems and passions of mankind, no grudge, no matter how stubborn, could at this point continue to put up resistance. The little stage of Via Mazzini displayed, to the left, emerging against the sun from the end of the street, the close and radiant ranks of the cycling girls; and to the right, motionless and gray against the wall where he was leaning, Count Lionello Scocca. How could you help but smile at such a spectacle, and at the light that enfolded it, as if of posterity? How could you not be moved at the sight of that kind of wise allegory that suddenly reconciled everything: the anguished, atrocious yesterday, with the today so much more serene and rich in promises? Certainly, on seeing the aged, penniless nobleman openly resume his former observation post, where a man with sharp eyesight and keen hearing, like his, could observe the whole extent of Via Mazzini and, at the same time, the adjacent Piazza delle Erbe, you suddenly lost the heart to reproach him for having been a paid informer of the Secret Police for years or for having directed, from 1939 to 1943, the local bureau of the Italo-German Cultural Institute.

He had allowed that little Hitler mustache to grow for the occasion, and he kept it still; now didn't it lead you to considerations tinged with fondness, and even—why not?—even with gratitude?

It seemed scandalous therefore that, with Count Scocca—a harmless eccentric, after all—Geo Josz, on the contrary, behaved in a way that not only showed no fondness or gratitude, but had to be considered lacking in even the most elementary humanity and discretion. And the surprise was all the greater because for some time it had become customary to smile benevolently, understandably at him and his own oddities, including his dislike of the so-called "war beards." To speak of Geo and his famous whims ("He's against beards! Well, if that's all it amounts to . . .") and to assume the resigned air of one harassed, who prepares to give in "just to make him happy," above all "to please him": this was the custom and this was, also, the profound truth. Though at the same time the city's beards fell one by one beneath the barber's scissors and, for this, much of the credit was his—since, I repeat, everything was done "to let him have his way," above all "to make him happy"—as so many gentlemen's faces dared finally reappear, naked, in the naked light of the sun. And it was true, entirely true, on this score, that Geremia Tabet, Lawyer Tabet, Geo's maternal uncle, hadn't yet cut off his beard, nor in all likelihood would he ever cut it off. But his case might have represented a valid exception only for those who couldn't mentally associate that poor little white goatee with the black wool tunic, the shiny black boots, the black fez, in which every Sunday morning, until the late summer of '38, to the very end of the "good old days," Geremia had gloriously displayed himself, between noon and one o'clock, at the Caffè della Borsa.

At first the incident seemed unlikely. Nobody believed it. It was positively impossible to picture the scene: Geo, coming without surprise, with his languid walk, into the eyeshot of Count Scocca, leaning against the wall; Geo, striking the old, resuscitated spy's parchment cheeks, with two sharp, peremptory slaps, "like a real Fascist bully." The event, however, actually did take place: dozens of people saw it. But, on the other hand, wasn't it fairly strange that various, even contradictory, versions immediately started circulating, about the course events had taken? One was almost tempted to doubt not only the authenticity of each version, but even the true, objective reality of that double slap, itself, *smack-smack,* so full and resounding, according to the general report, that it had been heard for a good part of Via Mazzini: from the Oratorio di San Maurelio, a few yards from where the Count was standing, all the way to the Temple and even beyond.

For many people Geo's act remained unmotivated, without any possible explanation. A few moments before he had been seen walking slowly in the same direction as the bicycling girls, letting them pass him. He never turned his face from the center of the street; and nothing in his face, where a mixed emotion of joy and amazement was legible, could have led anybody to imagine what was to happen a moment later. So when he came up to Count Scocca, and looked away from a trio of girls about to turn from Via Mazzini into Piazza delle Erbe, Geo, all of a sudden, stopped abruptly, as if the Count's presence, at that spot and at that hour, seemed, to say the least, inconceivable to him. His hesitation, in any case, had been minimal, just long enough for him to frown, purse his lips, clench his fists convulsively, mutter some broken, incoherent words. After which, as if operated by a spring, he had literally flown at the poor Count, who, for his part, had until then shown no sign of having noticed him.

Is that all? And yet there was a reason, there had to be, others insisted, pulling down their lips, dubiously. Count Scocca hadn't noticed Geo's arrival; and that, though in itself might seem strange, found all more or less in agreement. But how could one think that Geo became aware of the Count at the very moment when the three girls, at whom his eyes were greedily staring, were about to disappear on their bicycles into the golden mist of Piazza delle Erbe?

According to those others, the Count, instead of standing motionless and silent to watch the passers-by, concerned only with remaining absolutely identical to the image that he and the city, in a united emotion of fondness, both wanted, was doing something. And this something, which nobody who went by at a distance greater than two yards could have noticed—also because his lips, in spite of everything, persisted in shifting the toothpick from one side of his mouth to the other—this something was a soft whistling, so faint that it seemed not so much timid as accidental: a lazy, random little whistle, which would certainly have remained unobserved if the tune he was indicating had been something other than *Lili Marlene*. (But wasn't this, after all, the final, the really toothsome detail, for which one should be most grateful to the old informer?)

Underneath the lamplight, by the barracks gate . . .

Count Scocca whistled, softly but distinctly, his eyes also lost, despite his seventy-odd years, in pursuit of the cycling girls. Perhaps he too, breaking off his whistling for an instant, had briefly joined his voice to the unanimous chorus of praise that rose from the sidewalks of Via Mazzini, murmuring in dialect, following the goodhearted, sensual custom of the Emilian province: "Blessed by God!" or "Blessed are you and the mothers that bore you!" But as bad luck would have it, that idle, peaceful, innocent whistling—innocent to anyone, that is, except Geo—came at once to his lips. Needless to say, from this point on, the second version of the incident coincided with the first.

There was, nevertheless, a third version: and this, like the first made no mention of *Lili Marlene* nor of any other whistling, innocent or not, provocative or not.

If this last report was to be believed, it was the Count himself who stopped Geo. "Hey there!" he exclaimed, seeing him go by. Abruptly Geo stopped. And then the Count immediately started speaking to him, starting right off with his full name ("Why, look here, you aren't by chance Geo Josz, son of my friend Angiolino?"), because he, Lionello Scocca, knew everything about everybody, and the years he had been forced to spend in hiding, God knows how or where, hadn't in the least befuddled his memory or diminished his ability to recognize a face among thousands—even when it was a face like Geo's, which at Buchenwald, not in Ferrara, had become the face of a many. And so, long before Geo flung himself on the old spy and, heedless of his age and of everything else, slapped him violently, for a few minutes the two had gone on talking between themselves with great affability, Count Scocca questioning Geo about the end of Angelo Josz, of whom, he said, he had always been so fond, inquiring closely into the fate that had befallen the other members of the family, including Pietruccio, deploring those "horrible excesses" and at the same time congratulating him, Geo, on his return; and Geo, answering, with a certain embarrassed reluctance, true, but answering all the same: to look at, they were not unlike a normal couple of citizens, stopping on a sidewalk to talk of this and that, waiting for night to fall. What had driven Geo, then, suddenly to attack the Count, whom it was logical to credit with having said nothing to offend or in any way hurt his interlocutor, and, in particular, with not having hinted at even the slightest whistle all the oddness of Geo's character lay there, in the opinion of those who told such things, it all lay in this "enigma"; and the gossip and the suppositions on the subject were to continue for a long while still.

◆ *V*

No matter what really took place, one thing is sure: after that May evening many things changed. If anybody chose to understand, he understood. The others, the majority, were allowed at least to know that a turning point had been reached, that something serious had happened, something irreparable.

It was on the very next day, for example, that people could really become aware of how much weight Geo had lost.

Absurd as a scarecrow, to the wonder, the uneasiness and alarm of all, he reappeared, wearing the same clothes he had been wearing when he came back from Germany, in August of '45, fur hat and leather jerkin included. They were so loose on him, now—and, obviously, he had done nothing to make them fit better—that they seemed to droop from a clothes hanger. People saw him coming along Corso Giovecca, in the morning sun that shone happily and peacefully on his rags, and they could hardly believe their own eyes. So, during those months he had done nothing but grow thin, dry himself out! Slowly, he had shrunk to the rind! But nobody managed to laugh. Seeing him cross the Corso at the Teatro Communale, and then take Corso Roma (he crossed, looking out for the cars and the bicycles, with an old man's caution), there were very few who, in their hearts, didn't feel a shudder.

And so, from that morning on, never changing his dress, Geo installed himself, so to speak, permanently at the Caffè della Borsa, on Corso Roma, where, one by one, excepting the recent torturers and slaughterers of the Black Brigade, who were still kept hidden, distant, by sentences already "out of date," the old Fascist bullies showed up again, the remote dispensers of castor oil of '22 and '24, whom the last war had scattered and swept into oblivion. Covered with rags, he, from his little table, stared at the groups of them with a manner that lay between defiance and supplication. And his attitude contrasted, entirely to his own disadvantage, of course, with the shyness, the wish not to be too noticeable, that every gesture of the former tyrants betrayed. Old now, harmless, with the ruinous marks that the years of misfortune had multiplied on their faces and their bodies; and yet reserved, polite, well dressed: these men appeared far more human, more moving and deserving of pity than the other, than Geo. What did he want, this Geo Josz? many began to ask themselves once again. But the time of uncertainty and puzzlement, the time—which now seemed almost heroic!—when, before making the slightest decision, one paused and, as they say, split hairs: that time full of romanticism just after the war, so suited to moral questions and examinations of conscience, unfortunately, could not be called back. What did he want, Geo Josz? It was the old question, yes, but uttered without secret trembling, with the impatient brutality that life, eager to assert its rights, now forced one to adopt.

For this reason, except for Uncle Daniele, in whom the presence at those same tables, "so in the public eye," of some of the leading members of the local Fascist bands, former Consuls of the Militia, former Provincial Secretaries, former Mayors, etc. always aroused indignation and an argumentative streak (but his loyalty was too natural, too obvious: who could feel it was a real exception, a true consolation?)—for this reason, I say, the frequenters of the Caffè della Borsa still able to make the effort to rise from their wicker chairs cover the few necessary yards, and finally sit down beside Geo had become few.

There were some, in any case, more unwilling than the others to surrender to their inner repugnance. But the embarrassment they brought back each time from those voluntary *corvées* was always the same. It was impossible, they would cry, to converse with a man in costume! And, on the other hand, if they let him do the talking, he immediately started telling about Fòssoli, about Germany, Buchenwald, the end of all his relatives; and he went on like that for whole hours, until you didn't know how to get away from him. There, at the café, under the yellow awning which, whipped obliquely by the sirocco, had a devilishly hard time protecting the little tables and the chairs from the fury of the noonday sun, there was nothing to do, while Geo narrated, but follow with one eye the movements of the workman opposite, busy filling with plaster the holes made in the parapet of the Castle's moat by the shooting of December 15, 1943. (By the way, the new Acting Prefect, sent from Rome after Doctor Herzen's sudden flight abroad, must have issued precise instructions in this matter!) And meanwhile Geo repeated the words that his father had murmured in a whisper, before dropping exhausted in the path from the *Lager* to the salt mine where they worked together; and then, still not satisfied, he imitated with his hand the little gesture of farewell his mother had made to him, at the grim Station of their arrival, in the midst of the forest, as she was pushed aside with the other women; and then, going on, he told about Pietruccio, his little brother, seated beside him, in the dark, in the truck transporting them from the station through the fir trees to the huts of the camp, and how all of a sudden he vanished, like that, without a cry, without a moan, and nobody could find out anything more about him, then or ever. . . . Horrible, of course, heart-rending. But in all this there was something excessive, everyone declared, in agreement, returning from those too-long and depressing sessions, not without frank amazement, it's only fair to say, at their own coldness—there was something false, forced. It's the fault of all this propaganda, perhaps, they added, excusing themselves. It's true that countless stories of that sort had been heard, *at the proper time,* and to hear them thrust on one now, when the Castle's clock was probably striking the hour of dinner or supper, one simply couldn't fend off, honestly, a certain feeling of boredom and incredulity. As if, after all, to make people listen with greater attention, it was enough to put on a leather jerkin and stick a fur hat on your head!

During the rest of '46, all of '47, and a good part of '48, the more and more tattered and desolate figure of Geo Josz never stopped appearing before our eyes. In the streets, in the squares, at the movies, in the theaters, by the playing fields, at public ceremonies: you would look around and there he would be, tireless, always with that hint of saddened wonder in his gaze, as if he asked only to start a conversation. But all avoided him like the plague. Nobody understood. Nobody wanted to understand.

When he was just back from Buchenwald, his soul still tortured by dread and anguish, it was completely understandable, everyone admitted, that he would preferably stay in his house, or, on coming out, instead of streets like Corso Giovecca, so broad and open that at times it made even the most normal people feel a bit dizzy, he would instinctively turn to the winding alleys of the old city, the narrow and dark little streets of the ghetto. But afterward, removing the gabardine suit that Squarcia, the best tailor in the city, had made to order for him, and taking out again his lugubrious deportee's uniform, if he planned to turn up wherever there were people with a desire to enjoy themselves or, simply, a healthy wish to emerge from the shoals of that dirty postwar period, to go forward somehow, to "reconstruct," what excuse could be found for such outlandish and offensive conduct? And what should he care, he, who one August evening in '46 had had the bad taste to appear, in this guise, and extinguish the laughter on all lips, what should he care, for God's sake, if more than a year after the war's end they had decided to open a new outdoor dance hall, the one just beyond Porta San Benedetto, in fact, in the bend of the Doro? It wasn't one of the usual places, after all! As anyone had to admit, it was a very modern establishment, in the American style, with magnificent neon lighting, a fine bar and restaurant permanently open, kitchen always ready, which could provoke no more serious criticism (according to the article in the *Gazzetta del Po* written by that poor dreamer, the young Bottecchiari) than that it was located less than a hundred yards from the place where, in '44, five leaders of the underground National Liberation Committee had been shot in reprisal. Well, apart from the fact that the dance hall in the bend of the Doro was, as the crow flies, not a hundred, but at least two hundred yards from the little marble column commemorating the execution, only a maniac, a hater of life, could think of venting his wrath on such a pleasant and jolly place. What harm was there? The first months everyone went there, more or less, coming out of the movies after midnight, with the idea of a late snack. But often people ended by having supper there; and then they danced to the radio, perhaps, among transient groups of truck drivers, making merry and enjoying the good company until dawn. It was only natural. Society, shattered by the war, was trying to pick up again. Life was resuming. And when it does, of course, it pays no attention to anyone.

Suddenly, faces, bitterly interrogatory until a moment before, without a ray of hope, brightened with malicious certitude. And what if Geo's disguise and self-exhibition, so insistent and irritating, had a political aim? What—and they winked—if he were a Communist?

That evening at the dance hall, for example, when he started displaying left and right the photographs of his relatives who had died in Buchenwald, he reached such an excess of arrogance that he tried to grasp the lapels of some young people who wanted only, at that moment—since the orchestra, meanwhile, had started playing again—to fling themselves, embracing, onto the dance floor. These weren't tales, hundreds of people saw him. And then, what could he be getting at, with those gestures, those honeyed grins, those imploring—ironically imploring!—grimaces, that bizarre and macabre pantomime of his, in short, unless he and Nino Bottecchiari, having recently come to an agreement about the house on Via Campofranco, were now, *also in other matters and namely Communism,* hand in glove? And if that's how things stood, if he was only a useful idiot, wasn't it right, after all, that the Friends of America Club, where in the chaos and enthusiasm of the immediate postwar period somebody had officially signed up Geo also, should now arrange to drop him, as a measure of obvious prudence, from its list of members? Probably no one, to tell the truth, at least for the moment, dreamed of thinking about him, about

Geo Josz. But he *wanted* a scandal, that was clear: on that notorious evening when he had forcibly demanded entrance to the Club (it was in '47, in February), the waiters had seen appear before them not a decently dressed gentleman, but a strange character in the condition of a beggar, with a shaved neck like a prisoner—something, considering also the filth and the stink, very similar to Tugnin, the poor city beggar—who, from the vestibule full of overcoats and furs hanging in full view from the racks, had started proclaiming in a loud voice that he, being, as then proved quite correct, a regularly inscribed member of the Club, could visit it when he liked. And on what grounds, anyway, could the Club itself seriously be criticized, for having made such a radical decision toward Geo when in the autumn of the preceding year the assembly of members had expressed a unanimous desire for the organization to return as soon as possible to its former, glorious name, the Circolo dei Concordi, again restricting the membership to the aristocracy—the Costabili, Del Sale, Maffei, Scroffa, Scocca families, and others of the sort—and to the most select members of the bourgeoisie? If the Friends of America, *pro temporum calamitatibus,* had been wise to accept anybody at all without fuss, the Circolo dei Concordi had certain standards, certain long-established customs, certain natural exclusions—and politics had nothing to do with this—and, really, there was no reason to fear restoring them. Why? What was odd about it? Even old Maria, Maria Ludargnani, who in that same winter of '46–'47 had reopened her house of ill-fame in Via Arianuova (it had remained the only place, after all, where people could foregather, without political opinions cropping up to spoil friendly relations; and evenings were spent there as in the old days, mostly limited to gossip or to playing rummy with the girls . . .)—even she would have nothing to do with Geo, that night he came to knock at her door; she wouldn't let him in, nor would she move away from the peephole, her eye glued to it observing him for a long time, until she saw him go off in the fog. In short, if on that occasion nobody thought for a moment that Geo had been deprived of some right, then all the more reason to recognize that the Circolo dei Concordi had behaved toward him in the most correct and sensible fashion. Democracy, if the word had a meaning, had to safeguard *all* citizens: the lower ranks, of course, but also the upper ones!

It was only in '48, after the elections of April 18th, after the Provincial Office of the Partisans Association was forced to move into three rooms of the former Casa del Fascio on Viale Cavour (and this proved, belatedly, that the rumors about the owner of the house on Via Campofranco and his Communism were purely imaginary), it was only in the summer of that year that Geo Josz decided to leave the city. He disappeared suddenly, leaving not the slightest trace after him, like a character in a novel; and immediately some people said he had emigrated to Palestine, following the example of Doctor Herzen; others said to South America; others, to an unknown country "behind the curtain."

They went on talking about him for a few months more: at the Caffè della Borsa, at the Doro, in Maria Ludargnani's house and in many other places. Daniele Josz was able to hold forth publicly on the subject many times. Geremia Tabet, the lawyer, stepped in as administrator of the disappeared man's not inconsiderable possessions. And meanwhile:

"What a madman!" one heard repeated on all sides.

They would shake their heads good-naturedly, purse their lips, silently raise their eyes to heaven.

"If he had only been a bit more patient!" they would add, with a sigh; and they were again sincere, now, sincerely grieved.

They said time, which adjusts all things in this world, and thanks to which also Ferrara, luckily, was rising, identical, from its ruins, time would finally have calmed even him, would have helped him to return to the fold, fit in once more, in short—because, when you got down to it, this was his problem. But no. He had preferred to go away. Vanish. Act the tragic hero. Just when, by renting properly the now empty palazzo on Via Campofranco, and giving a good push to his father's business, he could have lived comfortably, like a gentleman, and, among other things, devoted himself to building a family again. Marrying, naturally; since there wouldn't have been a young lady in Ferrara, of the class to which he belonged, who, in the event, would have bothered about the religious difference (the years, on this score, had not passed in vain; in these matters people everywhere were much less strict than in the past!), no one would have considered it an insuperable obstacle. Odd as he was, he couldn't know that; but, with a ninety-nine per cent probability, this is how things would have gone. Time would have settled everything, as if absolutely nothing had ever happened. To be sure, you had to wait. You had to be able to control your nerves. But, instead, had a more illogical way of behaving ever been seen? A more inscrutable character? Ah, but to realize the sort of person he was, the kind of living enigma who had turned up in their midst, the Count Scocca episode, without waiting for all the rest, was really more than enough. . . .

◆ *VI*

An enigma, yes.

Still, on closer examination, when, lacking surer clues, we fell back on that sense of the absurd and, at once, of revealed truth, which at the approach of the evening any encounter can arouse in us, that very episode with Count Scocca revealed nothing enigmatic, nothing that couldn't be understood by a slightly sympathetic heart.

Oh, it is really true! Daylight is boredom, the deaf sleep of the spirit, "boring hilarity!" as the poet says. But let, finally, the twilight hour descend, the hour equally steeped in shadow and in light, a calm May dusk; and then things and people who a moment before seemed utterly normal, indifferent, can suddenly show themselves for what they truly are, they can suddenly speak to you—and at that point it is as if you've been struck by lightning—for the first time of themselves and of you.

"What am I doing here, I, with this man? Who is he? And I, who answer his questions, and at the same time lend myself to his game, who am I?"

The two slaps, after a few moments of mute wonder, answered like lightning the insistent though polite questions of Lionello Scocca. But those questions could also have been answered by a furious, inhuman scream: so loud that the whole city, as much as was still contained beyond the intact, deceitful scenery of Via Mazzini to the distant, breached walls, would have heard it with horror.

*Rachmil Bryks 1912–1974*  Bryks grew up in Scarzisk (Skarzhisko), a small Polish town near the city of Lodz. His budding career as a Yiddish poet (*Young Green May,* 1939) was interrupted by the years he spent in the Lodz ghetto and at Auschwitz. Bryks completed his long poem *Geto Fabrik 76 (Ghetto Factory 76)* in 1944 and when he recited it before a group of Jews in Lodz, he was placed on a transport to Auschwitz. When the Russian army approached Auschwitz, he was among those moved by the SS into Germany on the infamous death marches. He was eventually liberated from a labor camp in Germany by the American army. The poem was discovered in the ruins of the Lodz ghetto after the war and published in Yiddish and English in 1967.

Four novellas (Yiddish, 1952 and 1956) of the Lodz ghetto, written in Stockholm and New York after the war, were published in English as *A Cat in the Ghetto: Four Novelettes* (1959; film, 1970) and later in a revised version as *Kiddush ha-Shem* (1977). Two of his novels, *Der Keyser in Geto* (1961 and 1963) and *Di Papirene Kroyn* (1969), center on Mordechai Rumkowsky (1877–1944), who reigned over the Lodz ghetto by the grace of the Gestapo as head of the Jewish Council, the *Judenrat,* and strictly controlled the daily life of the ghetto inhabitants. Bryks's father, Tevya, his mother, Sarah, three sisters and their families were all murdered in the Treblinka death camp in 1942, and his brother, Yitzhak, perished in Auschwitz in 1942.

## ARTISTS IN THE GHETTO

Despite the resounding success of his recitation of "Plant 76" before a large audience, the poet Simcha Blaustein still had his doubts as to whether the composition was satisfactory. He felt the need of reading it to those who were experts

in literary matters, in order to get their opinion. This is just what he set about
to do.

It was shortly after the closing of the Ghetto. Blaustein had put in a day's
work at Marishin, a suburb of the Ghetto of Lodz, when he heard a violin
playing. Following the sound, he was led into a courtyard with an adjoin-
ing garden where almost twenty young people, men and women, were
gathering with musical instruments in their hands. The day was sunny.
Through the open windows and doors of a one story frame house, the strains
of a violin could be heard. Outside, at a table by a window, sat a young man
writing music. By the aristocratic look on their faces and the manner in which
they were dressed, Blaustein realized that most of the group did not come from
working-class families.

In the middle of the clear blue sky the sun was shining brightly. Trees and
plants stood in full bloom; insects were buzzing, butterflies were fluttering about;
sparrows and swallows were singing of the joy of the world. The garden, with
its vegetables of every kind, was cultivated by the musicians, who also lived in
the house on the premises. The group received a subsidy of bread, kashe and
oil-cakes, out of which they would cook soup. They were entitled to this because
they made up a collective that included a *gialke* (an assigned piece of land).
Blaustein felt himself somewhat ill at ease in his lime-spattered suit and shoes.
Nevertheless, he approached the young man who was absorbed in writing music.
The man's name was Yerachmil Piaskovsky. He wore a bright pair of long trousers
and a white shirt with short sleeves. He had long, thick, disheveled black hair,
a round face, a high curving forehead and green eyes which looked at one
with intelligence. Blaustein saw he was writing music for several instruments. Piaskovsky felt that someone was standing beside him, so he raised his
head and smiled. Blaustein offered him his hand. "How do you do? My name
is Simcha Blaustein."

"And mine is Yerachmil Piaskovsky," the other answered, taking his hand
firmly.

They chatted briefly and Blaustein learned that Piaskovsky had organized
a group of musicians under the name *Slonza* (sun) and was now preparing a
concert of classical music.

"Does this mean" Blaustein asked with delight, "that the Nazis have not
succeeded in dehumanizing us?"

"That they shall never accomplish!" Piaskovsky responded with assurance.

By this time more than forty people, their instruments in their hands, had
come together and were setting up their music stands. Piaskovsky distributed
the music to them. Some tuned their violins in preparation for the rehearsal.
The sun cast a pleasant warmth over all. Trees and plants smelled fragrantly.
Those assembled forgot that they were in the Ghetto and that, not far from
where they were sitting, armed German guards were circling the Ghetto fence.

The artistic impulse awoke in Blaustein and he spontaneously asked Piaskovsky, "Perhaps you would like to hear a good poem in denunciation of war?"

"Certainly, let's hear it," Piaskovsky encouraged him. "Here in our group we are always ready to see or listen to any work of art."

Blaustein placed himself in the middle of the courtyard and the group formed a half-circle about him. He felt uncomfortable in the clothes he was wearing, but straightening himself, he announced in a resounding, voice, " 'Trains' by Moshe Shulstein." Setting his right foot forward, he curled his hands into fists and began to motion rhythmically with his hands and body, like the rods of a locomotive that drive the wheels. Beginning very slowly, the tempo of his gestures gradually increased, becoming ever faster, and faster. His voice was also quiet at first, with the labored chugging of a locomotive when it starts rolling, but then it grew in intensity until a whistling sound could be heard. In a word, Blaustein transformed himself into a travelling locomotive.

> Trains are rolling, trains are rolling—
> Showing where, and shuffling after
> Every road and every village,
> Every district, every city.
> Trains already know their way, and
> Do not have to ask directions—
> Where ... where ... where ... where ....

Blaustein spoke with feeling and carried his listeners along with him. He concluded quietly, gently, with the rhythm of a locomotive drawing to a stop. The group thanked him with vigorous applause for the poem, and for his fine presentation. They asked him if he would continue, so he recited parts of Chaim Nachman Bialik's "The Slaughter Town." He began:

> From steel and iron—cold and hard and dumb—
> Forge out a heart, O mortal man, and come!
> Come to the slaughter town, that you may see,
> That you may touch and feel with your own hands
> On fences, poles, on towers and on walls,
> On stones and in the streets, on every board:
> The blackened, dried out blood, the spattered brains
> Of your own brother's heads, and of their throats.

Those present saw tears begin to appear in the eyes of the speaker. In the audience, some started to weep. Others were shaken by the images evoked. Blaustein paused, took a deep breath, and then continued with irony and sarcasm:

> God, with a liberal hand, has sent you twins—
> Slaughtering and spring.

> The garden was in bloom, the sun was shining,
> And the slaughterer was slaying.
> The knife was glistening, and from the wound
> Blood and gold were running. . . .

Each one felt as though the poet were describing his own life, as it was before the Ghetto, and now, in the Ghetto. When Blaustein had finished, no one made any motion to applaud. There was silence for several long moments. Then applause thundered, and all came forward to shake Blaustein's hand.

From then on, Piaskovsky and Blaustein grew very attached to one another. They became like brothers. Piaskovsky took Blaustein's romantic poems and set them to music. Once he sang them to Dargozshansky, the cantor of the German Synagogue, who was by now an old man and had since lost his sight in the Ghetto. When Dargozshansky heard the songs, he wept and said: "I am weeping for joy that something artistic is being produced in the Ghetto."

The Ghetto's first symphonic concert took place under the direction of Piaskovsky in the large hall of the synagogue on Yansheva Street in Marishin. The size of the audience made it necessary to remove the chairs from the hall. People stood cheek-by-jowl and crowded in at every door and window. Finally, it was announced that the concert would have to be repeated and hundreds of people were turned away from the box office, bitterly disappointed.

For possessing or listening to a radio, Jews would receive the death penalty. All the more, the audience trembled in ecstasy when the music began to sound, and many wept.

During the intermission, Blaustein presented greetings to the musicians and the public. "Although the Germans try to dehumanize us," he stated, "we still have retained the divine image. Our artists paint, our writers and poets continue to write, our musicians compose and perform. The works produced among us speak out against our terrible predicament and bear witness to what takes place here."

"Although the Germans murder us, we do not cast away the works of the best sons of the German people: Bach, Beethoven, and Mozart, whose music you have heard today, and others whom you shall hear in the future. And now, in your honor, I should like to read the first poem I ever composed in the Ghetto. It is entitled: 'Do Not Despair.'"

> It's but a passing wind—
> Do not despair, my child.
> We are old trees, deep and broad,
> Rooted in the earth,
> With large crowns

Which adorn the world.
Strong gusts
Can but tear the leaves from us
And break the branches,
But not the crowns.
Strong, deep-rooted trees
Cannot be torn by the wind,
Nor be uprooted.
We are eternal trees
Giving nourishing fruits to the world.
We shall be eternal
It's but a passing wind—
Do not despair, my child.

Blaustein put his soul into every word. He recited it with all the 248 limbs of his body. While the reading lasted, there was a smile of happiness and confidence on the faces of those crowded into the hall. When Blaustein had finished, the audience remained as though entranced. Blaustein saw that they were overcome with a joy which was not of this world. In order not to appear like an actor waiting for applause, Blaustein quickly walked from the stage. Only then was the audience deprived of its blissful dream. Thundering applause sounded for several minutes, until gradually the smiling faces turned back into hollow cheeks once again. Blaustein regretted having left the stage so soon. Had he stayed a few moments more, those poor beings might have dreamed their dream of faith and trust a little longer.

◆

Yerachmil Piaskovsky was the grandson of the noted benefactor Alter Piaskovsky, a manufacturer known all over Poland. The customer knew that if the Piaskovsky trademark is on the cloth, it must be of first quality.

Reb Alter Piaskovsky was a Hasidic Jew who had lived in richness and dignity. When the Germans occupied Poland, they drove him from his kingdom. Of his entire estate, all he was permitted to take with him was twenty marks.

Yerachmil was planning to return to his grandfather's village estate when the war was over. There he would rest and invite writers, painters, and musicians to join him in the out-of-doors. They could eat and drink and work amid natural surroundings, and each one would be given a small allowance, enabling him to lead a life free of care.

Before the war broke out, many artists had found refuge at the Piaskovsky's large, comfortable house. They would take their meals there, and frequently stayed overnight. His mother realized that these were creative people, who sometimes neglected the practical side of life.

The Piaskovsky's were one of the last families to enter the Ghetto. Like all Jews, they had thought that the war should be over any day now, and that the Germans would not take the trouble of establishing a Ghetto. For this reason, they did not even look for living quarters in the Ghetto during the period before it was sealed off. Instead, they were later on allotted a *paziat* (a little attic room with a stove) by the Lodging Agency of "Keyser" Rumkovsky. From out of a kingdom, they had fallen into a living grave. In summer, one could not breathe there because of the parching heat. The walls and furniture crawled with bedbugs and other insects. In winter, as no means of heating the room had been provided, it was as cold there as it was outside.

The first of them to die was a beautiful four-year-old boy whom they had adopted after his parents had been murdered by the Germans. They loved him like their own child, and Yerachmil's mother would always recount the clever things he said and did. They could never overcome his loss. A short time afterward Yerachmil's father died of starvation and Yerachmil himself became stricken with pulmonary disease.

When it was ordered that everyone in the Ghetto had to work, or else be subject to arrest, Yerachmil became a checking clerk in the "Old-shoe Division," where the Germans dumped the shoes of Jews who had been murdered. There the shoes were dismantled and that which might have been hidden there for a "rainy day"—money, gold, or even diamonds—was removed. Then the shoes were remodeled.

The workers, in their struggle to outlast the war, carried parts of the shoes, pieces of leather and other things out of the factory. Yerachmil's job was to check on them. He went about his business, but pretended not to see anything suspicious. Other checking clerks made fifty-fifty deals with the "smugglers," but Piaskovsky would not do so, considering such a thing beneath his dignity.

He had to walk a long way to work, as he lived in one corner of the Ghetto and the factory was located in the opposite corner. There was no means of transportation. In his condition, he would have needed plenty of rest, fresh air and good, wholesome food—none of which was available in the Ghetto. He always arrived on time, but he was gradually wasting away.

Piaskovsky had married a young girl who played violin in the *Slonza*. As a marriage bonus, they received four pounds of bread, horsemeat, and some other substances which might be cooked and eaten ("Keyser" Rumkovsky granted a special allotment of food for the wedding). The young bride refused to take advantage of her share of the bonus and gave everything to Piaskovsky. They were assigned a room next door to his mother. Both worked and his mother took care of the household.

Piaskovsky was glad that he could be together with those whom he loved, but with each day his ailing lungs got worse and worse. They had been married in midsummer, and by the fall he was already confined to bed.

*Rachmil Bryks*

The autumn of that year was a wet one. Day and night, heavy fog shrouded the Ghetto. Those suffering from diseases of the lung suffocated, and since the majority of the younger people had active tuberculosis, they perished in the course of that autumn.

When another friend of Blaustein's, the poet Moshe Schwartz (the first one to whom Blaustein had read "Plant 76"), died of tuberculosis, there was no one to report his death to the authorities. Blaustein, out of reverence to the dead, went to attend to this himself. As he was standing before one of the little windows and reporting the passing of his friend, he heard someone at a second window announce, "Yerachmil Piaskovsky." Thus he learned that Piaskovsky had died on that same day. All at once, Blaustein had lost his two closest friends. His eyes began to dim, his knees grew unsteady, and he felt as though he were about to faint. He reached out and grasped the window for support, and in a few moments he came to himself again.

Blaustein could not attend either of the funerals because he was compelled to be at work; otherwise, he would risk deportation from the Ghetto. This, however, he could not permit himself.

◆

Spring. When it grew warmer, Blaustein gathered whatever strength he had left and made his way to the Piaskovsky's. When he entered the attic room, he found the mother there alone. As soon as she saw him, she began to cry. Her thoughts went back to "Milekin," as she used to call her son. She was unable to control herself and cried openly. Blaustein already regretted that he had come.

Piaskovsky's mother was in her forties. She was still attractive; her face, though it had withered, still retained its aristocratic look. She was standing by the brick stove in Yerachmil's boots and winter coat, fastened round by a coarse belt, stirring a pot of water into which she had poured several ounces of burnt synthetic corn meal for flavoring. She was preparing this for the children, who worked in the textile factory. She remained standing with her face toward the kitchen, wiping her eyes. Her shoulders were trembling. Blaustein was still standing by the door and did not know what to do: should he go away?

When the woman had calmed down somewhat, he said with guilt in his voice, "Mrs. Piaskovsky, forgive me for having come. I did not realize that it would cause you such grief. I was one of Milek's best friends—that is true; but I am also a good friend of yours. I had to come, because I wanted to know how you were getting along."

"It does not matter" she answered, suppressing a cry. "You did right in coming here. I also wanted to know how you have been. But you did not attend Milushin's funeral?"

"You understand, Mrs. Piaskovsky, that I was forced to work on that day, or else risk deportation from the Ghetto."

"*Panie* Blaustein," she began, "I made a great mistake in giving my children a humanistic education. I should have raised them to be thieves, robbers, murderers—then they would have lived and enjoyed the good things of life!" She spoke painfully, her voice raised. Blaustein's heart was torn by her anguish. He knew she would not have wanted such children, but that this was the sorrow in her crying out.

When she had finished weeping, she asked in a calm voice, "What are you doing now, *panie* Blaustein? How are things? Do you still continue to write?"

"Yes, Mrs. Piaskovsky, I have written a number of new compositions."

Besides being a devoted mother, Mrs. Piaskovsky was an intelligent woman, and she had understood her "Milek." She took a photograph of him from her bosom and showed it to Blaustein. Blaustein gazed at the picture: a boy of seven or eight years with a violin and bow, a round face, a high curving forehead and a head of long, curly hair.

"Already then" the mother began sadly, "the professor with whom he studied wanted to take him on a concert tour throughout the country. But I would not permit it."

Mrs. Piaskovsky understood a great deal about music. Whatever Milek would write, he would first perform for her. She was his first critic, and she would encourage him. When the Jews had to turn their musical instruments over to the Germans, she wept over the violin that they had to surrender as much as did Milek.

She led Blaustein over to a chest of music which stood in a corner of the room.

"You see" she said, "these are Milek's Ghetto productions. Here, through his grief, he expressed the suffering and pain of the Jews in the Ghetto. In this my Milekl lives. I guard it like the apple of my eye. Perhaps it will be preserved and someday, someone may bring his work to life. . . ." She pondered, then asked: "Of course you, *panie* Blaustein, always carry what you have written with you, yes? If you have something that you would care to recite, I am prepared to listen."

"I know that your judgment is sound in these matters. If you might give me your opinion of my 'Plant 76,' I would be grateful." He took the manuscript from his pocket and asked, "Would you like to hear it?"

"Of course, with the greatest pleasure!"

Blaustein read the whole composition. He read with feeling; the rhythm echoed, and Mrs. Piaskovsky followed with baited breath. If she missed a word or did not understand a line here or there, she interrupted him and asked him to read it again. Blaustein felt that his words penetrated deep into her heart and he read with great satisfaction. When he had finished, she took his hand in both of hers and said:

"The composition has both a historic and an artistic value. I wish that it might be your lot to survive the war: you will make a great career as a Yiddish writer because you have a sensitive heart, a beautiful soul, and above all, you relate the truth, which mankind must know, in a simple, human style."

Blaustein was deeply moved by her words. He felt elated within. He thanked her and remained a while longer. Then he graciously took his leave and ran to work.

# BERELE IN THE GHETTO

It was several days before Rosh Hashana (5702) in the year nineteen hundred and forty-two—that the "Kaiser" of the Ghetto in Lodz, Mordechai Hayim Rumkovsky, spoke to the Jews assembled in the Firehouse Square.

"My dear brothers and sisters! As the Elder of the Jews I appeal to you and you are to obey me. You know that I am as a father to orphans and that the old and the young are the whole of my life. But the time has come when I must give away that which is most dear to me." (He always spoke unctuously, personally, possessively regarding everything in the Ghetto, even its inhabitants, as "his"). "Therefore I appeal to you to give up with a good will both the young and the old. They are to be taken out of the Ghetto. This is the will of the Government and a Jew must not rebel against the laws of the country."

The thousands of Jews who had gathered in the Square burst into a stifled lament. Young Berele, nine years old, childlike at the front of the crowd, joined in the lamentation but added a precocious curse and swore never to let himself be sent out of the Ghetto. Pushed this way and that by the agitated, frantic crowd, he was eventually able to join the stream of people escaping from the Square. Like many of them he was making plans to hide.

Rumkovsky had had his choice. Either the Gestapo would themselves carry out the "*Aktion*" or he could attempt to achieve bloodlessly the diabolical ends that they decreed. So for two days Jewish doctors and police themselves went from room to room, the house-guards carrying the register and the police checking whether all were present. Children under twelve and old people of sixty and over were taken away immediately. The remainder were examined by the doctors and the able-bodied were allowed to stay. The sick and weak were remorselessly seeded out and taken away.

But by the first day of Rosh Hashana, the Gestapo had become impatient of such methods. They proclaimed a blockade, a "*Sperre*," a curfew. Posters announced that for a period of seven days Jews were not to leave their quarters. The factories, offices and co-operatives were closed, and with this even the inadequate rations of soup and synthetic bread allocated to productive workers were ended.

The Gestapo went about their business of intimidation. They fired shots into the air, as a signal for people to leave their homes and come out into the street. On one gallows in the market place hung the bodies of eighteen Jews. They remained there for three days as a warning: "Those who conceal children or old people will be hanged." Nevertheless many were hidden and those that were discovered were shot out of hand as they cowered defenselessly in their dark corners. The terror continued remorselessly as the Gestapo, assisted by the Jewish police, the fire brigade, chimney sweeps and the "White Guard" (flour-carriers), who thus earned a craven respite for their families, went from yard to yard on their deathly mission.

Much of this was seen by young Berele from his hiding place. He saw mothers, running through the streets clutching their little ones and crying frantically, "*Where shall I hide you? Where shall I hide you?*" He heard his elders praying to God to relieve them of their souls and grant them a Jewish burial. He heard the all-pervading lamentation. His frightened but stubborn eyes saw men and women with their loved ones desperately jump from the highest buildings to their death. He felt the terror that they escaped. He saw the Gestapo ripping out doors and floors in their search, combing the garrets and cellars, taking now indiscriminately, the robust and healthy with the weak and ailing to the fictitious "recreation camps" in which nobody believed.

Then on the second day of Rosh Hashanah, Berele's own family were taken. They did not go voluntarily as so many had done: the police forced them out. But they had prepared for the inevitable: their pitiful bundles were already packed. There were his father, his mother, his three elder sisters, and little Simkhele, his younger brother. Only Berele himself remained hidden, terrified, breathless until they had gone. Then, still fearfully, he crept from hiding to the window, and peered into the courtyard.

He saw the people, his family, the neighbors, men, women, and children lined up in a row by the wall. He saw Gestapo Officer Schmidt picking out the Jews pointing with his forefinger, like the venomous tongue of a serpent: "*Right! . . . Left! . . . Right! . . . Left! . . .*" After that he saw him flourishing a white-gloved hand and a horse-drawn wagon drew up. The people were driven on to it as if they were cattle, as if they were indeed cattle to the slaughter. For some of them the spell of acquiescence was broken and they pleaded piteously. Others attempted to jump off the wagon but they were cruelly beaten back. There were many skirmishes as hysterical mothers crying: "*My only treasures! My life! How can I save you?*" were separated from their children. There were more wagons now. Some of the mothers succeeded in joining their children but most were kept back.

As the mobilization proceeded the pandemonium increased and suddenly Berele stiffened. He saw Simkhele jump off the wagon and remain as if glued to the ground. A policeman lashed at him but he refused to move. He was beaten again and again until he was besmeared with blood, unconscious, thrown back onto the wagon.

There seemed no hope for these condemned Jews. But a mixture of pity and corruption, a loaf of bread for the police and a discreet turning of the head on their part enabled some to escape: just as rumor had it that even at the final Gathering Point some were able to evade death if gold and diamonds changed hands.

Then Berele heard the voices of other children happily singing. These were the children from the orphanage. They were festively dressed, their hair washed and combed and they were carrying packets of food. In their innocence they thought they were off on a picnic. It was a merry, Polish song they were singing:

> The train that comes from far away
> It will not wait a second.
> So take us now, conductor, please,
> To Warsaw, for a holiday.

The Gestapo and the lusty Rollkomando Germans stood by. The children's singing merged with the wailing of the older ones as the procession of wagons moved away. Berele saw them go, his father, mother, his three sisters, and poor battered little Simkhele in the doomed cavalcade. He turned from the window with a heavy heart and cried bitterly. Now there was only his old aunt to whom he could turn. Somehow she had escaped the rounding up and he went to her. For some days they lived in sorrow together but they were nearly starving. In the end they had to venture into the open fields to gather grass for their food. There were many others reduced to the same plight. But even this was eventually denied them. There was a roar of engines and the Gestapo hurtled up in their lorries. They stopped. Then another sound spat out. The Gestapo's machine-guns mowed down the starving, distraught people. Berele saw his aunt fall. It was another grim sight for his young but no longer immature eyes. He lay pressed to the ground, his hands clutching the grass until his enemies went away.

Now he really had to plan where to hide. He thought of "*Shishkowice*." It was the place where the "big shots" ("*Shishkes*") lived. They were like the thorny berries that grew on the topmost branches of a certain tree and thus were they named. It was in the suburb Marishin. Here lived Rumkovsky in his summer palace, the officials, the commissars, the councillors, and others whom Amts-Leiter Hans Bibow (cursed be his name) had freed from the Resettlement. Here, too, were the orphanages and hospitals that had been liquidated and turned over to Bibow's favorites. There was food here and shelter of a sort.

Berele made his way there, climbed to the roof of one of the buildings and hid under a barrel.

At last the "*Aktion*" was ended and large posters proclaimed:

"Sperre Lifted I Order All Jews to Go to Work and Speed up
      Production for the Time Lost!
Amtsleiter Hans Bibow"★

Berele was freed now but sad and lonely. He was as lonely as a stone. He thought
of his father and mother; of how he used to play with his little brother; of how
they used to share their bits of bread and the watery soup. Even those harsh
days seemed kindly now. He was indeed alone. But many others were also
afflicted. There was the woman whose two children had died of typhus and
whose husband had been taken away by the Germans. She, too, was as lonely
as a stone. And so it came about that she and Berele adopted one another. She
lavished her love upon him and cherished him as her own. And he slowly and
gratefully became accustomed to his new mother.

There still remained problems. Only children of twelve and over were
allowed to work; and only those who worked were allowed to remain in the
Ghetto. So nine-year-old Berele, no longer innocently young, was registered
as thirteen years old. Thus ended the harrowing Autumn and Winter came
upon them.

◆

Winter. In the Ghetto the frost is as bitter inside as out. The Jews had been
intentionally moved into a wet area. No firewood could be found. The houses
are wet both summer and winter. In summer the walls rot and fungi begin spreading. The dampness is rancid. In the winter the walls, ceiling, and floors glisten
with white snow. In every utensil where there is a drop of water it turns to
ice. The windows are covered with a thick layer of ice and snow, as well as a
dark blanket—as air raid precautions—which is never removed because on leaving for work it is dark and on returning home from work it is also dark.

Berele must get up each day at five-thirty in the morning. He shudders
with cold and never warms up. When one's hungry, one is cold. Ever since Berele
has been in the Ghetto he has never had a full meal.

He would like to lie curled up a while longer under the cover, but he must
dress and be off to work. Dress? Because of the cold he sleeps with his clothes
on. It would be silly to undress in this frost when it is as cold inside as out.
While it is still dark Berele lifts the heavy wooden-soled shoes onto his feet,
and putting on his coat, makes his way over the slippery, broken pavement, the
clattering of his sabots sounding in the distance. With a pot hanging by a string

---

★A few days later German newspapers carried pictures with these captions: "Jewish mothers in the Ghetto of Lodz abandoning their children and the SS taking pity on these
Jewish children."

around his neck, he hurries to work at the "*Resort*" (factory) together with tens of thousands of other Jews.

The wind flails Berele's body. The frost cuts his face and pricks the skin under his fingernails. A full moon and scattered stars shine down from a blue, darkening sky. The snow plays about under Berele's feet.

Clip-clap, echoes a rataplan of sabots. The tooting of a locomotive and the clattering of coaches is heard coming in. One rooster crows—a second answers. Dogs are heard howling. This reminds Berele that not far off there is a world, a free life. A yearning for freedom gnaws at his heart, but he consoles himself with the thought that the war cannot, after all, last forever and soon he will be back with his parents.

Berele's each step is accompanied with fear lest the Germans who stand guard by the barbed wire will, God forbid, decide to amuse themselves by shooting at him, as they do so often with the Jews.

Berele must be at the factory on time. Everyone must be at work at seven o'clock. He has a long distance to walk and if you're late your punishment is— no soup. The soup consists of a few pieces of dried-up kohlrabi afloat in half an ounce of water (three-quarters of an ounce for children). Fresh kohlrabi is used as food for cattle, but when you cut up the kohlrabi and dry it out it becomes wood. This soup—was the mainstay of daily life.

◆

Berele worked in a children's garment factory. Only children worked there. One adult, the instructor, supervised the work. Up till the "*Sperre*" this building had been a children's hospital. On the third anniversary of the war's outbreak the Germans liquidated all the hospitals in the Ghetto of Lodz. The Gestapo came round in trucks, surrounded the buildings and threw the patients (both the grown-ups and children) out of the windows, like logs of wood. The more sturdy ones who tried to run away were shot on the spot. During the "*Sperre*" the Germans turned these buildings into Gathering Points for the victims. Here, in the wards of the former children's hospital stood two rows of machines. Each child sewed one part of a military uniform. Some children sewed by hand, some by machine and others pressed.

The children turned out first-class work. They put their whole soul into it, turning out by the thousands, uniforms for the German military. They had a special production quota to meet. They were responsible for each uniform, just like adults. The smallest defect was regarded by the Germans as sabotage. When a German commission came to inspect this children's garment factory, they were dumbfounded at the productiveness of the Jewish children.

Berele was called "*Kleopsedry*" (Death-Notice) because he had the appearance of a death head. He could barely support himself on his thin little legs and could just manage to move around.

When a German commission came to the factory, Berele hid himself because of his poor appearance.

◆

There was at one time a frightful famine in the Ghetto. Apart from the piece of synthetic bread and watery soup there was nothing else to be obtained. Like the adults, the children grew weaker and weaker, and they found it impossible to turn out the required quota.

The factory supervisor ordered the soup portions to be discontinued. The children argued: "If you take our soup away we will not be able to turn out the work."

The majority of the children belonged to the Underground Movement of all the united parties in the Ghetto. Berele also took an active part in the Underground Movement. The children were told stories of heroes who sacrificed their lives for freedom. Also stories of the oppressed who fought for and achieved their freedom. The children were fired with the spirit of fighting for their rights. Berele's dream was to become a Judah Maccabbee.

Berele's parents had been socialists, so he knew how to organize a strike.

When the supervisor saw that the children were of one will he decided to spread envy and hatred amongst them by distributing fifteen soup-coupons for more than one hundred children. Berele jumped up on a bench, waving his coupon. With his weak voice and like a prophet he roused and fired the hearts of the children.

"Friends: We must be as one with those who did not get any soup, for are we then any better than they? Do they not hunger as much as we? My advice is for no one to take any soup till everybody gets a portion. One for all, and all for one."

"Bravo! Bravo!"—all the children cried out cheerfully.

When they brought pots of soup not a single child went up, even though they were all frightfully hungry. Most of the children hadn't eaten since yesterday.

The pots stood open and the steam drifted out from them. The taste of soup spread all over the room, teasing the stomach.

The soup distributors could not understand what had happened to the children. Everyday there is a mad rush for the bit of soup, everyone wants to be first in line. Today—nobody moves, all are silent; no one wants his portion. They did not know that this was Berele's work.

◆

The factory manager immediately phoned the "Kaiser" of the Ghetto, Mordechai Hayim Rumkovsky, to let him know what was happening.

The "Lunatic" (that is what the Jews called him) came running in his cab.

The first thing he did was to castigate several boys, in order to instill fear into the children. Then he jumped on one boy—with his left hand he held on to his eyeglasses and with his right he beat the boy, shouting at him with his Lithuanian-Jewish accent: "Shpeak, who are the unionishts?"

The youth answered nothing.

The blood rushed to the "Kaiser's" face. His brow wrinkled up and his silver, philosophic mane trembled. He went at a second boy, and at a third. He lashed and kicked with his officer's boots, yelling spasmodically: "Shpeak! Who are the unionists? I'll kill you all!"

The children said nothing.

The "Kaiser" regained his breath, and then appealed to those children whom he had not beaten:

Tell me children, for you are the whole of my life (the Governor's favorite expression) who be those who won't let you eat the bit of soup?" With a fawning smile he looked each child in the eyes. No one answered him. The "Kaiser" became enraged and cried out: "Are you telling, or not? If not, I'll have you all whipped!" (In the Ghetto they whipped people for the smallest transgression.)

The children remained silent.

"My children," he suddenly said fawningly and in a tone of voice one used when about to reveal a secret, "whoever tells me who the unionists are, I will give him a half-pound salami. Well, who'll be the first to tell?"

Such a gift was, in the Ghetto, like the requittal granted to a condemned man who is already on his way to the gallows. With this offer the Governor felt certain he had caught his prey. But he was disappointed. With great fury he picked out ten boys: "You! You! You! three days' *fekalie* cleaning (to clean out with scoops the toilets, and carry the barrels of refuse tied to one's back through all the streets of the Ghetto). And today you'll get the *plague* (another of the Governor's favorite words), not soup! Like dogs you'll lie here in the factory till nine o'clock at night! Not a speck of food will *I* allow to be brought to you! Only the *plague!*"

The children accepted the punishment in silence.

When the old man rode away, Berele started singing and all the children after him:

> Hayim, our Governor is a real fine guy,
> He'll have us eat yet rolls, butter and pie.
> Rumkovsky Hayim is Elder of Jews
> With the Gestapo he's quite chappy,
> Really feels as brother to us—
> And supplies us with some pappy . . .

# BREAD

Comrade Zeide and Bluestein always went together for bread. Zeide took a sack with him; he had, after all, eleven mouths to feed, a wife with nine children.

It was just after *Succos*. The ghetto was drenched in rain. Cold winds thrashed the dried-out bodies. Scarcely anyone had warm clothes or good shoes. Nor was there anything with which to heat the house. The "King" of the ghetto, Rumkowsky, stopped the packages which relatives sent. Jews of Sosnov wanted to send coal but he did not permit it. When asked why he didn't want coal, he answered it was nobody's business, he wouldn't tell why. He wanted all the Jews to be dependent upon him.

Soreleh and Bluestein were sitting by the window, looking at the rain beating on the window pane, their mood as sad as the day. Then Zeide came along outside their window with his heavy soldier-stride, his hands deep in his pockets, his sack under his arm. Stretching his head out from under his turned-up collar, he called out, "Nu!"

That meant, "What are you sitting for? Why aren't you ready to go?" Bluestein quickly grabbed his coat and his cloth bag and ran out.

By the time they reached the bakery, the rain had stopped and they found the yard filled with men, women, and children, enraged because the baker refused to sell them bread. He informed them they would have to wait, he would sell later. Why? He didn't say.

The crowd shouted, "What do you, mean—later? We need bread now!"

"It's easy for you to say 'later' because you have already eaten."

"My children have had nothing in their mouths since yesterday!"

"Our only food is this miserable bit of pasty bread!"

And again they yelled, "The baker wants to get rich! He wants to speculate. He wants to raise the prices!"

"Let's break in and loot the bread!"

"No, comrades, no," thundered Comrade Zeide in his deep voice. "No looting!"

"No—no," shouted many, in support.

Suddenly, as if from heaven, there sounded the voice of a young man, shouting, "In front, the store's already open! They're selling bread!"

In the twinkling of an eye, the crowd rushed out of the yard, each one pushing ahead of the other. Everyone wanted to be first, lest there not be enough bread for all. But there too they found the store barred and locked. So they realized the young man fooled them. They rushed back but now the gate to the yard was also locked. The crowd yelled again. Whoever could, climbed over the high fence. The little ones climbed up and sat on the gate and on the fence.

The crowd cursed and hurled insults at the unknown young man who enticed them out of the yard.

"Comrades—let's crash the gate! Nu!" shouted Zeide, and he and Bluestein pushed at the gate. The mob hurled itself at the gate and stormed—"ah ah-ah-ah!" Together with their outcry was heard the groaning of wood and iron—and the gate broke open. Half of it remained hanging, the other half fell to the ground and the mob poured into the yard with a wild cry, "Let's break into the bakery!

"Yes! Yes! Hurrah!" And the mob rushed to the door.

"No, comrades, no!" Comrade Zeide thundered again in his deep voice.

He and Bluestein ran ahead and faced the crowd with outstretched arms, as one stops a runaway horse.

The mob did not heed them.

"Get away, Rumkowsky's stooges!" were shouted at Zeide and at Bluestein. But they did succeed in restraining a few.

"Comrades, don't do it, don't loot!" Zeide still continued to plead. His words were drowned in the shattering of the window glass in the bakery.

Suddenly, with much whistling and shouts of vile language, in stormed a wagon with the "King's" police thrashing about with their sticks. In great terror, the crowd cleared the yard and ran off.

When Bluestein and Zeide returned to Soreleh with empty bags and faces looking as though they were fleeing from a catastrophe, she asked, frightened, "What happened? What's going on outside?"

"May he burn like kindling," Zeide cursed, "that crazy Rumkowsky, with his bakeries, with his police and with his entire government."

"Don't worry, we'll outlive them all," said Bluestein with his usual smile.

This was the story: Since the stale, mouldy flour had already been used up by the Jews, the Germans cut off the flour order, leaving the bakeries only a last few bags. And so the "King" ordered the bakeries not to bake any more and not to sell the bread they had. One of the "King's" policemen guarded the bakery until more police came with a horse and wagon and carried off all the bread and the flour. Even the baker was not permitted to take any.

Rumkowsky rationed this bread out to the hospitals, orphanages, old-folks homes, and to his police and officers.

For several days the ghetto was without bread and without soup, because the "King" closed down the kitchens, too; there was nothing to cook. If, somewhere, a bakery did operate, half-a-loaf was given only to those who had pull.

From five in the evening until nine in the morning no Jew was allowed to be seen outside the house where he was registered. Nevertheless Zeide and Bluestein decided to wait outside the bakery all night, to be first to get bread. These two heroes thought they would be the only ones in front of the bakery, but they found a long line there. They waited all night and into the following afternoon.

While standing on line, people conversed about everything in the world. Some read books. Religious Jews studied their holy writings. Members of families took turns several times. Soreleh took Bluestein's place and Zeide's oldest daughter, her father's. After a short rest they returned to the line and those in back of them saw to it that their stand-ins should not remain with them.

Finally in the afternoon, the bakery opened up. They began to let people in, and soon half-loaves were being carried out, steaming and fresh-smelling. This teased all the more the hungry stomachs of those who were standing on line, and of those who were besieging the yard outside the line.

Those who could afford it, paid many times more than the baker's price—they bought up bread from the poor ones who were standing in line, or from those who got bread through pull.

Zeide and Bluestein became upset. They could not understand how it was that they saw bread being carried out and the line wasn't moving a step.

At last Bluestein got to the door, and was about to go in, when along came several toughs and fought their way in ahead of him, with the help of the "King's" policeman, who faced the line and, raising his stick, shouted in Polish: "Get in line! Order, now!" In the meantime, behind his back and with his connivance, the toughs got in. Bluestein and Zeide noticed this collusion.

"I've been here all day and all night," Bluestein protested, "and they barge right in. What kind of a policeman are you to admit some one out of line?"

"Shut up! Where? What? When?" The policeman waved his stick.

"What do you mean Where? What? When?" called out Zeide, "don't be so innocent! I could knock you off your high horse! Let's hand it to him, the swindler!"

He rushed up and punched him in the jaw. Bluestein grabbed his stick and hit him with it. The crowd was carried away and let out its accumulated wrath upon the policeman:

"Take this, and this—I stand on line day and night and you admit your cronies?"

"Give it to him! Give it to him—Rumkowsky's stooge!"

"Tear off his cap!"

"Rip off his arm-band!"

The policeman lay there, all beaten up. Whoever could, punched and kicked him. The half-loaves of bread which the toughs had carried out were torn up and stamped on by the incited mob. Some hungry ones picked up bits and devoured them. The mob seethed and roared. The bakery bolted its door, and then were heard real wailing and outcries. In the confusion, Bluestein and Zeide, together with some others who took part in the fight, left and got home with empty bags, angered and embittered at Rumkowsky's regime.

A while later Rumkowsky appeared, riding in his "beautiful" carriage, followed by a commissar and several policemen. The battered policeman was immediately carried away. The commissar shouted: "To hit the police is forbidden! They are authority. Those who took part in the attack should be reported. The rebels must be punished."

No one answered him.

Another line was formed, standing quiet, in fear. Then the "King" addressed them from his coach:

"My sisters and brothers! I do my best for you. Do not allow yourselves to be incited by the bums! by the rebels! In *my* ghetto there must be quiet and order! *My* ghetto will run like a clock! Be calm, I have enough to eat, only be obedient, then you will lack nothing with *me*, in *my* ghetto!"

The crowd listened with silent contempt to his speech. The commissar stationed several policemen along the line and two at the door, which he ordered to be opened. Quietly and silently the line moved. Now, only quarter loaves were brought out—that was the order of the "King" so that every one would get something. The "King" sat in his carriage, and looked on.

"Yes," he thought, "*my* ghetto will run like a clock. In *my* ghetto it must be quiet." And he was pleased.

Zeide's six children stood on line at several bakeries and each brought home a quarter-loaf. At night the neighbors brought a quarter-loaf to Bluestein and to Zeide. Tears came to the eyes of both when they saw that there were still some people who appreciated their integrity.

# CHILDREN OF THE LODZ GHETTO

Tobtche was tall, slender, with long chestnut hair, a ready smile on a slightly elongated face, and black eyes which sparkled with green and brown tints. At eighteen, Tobtche had already spent much time with the children in the courtyard, both as their teacher and their playmate.

The smaller children, whom she cradled in her arms and fondled, loved to caress her silken tresses. She played with them "ring-around-the-rosie," told them stories, sang for them Hebrew, Yiddish and Polish folksongs, danced for them, and taught them to participate.

She frolicked with them and blithely joined their games and plays. She did their tricks, jumped rope, made rag dolls, played hide-and-seek and blindfold guessing. She loved them abundantly, and they returned her love by clinging to her.

Playfully, she would place a five-year-old boy in her lap, and ask him solemnly:

"Yossele, have you learned the *alef-bet*?"

"Yes," the child assured her.

"Well, so let me hear it."

The little boy would lead off with a *heder* tune.

> *Alef, bet, gimel—*
> There is a God in *himel* (heaven);
> *Daled, hay, vov—*
> We are all His *shof* (sheep);
> *Zayen, khess, tess—*
> In Him our trust we profess;
> The tenth letter is *Yid—*
> God, the Shepherd *hit* (watches);
> *Kof, lamed, mem—*
> The words of Torah *farnem* (absorb);
> *Noon, samehh, ayin—*
> In *heder* you must not *shreien* (yell);
> *Pay, tsadik, koof—*

We obey our parents *roof* (call);
*Raish, shin, toov*—
Be good, and to God you *hoof* (hope) . . .

When the child finished, Tobtche applauded, and the children stamped their feet with glee.

To a large degree the children's games reflected life in the ghetto. They set up a "kitchen" and a "cooperative," like the adults. But they also had their own folklore. They took a long rope, called it a "ghetto fence," and chanted:

Rumkowsky, Hayim
made a "ghette"
with a "mette" (border) . . .

Inside the "fence" they stationed a little boy with a short stick—the "ghetto policeman." To the other side they assigned a boy with a longer stick—a "rifle;" he was the "German guard." The two exchanged no words, following a strict German rule. Further away they perched a boy on a rock; he was "Kaiser Rumkowsky." Then the rest of the children formed a line, the "Kaiser" appeared and handed each a "food card" for the "kitchen," or the "cooperative."

The children hated the roles of the wicked characters, but when Tobtche cast them in the parts, they accepted because she was goodness itself.

After they received the "cards" they formed a second line close to Tobtche. She served make-believe soup, rations of flour, sugar, vinegar, salt and washing soda, using sand, pebbles, crushed red brick, leaves and grass. The children pretended to take the "food" to their mouths, and made chewing motions. They would push, screech and jostle one another just as their elders in the ghetto did. At this point the "ghetto policeman" restored order. He shouted: "Quiet! Shut your traps!" and he lashed out with his little stick.

Then "Kaiser Rumkowski" came on the run to "control the situation," to see if the "food" was properly divided. The boy enacting the part, imitated his heavy tread, and manner of speech. The children "complained" to him:

"Mr. Kaiser, the soup is cold."
"Mr. Kaiser, I couldn't find a speck of potato in it."
"Mr. Kaiser, she cheated me on the measure," a little girl whined, pointing to Tobtche.
"Mr. Kaiser, how can we live on vinegar and washing soda?"

One child improvised a ditty, and the other children picked it up:

Rumkowsky, Hayim,
gives us "mayim!" (water),
he gives us pepper,

he gives us poison . . .
He made a "ghette"
with a "diette!" (diet).
He made a "ghette"
with a "mette"(border).
And he *screams* that he is just . . .

"Kaiser Rumkowsky" shrieked with his peculiar Lithuanian accent:

"Quiet, little rebels! I have enough food around here! There's enough of everything in my ghetto. Shut their mouths!" he commanded the "militia-man," and without waiting, wrested the stick from the boy, and struck them himself.

The children fought back, yelling: "Crazy man! Crazy man!"

"Silence, bastards!" the "Kaiser" raged, "I will have you flogged!"

A feeling of vengeance seized the children and they fought him. The "ghetto policeman" tried to intervene, and they attacked him, too, with anger. After the "Kaiser" and his "orderly" had taken sufficient punishment, the "German guard"—the boy with the longer stick—entered the fray, barking:

"Crazy Jews! What are you doing to your chief? *Donnerwetter*, Jewish swine!"—and he took aim with his "rifle"—bang! bang!

The "German" is shooting!—the children cried, and ran for cover.

◆

Simkhe Bluestein would often talk with Tobtche about Jewish suffering, literature, and politics. He sensed in her sensitive soul much craving for beauty.

Then Tobtche came down with a high fever. She lay motionless, her pretty, smiling face stained with tears. She had contracted tuberculosis, a disease which ravaged the majority of the young people of the ghetto.

On a warm day they helped Tobtche out of her bed and placed her under a tree so that she would have fresh air.

No one in her family was working. They subsisted on the "nine-mark notes" which "Kaiser Rumkowski" was supposed to mail out to the ghetto dwellers on the first of each month, but seldom did. Without the scrip the Kliegers, like the others, were unable to buy their rations. Once in eight days the "Kaiser" allotted them a loaf of bread, but it was usually devoured at one meal.

In no time Tobtche's well built body was reduced to skin and bones. Frequently Bluestein shared with her his bread-loaf on a loan basis, until her mother obtained her own. Tobtche grew weaker. Her mind remained alert and her feelings were sharp. She listened intently to the optimistic talk of the neighbors and to Bluestein who tried to raise her hopes with information that the war would soon end; he himself did not believe a word of it.

Tobtche and her family dreamed of the day when she would get a ration of butter, fats, and nourishing food to cure her lungs. Only one doctor was authorized to issue such an order, and he took his time in coming. He would appear only after the other physicians reported the patient was beyond help. Finally, the doctor for whom they were anxiously waiting—a woman— arrived. She did not examine Tobtche too closely: one look at her wasted body and the way she drew her breath, convinced her that Tobtche could not last much longer. Nevertheless, in a spurt of generosity, she wrote out an order for a month's allotment of the necessary foods, and promised to do so once every month until Tobtche recovered her health. The family's joy was bound-less. They brought in the first week's supply: canned meat, fat, creamery but-ter, a bottle of oil, sugar, Swiss cheese and a little stove for cooking. Tobtche's mother beamed. She cooked and fed the inert girl as though she were a baby, prodding her:

"Eat, eat, Tobtche darling, in good health! At long last God has heard my prayers and rewarded us with a food-order. Now you will surely regain your health. Do you see, Tobtche dear? The meat, the fat, the butter, and the oil will, with the help of God, cure your lungs."

On the third day there was a visible improvement in Tobtche. She was able to sit up. Her face grew animated, her cheeks gained color. "Do you see the power of a food order?" rejoiced the mother. "What a pity it didn't come sooner!"

That night Tobtche could not fall asleep. She felt very ill. The mother hov-ered over her, bent on packing the food into her ailing daughter. But Tobtche had completely lost her appetite. Secretly the mother wiped her tears, and sighed: "Now that there is so much food—and there is no scarcity, it is no good. This is a bad sign."

The following morning Tobtche was in a coma. The eyes in her emaci-ated face were glazed. Her chest heaved violently. Her breathing turned into a death-struggle. The family was by her bedside, and prayed for a miracle. Her agonies were frightful. Then an expression of regret settled on her parchment face.

Neighbors gathered outside under the window. One woman suggested: "They ought to place two lighted candles to her eyes to ease the departure of the soul." Another chimed in: "Yesterday, when I saw signs of improvement in her, I knew it was a bad omen—before dying the sick always look better. The color in her cheeks was the bloom of death. Her lungs were gone yesterday. I know. Misfortune made me an authority on such things. . . ."

The women outside chattered on, offering all sorts of advice on what might or should have been done. None dared to step inside. When the sun was glid-ing down in the west, a piercing scream rent the twilight: "Tobtche! Tobtche!"

Old man Itzik fingered his long grey beard. Leaning on his cane, he limped into the house. "Quiet! Leave the dead!" He waved everybody aside.

He pulled a feather from the pillow, held it to Tobtche's nose for several seconds with an air of performing a sacred mission. Seeing it did not stir, he pronounced with a choked-up voice: "She's dead! Praised be the true Judge! God
gives life, and takes it away." Tobtche's eyes were closed and an expression of
peace was on her face.

Old Itzik drew the cover over her face, and commanded: "Light two candles!" He was handed the tapers and matches, kindled them, and placed them
at the head of the dead girl.

But news of her death was withheld. Next morning bread loaves were to
be issued, and Tobtche's younger sister appeared early at the cooperative to claim
it on Tobtche's card. Afterwards her brother-in-law hastened to the burial service office, reported the death, and surrendered her card.

Tobtche's death raised a commotion. Her body was washed at home, according to ritual. The funeral took place the following day. The casket was carried
all the way to the cemetery. Among the weeping mourners, trailing in the procession, were the crying children whom Tobtche had befriended.

Two days later the father died. Keile Klieger, the widow, dressed in black
and wrapped in a dark, silken shawl, paced the moist, dismal, earthen floor in
stockinged feet, and tearfully addressed the Master of the Universe: "Tell me,
Father in heaven, why have I deserved two funerals in my house in one
week?" Looking shrunken, she sat down on a low bench to begin the seven-
day period of mourning. The gloomy, dripping walls smelled of wild mushrooms that were growing outside.

She opened the Book of Job, translated into Yiddish, and read with a quivering voice:

"There was a man in the land of Uz whose name was Job . . ." Her dole-
ful prayer-tune carried into the street, and penetrated Bluestein's heart.
"Hm," he reflected with a heavy sigh—"we have a King above who rules
the world, and a 'Kaiser' below who runs the ghetto. Alas, both assist the Germans in annihilating the Jews."

# THE LAST JOURNEY

In the same train in which the deposed "Kaiser" Mordechai Hayim Rumkovsky rode along with those closest to him, there also traveled Blaustein and his wife, Sarahle. The Germans had captured them in the place where they lay in hiding. Both were now sitting in the cattle car upon Blaustein's knapsack, which held a few necessities, as well as manuscripts of his poems and stories, several Hebrew volumes and books.

Blaustein's former director, Yeszhe Ferst, his wife Marisha and both of their families, together with all those whom Ferst had put up in the factory, Resort 76, traveled in the same car. Ferst carried along the gold, diamonds and foreign currency which Jews had given him in order that he either hire them, thus not having them deported from the Ghetto, or put them up in *his* factory while the Ghetto was being liquidated. Ferst also had brought along bottles of alcohol and liquor from *his* factory, along with expensive garments and underwear for himself and his wife.

The German-Jew Edelmann, the watchman at his factory, also accompanied him, and here, too, was at his constant beck and call.

Also riding with them was the manager of the factory, Schlomo Fein, a coarse person who was convinced that everything belonged to him and that, in the end, everything would be left over for him. He had mercilessly tormented the workers, but by now he was already a bent and broken man. No one knew where they were going. The Germans had said that the transport was destined for work in Hamburg.

Blaustein had heard a rumor to the following effect: from a crack in an empty box-car which had returned from transporting a group of Lodzer Jews, another Jew who worked at the Radogodsh-Marishin railway station (from which the Jews of the Ghetto were deported) had pulled out a slip of paper with the inscription: "We arrived at Oswiecim (Auschwitz)!" It was from one of his relatives. They had talked about doing this before; this information was now made known only to certain individuals.

The religious poet, Alter Schnur, could also be found here. One of his hands was bandaged in a towel tied around his neck. He would not let go of his Tallis bag, which held his prayer shawl and phylacteries, and his prayer book with the vernacular translation, as well as his Hebrew and Yiddish manuscripts. In his knapsack he carried—in addition to some bare necessities—the Five Books of Moses in Hebrew and Yiddish, the Festival Prayerbook, the *Code of Jewish Law,* stories about the Baal Shem Tov in Yiddish, and the *Tanye.*★ He sat upon his knapsack with his lovely dark-complexioned wife, and they worried together.

Blaustein, on seeing his bandaged hand, had a premonition that the Germans would send him directly into the oven because of it. (When the *Aktion* intended at rounding up the Jews had gotten under way, Alter Schnur ran to hide himself. He climbed to a rooftop and leaped from one roof to another, until he fell and sprained his left hand.)

Several days ago, Blaustein had gotten five kilos of potatoes. Carrying home the treasure, he met Alter Schnur on a street which had already been cleared of Jews. He opened the bag and said: "Take half of it; I'll share it with you. Go home *now,* bake them and eat!" Alter took the potatoes, and Blaustein went along his way contented.

The more than one hundred souls who were squeezed into the cattle car silently looked to each other for consolation. Through the window openings, whose length and width were spanned with barbed-wire, a bit of light seeped into the dark car. The twilight cast even more gloom upon the surroundings.

Alter Schnur sighed: "Well, Germany, the land of the poets and philosophers, doctors, professors and technicians—educated people! Well, you see now what her universities have made out of the human being! He murders in the most refined, scientific way. He can already fly to the highest heavens with airplanes. I am afraid they will yet invent a bomb with which to destroy all of mankind. But let them produce something to save mankind, to make man control his savage instincts! Man should first of all learn to be human—not to steal, not to rob, not to kill, to love his neighbor because he is like himself, with all his faults. But meanwhile modern science has not found a way to improve the human being. On the contrary, it has turned him into the most cunning, bloodthirsty savage. Only the Torah can perfect man. But, Jews, don't give in! Any moment may bring the Messiah."

"Do you know what I'll tell you?" Blaustein answered him. "When all of mankind will be able to live according to the moral laws of the Torah, then mankind itself will have become the Messiah, and then the Messiah will not have to come any more."

All those who were listening agreed, and reflected upon what had been said.

---

★Popular philosophical treatise by the founder of the Lubavitsher Hassidim.

The clatter of the turning wheels on the steel tracks became audible. Alter Schnur broke the silence once more: "Well, praised be God that we have come so far. 'The Guardian of Israel neither slumbers nor sleeps.' He who has helped us until now will continue to stand by us . . ."

"Jews, it is a lie!" Blaustein called out painfully. "No! There is no Guardian of Israel! If there were, He would not permit the murder of a whole people—His 'Chosen People'!" he said sarcastically.

" 'God is good to those who wait for him', so says Jeremiah in Lamentations," answered Alter Schnur, "and we Jews have sinned."

"In what did we sin more than all the other nations?!" Blaustein cried angrily. "Because we did not murder? Because we did not rob? Because we do not fight wars? By not glorifying weapons? How did we sin against Him? By being the first to acknowledge that there is only one God? *One?!* By accepting the Holy Torah? By giving mankind the highest moral laws, the Ten Commandments? What was the sin of the Talmudic scholars, truly righteous men who studied God's Torah by day and by night, fasting and mortifying their flesh, in order not to sin? They were not concerned with money. They did not enjoy anything of this world. And they were the first whom the Germans murdered in the cruelest ways. In what did the Jews sin?"

Blaustein caught his breath and continued angrily: "What were the sins of our little children, the tiny infants? And how did I sin? Since I was twelve years old, I worked hard and went hungry. I can say with a clear conscience that I have never impoverished anyone. On the contrary, all of my life I have always been the one to be made the poorer, but I have kept quiet for the sake of peace. After all, the majority of Jews in Poland lived in need and distress, and bore their poverty in dignity. The main thing for them was Torah, spirit. They breathed with the faith that any minute now the world would be saved. For what did they deserve to be murdered? Why? How does Bialik put it in 'The City of Slaughter': 'Does then a shadow on the wall sin, or a broken potsherd, or a dead worm?' Again and again I ask: in what did the Jews sin more than any other nation? And I ask even further: cannot God make it so there be no more wars, that dictators should not be born, neither those who deceive whole nations, but that the world should be a paradise? Is not everything possible for Him and are we not all His children? What true father would so incite his children that they kill one another? I have only one complaint to God: If You saw fit to create man, why then did You not create him with wisdom, with reason, that he might know how to live? Man alone is a foolish creature, perhaps the most foolish, most unhappy creature. He means to do good and he does evil. Surely he comes from an animal: the animal instinct rules over him, the heritage of his progenitors. It is said that man is created in the image of God. Some fine appearance we ascribe to the Creator! Indeed, man is the most foolish and most miserable creature, despite all of his cleverness. For this reason, our Sages tell us: 'No man should boast of his wisdom,' because even a wise man deceives himself. And how many wise men are there in the world, anyway? This is why they did not say: 'No *man* should boast of his wisdom'—because, as far as the general lot of mankind is concerned, there is nothing at all to speak of!"

"There is a haggadic legend," remarked Alter Schnur, "that when God created the world, He wrapped Himself in a white garment which radiated such a great light that one could see it from one corner of the earth to the other. But He kept this light to Himself because He saw in advance that mankind would degenerate and sin, and would try to do as much evil as possible. The question is: until when will this light continue to be withheld? When men shall become wise and honest, then they themselves will want to find such a light. And when they will have become wise enough not to use their knowledge to do evil, not to deceive, not to murder—then they will be able to find out the secret."

"Then the Messiah will have already come!"

"It is a shame that we were born too soon."

"The tragedy of the world is that a minority is always born too early, and a majority too late," philosophized Blaustein.

"If the Messiah will only then have come when humanity will have begun to live according to those moral laws enunciated by the prophets, that means that mankind itself must be the Messiah. There is, nevertheless, a saying that 'When the Messiah comes, every sick person will be cured, except the fools.' But if a majority of fools continues to be born in every generation, how then can the Messiah come?"—Shmulik Stzshizshevski argued with a Talmudic intonation.

"And there is yet another Jewish legend—that the Messiah will come riding on a donkey. Do you know why? Because all those who wait for him are asses. . . ."

Everyone felt himself hurt.

"This is a deceitful world," replied Alter Schnur, "the corridor to the true world. The more a Jew suffers in this world, the better it will be for him in the next world. I am not afraid of death."

"I envy you. But when can one make peace with your outlook? In normal times, when one is able to live out the years which God had intended for us and one leaves children behind. . . . But today the entire Jewish people is being wiped off the face of the earth."

"So, what can we do?!" Schlomo Fein interrupted angrily.

"Now you ask?" answered Blaustein, "when we are already deep in the lion's jaws? Perhaps in the Ghetto there still would have been a way out—if we could have fought with guns against the Germans and their Jewish collaborators: the 'Kaiser's' police, the *Sonder* (Jewish Gestapo), the fire brigade, the chimney-sweepers, the 'White Guard' (those who carried sacks of flour)—that whole underground crew! And also the trash that wore the yellow badge in the shape of the Star of David. They all belong together. 'Let my soul then perish along with the Philistines'! That is the Jewish tradition."

Blaustein paused for a while and then continued heatedly: "Not one party in the Lodzer Ghetto aroused the people to fight. All their activity consisted in running to obtain the best positions for themselves. They put their people into the administration and in great secrecy used all the means at their disposal so that they and their followers should not go hungry. Through various machinations, they obtained food rations. They simply took the little that others had out of their mouths, and did everything possible to prevent themselves or their people from being deported from the Ghetto to a certain death. And then, after the war, each party will record in its history that it was the one and only party which helped the people, and which fought for righteousness and justice."

Blaustein breathed deeply and, with a sorrowful voice, continued: "Leaders, honest leaders—that is what we needed in the Lodzer Ghetto. What is a people? 'Clay in the hands of the potter.' We remained like sheep without a shepherd. The Jewish leaders all fled, because Hitler was out for their heads; and those who could not escape were murdered by the Germans in the cruelest ways. What remained was a blind mass without leadership? Sheep gone astray.

"The Germans knew full well that Rumkovski was unstable and a degenerate, and that is why they appointed him *Fuehrer* of the Lodzer Jews. A confused fellow who chased after power all of his life. . . . And now, under the Nazis, he achieved the longed-for career which had been his ambition. His virtuosity in this area came into full play. He imitated Hitler in every way, but first of all in surrounding himself with the underworld. He was only missing a Horst Wessel, because such a thing cannot take place among Jews. By order of the Germans, he established a clique of blood-suckers. Only now, after the *'Jude'* has done his work, have we all become *'yidn'* once again.

"There, in all his misery, lies Garfinkel, the Police Commissar of the Third District. Just look at what has become of him! Only the day before yesterday, he was still ordering us around. He thought that the world was his. And over there sits my former director, Yeszhe Ferst, who sent many of his workers to their death. Their lives were all in his hands. He wanted to have me murdered also, but now we are equal. And here is Ptakul, the Bundist, who is honesty personified—a fighter for a Socialist world and for Jewish territorial rights in those places where Jews live, and a passionate advocate of the Yiddish language and Yiddish literature.

"Here is also Shmulik Stzshizshevski, the Communist, an accomplished man, a former Yeshiva-student, a genius steeped in Gemara and world literature, who has brought a library along with him. He believes in a Communism which would be in accordance with the spirit of our prophets. And here you have Wishlicki, the Zionist-Laborite, a fighter for a Jewish homeland in Palestine.

"Over there is Sandberg, the territorialist; he is looking for a territory for the Jews in the non-Jewish world: let men take pity on us and give the Jews a tract of land in a wilderness somewhere. And here are three sisters, the Mizrachi women, Rebecca-Hannah, Chayeh-Sarah and Miriam Leah—religious Zionists all. And Alter Schnur there,"—he points him out with his finger—"the deeply pious Jew.... In the eyes of the Nazis we are all the same: Jews; and Jews—so they hold—must be wiped off the face of the earth. I still believe that if we would have begun a revolt, the servants, police and supervisors would have joined up with us."

"It is forbidden to shed blood," stated Alter Schnur with a trembling voice.

"According to Jewish law, and—it goes without saying—according to the law of human decency: 'If someone comes to kill you, you are to kill him first.' I believe it is even a legal precedent. Did not the great Rabbi Akiba gather his students to fight against the Romans? And Bialik in 'The City of Slaughter' cries out: 'Where is a fist? Where is a thunder peal which would avenge the generations?' We Jews of the Lodzer Ghetto did not—God forbid—bring shame to our tradition of fighting. The Germans arranged things so that we had to wage our entire battle against their Jewish servants: the administrators and supervisors, Rumkovsky and his clique."

"In the sacred Torah," interrupted Alter Schnur, "it is written that the administrators and supervisors in Egypt were also Jews, so that neither Hitler nor our times have produced anything new. The Torah conceals nothing."

"Yes, this too was a fight against the Germans," Blaustein continued, "because a fight against those who serve the Germans is a fight against the Germans themselves. Who does not recall the first summer in the Ghetto in 1940, when the hungry Jews demonstrated spontaneously against Rumkovsky and his *Judenrat*? They were demanding work and bread when the Germans came in and fired at the demonstrators, and victims fell. I suppose that the insurgents of the Warsaw Ghetto did not even liquidate one Jewish policeman or one Jewish informer who served the Germans. At least, in the Warsaw Ghetto Jews were able to communicate with the Aryan side and obtain weapons through the canal system and through holes under the wall surrounding the Ghetto. But the Lodzer Ghetto was completely cut off from the outside world because it was encircled by barbed wire. In this way the German guards could easily see whether anyone approached the Ghetto fence, and what was going on within the Ghetto. Only Germans were allowed to live along the perimeter of the fence—and Lodz had no underground canals. In the Lodzer Ghetto we fought twenty-four hours a day: first, with hunger, in the rationing of soup and synthetic bread—this rationed food allowance which was 'scientifically' calculated to make one's body swollen. People's limbs began to ooze with puss, and they would die in terrible agony. So we became inventors: from the rations we made such diverse dishes as cannot be imagined, just to live a little longer. This was a hard-won victory over the enemy. And was not concealing oneself during the deportations from the Ghetto a fight against the bloodthirsty enemy? And the street demonstrations against the Rumkovsky administration—were they any small act of heroism?

"And the fact that we succeeded in maintaining ourselves in accordance with the image of God, in spite of starvation and under such horrible conditions—was this anything less than heroism? Imagine if other people were to find themselves in our predicament, how many robberies, murders and even suicides would take place! And the Cantor of the Wolliner Synagogue, Reb David Toffel, who smuggled a radio into the Ghetto, and who day and night for four and a half years listened to the news from London and Moscow, and by spreading these reports kept our courage alive . . . In the end he fell like a soldier on the battlefield. The Gestapo caught him at the radio with two other Jews. You can imagine how they were tortured in the Gestapo's inquisition-cellars for this revolutionary act. Our Comrade Zeide waged a daily fight against the injustice of Rumkovsky and his clique, as did Comrade Regina as well, until they, too, fell victims to the Gestapo. Comrade Zeide! Comrade Regina! Every moment of your lives you gave your strength and talents for your people, and so you have also perished for your people. How many workers have paid with their lives because they did not want to yield to their supervisors, and for this they were sent to their death? Other peoples, under such circumstances, would also not have been able to fight directly against the Nazis. But perhaps they, in addition, would neither have fought against a Rumkovsky of their own, or against *their own* police, because they would have been accustomed to carrying out orders given by their own police. But we Jews, who lived for generations under the terror of foreign peoples, were unable to reconcile ourselves to terror wielded by our own brethren. We do not tolerate any dictator, and so we have ridiculed, mocked, protested and fought against them. Fighting against Rumkovsky and his clique was a fight against the Germans."

Blaustein grew silent. Everyone who had heard him thought to himself: "He must think he discovered America!" And yet they pondered over the truth of his words.

The train rode over the Polish fields and woodlands. It became darker and darker. Night began to fall. The SS who guarded the front of the train kept a closer watch on the windows of the cars, in order that no one might escape.

*Chaver Paver 1900 (1901?)—1964*  Chaver Paver is the pen name of Gershon Einbinder who was born in Bershad, Podolia, Russia. He wrote his first story, in Hebrew, at the age of twelve, but when his *cheder* teacher read it aloud and the boys laughed at the author, not the story, he did not write again until the Russian Revolution and the subsequent pogroms. While teaching refugee children in Kishinev, he wrote his first Yiddish story for the kindergarten children (who loved it), and took the name Chaver Paver from the first two words of a children's song.

Chaver Paver came to America in 1923, taught children in Yiddish schools, and continued writing Yiddish children's stories, including *Chaver Paver's Mayselekh* (2 volumes, 1925), stories for little children, *Fun Yener Zeit Teich* (*Across the River,* 1930), the story of a Jewish boy caught in war and revolution, and *Labzik* (2 volumes, 1935–1937), the life of a Jewish family in New York during the Depression as seen through the eyes of the family dog. He wrote a Yiddish novel about Jewish partisans in Poland during the Holocaust (*Giboyrim Fun Der Nakht,* 1950), numerous plays and novels for adults, including *Clinton Street* (Yiddish 1937; English 1974), depicting Jewish life on New York's Lower East Side.

## THE BOXING MATCH

The Commandant himself made the selection from the fresh transports of Jews brought in daily to the death camp. Flanked by a swarm of guards swinging bludgeons, in his parade uniform, with the many medals proudly displayed on his chest, he walked leisurely in front of the long rows of anguished, broken Jews, and with a quick experienced glance appraised each victim—the weaker ones for the gas-chamber, the stronger ones for slave labor. A motion of his white-gloved hand to the right meant death in the gas-chamber, a motion to the left, a few weeks of life yet for hard labor in the camp.

Through with this routine, he made a second selection, a more careful one now. Those that had been sent to the left were again lined up, and the Commandant halted before each one he considered a good possibility, inspected him closely, felt his muscles, and picked out the strongest of the strong to be taken to a special barracks. These were used as material for the "boxing matches."

Commandant Friedrich Zibler before the war had been a professional boxer in his native Hamburg, and a good Nazi party comrade from the old days when they had to beat up communists and Marxists at street demonstrations. For his good services to the cause he had been assigned the responsible post of head of a death camp.

But here in the death camp, the poor man was bored by the monotonous daily routine of exterminating people and the "boxing matches" were life-savers for him. Without them, God forbid, he would have gone crazy. He staged these matches not only for entertainment but also for educational purposes. He secured experienced cameramen who took films of the matches and those films were mailed to the propaganda ministry in Berlin, which distributed them to moving-picture theaters all over Germany to show how a subhuman race behaved in sports.

The truth must be said about our Commandant that he was quite fair to his victims. He gave them boxing gloves and ordered them to resist, to dodge his blows and even to hit him back. The trouble with the Jews though was that they tried to cheat him. They collapsed after the first few blows and pretended they were knocked out. But Zibler was no fool either; he always had the camp doctor at these fights to see that there should be no cheating.

◆

In the latest transport, the commandant's experienced eye spotted among the new arrivals a highly prized victim—a very tall, broad-shouldered young fellow with a fiery black beard and thick curly forelocks who held himself very proudly and defiantly. His fiery almond-shaped black eyes looked at him threateningly as if they were saying, "Wait, you beast, the hour of reckoning will come yet."

Those proud and defiant Jews in the transports always puzzled our Commandant. He knew very well the whole process they had to undergo before reaching his death camp, a process which had begun two years back when the German army invaded Poland, a process planned by the best brains among German scientists and statesmen systematically to break the Jew physically and mentally so that when he reached the death camp, not a shred of resistance and human dignity was left in him. But the odd thing was, our Commandant noticed, almost in every fresh transport there were quite a few who looked hardly touched by the process. Such people were usually those the Commandant picked for his boxing matches. For such people our Commandant had a passion. He wanted to prove to himself that what the planned process couldn't accomplish with them in two years, he, Friedrich Zibler, in his death camp could accomplish in a few short days.

Friedrich Zibler felt very good that day. This bearded, insolent young fellow would be a worthwhile target for his skill. He would prolong the fight for many, many rounds and order the cameramen to make a real feature of this show and take shots of each move the Jew made in the ring, showing how step by step under the impact of his powerful blows, the bearded fellow lost his false pride and stupid defiance and became frightened, forlorn and despairing like any other slave in his death camp.

◆

It was near sunset. The orchestra of slaves made up of former professional musicians was playing Zibler's favorite selection, Beethoven's *Turkish March*. All the 2,000 slaves of the camp, men and women, with closely shaven heads, in dirty grey and yellow striped jackets and trousers and with wooden sandals on their bare feet, were lined up around the ring in rigidly straight lines, watched by heavily armed guards. On the roof of the Commandant's headquarters stood the cameramen taking shots of the preliminaries.

Always before the Commandant himself made his appearance in the ring, short preliminary matches of a grotesque nature took place. Very short Jews were picked out from among the slaves and matched against the tallest of the camp guards. The very tall, husky, well-fed guards didn't hasten to finish off their bewildered, half-starved victims. They prolonged the fun.

The preliminaries also included the fight of naked slaves. They matched a young one against an elderly one, stripped them entirely naked, and ordered them to pound at each other with all the vigor left in their bodies. Instead of clown's hats, the naked boxers were decorated with *streimlich*, traditional rabbinical fur hats made of animals' tails. The slave orchestra had to play Jewish wedding songs while the naked boxers, lashed on by the hilarious guards with their long smarting whips, swung unwilling blows at each other.

The Nazis reeled with laughter. The two thousand slaves reeled with laughter too. The guards saw to it they should laugh and put feeling into their laughter.

Then at a signal from the Commandant, the hilarious roaring of the Nazis and the dry, hollow laughter of the slaves ceased. The blaring of the orchestra stopped abruptly. The two naked slaves were dragged out of the ring. The slaves stood at attention amid a foreboding silence.

The Commandant, a mighty athlete, leaped up on the platform and clasping his gloved hands, condescendingly and conceitedly waved them to the crowd as it greeted him with noisy applause. The slaves applauded him too; the guards saw to it they should applaud and put some feeling into their applause.

The bearded young Jew leaped up on the platform too. With a menacing agility he leaped upon the platform. The hearts of the 2,000 slaves sank, for they detected wrath and stubbornness in that menacing agility. The 2,000 slaves were very much worried about today's spectacle. They had learned that this tall, broad-shouldered young man was famous for his strength in his native town of Sosnowice and that he knew boxing too. The son of a rabbi, he had gone contrary to his father's wishes to study for a rabbinical career. The rebellious son was fired, as were many of his generation, by the dream of Palestine—to settle the country with strong, hardy men. To make himself fit for the hard life of a pioneer, he had steeled his body by heavy labor on peasant farms, by sleeping outdoors, by walking bare foot a whole summer and part of fall, by satisfying his hunger with a minimum of food and also by athletics—swimming, horseback riding and boxing.

The inmates of this camp had sought vainly a whole day to come in contact with him and ask him not to resist the Commandant too energetically in the boxing match. If he hit Zibler with too powerful a blow, the guards would afterwards massacre them. They succeeded only in smuggling to him in the special barracks, where he was kept well-guarded, a note from his aunt, who was the only survivor of their large family. "Moishe, for the sake of all the Jews in this camp, don't hit him back too hard. Allow yourself to be beaten," said the note.

Two thousand pairs of eyes now looked toward that black-bearded young man and silently cautioned him. His aunt, tall, bony, with a sack-cloth shawl over her shaven head, with weeping lips, stood among the crowd too and talked to him with her tortured black eyes. Her eyes seemed to say: "Only we two have remained alive of all our kin. Let us cling to life, no matter how. Maybe with the help of God, we will survive this gruesome nightmare—we, the last two remaining members of our large family. . . . So don't lose your head."

A guard removed the Commandant's brown swastika-besprinkled silken robe and he remained standing before the crowd in his bronze nakedness, a very compact muscular blond giant.

Another guard took off Moishe's robe, a blue and white striped robe besprinkled with many stars of David, and he remained standing before the crowd in his pale nakedness, a tortured brunet giant. All the ribs on his lean body could be counted—broad massive ribs. In the broad massive ribs of that tortured lean body lay a mighty power, a lightning swiftness. He looked proud and handsome in his tallness, in the slenderness of his hips, in the towering height of his shoulders.

They stood facing each other, the powerful Jew and the mighty blond beast, on the platform amidst the fearful silence of the 2,000 slaves. Zibler, in all his boxing matches at his camp, had never fought his adversaries with hatred in his heart. He didn't hate these inferior people, he despised them. But toward this thick-bearded giant, he felt a burning hatred. That Jew looked at him as if he, the Commandant, were the contemptible being, one of an inferior race, not he, the slave.

With the other victims, he usually played around at first, exhibiting the fine points of his art and only in the last round would he start to deliver his deadly blows. This fellow he wanted to hurt right away. . . . He aimed at his eyes—those detestable, insolent Jewish eyes. . . . He let go his right fist with all his force and fury. But quicker than lightning, the other dodged—and the Commandant's intended blow hit the air.

The eyes of the Jew were blazing now with the most expressive contempt. They looked at him as upon a repulsive rodent. The Nazi aimed again at those accursed, haughty, mocking eyes—and again his furious blow hit the emptiness. Zibler threw a swift glance at the crowd and it seemed to him the 4,000 eyes of the slaves were mocking him too.

◆

The sun was setting. . . . The walls of the barracks and the gas chambers were a glowing red. . . .

For a fraction of a second, Moishe took his eyes off the Nazi. They wandered, Moishe's eyes, to his unfortunate brethren who stood rigid and frozen, looking with the fear of death toward the ring. Moishe's eyes also wandered away in that fraction of a second to the western sky. . . . Was this the last time in his life he'd see how the sun was setting?

In that fraction of a second, the Commandant got him with the impact of a thunderbolt right on the chin. Moishe collapsed on the boards of the platform. His limbs fainted. Only his mind remained conscious. His tortured limbs wanted to lie where they were and never rise again, to dissolve and live no more in that vicious world. But a voice from somewhere spoke to him. It commanded him to rise, to mobilize all his strength, to stand against the murderer and laugh again straight in his face.

Moishe was again on his feet and his eyes had regained supreme strength, the strength to disdain death. He now looked at the Nazi with an entirely different look—not the look of mocking, but of deadly hatred.

The boundless hatred shooting from that Jew's eyes burned the Commandant as if his flesh had been seared by hot coals. He threw himself upon Moishe, no longer the carefully calculating boxer, but a desperate murderer. . . . He was met by a lightning blow on the ear.

The hearts of the 2,000 slaves rose when Moishe landed that lightning blow on the Nazi's ear. Moishe's heart too rose. He felt in his body the strength not only of his own self but of all his tortured people.

The Jew Moishe became a whirlwind of wrath. Every cell in his starved giant body yearned to take part in the act of vengeance and dispatched into his very broad shoulders, into his massive ribs and into his swift hands every last bit of energy and strength still in reserve.

The 2,000 slaves, seeing the unresisted blows Moishe rained on the murderer of their whole people, too rose above death. They cared no longer about the terrible tortures they would undergo at the hands of the maddened guards. They didn't shout exultantly but breathed deeply and Moishe felt in their deep breathing that they were blessing him. He felt in their deep breathing waves of love flowing toward him.

The guards were uneasy. Friedrich Zibler was bleeding from both ears, his mouth and his nose. They didn't know how to act without a command. The cameramen had stopped shooting; they had to stop, for the shots wouldn't have been any credit to the Third Reich. . . .

◆

In the western sky, the last bit of light was fading. . . . Dark was closing.

Before the guards collected themselves and started firing at him, Moishe must deliver the last blow of reckoning. He leaped, the very tall, tortured Moishe, with his pale nakedness and his steely broad ribs—he leaped, in his body the collective strength of all his brethren, and loosed the last blow. . . .

The Nazi reeled and fell to the floor, not knowing what had hit him. . . . He would never know what had hit him. . . .

And then? Then it became very dark—and also very light. . . .

The guards were firing at Moishe from all sides. . . .

## *Ida (Stein) Fink 1921–*

Born and raised in Zbaraz, Poland, Ida Stein was studying at the High School of Music in Lwow, Poland, when the Nazis occupied her homeland. She spent some time in a ghetto, and from 1942, when she escaped, until the end of the war, managed to remain safely hidden. In 1948 she married Bruno Fink and moved to Israel in 1957. It was there that she began to write stories as well as plays for European and Israeli radio and television. She also became active at Yad Vashem, the Holocaust memorial and museum in Jerusalem, and taped interviews with many survivors.

Twenty-one of her Polish stories and a play for radio and television appeared in Hebrew (1974), Polish (1987), and English (1987) translations. *A Scrap of Time and Other Stories,* a semi-autobiographical collection of stories about the Holocaust, received the first Anne Frank Prize for Literature in 1985. Her novel *Podroz* (1990) was also translated into English (*The Journey,* 1992, 1993) and Hebrew (1993).

# THE DEATH OF TSARITSA

The death of Tsaritsa would have remained one of a million anonymous deaths were it not for the fact that it happened on a beautiful mild day. (I have imagined that mildness, much of what I write is the product of my imagination, but only the scenery, not the actual skeleton of events.) It happened in the very early evening, when the trees cast long shadows and the air is filled with a light blue haze which becomes deeper and darker by the minute, although there is a still long time to go until nightfall. It happened at just the sort of hour that makes people who are worn out after their day's work like taking a stroll through town.

B's decision to go for a walk through the streets that already lay under the long shadows of the setting sun rescued this death from anonymity; it summoned a witness and located the death accurately in time and space. When B. bent down, Tsaritsa was still alive. But immediately afterwards, she stopped breathing.

She didn't look at all like a Tsaritsa. She was more like a buxom village girl, because she was always ruddy and had a round face with dimpled cheeks. Her hair was coarse and thick. She laughed a lot and when she did that she showed her very small, very white teeth. Her laugh was light and playful, but she herself was dignified and stately. We called her "Tsaritsa" in obedience to a certain vision. It was winter. The poet was drinking beaten raw eggs when Stefania entered the room covered with frost, all rosy from the cold, wearing a sheepskin hat and high boots. The poet put the eggs down on the windowsill and cried out, "Tsaritsa!" He was skinny and sported a pointed little beard, and looked like a dwarf next to Stefania. So she became "Tsaritsa", since the poets' power is great over us even when they see a crown and a throne where we see a haystack. She was very pleased by this; she burst into merry satisfied laughter, and that was probably how she laughed when she saw Kürch coming towards her down the street—astonished, incredulous, Kürch who, I imagine, cried out, "Stefania!" when he saw her. He called her his Stefania, in the Polish way, not Steffi, which was one more proof of his kindness. The other policemen (she worked as a cleaning woman for the Feldgendarmerie) called her Steffi.

I don't know what street it was, probably one of the main streets, very likely the main street itself, a sort of avenue between a double row of trees that overhung the walkway between them. The street ended in a rounded square with a fountain, gleaming towers and cupolas. That's where I place their meeting, the meeting between Stefania and Kürch, the sickly German with the bald, pear-shaped head, with his round eyeglasses and dressed, of course, in the uniform of the Feldgendarmerie. What is more, it seems to me that it had to take place precisely in the vicinity of that square with its fountain, with the benches placed around the fountain, and the jasmine bushes, since that is where the mothers usually sat with their children, and no doubt Stefania was there with the child. I don't know if the child was a boy or a girl, but I do know what Kürch looked like because I saw him once.

I saw him in the peasant hut where Stefania and her parents were living after their forced move. It was on the outskirts of the little town (Stefania's home town and mine) in a garden, and it was so low that the mallows and other red flowers reached to the window. It was a picturesque hut filled with the smell of weeds and mint. Only now do I notice its picturesqueness; at that time I thought, it's well situated, close to the forest.

Stefania's mother, a small woman, had just lit the oil lamp (there was no electricity in the hut) and we were drinking tea brewed from the petals of the roses that grew in the garden. The tea was fragrant, though weak. The sky was growing dark, and footsteps were heard in the yard. The mother and daughter exchanged a knowing glance, both said *"Bitte"* out loud, and Kürch entered the room. His glasses glittered in the light from the oil lamp; he said *"Guten Abend,"* not *"Heil Hitler,"* in the accent of a Saxon peasant. I assume that he felt at home in that peasant hut; perhaps it reminded him of his home in Saxony. Stefania must have known and remembered that. He placed a flask of wine on the table, he did this discreetly, with a certain embarrassed air, and smiled, *"Na ja ... wie geht's ... na ja ..."* That was when I saw him.

He slurped his tea and his nose turned red. He didn't stay long, perhaps because I was there, because I was gaping at him wordlessly. He talked about a letter he had received from his home. He didn't show any photographs; no doubt they had already seen them. He stood up reluctantly, took a long time to make his farewells, and Stefania smiled her kind, merry smile.

"A decent man," she said afterwards, as we stood by the window and watched him walking down the road towards town, "he's ashamed of all this, he sympathizes with us ... It pains him that I have to wash floors for them. He visits us often, and it's thanks to him that I'm still working there and have a good *Ausweis* ..."

What did her parents say to Kürch when their daughter suddenly disappeared? I assume there was no such conversation. Stefania disappeared from our town the day before everyone had to move into the ghetto. Where did she go? How? She was the first who dared to take such a step. No one knew; no one asked.

Only after the war B. (not her parents, who were killed) told us that she had worked as a nanny for a German family in a town that was some 200 kilometers from our town. He had lived in the same part of town and had seen her often, usually by chance; she spent a lot of time in the fresh air, in the parks and squares.

So when she saw, coming towards her along that street that keeps insinuating itself into my imagination, a sickly man with a pear-shaped skull, she didn't hesitate for even a moment, perhaps she even quickened her pace. I know she didn't hesitate, because even if she couldn't avoid that meeting which, unknown to her, was her fate, she didn't have to say anything. But she did. The village hut in which he had sat at her parents' table, slurping tea or drinking wine, surfaced from out of the darkness of that other world that was as distant as another planet, but that suddenly existed once again close by. Kürch in his Feldgendarmerie uniform was not just Kürch, he was a composite of images that swirled around her—her home, her parents, her native town, her mother's voice, and undoubtedly his voice, too, Kürch's voice, sympathizing with them, grieving over their fate. I am certain that she did not hesitate and that he—astonished, incredulous, when he recognized the smiling girl leading a well-fed child by the hand that same Stefania, whom he had probably long since thought of as no longer existing, as exterminated, when, looking closely at her, he noticed the absence of a white-blue armband on her sleeve—first shouted out her name in amazement (it had to have been that way!) and only later, I'm not certain of the exact moment, if it was when she held out her hand to him with a carefree smile, or afterwards, when she was telling him about everything, he again reacted in astonishment, this time at the confused order of things. And he told himself the rest.

She ought to have expected it and been afraid, but she didn't expect it, and she wasn't afraid. It's amazing, how unscarred she was by the time, how alien to her were its laws and its sacred regulations. She preserved her sense of trust, and in those days trust was founded on a lack of imagination.

I even suppose she told her employer about the meeting, which provided a desirable alibi, and let her know that she was expecting a visitor.

B. told us that he went out for a stroll around town before dark, so it must have occurred, as I mentioned, at that time before nightfall, when the sun is setting and a thin mist hangs over the town and the shadows of trees lie on the streets.

How they came in, the words they used, even the expression on Tsaritsa's face (now she has become Tsaritsa again for me), the glimmer of terror at the moment when she became conscious of what was happening, I have never been able to picture to myself, although, without being a witness to her meeting with Kürch, I have been able to visualize it clearly.

Only the jump itself, that hurtling of the body—there were three of them, Kürch and two others, they were standing in the middle of the big room with its window open over the trees on the tranquil street, a fourth-floor window—only the jump itself, the hurtling body and its flight towards the ground and the violent upward gliding of the sky, the flight that ripped her from the laws of that time and returned her to the everlasting law of gravity, which applies equally to everyone. Now, at the moment of her death, I feel no contempt for the poet's exclamation.

B., walking along the quiet street, heard shouts, and then he saw a crowd of people, among them three Germans in uniform. Guided by instinct, he made his way through the crowd and bent over the woman who was lying there. Tsaritsa was still alive. Her eyes were open, staring at the sky, which had soared during her leap and then stopped, suspended overhead, the instant her body made contact with the earth.

## Pierre Gascar *1916–*

Gascar was born in Paris as Pierre Fournier. He served in the French army during World War II, was taken prisoner by the Nazis, escaped and was recaptured twice, and was finally taken to the Rada-Rusk concentration camp in the Ukraine. After the war, he combined journalism and literary criticism, but also published fiction and nonfiction prolifically. *Les Bêtes* (1953), a collection of six short stories and one novella ("Le Temps des morts"), which is filled with images of menacing animals and men hunting men as if they were beasts, won the Prix Goncourt in 1953. It was published in English as *Beasts and Men* (1956) together with the novella "The Season of the Dead," a portrayal of *l'univers concentrationaire* as observed from a prisoner-of-war cage near a small Ukrainian town. In 1960, *Beasts and Men* was published together with *The Seed* (*La Graine*). The prisoner of war theme is preserved in *The Fugitive* (1964), and the story "The Season of the Dead." Gascar has received numerous French literary awards.

# THE SEASON OF THE DEAD

◆ *I*

Dead though they be, the dead do not immediately become ageless. Theirs is not the only memory involved; they enter into a seasonal cycle, with an unfamiliar rhythm—ternary perhaps, slow in any case, with widely spaced oscillations and pauses; they hang for a while nailed to a great wheel, sinking and rising by turns; they have become, far beyond the horizons of memory, rays of a skeleton sun.

We had reached the first stage. We were opening up the graveyard—in the sense in which one speaks of opening up a trench; in this place, there had only been life before there was death. And this freshness was to persist for a long time, before the teeming dust of the charnel should dim it, before, eventually, when all the earth was trodden down, oblivion should spread with couch-grass and darnel, and the writing on the tombstones should have lost its meaning; and the arable land should regain what we had taken from it.

For a graveyard to become a real graveyard, many dead must be buried there, many years must pass, many feet must tread on it; the dead, in short, must make the ground their own. We were certainly far from that point. Our dead would be war dead, for whom we had to break open a grassy mound. It was all, in short, brimful of newness.

War dead. The formula had lost its heroic sense without becoming obsolete. The war had lately moved away from this spot. These men would die a belated and, as it were, accidental death, in silence and captivity, yielding up their arms for a second time. But could one still use the word "arms"?

From the slope of the mound where the new graveyard lay I could see them walking round and round within the barbed wire enclosure of the camp, looking less like soldiers than like people of every sort and condition brought together by their common look of sleeplessness, their unshaven cheeks, and the cynical complicity of gangsters the morning after a raid. Following several abortive escapes through Germany, some thousand French soldiers had just been transferred to the disciplinary camp of Brodno in Volynia. It was a second captivity for them, a new imprisonment that was more bewilderingly outlandish and also more romantic. That word gives us a clue: it was an imprisonment for death.

I had been granted the title of gravedigger in advance of the functions. When you dig a ditch, it's because you have already found water. Just now there was nothing of that sort. The ditch we were digging was too long to have a tree planted in it, too deep to be one of those individual holes in which, at that time, throughout Europe, men in helmets were burrowing, forming the base of a monolithic monument which was hard to imagine, particularly here. It could only be a grave. Now we strengthened it with props, we covered it with planks. Nobody was dead. The grave was becoming a sort of snare, a trap in which Fate would finally be caught, into which a dead man would eventually creep. He would thus have been forestalled and would glide into the darkness through wide open doors, while we would shrink back as he passed, hiding our earth-stained hands behind our backs.

The German N.C.O. had rounded us up in the camp. He needed six men. When he had got that number he took us to the gate and handed us over to an armed sentry. We skirted the wall outside the camp until we came to a small rough road which, a little further on, led over the side of a hill. At this point a track took us to the verge of the forest. The N.C.O., riding a bicycle, had caught up with us. He went to cut a few switches from an elm-tree.

"Who knows German?" he asked without turning round.

"I do."

He called me to him. He was trimming the leaves from the switches with vigorous strokes of his penknife. I disliked the sight: swift-working fingers, pursed lips, and at the end of the supple, swaying branch a ridiculous tuft of leaves dancing as though before an imminent storm. There is no wretchedness like that of flogged men.

"There's to be a graveyard here," he said to me, suddenly handing me the trimmed branches. "Your own. Follow me and tell your mates to pull off some more branches."

I passed on the order and followed the N.C.O. to a place where the skirt of the wood dipped down into a narrow combe at the end of which lay a round pond like a hand-mirror. The German dug the heel of his boot into the grass: "Here." As carefully as a gardener I planted a branch at the spot he showed me. Then he straightened his back and made a half-turn; staring straight in front of him, he walked forward, stopped and dug his heel into the grass, started off again and stopped again. My companions came up with their arms loaded with leafy branches. The task of planting began, and soon the branches stood lined up there in the still morning, marking the footsteps of the man as he doggedly staked his theoretical claim.

When the enclosure was thus demarcated, the German called me. We had to mark the site of the first grave. When this was set out my companions, in a fit of zeal, immediately began to lift up clods of turf. Then the earth suddenly appeared as it really was; it lay there against the grass like a garment ready to be put on.

"That's enough, you can dig it tomorrow," the German told us. "We must always have one ready. Death comes quickly these days. War's a shocking thing."

He collected us together and the sentry took us back to the camp. As we were going through the gate one of us got from him, after some pleading, a leaf from his note-book with his signature. We rushed to the kitchens where extra rations of soup were sometimes distributed to the men who were working in gangs about the camp.

"Graveyard!" cried the prisoner who held the voucher, waving it. The man with the soup-ladle looked at us uncertainly for a moment, as though trying to remember to what burial-ground this irregular privilege could suddenly have been allotted.

"Camp graveyard!" someone else repeated. The man took the can that was held out to him and filled it. Death had spoken; moreover, Death's voucher was in order.

From that day, and still more from the following day when the first grave had been dug and shored up, I began to look out for Death in the faces of my comrades, in the weight of the hour, the colour of the sky, the lines of the landscape. Here, the great spaces of Russia were already suggested; I had never known a sky under which one had such a sense of surrender.

Sometimes the earth, dried by the early spring sunshine, was blown so high by the wind that the horizon was darkened by a brown cloud, a storm-cloud which would break up into impalpable dust, and under which the sunflowers glowed so luminously and appeared suddenly at such distances that you felt you were witnessing the brief, noisy revenge of a whole nation of pensive plants, condemned for the rest of their days to the dull quietness of sunshine.

Close to us, the town was shut in with a white wall above which rose a bulbous church spire, some roots, and the white plume of smoke from a train, rising for a long time in the same spot, with a far-off whistle like a slaughtered factory.

We had reached Brodno one April morning. The melting snows and the rain had washed away so much earth from the unpaved streets that planks and duckboards had been thrown down everywhere to let people cross, haphazard and usually crooked, looking like wreckage left after a flood subsides. The sentries could no longer keep the column in order and we were all running from one plank to another mingled with women wearing scarves on their heads and boots on their feet, with German soldiers, with men in threadbare caftans; and here and there jostling one of those strange villagers who stood motionless with rigid faces, their feet in the mud, idle as mourners, with white armlets on their arms as though in some plague-stricken city.

It might have been market-day, and the animation in the main street of the village might have been merely the good-humoured bustle of the population between a couple of showers, such as one sees also on certain snowy mornings, or on the eve of a holiday.... In any case, that first day, the star of David, drawn in blue ink on the armlets of those painfully deferential villagers who looked oddly Sundayfied in their dark threadbare town clothes amongst that crowd of peasants, seemed to me a symbol of penitence, somewhat mitigated, however, by its traditional character.

It was not until later on that their destiny was clearly revealed to me. Then, when I saw them in a group away from the crowd, they ceased to be mere landmarks; exposed to solitude as to a fire, that which had been diluted among so many and had passed almost unnoticed acquired sudden solidity. All at once, they became the mourners at a Passion: a procession of tortured victims, a mute delegation about to appeal to God.

A certain number of Jews had been detailed by the Germans to get the camp ready before our arrival. When we entered the gates they were still there, carefully putting the last touches to the fences, finishing the installation of our sordid equipment, and thus implacably imprisoning themselves, by virtue of some premonitory knowledge, within a universe with which they were soon to become wholly familiar.

The camp consisted of cavalry barracks built by the Red Army shortly after the occupation of Eastern Poland at the end of 1939. A huge bare space separated the three large brick-built main buildings from the whitewashed stables which housed the overflow of our column, according to that mode of military occupation that disdains all hierarchy of places—thus identifying itself with the bursting of dams, the blind and inexorable progress of disasters.

Inside every building, whether stable or barracks, wooden platforms, superimposed on one another, had been set up the whole length of the huge rooms, leaving only a narrow passage along the walls and another across the middle of the structure: tiered bunks like shelves in a department store, where the men were to sleep side by side. Our captivity thus disclosed that homicidal trend which (for practical rather than moral reasons) it usually refused to admit: for the Germans, the unit of spatial measurement was "a man's length."

The great typhus season was barely over at Brodno. It had decimated the thousands of Russian prisoners who had occupied the place before us and who had left their marks on the whitewashed walls—the print of abnormally filthy hands, bloodstains and splashed excrement—messages from those immured men jostling one another in the silent winter night, while Death and Frost exchanged rings: faintly-heard calls from far away. Because of the lingering typhus and the risk of propagating lice, we were given no straw.

We were given little of anything that first day. The Germans, except for a few sentries established in their watchtowers, had retired no one knew whither, as though it were understood that at the end of our trying journey we must be granted a day's truce, an unwonted Sunday that found us standing help-less, leaning against the typhus-ridden bunks with our meager bundles at our feet. A louse crawled up one's spine like a drop of sweat running the wrong way, and within one there was that great echoing vault, hunger.

In the afternoon, however, a few dixies full of soup were thrust through the kitchen door. A thousand men lined up on the path of planks that led to it. Hardly any of us had a mess-tin, but a great rubbish-dump full of empty food-tins supplied our needs. When the tins were all used up we unscrewed the clouded glass globes covering the electric lamps in the building, and made empty flower-pots water-tight by plugging the holes with bits of wood. When these uncouth vessels appeared in the queue they were greeted with shouts of envy, provoked rather by their capacity than by their grotesque character. A sort of carnival procession in search of soup took place, and the owner of an empty sardine-tin might be seen gauging a piece of hollow brick half-buried in the mud, wondering if those four holes like organ-pipes might perhaps be stopped up at the base, and turning over the problem with his foot while the column moved on a few yards. Fine rain was falling.

"It's millet!" shouted a man coming towards us from the kitchens, clasp-ing his brimming tin in both hands.

A cry of joy, in an unknown voice: a fragmentary phrase, as though cut out of its context, which, uttered in the dying afternoon in the heart of the

Volynian plain, seemed to have escaped from a speech begun very far away, many years earlier, and to have returned now—just as, in the hour of death, words half-heard long ago, neglected then and despised, recur to one's memory, suddenly whispering out their plaintive revenge, suddenly gleaming with a prodigious sheen because they hold the last drops of life.

◆ II

It was not until much later that somebody died.

From the time of that first burial I felt certain that death would never move far from our threshold. A dead body is never buried as deep as one thinks; when a grave is dug, each blow of the pickaxe consolidates the boundaries of the underground world. Though you lie sepulchered in the earth, like a vessel sunk in quicksand, and the waves of darkness beat against you from below, your bones remain like an anchor cast.

That day a group of German soldiers accompanied the convoy. They were armed and helmeted. They fell into step with the handful of Frenchmen—the chaplain, the medical orderly, the *homme de confiance*★—who were walking behind the *tarantass* on which the coffin was laid. They moved very fast and they seemed to be upon us in a few minutes, as we stood watching from the graveyard on the side of the hill (had they remembered to bring the cross and the ropes?); they were charging on us, a crowd of them, two by two, clad from head to foot; they were coming for us, making us realize in a flash what a terrible responsibility we had accepted when we dug that hole, what echoes our solitary toil had roused over there.

We had to face them, to lay the ropes down side by side on the spot where the coffin would be placed, to put down the two logs at the bottom of the grave on which it would lie so that we might afterwards haul up the cords, the ends of which would flap against the coffin for a minute like the pattering footsteps of a last animal escaping. The chaplain recited prayers. The medical orderly sounded the Last Post on a bugle, picked up somewhere or other. We grasped our ropes and, leaning over the grave, began to slacken them. At an order from their N.C.O., the German soldiers, who were presenting arms, raised the barrels of their guns towards the sky and fired a salvo.

There is always somebody there behind the target of silence. A shout or a word uttered too loud or too soon, and you hear a distant bush crying out with a human voice—you run towards a sort of dark animal only to see it clasp a white, human hand to its bleeding side; it's the tragedy of those hunting accidents where the victims, emerging from silence, are the friend or stranger—

---

★One of the French prisoners chosen by the rest to represent their interests in dealing with the Germans.

equally innocent—who happened to be passing by; there's always somebody passing just there, and we are never sufficiently aware of it.

The Germans' salvo re-echoed for a long time. We had lifted our heads again. Lower down, on the little road, some peasants and their women, coming back from the town, who had not witnessed the beginning of the ceremony (at that distance, in any case, they could not have observed its details) began to walk suddenly faster, casting a quick look back at us. Some women drew closer together and took each other's arms, a man stumbled in his haste, and all of them swiftly bowed their heads and refused to look at what was happening in our direction.

They seemed possessed not so much by anxiety as by a kind of shuddering anticipation, making them shun a spectacle which they dreaded as though it were contagious and hurry slightly despite their assumed indifference. They betrayed that tendency to deliberate withdrawal which, at that time, was making the whole region more deserted than any exodus could have done. Had we run towards them, clasped their hands, gazed into their faces crying "It's all right, we're alive!" they would no doubt still have turned away from us, terrified by fresh suspicions, feeling themselves irremediably compromised. . . . Now they had vanished. The Germans slung their rifles. We stood upright round the grave, like a row of shot puppets.

This incident and others less remarkable gave us a feeling of solidarity. We tried to secure official recognition for our team from the camp authorities by presenting a list of our names to every new sentry—to those that kept guard over the gates, those that supervised the kitchens, those that inspected our block. Every week we made out several lists, in case the camp administration should prove forgetful. We gave notice of our existence to remoter authorities, to prisoners' representatives, shock brigade headquarters, divisional commanders, with the stubborn persistence of minorities ceaselessly tormented by the nightmare of illegality.

We guessed that our proceedings met with secret opposition from the Germans, who were unwilling to give public recognition to this peculiar team, the granting of legal status to which would for them have been equivalent to admitting criminal premeditation—and from the prisoners too, since they did not need so realistic a reminder of the gruesome truth.

Between two deaths, it was only owing to the force of habit and the routinist mentality of the guardroom officer that we found a couple of sentries waiting each morning to take us to the graveyard. This, lying on the side of the hill amongst long grass, was in such sharp contrast to the almost African aridity of the camp as to enhance the feeling of separateness and even of exclusion which the failure of our advances to the administration had fostered in us. We belonged to another world, we were a team of ghosts returning every morning to a green peaceful place, we were workers in Death's garden, characters in a long preparatory dream through which, from time to time, a man would suddenly break, leaping into his last sleep.

In the graveyard we led that orderly existence depicted in old paintings and, even more, in old tapestries and mosaics. A man sitting beside a clump of anemones, another cutting grass with a scythe; water, and somebody lying flat on his belly drinking, and somebody else with his eyes turned skyward, drawing water in a yellow jug. . . . The water was for me and Cordonat. We had chosen the job of watering the flowers and turf transplanted onto the first grave and amongst the clumps of shrubs that we had arranged within our enclosure.

Its boundaries were imaginary but real enough. We had no need to step outside them to fill our vessels at the pond which, from the grave side, could be seen between the branches, a little lower down; there, the radiance of the sky reflected in the water enfolded us so vividly, lit up both our faces so clearly, that any thought of flight could have been read on them from a distance, before we had made the slightest movement, before—risking everything to win everything—we had set the light quivering, like bells.

The only flight left to us was the flight of our eyes towards the wooded valley at the end of which the pond lay. The leaves and grass and tree-trunks glowed in the shadow, through which the sunbeams filtered and in which, far off, a single leaf, lit by the sun's direct fire, gleamed transparently, an evanescent landmark whose mysterious significance faded quickly as a cloud appeared.

Flowers grew at the very brink of the pond, violets, buttercups, dwarf forget-me-nots, reviving memories of old herbals; only the lady-bird's carapace and the red umbrella of the toadstool were lacking to link up the springtime of the world with one's own childhood. When we had filled our bottles, Cordonat and I would linger there gazing at our surroundings, moved by our memories, and in an impulse of greedy sentimentality guessing at the beech-nut under the beech-leaf, the young acorn under the oak-leaf, the mushroom under the toadstool and the snail under the moss.

Sometimes the sun hid. But we could not stir, for we had fallen down out of our dream to such a depth that our task—watering a few clumps of wood-sorrel in a remote corner of Volynia—appeared absurd to the point of unreality, like some Purgatorial penance where the victims, expiating their own guilt or original sin, are forced to draw unending pails of water from a bottomless well, in a green landscape, tending Death like a dwarf tree—just as we were doing here.

Actually, I did not know whether Cordonat's dream followed the same lines as my own. I had lately grown very fond of Cordonat, but he was so deeply consumed by nostalgia that maybe I only loved the shadow of the man. He was ten years older than I, married, with two children; home consists of what you miss most. This vineyard worker from Languedoc showed his Catalan ancestry in his lean, tanned face, with the look of an old torero relegated to the rear rank of a *cuadrilla*, his delicate aquiline nose and wrinkled forehead with white hair over the temples which predestined him for the loneliness of captivity.

It so happened that, with the exception of myself, all the men of our grave-yard team, who belonged to the most recent call-up, were natives of the South of France, and all showed a tendency to nostalgic melancholy which was highly appropriate not only to their new duties but to our peculiar isolation on the fringe of camp life. This distinction enhanced a characteristic which was common to all the prisoners of Brodno, who, by their repeated attempts to escape from Germany, had in effect escaped from their own kind. At a time when under cover of captivity countless acts of treachery were taking place, they had set up on the Ukrainian border, in a corner of Europe where the rules of war were easily forgotten, a defiant Resistance movement, a group of "desert rats" whose most seditious song was the Marseillaise.

Homesickness creates its own mirages, which can supersede many a land-scape. But that amidst which we were living now was becoming so cruelly vivid that it pierced through all illusory images; it underlay my companions' dreams like a sharp-pointed harrow. This only became clear by slow degrees.

When Cordonat and I were sitting by the pond, we would look up and see peasants and their wives on their way back from the town, passing along the path through the trees and bushes at the end of our combe. We would stand up to see them better and immediately they would hurry on and vanish from sight, imperceptibly accentuating the furtiveness of their way of walking, stooping a little and averting their eyes as though they were eager to avoid the sight of something unlucky or, more precisely, something compromising.

As we stood at the foot of this hillock, somewhat apart from the other prisoners, we must have seemed to be in one of those irregular situations which were not uncommon here, like cases of some infectious disease. Were we escaped prisoners, obdurate rebels? Were we in quarantine, or about to be shot? In any case we were obviously trying to make them our accomplices, determined to betray them into a word or a look and thus involve them in that contamination that always ended with a shower of bullets and blood splashed against a wall. And the forest in which, only a minute before, spring flowers had awakened childhood memories, now emerged as though from some Hercynian flexure, darker and denser, more mysterious and more ominous, because of the fear and hunger of men. Fear can blast reality.

But it was when we left the skirt of the forest and reached the plain where the town lay that this devastating power of fear seemed actually to colour the whole landscape. The white road, the far-off white house fronts, the lack of shadows, all this was deprived of radiance by the subdued quality of the light; but it exuded a kind of stupor. At first, you noticed nothing.

But when we drew near we would suddenly catch sight of a man or a woman standing motionless between two houses or two hedges, and turning towards us in an attitude of submission, like people who have been warned to prepare for any danger. The man or woman would stare at us as we passed with eyes that revealed neither curiosity nor envy nor dread, a gaze that was not dreamy, but enigmatically watchful. A few men, also dressed in threadbare town clothes, were filling up the holes in the pavement. They did not raise their heads as we went by; they kept on with their work, but performed only secondary, inessential tasks, like factory hands waiting for the bell to release them from work and only staying at their posts because they have to.

In every case we were aware that, as we approached (or more precisely as our sentries approached), some final inner process of preparation was taking place (but maybe it had long since been completed?) and that one of the Germans had only to say "Come on!" load his gun or raise the butt to strike, for everything to take its inevitable, unaltering course. The tension of waiting was extreme.

They had long ago passed the stage when your pulse beats faster, spots dance before your eyes, and sweat breaks out on your back; they had not left fear behind, but they had been married to it for so long that it had lost its original power. Fear shared their lives, and when we walked past with our sentries beside us it was Fear, that tireless companion, that began, in a burst of lunatic lucidity, to count the pebbles dropping into the hole in the pavement, the trees along the road, or the days dividing that instant from some past event or other—the fête at Tarnopol, or Easter 1933, or the day little Chaim passed his exam: some other spring day, some dateless day, some distant day that seemed to collect and hold all the happiness in life.

Sometimes, in the depth of their night, fear would flare up and wake them, like the suddenly remembered passion that throws husband and wife into each other's arms; then they would embrace their fear, foreseeing the coming of their death like the birth of a child, and their thoughts would set out in the next room the oblong covered cradle in which it would be laid. Morning would bring back their long lonely wait, *tête à tête* with fear. They tied round their arms the strip of white material with the star of David drawn on it. Often the armlet slipped down below the elbow, and hung round the forearm slack and rumpled and soiled like an old dressing that has grown loose and needs renewing. The wound is unhealed, but dry. But why should I speak of wounds? Hunger, cold, humiliation and fear leave corpses without stigmata. One morning we saw a man lying dead by the roadside on the way to the graveyard. There was no face; it was hidden in the grass. There was no distinguishing mark, save the armlet with the star of David. There was no blood. There is practically no blood in the whole of this tale of death.

◆ *III*

One Monday morning two new sentries came up to join us at the camp
gates. They belonged to a nondescript battalion in shabby uniforms which had
been sent from somewhere in Poland by way of relief, and had arrived at Brodno
a few days earlier: one of those nomadic divisions to which only inglorious
duties are assigned, and whose soldiers only get killed in defeats.

Our two new sentries were a perfect example of the contrasts, exaggerated to the point of grotesqueness, which are always to be found among any
group of belatedly conscripted men, since neither regulation dress nor esprit
de corps nor conviction can replace the uniformity of youth. One of the two
soldiers was long and thin, with a high-coloured face; the other, short and squat,
was pale.

Each morning, when we went into the enclosure, we would quickly dismiss and, one after the other, go and stand before the graves giving a military
salute; it was the only solemn moment of the day. That morning, as I was walking after my comrades to pay my homage to the dead, I heard a click behind
me: the taller of the two soldiers was loading his gun. We had been running
rather quickly towards our dead, because it was Monday and we felt lively. He
had been afraid we were trying to escape or mutiny. But we were merely hurrying towards the graves like workmen to the factory cloakroom, discarding discipline and, at the same time, hanging up our jackets on the crosses.

There were only three graves at this time. We made up for this by working on the flower-beds, those other plots of consecrated, cultivated ground.
Cordonat and I were already grasping our bottles, eager to resume our rever-
ies beside the pond, at the bottom of which could be seen a rifle and a hand-
grenade thrown there by a fugitive Russian soldier. This filthy panoply, sunk
deep in the mud, mingled with our reflected images when we bent over the
water, as though we had not been haunted enough for the past two years by
the memory of our discarded arms.

I went up to the short German soldier (the other had alarmed me by that
performance with his rifle a little while before) and explained to him that it
was our custom to go and draw water from the pond. He nodded, smiling but
silent; then, before I went off, he said to me in French: "*Je suis curé.*"

The word, uttered with an accent that was in itself slightly ridiculous, had
a kind of popular simplicity that, far from conferring any grandeur on it, seemed
to relegate it to the vocabulary of anti-clericalism, made it sound like the admis-
sion of a comic anomaly. Such a statement, made by this embarrassed little man
wearing a dreaded uniform in the depth of that nameless country, suggested
the depressing exhibitionism of hermaphrodites, the sudden surprise of their
disclosure. I could find nothing to reply.

"Protestant," he went on in his own language. "In France, you're mostly
Catholics."

So he was a pastor. The rights of reason were restored—so were those of the field-grey uniform, since I found it easier to associate the Protestant religion with the military profession. I acquiesced: we were, apparently, Catholics. Generously, the Germans granted us this valid historical qualification; we might graze on this reprieve. The little pastor, however, did not try to stop us from going to draw water for our flowers; he encouraged us to do so and walked along with us down the path leading to the pond.

Without giving me time to answer, he chattered in his own language, of which Cordonat understood barely a word. I had never before heard German spoken so volubly; it poured forth like a long-repressed confession, like a flood breaking the old barriers of prejudice and rationalism, and the clear waters rushed freely over me, carrying the harsh syllables like loose pebbles. He was a pastor at Marburg. His family came from the Rhineland and one of his ancestors was French. In the Rhineland they grew vines; the country was beautiful there. Marburg lay further east; and there they still remembered Schiller and Goethe and Lessing (nowadays people seldom talk about Lessing). The pastor's wife was an invalid. On summer evenings he would go into the town cafés with his elder daughter. They were often taken for man and wife.

He went on talking. It was a sunny June morning. The Ukrainian wheat was springing up. By the side of the sandy roads, you could sometimes see sunflower blossoms thrown away by travelers after eating the seeds. And we carried on our Franco-Rhenish colloquy, squatting at the foot of the hillock, beside the pond, in the shade of the trees, while the peasant women, suspecting some fresh conflict, some subtle and wordy form of bullying, hurriedly passed by higher up with a rustle of leaves under their bare feet.

In order to keep our hands occupied and to justify our long halt by the pond in the eyes of the other sentry, Cordonat and I had begun to scour our mess-tins. We always carried them about with us. I had fixed a small wire handle to mine so as to hook it to my belt. This habit was partly due to the constant hope of some windfall, some unexpected distribution of food, but also no doubt it expressed a sort of fetishistic attachment to the object that symbolized our age's exclusive concern with the search for food. These mess-tins, which had only been handed out to us on our second day in camp, were like little zinc bowls; we went about with barbers' basins hanging from our waists. As part of this instinctive cult, we felt bound to polish them scrupulously. Cordonat and I were particular about this, to the point of mania. It was largely because of the fine sand on the edge of the pond and also because we were waiting—waiting for better days to come.

"*Ydiom! Ydiom!*" (come on!) we heard a peasant woman on the hill above us calling to one of her companions, who must have been lingering in the exposed zone.

The little pastor kept on talking.

"What d'you think of all this?" I asked him.

"It's terrible," he said. "Yes, what's happening here is terrible."

That simple word assumed the value of a confession, of a dangerous secret shared. It was enough in those days (a look, a gesture, a change of expression would have been enough) to lift the hostile mask and reveal the pact beneath. However, I dared not venture further and I began pleading our cause, describing our destitution, making no major charge but only such obvious complaints as could give no serious offence to the Germans. The petty sufferings we endured acted as a convenient salve for one's conscience; I realized this as I spoke and I resented it. Even this graveyard, so sparsely populated and so lavishly decorated, had begun to look like "a nice place for a picnic," with its green turf overlying the great banqueting-halls of Death.

"Terrible, terrible," the little pastor kept saying. It was the word he had used earlier. But it had lost its original beauty.

◆ *IV*

Back in camp, after the midday meal of soup, I waited impatiently for the two sentries to come and take us to the graveyard. I looked forward to seeing Ernst, the pastor (he had told me his name), with a feeling of mingled sympathy and curiosity that was practically friendship; it only needed to be called so.

I was not surprised when, on reaching the graveyard, Ernst took me into the forest, explaining to his mate that we were going to look for violet plants. It was high time, the last violets were fading. The other German appeared quite satisfied with this explanation. Since the morning, he had been so good-humoured that I felt inclined to think that that sudden business with the rifle had been an automatic gesture; a gun never lets your hands stay idle. He had a long shrewd face.

"I'm a Socialist," he told my friends while I walked away with Ernst.

Cordonat watched me go; was he envying me or disowning me? He sat there beside the pond like some lonely mythological figure.

But now the forest was opening up in front of me: that forest which hitherto I had known only in imagination, which had existed for me by virtue not of its copious foliage or its stalwart tree-trunks but of its contrasting gloom, the powerful way it shouldered the horizon and above all its secret contribution to the darkness that weighed me down. We walked on amidst serried plants; he carried his rifle in its sling, looking less like an armed soldier than like a tired huntsman, glad to have picked up a companion along the homeward road. But already the forest and its dangerous shadows had begun to suggest that the journey home would be an endless one, that our companionship was forever; once more, in the midst of a primeval forest, we were shackled together like those countless lonely damned couples—the prisoner and his guard, the body and its conscience, the hound and its prey, the wound and the knife, oneself and one's shadow.

"Well, when you're not too hungry in camp, what d'you like doing? You must have some sort of leisure. Oh, I know you don't like that word. But I don't know any other way to express the situation where I'd hope to find your real self—for hunger isn't really you, Peter. Well, what else is there?"

He pushed back from his hip the butt of his rifle, which kept swinging between us.

"I walk round the camp beside the barbed wire, or else I sleep, and when I find a book I read it...."

"And sometimes you write, too...."

I looked at Ernst suspiciously.

"A few days ago," he went on. "I was on guard in one of the watch-towers. I noticed you. You stopped to write something in a little note-book. This morning I recognized you at once."

This disclosure irritated me.

"You see, I can't even be alone!" I cried. "Isn't that inhuman?"

"But you were alone. You were alone because at that moment I didn't know you, and you didn't know me. Really, nothing was happening at all."

He was beginning to sound a little too self-confident. It was a tone that did not seem natural to him; there was a sort of strained excitement about it. I did not pursue the matter; without answering I bent down to pick up my violet plants. Ernst stood in silence for a while then, returning to the words I had spoken a few minutes earlier, as though his mind had dwelt on them in spite of what had followed:

"Books," he repeated with a schoolmasterish air of satisfaction and longing. "They were my great refuge, too, when I spent a few months in a concentration camp two years ago. I'd been appointed librarian, thank heaven.... Look here," he went on in a livelier tone, as though what had been said previously was of no importance, "put down your violet plants. Come and I'll show you something."

He was giving me line enough, as fishermen say; but I was well and truly caught this time. I stood up. He had started off ahead of me along a path that led to the right. I caught up with him: "I suppose the camp was on account of your political ideas?"

"Political ... well, that's a word we don't much care for. Rather on account of my moral views. However, they did let me out of that camp. It was just a warning. I need hardly tell you that I haven't changed.... You see that wall?"

I saw the wall. It was decrepit, overgrown with moss and briars, its stones falling apart, and it enclosed a space in which the forest seemed to go on, to judge by the tree-tops that appeared above it. We walked some way round the outside and came to a gap in the wall. Within the enclosure grey stones stood among trees which were slighter than those of the surrounding forest, contrary to my previous impression. Here and there, pale grass was growing; it had begun to take possession of the ground again. The upright stones marked Jewish graves, a hundred years old no doubt. Eastern religions lay their dead at the foot of slabs of slate, stumbling-blocks for the encroaching wilderness. Time had jostled many and overthrown a few of these old battlements of death, monoliths on which Heaven had written its reckoning in the only tongue it has ever spoken.

Ernst knew a little Hebrew. His small plump hand was soon moving over the stone, beginning on the right as in fortune-telling by cards. He read out some long-distant date, lazily coiled up now with a caterpillar of moss lying in the concavity of the figures, some name, with the knowledgeable curiosity of an accountant who has discovered old statements, bills yellow with age that have been settled once and for all. His religion was based on the belief that death belongs to the past and, when he looked at a grave, whether worn down by time or black with leaf-mould, he would say to himself with visible gladness that "all that's over and done with." Meanwhile I was overwhelmed by the symbolism of these graves; on most of the stones there was carved a breaking branch—you could see the sharp points at the break and the two fragments about to separate forming an angle, a gaping angle like an elbow. It was like the sudden rending that takes place high up in the tree of life, its imminence revealed by the flight of a bird, of that other soul which has hitherto deafened us by its ceaseless twittering, whereas our real life lay in the roots. On the stone, the branch was endlessly breaking, it would never break; when death has come, has one finished dying? Ernst raised his head and straightened his back.

"I've been re-reading your classics," he said to me with a smile.

I did not understand.

"I mean that this ancient, traditional burial-ground, close by your own fresh and improvised one, is rather like the upper shelf in a library. . . ." He laid his hand on a carved stone. "The preceding words in the great book . . ."

"Who can tell? Perhaps the moment of death is never over," I replied, thinking of the symbol of the broken branch. "Perhaps we are doomed to a perpetual leave-taking from that which was life and which lies in the depth of night, as eternal as the patient stars. Perhaps there is no more identity in death than in life. Each man dies in his own corner, each man stays dead in his own corner, alone and friendless. Every death invents death anew."

"But I believe in Heaven and in the communities of Heaven, where no echo of life is heard," replied Ernst joyfully. "In the peace of the Lord."

"I cannot and will not believe that those who are murdered here cease their cries the moment after. . . ."

"Their cries have been heard before," said Ernst. "What do you mean? Do you need to hear dead men's cries? Isn't it enough that God remembers them, that we remember them? I will tell you something: they are sleeping peacefully in the light, all in the same light."

"That's too easy an answer!" I cried. "That's just to make us feel at peace."

"Don't torture yourself," Ernst replied. "In any case, neither you nor I is to blame."

We were not to blame. I had taken up my violets again from the place where I had left them a short while before and, with this badge of innocence, my flowers refuting what Ernst's rifle might suggest, we made our way to the graveyard through the silent forest.

"Tomorrow we'll go for another walk," Ernst said. "We might take the others too. We'll find some pretext."

◆ *V*

But next day we were deprived of any pretext. Two men had died in the camp. Graves had to be dug; the dead had to be buried.

Ernst directed our labors skillfully and with pensive dignity. It was he who taught us that in this part of Europe they lined the inside of graves with fir-branches. Not to lag behind in the matter of symbolism we decided to bury the dead facing towards France. As France happened to be on the further side of the forest against which the first row of graves had been dug, we were obliged to lay the dead men the wrong way round, with their feet under the crosses.

These two deaths occurring simultaneously aroused our anxiety. Sanitary conditions within the camp had worsened; underfed and weakened by their sufferings during the escape and the subsequent journeys from camp to camp, the men gathered in daily increasing numbers in a huge sickroom. A few French doctors had been sent to Brodno by way of reprisal; lacking any sort of medicaments, they went from one palliasse to the next making useless diagnoses, reduced to the passive role of witnesses in this overcrowded world whose rhythm was the gallop of feverish pulses and where delirious ravings mingled in a crazy arabesque, while men sat coughing their lungs out.

We buried four men in the same week. June was nearly over; it was already summer. By now, the white roads of the invasion spread like a network over the Russian land, far east of Brodno, right up to the Don, then to the Volga, to the Kuban, milestoned with poisoned wells. The woods were full of hurriedly filled graves, and the smoke rose up straight and still from the countryside, while the front page of German illustrated papers showed bareheaded soldiers, with their sleeves rolled up, munching apples as they set off to conquer the world. Hope dried up suddenly, like a well.

The Germans' victorious summer, as it rolled eastward, left us stranded on that floor formed by the hardened sediments of their violence, their extortions, their acts of murder, which already disfigured the whole of Europe. The drift of war away from us had only removed the unusualness of these things; the things themselves remained, only instead of seeming improvised they had assumed a workmanlike character; ruins were now hand-made, homes became prisons, murder was premeditated.

The Jews of Brodno had practically stopped working inside the camp, where everything was now in order. Those who were road-menders spent their time vainly searching the roads for other holes to fill; the saw-mill workers, whom we used to see on our way to the graveyard, kept on moving the same planks to and fro, with gestures that had become ominously slow. More and more frequently you could see men and women, wearers of the white armlet, standing motionless between houses or against a hedge, driven there by the somnambulism of fear.

Inside the camp the same fatal idleness impelled the French to line up against the barbed wire, with their empty knapsacks slung across their backs and clogs on their bare feet. To Jews and Frenchmen alike (to the former particularly) going and staying were equally intolerable fates, and they would advance timidly towards the edge of the road or of the barbed wire, take one step back and move a little to one side, as though seeking some state intermediary between departure and immobility. They would stand on the verge of imagined flight, and in their thoughts would dig illusory tunnels through time.

The tunnels we were digging might well have served them as models. Only ours had no outlet.

"Indeed, yes, Peter, graves have outlets," Ernst told me.

He had just brought me the stories of Klemens von Brentano. Death having left us a brief respite, we had gone off for a walk in the forest. A little way behind us, my comrades were gathered round Otto, the other sentry.

"What's he saying?" they shouted to me. I turned round. Otto repeated the words he had just uttered.

"He says that at home he was the best marksman in the district," I translated.

"Yes, we got that, he won some competitions. But he said something about birds . . . ."

"He can kill a bird on a branch fifty meters off with one shot. He's ready to prove it to us presently."

Otto was smiling, his neck wrinkling. His boast sounded like a public tribute when repeated as an aside by somebody else. I went back to Ernst.

"He's a nuisance with his stories of good marksmanship! Shots would make too much noise in the forest and in these parts they mean only one thing. I was going to take you to see the girls who work where the new road's being made. If he shoots we shall find them all terrified. . . ."

The project had a frivolous ring but Ernst forestalled my questions:

"They are young Jewish girls, unfortunate creatures. I've made friends with one of them. Every evening I take her some bread—a little bread; it's my own bread—at least, part of my own bread," he added in some confusion, recalling the daily agony of sharing it, his hunger and his weakness.

"Why are we going to see them?" I asked him. "We can't do anything for them. You know that."

"You are French, and the point is this: these are girls from the cultured classes of Brodno. They are better dressed than the peasants, they don't speak the same language, they had relations in various other countries, and now they are isolated, as though by some terrible curse. Nothing can save them from their isolation. Even if tomorrow the peasants round here were to be persecuted, the girls would find no support amongst them, no sense of kinship, no co-operation. Believe me, they've always been exiles in the East, even before the Germans settled here. And perhaps only you and I share what they've got, what makes them different. So don't run away."

"How could I run away?" I pointed to his gun. Ernst reddened with anger and shook his head. Behind us, big Otto had seen my gesture: "Don't talk to the pastor about his gun," he called out to me. "He thinks it's a fishing-rod."

I turned round. "Please note that I'm just as much a pacifist as he is," Otto said. "Only I know how to shoot!"

He burst out laughing. Cordonat was near him and beckoned to me. "Ask him to choose a biggish target," he said as I came up, "a rabbit for instance or a jay or a rook. Let's at least have something to get our teeth into!"

I passed on the request to Otto.

"But then it wouldn't be a demonstration," he cried. "It's got to be quite a tiny animal."

I tried to explain to him that he could still keep to the rules of the game if he stood further away from his living target. The argument seemed likely to go on indefinitely.

Ernst walked on ahead of us, indifferent to our conversation, with his back a little bent, like a recluse, and in addition that pathetic look that small men have when they are unhappy. He was going forward through the forest without keeping to the paths, and the forest was growing thicker. Already, we felt cut off from the outside world here, just because the shadows were a little deeper and the ground was carpeted with dead leaves, moss, myrtles and nameless plants. For us, as for millions of others, war meant "the fear of roads." These enslaved men looked at you sometimes with eyes like horses.

There was still the sky, the sky between the branches when you raised your head, an unyielding sky, still heavy with threats. Daylight is up there. I must be dreaming. It was as if when you pushed open the shutters after a night full of bad dreams the influx of light proved powerless to dispel the terrifying visions of the darkness from your eyes. And yet everything is there, quite real. You need a second or third awakening, the maneuvering of a whole set of sluice-gates, before the morning light yields what you expect of it—not so much truth as justice.

After a few minutes I caught up with Ernst. I was afraid of disappointing him by showing so little interest in the visit he had suggested to me. Perhaps he had given it up; the thought caused me no remorse, for he was a man with too clear a conscience, too easily moved to compassion. But even if I had interfered with the execution of his plans, I did not want him to think me indifferent or insensitive.

"I'm hungry," I said as I drew near him, so as to avoid further explanations.

"So am I. But we shall soon find these girls, and they'll give us some coffee—they make it out of roasted grain. That'll help to appease our hunger. Afterwards we'll go and fell the trees. And then Otto will have plenty of time to fire his shots."

The trees that we were to fell were intended to build a fence round the graveyard. Ernst had discovered this excuse to justify our walks. We were now on a path that led down to the verge of the forest. The new road that was being made skirted it at this point and the workmen had set up a few huts for their gear and for the canteen. Eight Jewish girls worked here under German orders on various tasks, and two of them kept the canteen.

These were the girls we saw first when Ernst, telling his mate we were going to get some coffee, led me towards the hut. The two girls had come out over the threshold. They were wearing faded summer dresses whose original colors suggested Western fashions and cheap mass-production. That was enough to introduce into this woodland setting an urban note which would have struck one as strange even without the added impression of bewilderment and weariness conveyed by the pale faces and wild eyes of the two girls. In spite of their youth, their features were devoid of charm. Beautiful faces were rare in this war; those faces which were daily taken from one were like commonplace relatives full of modest virtues, known intimately and loved and now gone into the night, unforgettable faces with their freckles and their tear-stained eyes.

When they recognized Ernst the two girls nodded gently. They stayed close together on the door-step. Ernst spoke to them, calling them by their names. We were Frenchmen, he told them, prisoners too, hungry and unhappy. "Nothing was happening." We looked at each other, helplessly. What conversation could we hold? Everything had been said before we opened our mouths. It was not to one another that we must listen but to the far-off heavens, to which some day perhaps would rise the noise of our deliverance.

"We can't give you coffee," said one of the girls to Ernst. "The *meister* hasn't given us any grain today."

Ernst had poked his head inside the hut to peer round. "Who's that?" he asked in a whisper. I looked too. In a corner of the room, a man in black was leaning over a basin, with his back towards us. He was dipping a rag in water and from time to time raising it to his face. One could guess from the stiff hunching of his shoulders and the timidity betrayed by his slow awkward gestures that he felt our eyes upon him.

"It's a man from the saw-mill," quickly replied one of the girls. "He hurt his face at work."

"But he doesn't work up here," said Ernst. "If the *meister* finds him here there'll be a row."

"He'll go away when you've gone," said the smaller of the two girls, speaking for the first time and with an ill-disguised nervousness. She was dirty, with untidy red hair hanging down each side of her face. "The other sentinel mustn't see him," she went on in a low voice. "Please, Herr Pastor, be kind and take your Frenchman further off."

"Where is Lidia?" asked Ernst.

"She's working on the tip-trucks," said the other girl. "She's being punished because she broke the cord of the hooter this morning."

"It's not fair!" went on the smaller girl, with bitterness. "The cord was rotten. When she tried to stop the hooter, at seven o'clock, the cord broke off in her hand. The hooter went on wailing long after everybody was at work. All the steam was being wasted. The *meister* called it insubordination. It's not fair . . . Yesterday they hanged four more men at Tarnopol."

"The way that hooter went on wailing," said her friend. "There was something sinister about it—it was like a warning. But what was the use of warning us? How could we move? What could we do?" she added anxiously.

Ernst did not answer. He stood with downcast eyes.

"Perhaps I'll come back tonight," he said after a while. "Tell Lidia. God be with you."

We joined the group of prisoners who were waiting for us, guarded by Otto, and plunged once more into the forest.

"Somebody must have hit him," muttered Ernst as I walked at his side. "I'm speaking of that man we saw in the hut," he added, with a look at me. "He didn't want us to see the blood."

"Why not?"

"Because they feel that to let their blood be seen is not only a confession of weakness, of impotence, but moreover it marks them out as belonging to the scattered herd of bloodstained victims who are being ruthlessly hunted down. While they are whole, they'll carry on as long as their luck holds; when they're wounded, they go out to meet their own death. The order of things that has been established here is all-embracing, Peter. If a civilian— if one of these civilians is found with blood on him, the authorities think the worst. Where did he get it, who gave him leave to move about? Why is he branded with that mark, and why is he not with the herd of the dead?

There's something suspicious about it. That man was well aware of this. He was hiding. He'd 'stolen' a beating. . . ."

"Do you think those girls are really in danger?"

While I was asking Ernst this question I realized that I had no wish to learn from him whether their danger was great or small. For the last few minutes I had experienced that slight nausea which, at the time, was more effective than any outward sign in warning me of imminent peril. Before Ernst could answer me a shot rang out behind us. Otto lowered his rifle and Cordonat ran towards a bush: "It's a jay!" he called out to me.

But I was observing the amazement created all around us, in the lonely forest, by the sudden report. I thought I caught sight of a grey figure disappearing swiftly between distant tree-trunks. Then everything was as it had been, unmoving. I did not want to talk any more, and Ernst seemed not to want to either. That rifle-shot had been like a blow struck with a clenched fist on a table, a call to order, silencing all chatter, even the private chatter of the heart. Otto was looking at us with a smile. He was looking at Ernst and myself. The bullet had passed just over our heads. He stopped smiling just as I was about to speak, to try and break out of that clear-cut circle which henceforward would enclose the three of us and within which we were now bound to one another by the dangerous silence that had followed our commonplace words.

◆ *VI*

The dead used to be brought to us in the morning, like mail that comes with habitual irregularity and provides no surprises; their belongings had to be classified, bills of lading for ships that have long since put out to sea; a cross had to be provided, with a name and a date. Now the coffins no longer showed those once ever-present wooden faces like those of eyeless suits of armour. Now a dead man in his coffin was no longer a human being wrapped in a door.

All we knew of the dead was their weight. However, this varied enough to arouse in us occasionally a sort of suspicion that somehow seemed to rarefy this inert merchandise. Unconsciously one was led to think in terms of a soul. A dead body that felt exceptionally heavy or, on the other hand, too light, reassumed some semblance of personality, smuggled in, as it were, in that unexpected gap between the weight of an "average" corpse and that of this particular corpse.

Things had begun to take their course. We might have been tempted to open the coffin, to examine the inscrutable face, to question the dead man's friends and search out his past history. But it was too late; the coffin was being lowered on its ropes; it lay at the bottom of the grave on the two supports we had placed there; the body was laid down, laid on its andirons and already more than half consumed with oblivion, loaded with ashes.

By now our burial-ground comprised seventeen graves. The flowers had grown and we were preparing to open a new section. It would be another row of graves set below the first, which lay alongside the verge of the forest. We were thus tackling the second third of the graveyard, for its limits had been strictly set from the beginning. Hardly two months had passed since our arrival at Brodno and we were already beginning to wonder if the graveyard would last out as long as we did, or if it would be full before we left the camp, so that some day we might find ourselves confronted with an overflow of dead bodies which would have to be disposed of in a hasty, slap-dash, sacrilegious way.

We foresaw that times would have changed by then; we might have a snowy winter, for instance, full of urgent tasks, and the fortunes of war would be drooping like a bent head. The limits of the burial ground, in a word, were those of our future, of our hope; all summer was contained within them. This summer had begun radiantly.

Fed by marshlands, fanned by the great wind blowing off the plain, the forest was aglow with its thousands of tree-trunks—beeches and birches for the most part—and its millions of leaves; carpeted with monkshood and borage, it projected into the middle of the wide wilderness, somewhat like a mirage no doubt, but above all like a narrow concession made to the surrounding landscape, to the past, and, in a more practical sense, to the dead.

We had gone through it now in all directions. As soon as a funeral was over Ernst and Otto would take us off to the hamlets that lay on the other side of the forest. There we would buy food from the peasants in exchange for linen and military garments from our Red Cross parcels; the barter took place swiftly and in silence, as though between thieves. We brought home a few fowls or rabbits, which we hurriedly slaughtered in the forest, using our knees and cursing one another, while the sentries guarded the paths.

We would wipe our hands with leaves. Then the dead creature had to be slipped inside one's trousers, between one's legs, held up by strings tied round the head and feet and wound round one's waist. The volume of the body, the feel of fur or feather, the temporary invasion of the lice they harboured, the smell of blood and a lingering warmth made us feel as though we were saddled with some ludicrous female sexual appendage, as though we had given birth to something hairy and shapeless that obliged us to walk clumsily, with straddled legs.

This stratagem enabled us to get back into the camp safely; I had no hesitation about resorting to it under the eyes of Ernst, since the very vulgarity of my movements, my grotesque gait, freed me from the mental complicity that bound me to him. It was a sort of revenge against despair. Sometimes, on the way back, we would catch a distant glimpse of the men and women at work on the new road. Ernst pointed out Lidia to me; she was wearing a light-coloured dress and pushing a tip-truck full of earth. Rain was threatening: "She's going to get soaked to the skin," Ernst muttered.

"Why Lidia?" I asked.

"Yes, why Lidia ..." he echoed, in torment, his head downcast.

"I meant why are you particularly interested in her?" It was hard to keep up this tone with a barely dead fowl stuck between your thighs.

"One has to make a choice, Peter," Ernst murmured. "One can't suffer tortures on every side at once. Mind you, that doesn't mean ..."

Otto was behind us, though far enough not to catch our words. I felt sure that if we went on talking like this he would soon shoot at a jay, a magpie, the first bird he saw. There's always one ready to fly off from an empty branch over your head, a little way in front of you or to one side. At every word, like involuntary beaters, we "put up" a covey of pretexts, birds with strange plumage and taunting cries. I turned round; Otto was smiling. Since I had begun carrying slaughtered animals between my legs his smile had grown broader; I was a "Kerl." Suddenly his smile froze: "Halt!" he called to me, pointing into the depths of the forest. Two figures were rapidly disappearing between the trees.

"Partisans," he said, hurriedly smiling again.

The word "partisans," as he spoke it, seemed to indicate some species of big game, rare and practically invulnerable, some solitary stag or boar shaking the unmysterious undergrowth with its startled gallop. Yet my heart had leapt. One morning, when we reached the burial-ground, we caught sight of black smoke drifting over a hamlet in the plain. Otto explained to me that some partisans, having been given a poor reception there in the night, had burnt it by way of reprisals. After that the open German cars that drove through Brodno assumed a warlike aspect, despite their gleaming nickel and brightly polished bodies. For beside the officers they were carrying sat two helmeted soldiers armed with tommy-guns.

We did not see them for long; the partisans seemed to have disappeared. In the villages, the Germans had distributed arms and formed militias. A watchman blew a bugle at the first alarm; it was a sort of long wail in the depth of the night which, generally without cause, made those who had taken refuge in treachery stir in their uneasy sleep. During the day Ukrainian policemen passed along the little path below the graveyard. They wore a black uniform with pink, yellow or white braid and badges of the same colours in checks, circles or triangles, like the gaudy signals of some obscure code hung out on the semaphores of terror.

The Germans acknowledged the stiff salutes of these liveried men with a nonchalant air. The Jews shrank back when they drew near; the Ukrainian policemen had the wild cruelty of certain sheepdogs, and above all their eyes and their voices recalled traditional pogroms. A few days earlier they had killed three prisoners who had escaped from the camp, shooting them down in the wood.

When they passed near us, Cordonat would taunt them under his breath in the patois of Languedoc. These muttered insults showed the total disconnectedness of everything; what mazes of recent history one would have to explore to account for this absurd conflict between a Ukrainian peasant dressed in a stage uniform and a *vigneron* from the South of France who, before the war, used to vote anti-Communist and who was now talking, in his patois, about joining the Volynian partisans.

Otto made fun of the Ukrainian policemen out loud when they had gone past us, and embarked on a conversation with Cordonat in which gestures to a large extent filled the gaps in their vocabulary; after a lengthy exchange of namely pacifist opinions, they had ended by discussing hunting, poaching and mushrooms.

Ernst appeared to be growing somewhat mistrustful of his companion. In order to be able to speak freely to me, he evolved the plan of taking me almost every day to the sawmill to get our woodcutting tools sharpened. I had never expressed any wish for these *tête-à-tête* conversations. They only lasted, actually, during the time we took to walk from the burial-ground to the saw-mill. This saw-mill was worked on behalf of the Germans by a Jewish employer and his men. I met there the man with the wounded face of whom we had caught sight a few days earlier in the girls' hut.

I had asked the boss of the saw-mill for a glass of water, as he stood talking to us in front of the workshop door. He turned round and asked someone inside, whom I could not see, to bring me one. A few minutes later Isaac Lebovitch came up to me carrying a glass of water. It was a glass of fine quality, patterned with a double ring, the remnant of a set no doubt, and its fragility and bourgeois origin made me uneasy. In this token of hospitality I recognized an object which might have been a family heirloom of my own. Isaac Lebovitch (he was soon to tell me his name) seemed to be about thirty years old. He had a long face with a lean beak of a nose. His dark curly hair, already sparse, grew low on his forehead. He stood beside us while I was emptying my glass.

"It may be that our hour has struck," the master of the sawmill was saying to Ernst. "It may be that the end of our race is in sight. There are things written up there," he added, pointing to the sky which was empty of birds, empty of hope.

I noticed a vine climbing round the door of the saw-mill. In that region where vines had never been cultivated it looked strange, like a Biblical symbol.

"And yet," the saw-mill boss was saying, "I myself fought during the last war in the Austro-Hungarian army. I was an N.C.O. and I won a medal. That means I was on your side, doesn't it?"

I felt embarrassed as I listened to his words. He was quite an old man, no sort of rebel against order or established authority, ready to accept a strict social

hierarchy and even a certain degree of victimization to which his religion exposed
him. . . . But not this, not what was happening now! These things were on the
scale of a cosmogony. Or worse: they took you into a universe which perhaps
had always existed behind the solid rampart of the dead, and of which the
metaphors of traditional rhetoric only gave you superficial glimpses: where the
bread was, literally, snatched from one's mouth, where one could not keep body
and soul together, where one really was bled white and died like a dog.

Like novice sorcerers inexpert in the magic of words, we now beheld the
essential realities of hell, escaping from the dry husks of their formulae, come
crowding towards us and over us: the black death of the plague, the bread of
affliction, the pride of a louse. . . . Seeing that Ernst was listening, with a look
of deep distress, to the old man's words, Lebovitch plucked up courage to speak
to me. He first addressed me in German, asking me whereabouts in France I
lived, what sort of job I had, whether my relatives over there suffered as much
from the German occupation as the people here did; then he suddenly spoke
a sentence in English.

It was quite an ordinary sentence like "life isn't good here." There was really
no need to wrap it up in the secrecy of another language, since it was no more
compromising than the words that had preceded it; and no doubt he had only
had recourse to these English words for the sake of their foreignness. A language does not always remain intact; when it has been forced to express
monstrous orders, bitter curses and the mutterings of murderers, it retains for
a long time those insidious distortions, those sheer slopes of speech from the
top of which one looks down dizzily. In those days the German language was
like a landscape full of ravines, from the depths of which rose tragic echoes.

"No, life isn't good here," I answered in German. "But over there in the
forest . . ."

"I don't go there any more. The other day . . ." Lebovitch showed me the
dry wound on his forehead. "Besides, you saw . . ."

"Probably you didn't go far enough, you didn't venture into the
depths. . . ."

"I had just gone to see Lidia," said Lebovitch, surprised by my remark. "I
had no reason to go further. You're liable to meet the partisans. . . ."

"That's just what I meant."

He stayed silent for a moment. We had moved a little further off and had
turned our backs on Ernst and the old man. Lebovitch stepped still further to
one side and, realizing that he wanted me to come away from the other two,
I went up beside him.

"The partisans," he said with an anxious air. "I'll tell you this: we don't
know much about them. If they saw me coming up to them they might shoot
me down. And how could I live in that forest? I've got no strength left," he
gasped, striking his thin chest with his fist. "And then there's so much vio-

lence, so much bloodshed every day, and all those farms set on fire. . . . After all, we're managing to hold out here. I've held out up till now. Perhaps we've been through the hardest part now. Listen, I may perhaps be dead tomorrow but I think it's better for me to save my strength. Don't you think that's best for you too?"

It would have been cruel to tell him that the dangers that threatened us seemed less terrible than his own, and I left him to his patience.

"That girl you call Lidia, who works on the new road," I remarked, "isn't she the one my sentry knows?"

"He ought to stop trying to see her. She told me so. It's likely to do her a lot of harm. I think she's had herself sent to the tip-trucks on purpose because of him, so that he can't try to see her during the daytime. What's he want with her, anyway? He knows that relations of that sort are forbidden. He'll only get her hanged, and himself after her."

"He wants to help her."

Lebovitch grasped me by the arm, after making sure that the other two could not see him: "Let me tell you this, Frenchman: the Germans can help nobody, d'you understand, nobody. They couldn't if they wanted to, they couldn't any longer. Imagine a hedgehog struggling to stop being a hedgehog; you wouldn't want to go near him then!"

Ernst called me. The tools were ready. We had to get back to the grave-yard. As I left Lebovitch, I was careful not to tell him that we would soon be back. It was no doubt bad for him and his friends that we should be seen at the saw-mill too often. We must each keep to his own solitude; fraternization had become conspiracy.

As we walked back, I spoke to Ernst about Lebovitch. "He's a friend of your Lidia's," I told him. "He's afraid that your interest in her may compromise her in the eyes of the German authorities."

"He's wrong," replied Ernst in an offhand manner. "You know I'm a pastor, and although I'm not a chaplain, the Commandant, who comes from my home town (only yesterday he was asking me for news of my family), gives me tacit permission to make some approaches to these people in a priestly capacity, to behave with a little more humanity in other words. . . ."

"Humanity," I echoed.

"I know what you're thinking, Peter," murmured Ernst. "Well, even if your thoughts correspond to the reality, what about it? Won't you ever understand?" he cried, appealing, far beyond me, to some unknown body of critics. "We are all lost. There's nothing for us to fall back on; there never will be. Even the earth has begun to fail us. In such conditions, who can forbid me to love in whatever way I can? Who can forbid me? This is the last form of priesthood open to me, Peter—the last power I've got. It's inadequate and clumsy, it needs to be exercised upon a living object, a single object. . . ."

His lips went on moving. I said nothing. I would not have known what to say. And then Otto was already watching us come, from the top of the burial-ground; the evening sun was behind his back and we could not see his face. He was standing motionless with his rifle on his shoulder. Behind him the graves were casting their shadows to one side, like beasts of burden relieved of their packs.

◆ *VII*

From that time on, discovering into what abysses I might be dragged if I followed Ernst, I fell back on the position of safety provided by the graveyard. Here was the only innocent place. Here we seemed to find a sort of immunity. When an officer came to inspect us we each bent as low as possible over a grave, assiduously weeding it as though pressed for time, without raising our heads, and the visitor refrained from speaking to us, wondering (probably for the first time in his life) if we were acting thus in response to some urgent appeal from the dead, such as he himself might perhaps have heard (it suddenly came back to him) in the middle of the night, in the days when he still felt remorse.

"The weeds are the white hair of the dead," Cordonat would say, and his words savored of that senile cult whose hold on us grew in proportion to the dangers that threatened us.

These dangers now assumed the shapes and sunburnt faces of SS men and military policemen, a few detachments of whom had recently arrived in the region of Brodno. But it was above all the growing silence of that summer, the pallor of the sun at certain hours, the oppressive heat that secretly frightened us. Our religion, which had never actually been a cult of the dead, was becoming a cult of the grave. As we dug and shell filled up our pits, we appeased some haunting dream of underground.

With our twenty-two dead, we had already opened up and explored a real labyrinth. We were familiar with its passages, its detours, its angles. It was a sort of deep-down landscape. We knew just where a tangle of hanging roots clutched clods of earth, where you could catch the smell of a distant spring, where you passed over a slab of granite. In the course of our work of excavation we had grown used to the coolness of this universe of the dead and we found our way about it mentally with the help of these particularities of structure rather than with the help of the names of the dead men who had drifted there accidentally, like foreign bodies.

This longing for the depths, unsatisfied by our task of weeding on the surface of the graves, impelled Cordonat and myself to try and open up a trench which would run a few yards into the forest and drain away the rain-water that poured down on to the graves and scored deep furrows in their unstable earth. Since we now no longer left the burial-ground to walk in the forest, which was patrolled by the soldiers who had recently come to Brodno, I was looking for an occupation.

Digging this trench had another very different result; it was through this narrow channel that I happened on something that I had been anxiously anticipating for many months. It began under my feet, like a forest fire. Right at the start, we had got on fairly fast with our trench and were now digging in the sandy soil of the forest, among the live roots of the trees. Below us our comrades were lying beside the graves, plucking the weeds from off the dead with one hand. Otto and Ernst were sitting in the shade of the trees, Ernst reading *Louis Lambert,* which had just been sent to me and which I had lent him. As we worked, Cordonat was telling me about his Landes. When we stopped to change tools, for we used pick and spade in turn, we shared out a little tobacco. The war seemed endless but here, at this precise moment, under this white silent sky, it had a flavor of patience, a flavor of sand; it bore the same relation to life as a fine sand to a coarser sand.

It was not with the pickaxe but with the sharp edge of the spade that I cut open the arm of the corpse. It was lying flush with the side of the trench and as I was leveling the walls I struck right into the flesh. It was pink, like certain roots, like a thick root covered with black cloth instead of bark. My blow had ripped off a bit of the sleeve. I started back, spellbound with horror. Cordonat came up and then called the sentries. Everybody was soon gathered round the unknown corpse. A little earth had crumbled away and his elbow and wounded arm were now projecting into the void; he was literally emerging from a wall.

"Cover it up with earth," said Otto.

"We'll make a cross of branches," murmured Ernst.

They went back into the graveyard with our comrades; the problem of burying this corpse was beyond them. It is easy, it is even tempting to throw earth on a dead body. Often, after our burials, we managed, using boards and spades, to push into the earth at one go most of the heaped-up earth that lay at its brink. Here, one would have had to cover over the arm that projected from the wall of earth, to enclose it in an overhanging recess. We therefore decided to fill up our trench and start it again lower down, skirting round the corpse. I did not know what name to give it. But all the indications (the colour of the clothes, their "civilian" appearance) suggested that the body was that of a Jew who had been killed there before our arrival or during one night, or maybe on a Sunday, very hurriedly no doubt, in a hush like that of a suicide.

I felt slightly sick. It was very hot. We were working with fierce concentration now, in silence. A few hours later, when we were digging our trench at some distance from the corpse, Cordonat, who was wielding his pickaxe ahead of me, suddenly started back. A sickly, intolerable smell arose; he had just uncovered a second body. This one was lying at the bottom of the trench, slightly askew and concealed by a thin layer of earth, so that Cordonat had trodden on it before, surprised by the elasticity of the soil, he exposed its clothing and the upper part of a mouldering face.

I was overwhelmed by the somber horror of it and the truth it revealed. This was death—these liquefying muscles, this half-eaten eye, those teeth like a dead sheep's; death, no longer decked with grasses, no longer ensconced in the coolness of a vault, no longer lying sepulchered in stone, but sprawling in a bog full of bones, wrapped in a drowned man's clothes, with it hair caught in the earth.

And it was as though, looking beyond the idealized dead with whom I had hitherto populated my labyrinths, my underground retreats, I had discovered the state of insane desolation to which we are reduced when life is done. Death had become "a dead thing," no more; just as some being once endowed with great dignity and feminine mystery may, after a slow degeneration, surrender to the grossest drunkenness and fall asleep on the bare ground, wrapped in rags; here, the rags were flesh. Death was this: a dead mole, a mass of putrefaction sleeping, its scalp covered with hair or maybe with fur: wreckage stranded in the cul-de-sac of an unfinished tunnel: surrender at the end of a blind-alley.

Cordonat discovered three more bodies. We had struck the middle of a charnel, a heap of corpses lying side by side in all directions, in the middle of the wood, a sort of subterranean bivouac which even now, when he had exposed it to the light, lost none of its clandestine character. We shouted, but in vain; this time nobody came to us. We turned over the earth till we were exhausted in an effort to cover up the bodies. We were practicing our craft of gravedig-gers in sudden isolation. And now it had assumed a wildly excessive charac-ter; we were gravediggers possessed by feverish delirium. Night was falling. We had ceased to care who these men were, who had killed them or when; they were irregular troops on the fringe of the army of the dead, they were "par-tisans" of another sort. We should never have finished burying them.

Their very position close by our own graveyard cruelly emphasized its pru-dent orderliness. Our dead, meekly laid out in rows, suddenly seemed to exude servility and treachery, wearing their coffins like a wooden livery.

The appalling stench of these accidentally exhumed corpses persisted for a long time in the forest, and spread over our graveyard. It was as though our own dead had awakened for a moment, had turned over in their graves, like wild animals hazily glimpsed in the sultry torpor that precedes a storm. There could be no doubt that something was going to happen. The smell warned one that the tide was about to turn.

The thundery heat and the horror of my discoveries made me feverish. Back in camp, I lay prostrate for several days on the wooden bed. Myriads of fleas had invaded the barrack-rooms and were frenziedly attacking us, while in the shadow of my clothes I traced the searing passage of my lice. Towards the evening Cordonat brought me a little water. This was so scarce that at the slightest shower all the men would rush outside clutching vessels, bare-headed, like ecstatic beggars, and when the rain stopped they sprawled on the ground, still jostling one another, round the spitting gutters. Then my fever dropped. When I went back to the burial-ground the first trains had begun to pass.

### ◆ VIII

A railway line ran over the plain that we overlooked from our mound. It was only a few hundred yards away. Until then we had paid little attention to it, for the traffic was slight or non-existent. During my absence it had increased without my noticing it; these trains sounded no whistles. If they had, I should have heard them from my bed in the camp; I should have questioned my com-rades and they could have enlightened me, for from certain windows in the building you could see a section of the line, beyond the station which was hid-den by houses.

The first trains had gone past behind us, full of stifled cries and shouts, like those trains that pass all lit up, crammed with human destinies and snatched out of the night with a howl while, framed in the window of a little house near the railway, a man in his shirtsleeves stands talking under a lamp, with his back turned, and then walks off to the other end of the room. And now, from the graveyard, I could see them coming, panting in the heat of the day, inter-minable convoys that had started a long time ago, long goods-trains trickling slowly through the summer marshalling-yards, collecting men on leave and refugees like a herd of lowing cattle.

I could hear their rumbling long before they appeared past the tip of the forest, and then when they were in sight (sometimes almost before) I could hear another sound, superimposed and as elusive as a singing in one's ears, a buzzing in one's head, or the murmur in a sea-shell: the sound of people call-ing and weeping.

The trains consisted of some twenty goods vans sandwiched between two passenger coaches, one next to the engine and one at the rear. At the windows of these two regular coaches (they were old ones, green, with bulging body-work) stood uniformed Germans smoking cigars. All the rest of the train was an inferno.

The cries seemed transparent against the silence, like flames in the blaze of summer. What they were shouting, these men and women and children heaped together in the closed vans, I could not tell. The cries were wordless. The human voice, hovering over the infinite expanse of suffering like a bird over the infi-nite sea, rose or fell, ran through the whole gamut of the wind before it faded into the distance, leaving behind it that same serene sky, that store of blue that bewildered birds and dying men can never exhaust. On the side of each van a narrow panel was open near the roof, framing four or five faces pressed close together, with other halves and quarters of faces visible between them and at the edges, the clusters of eyes expressing terror.

But it was more than terror, it was a sort of death-agony of fear; the time for beating their breasts was over and now they watched the interminable unrolling of that luminous landscape which they were seeing for the last time, where there was a man standing free and motionless in the middle of a field, and trees, and a harvester, and the impartial summer sun, while your child was suffocating, pressed between your legs in the overcrowded van and weeping with thirst and fright. Here and there a child was hoisted up to the narrow opening. When its head projected, the German guards in the first carriage would fire shots. You had to stand still there in front of the opening and bear silent witness to what was going on in the dense darkness of the van: women fainting, old men unable to lie down, newborn babies turning blue, crazed mothers howling—while you watched the symbols of peace slowly filing past.

The trains followed one another at short intervals. Empty trains came back. Beside the narrow openings the deported victims had hung vessels in the hope of collecting water—mess-tins, blue enamel mugs—like pathetic domestic talismans which a mocking Fate kept jingling hollowly as the train disappeared in the dusty distance. They had no thought of displaying sacred draperies or waving oriflammes at this window; death was yet another journey, and they set out armed with water-bottles.

Empty trains came back. I recognized them by the sound of the engine's panting.

"Now then, get busy, boys," Otto would tell us.

We had been given a third sentry. Brodno was crammed with troops and they had to be made use of. Ernst was some distance away from us, pale, his lips tight.

"Do you know why they're being taken off and where they're being taken to?" I asked the sentry whom I did not know.

"Delousing," he answered calmly. "Got to make an end of this Jewish vermin. It's quickly done. It happens some thirty miles away. I'm told it's with electricity or gas. Oh, they don't suffer anything. In one second they're in Heaven."

This man, as I learnt later, was an accountant from Dresden. He might just as well have been a blacksmith from Brunswick, a cobbler from Rostock, a peasant from Malchin, a professor from Ingolstadt, a postman from Cuxhaven, or a navvy from Bayreuth; he would have used the same language. And he did use the same language under all these different aspects, shifting from one to another like an agile actor impelled by Evil, altering his voice to suit each of these thousands of masks, imbuing it with the atmosphere of profound calm appropriate to Ingolstadt, Malchin, Bayreuth and countless other equally humane cities, and repeating, "Oh, they don't suffer, they don't suffer!"

Trains came down from the far depths of Volynia and the Ukraine, loaded with death-agonies, with tears and lamentations. At one stop, further up, the German guards had tossed dead children on to the roofs of the vans; nothing had to be left by the way, for each train was like the tooth of a rake. High up in the wall of the van, a little to the left in the narrow opening, there was a face; it seemed not living, but painted—painted white, with yellow hair, with a mouth that moved feebly and eyes that did not move at all: the face of a woman whose dead child was lying above her head; and beside the opening the little blue enamel mug, useless henceforward, shaken by every jolt of the train. Death can never appease this pain; this stream of black grief will flow for ever.

Towards the end of the morning I succeeded in drawing near to Ernst, who had moved away from the other two soldiers.

"It had started three months ago, at Brest Litovsk, when I was there," he told me in a low, tense voice. "But it wasn't on this scale. In a few days, tomorrow maybe, they'll begin on the people of this place. Do you think she ought to go away? To take refuge in the woods?"

He was looking at me bewilderedly, seeming more like a priest than ever with his smooth, babyish face, his indirect glance.

"It's probably the only chance they've got left," I muttered, bending towards the turf on the grave, since the new sentry was slowly coming towards us.

"But you've seen her, she's not strong, she'll never stand up to such an ordeal!" cried Ernst without noticing that the soldier was now standing quite close to him.

The soldier looked at Ernst in some surprise and then went off, humming. I stood silent.

"Won't you speak to me, Peter?" asked Ernst humbly. "You're saying to yourself: he thinks only of her. . . ."

"I mistrust the other sentry," I answered. "You're exposing yourself unnecessarily. If you're willing to run the risk, throw away your gun and go off into the forest with her."

"I've thought of that," said Ernst, hanging his head. "I've thought of that. And then nothing gets done. You're horrified and you stay where you are. In this war, every man looks after himself. But we ought to realize that there can't be any true life afterwards for us, who have endured these sights. For me, there'll be no more life, Peter, do you hear, no more life. . . ."

His two companions called him and he went off abruptly. I lifted my head. Down below, there were only empty trains passing along the line. Towards evening all traffic ceased. Ernst did not speak another word to me as we went back to the camp. And I never saw him again.

◆ IX

Next day, when our gang turned up at the guardhouse, the Germans sent us back to our barracks. Soon rumours reached us: the Jews of Brodno were going to be taken away in their turn. Towards noon, looking out of the windows of our building, we saw the first procession of doomed victims appear on the little road leading to the station. Many of them—nursing what hopes, trusting in what promises?—had brought bundles and suitcases. The hastily knotted bundles frequently let drop pieces of underlinen or scraps of cloth that nobody had time to pick up, since the soldiers were continually hurrying on the procession, with curses on their lips and rifle-butts raised. Other victims, arriving later, thus found themselves confronted with a scene of dispossession whose causes were as yet unknown to them, with the signs of ominous disorder.

The same signs were visible within their own group, where old men, children and adults were mingled; clearly there had been no attempt to sort them out, as had always happened hitherto before the removal of groups of workers or some other utilitarian deportation. The German soldiers from time to time struck at the sides of the column, but as we could only see them from a distance their gestures seemed to be slowed down: silent, clumsy blows, aimed low, more like stealthy misdeeds than like acts of violence. I had turned away from the window.

"Here are more of them!" somebody cried behind me.

Should I see Lidia, her friends, Lebovitch or the old man from the sawmill in this group, or the man who mended the road, or the fair woman who often stood waiting between two houses? Their packs made their silhouettes misshapen. Some of the women hugged them against their stomachs like bundles of washing. The dust was rising and I could not make them out clearly. Somebody said: "It's their children they're carrying. . . ."

Somebody said: "One of them has fallen. The guards are hitting him. . . . Now he's up, he's starting off again. . . ." Somebody said: "Oh, look at that woman running to catch up with the group!" The untiring commentaries, despite transient notes of pity, disclosed a sort of detachment, for passionate feeling will not allow you to see things through to the end, whereas these men followed the whole business with the mournful eagerness of witnesses. Evening drew on. I lay stretched out on the wooden bunk. At my side Cordonat was smoking in silence. Later on, flickering lights and distant rumblings rent the night. It was a stifling night, tense with anguish, and you could not tell whether those distant flares came from thunderclouds or from armed men on the march, carrying torches.

The arrests went on all next day. We were told by sentries that the cottage doors had been smashed in with axes and the inhabitants cleared out. Towards noon stifled cries were heard from the direction of the station. The victims, who had spent all night packed together in the vans standing in the sidings, were clamoring for water. By evening not a single train was left in the station. One man was walking along the track, bending down from time to time to check the rails. He went off into the distance, till he was almost invisible. Beyond, the pure sky grew deeper.

It was not until three days later that we set out once more on the road to the burial-ground. Two new sentries accompanied us. The road was empty, and most of the houses shut up. In one of them some Poles were setting up a canteen. A few men were working in front of the saw-mill. I recognized none of them.

At least we still had our dead, that faithful flock, each of whom we could call by his name without raising up a murdered man's face staring wide-eyed in the darkness. Our dead were already beginning to get used to their earth. After each of our absences they had "put on green," as we said when the grass had once more invaded the graves. Our cult of the dead consisted in wiping away the shadow of a meadow, day by day. And once more the sentries surrendered.

They had come to the graveyard armed with mistrust. But here, amongst the dead, we got the better of them. In front of our tidy graves, so tirelessly tended, their antagonism dropped: our accounts were in order. The liquidations (in the business sense of the word) which the Germans were carrying on all round us only took place spasmodically, as though at an auction, in an atmosphere of anger and excess which, once the payment had been exacted, increased the insatiable credit of the murderers with a debt of bitter resentment; they found it hard to forgive their victims. Our dead, on the other hand, had needed no dunning. Although the Germans were never paid fast enough, these had not worn out their patience like the others; nobody was conscious of having forced them to die.

Then, too, they seemed to be lying at attention under their three feet of earth in properly dressed lines, whereas the others, who had been shot point-blank, hid their heads in the crook of their arms; they had to be pulled by the hair, in fact it was an endless business bringing them to heel.

When the charm of the graveyard had worked, I plucked up courage to ask one of the two soldiers if he knew what had become of Ernst.

"Oh, the little pastor!" he replied. "He got punished. He's been sent to a disciplinary company. He knew a Jewess. They even say he burst out crying in the Commandant's office. Oh, don't talk to me about such people! Anyhow, I'm a Bavarian myself; so you see I'm of the same religion as you. I'm a Catholic, yes, but one's country comes first! Now get along and see to your graves."

I had no had time to inquire about the fate of Otto. In any case I was not deeply concerned about it. I felt calmer; the punishment inflicted on Ernst seemed a light one. Moreover, it cemented our friendship more firmly. He stood beside me now in the rebels' camp, like those guests at a party who you've expected for a long time, wondering whether they'll come, and who suddenly appear, all made up and grotesquely disguised, with their familiar kindly, serious eyes looking at you from under their hats, when the music has already started and the dark wine is being poured out all round you.

All this was happening in 1942. Our friendship needed some discipline, imposed from without, naturally. I was thinking of Lidia, too. Her relations with Ernst seemed to me solid ground, but there were stars, too. They still wheel round in my dreams. I do not know what became of them on earth, but in the map of heaven, and in the map of my heart, I know where to look for the distant glimmer of that unattainable love.

We never went back to the new road. Our kingdom grew narrower. No more walks in the forest; we only went down to the pond with sentries on either side of us, and we were forbidden to linger there; we were more than ever confined to the burial-ground. Otto and Ernst had already passed into a previous existence, threatened with oblivion, when we got news of the former, he sent us a corpse.

This was a fellow that I knew fairly well, a sullen-faced lad from Lyons obsessed by the urge to escape. Seeking an opportunity, he had asked me a few days earlier to let him take the place of a member of our gang who was too sick to leave the camp. He hoped to be able to make an easy getaway from the graveyard. I managed to get him accepted by our sentries. Underneath his uniform he was wearing some sort of escape outfit, and round his ankles there dangled long white laces belonging presumably to the linen trousers formerly issued to the French army. These were only too obvious. Silent, his jaws stiff with anxiety or determination, he thus attracted the guards' attention immediately. They never took their eyes off him and, that evening: he came back to the camp with us.

A few days later he got himself engaged in a gang of "road commandos" (prisoners employed on road-mending at some distance from the town) guarded by several sentries, among whom was Otto. Otto, being indirectly involved in Ernst's punishment, had been posted in charge of this detachment, which performed the duties of a gang of convicts and was rated as such. One evening, as the group was about to pass through the town on its way back to the camp, the young Lyonnais broke rank abruptly and began to run off into the fields. Otto promptly shouldered his gun and fired. The fugitive dropped; the bullet had gone in through his back and pierced his heart.

It was our first violent death. On the day of the funeral the Germans sent a wreath of fir-branches tied with a red ribbon. The wooden cross bore the inscription "Fallen" instead of "Died." Our graveyard had been sorely in need of this heroic note, as I suddenly realized; it was as though it had received the Military Cross.

"You shall soon have some stones, too," a sentry told me. "I know that in the camp they've been asking for a stonemason. It's the Jews' tombstones you're going to get; their graveyard's full of them, down there in the forest. We shall use them for the roads too. You people can't complain, your graveyard's much finer than the one where our own men are buried. . . ."

It was quite true. With its ever green turf, its flowerbeds, its carefully sanded paths edged with small black fir-trees which we had transplanted, with its rustic fence of birch-boughs, against the dark background of the forest verge, our graveyard seemed an "idyllic" place, as the Germans put it. On Sunday the soldiers from the garrison used to come and photograph it. The more we adorned it the greater grew its fame, and it aroused a wave of curiosity like that which carries crowds to gaze at certain baroque works of art or at others which, devoid of any art, are yet prodigies of patience and skill: houses built of bottle-ends, ships made of matches, walking-sticks carved to fantastic excess—monstrous triumphs of persistence and time.

On the fringe of the war, on the fringe of the massacres, on the fringe of Europe, sheltering behind our prodigious burial-ground, we seemed like hollow-eyed gardeners, sitters in the sun, fanatical weeders, busily working over the dead as over some piece of embroidery.

But the thought of those stones horrified us. We did not want to rob the Jews of their steles; that savoured of sacrilege and also of an incipient complicity with the Germans; and anyhow it "wasn't playing fair." We had made our graveyard out of earth and grass and to bring in marble would have been cheating. I went to lay the problem before the prisoners' French representative, the *homme de confiance* as we called him. He promised me to protest to the Germans. A few days later, in one corner of the camp, I saw a man sitting on the ground sawing and planing tombstones on which was carved a breaking branch.

He seemed in some doubt. Should each of the slabs of marble or granite intended for the graves (merely for epitaphs, not for funerary flagstones) represent an open book, a cushion (he could quite well picture a cushion slightly hollowed out by the weight of an absent head) or a coat of arms? He asked for my opinion. I told him angrily that I wasn't interested in his stones and that they should never cross the threshold of the graveyard. However, he went on cutting them, full of delight at getting back to his trade, heaping them one on the other when they were ready, although the Germans were now busy with something else and never came to ask for them. In any case, he could not have handed them over as they were for the essential part of the inscription was missing.

Though my ill-will discouraged him at first, he soon tried to get from one of us the names of the dead and the dates which he needed. He met with the same refusal. Besides ourselves, only the Germans possessed these essential facts, but no prisoner had access to their offices. Thenceforward, he began a patient investigation, going from one building to the next, questioning the men on the deaths that had taken place there. I soon got wind of this. It made me angry. The stonemason's obstinacy, although of a purely professional character, had begun to look like an intrusion into our field. For the last few months we had managed to keep our tasks secret, and now I felt this secrecy threatened by the publicity that he was causing by his noisy investigation of our past.

One day I saw him turn up at the graveyard, following a funeral. The man we were burying that day had come most opportunely in the nick of time, after the lad from Lyons, who, having introduced an appropriately heroic note into the place, had since seemed to be inaugurating a sequence of violent deaths. For here the latest corpse set the tone; it was in front of the latest corpse that we made our military salutes each morning; it was his bare, sparsely sown grave that attracted the attention (albeit vacuous) of visitors. It seemed important therefore that the tone thus set should not be, for too long, that of violent death: after all, a habit is easily acquired. And so I should have been quite glad to welcome this newcomer who restored order to things had I not perceived, among the handful of Frenchmen walking behind the cart, the stonemason, sporting a swordbelt.

He had probably managed to slip into the procession by posing as one of the dead man's friends; he may even have been one really. . . . But we were already convinced of one thing: he had come to the graveyard to take measurements and pick up names. We decided to keep an eye on him, and we buried the corpse in a state of nervous tension although, in the depths of our innocent hearts, we had longed for it. We did not take our eyes off the man during the whole ceremony which, with its dying bugle-call and the report of arms fired into the sky, was like that which marks the close of a war. When the burial was over the Germans and the Frenchmen who had formed the procession hung about. As the fame of our graveyard increased, funerals had tended to become, for those who were able to attend them, a sort of summer excursion, a trip into the country from which you might well picture yourself returning with armfuls of flowers picked on the spot. The stonemason had moved towards the first row of graves. I followed him. He was already taking a notebook out of his pocket.

"What are you doing there?" I asked him, my voice distorted with anger.

"I've been told to make tombstones!" he said, very loud. "You shan't prevent me! They don't belong to you, after all!" he added, indicating the graves of the dead.

"More than to you, anyhow!" I answered. "We wouldn't go and put stolen stones on their graves. . . ."

"Stolen?" He shook his head. "They're given to us and it's not our business to ask where they come from. . . . Well, I know, of course!" he went on, seeing that I was about to answer. "And so what? Would you rather see them laid on the roads?"

"Yes, I'd rather see them laid on the roads. I suppose you get soup and bread from the Germans for doing this job?"

"Oh, don't you talk about that!" cried the stonemason. He brought his angry face close to mine. "Everybody in the camp knows what you've wangled with your famous graveyard!" He stopped suddenly.

"Well then, tell me! Tell me!" I cried.

"Listen to me," went on the stonemason in a quieter voice. "Can't we make peace?"

Everything seemed conducive to this. The heat of the hour had led Frenchmen and Germans, in separate groups, to sit down beside the graves, where the forest trees cast their shade. Only our words disturbed the silence.

"Don't expect to get the names of the dead, whatever happens," I answered.

"You can keep them," said the stonemason, sitting down. He was a thin-faced man a little older than myself, with short greyish hair. "We're an obstinate pair. After all, I understand your feelings; you don't want it to be said that those stones had names taken off them in order to carve these on. Well, I'd never have had the courage to take them off myself if they hadn't been written in Hebrew. But in Hebrew they mean nothing! I'm not even sure that they were names and dates. And then the stones were there in the camp, without anybody lying beneath them. Put yourself in my place! I'm bored, I need to keep my hand in for after the war, and I'm presented with tools and stones! But it's all right; I give up the names," he added, pulling out his tobacco pouch and handing it to me.

I rolled a cigarette and he did the same.

"I give up the names," he went on, puffing at his cigarette, "but all the same, something really ought to be done with those stones—they're not all in good condition, you know, some of them are mouldering away. Besides, the dead people or their relations, if there are any left, wouldn't see any harm in our making use of these stones now that the Germans have pulled them up. They'd surely like that better than to see them crushed and scattered on the roads. . . . After all, we're on the same side as they are, aren't we? . . . So this is what I thought. Let's not talk of carving names on them, but let's make them into little ornaments, corner-stones for instance. We must think of our own dead too. I needn't comment on what you've done for them; it's quite unbelievable. But after all, there's nothing permanent about it. Suppose they take us off into Germany next month; after a single winter there'll be no sign of your graves. The rains and the melting snows will have washed all the earth away, and grass and briars will have grown over it. But with stones . . . Oh, I'm not suggesting making monuments," he cried, raising his hand to forestall objections. "I assure you, very little is needed. And I'm speaking from experience—I'm in the trade. A little pyramid at each corner of the grave for instance, or a ball on a little pedestal if you prefer, although that's much harder to make, or else carved corners joined together with chains, only unluckily we haven't any chains ... well, you get the idea, something not very high, firmly fastened into the ground preferably with cement, and above all something decently made. . . ."

But I was no longer listening to him. For the last few minutes I had been listening to the rumble of a train and now it was growing louder. The train was about to emerge round the tip of the wood. I could tell, without waiting for it to roll past before my eyes, what sort of freight it carried. Its slow jolting sound warned me of the other sounds that would follow although for the moment a contrary wind delayed them. I should soon hear the weeping, the cries of despair. The silence, no doubt, was due to the wind, but perhaps, too, those who were being transported, knowing what fate awaited them, had deliberately refrained from sending out their lamentations into that empty, sun-baked plain, in which the great migrations of death had never yet awakened any lasting echo.

### ◆ X

And so it all began again. Every day one or two convoys crossed the plain, and then were no more to be seen, and when night fell a train would rumble, too slowly, through the silence. New processions appeared on the little road that led to the station. They were smaller and more infrequent than the previous ones and seemed to be made up of belated recruits, of survivors from some ancient and now almost forgotten disaster, of beggars or vagrants rounded up in the middle of their wasted summer. Nothing rolled out of the bundles this time; nobody seemed to be in a hurry now, and the soldiers who struck at the sides of the column did so with the lazy indifference of cowherds.

The massacre was drawing to a close, but it lingered interminably like the raw gleam of a lurid sunset on walls, between patches of shadow. We said to ourselves: "Surely this must be the end of these torments." The plain seemed to have nothing left to offer Death save its quota of vagrants. We were wrong. On the contrary, those whom the Germans were now despatching to be slaughtered had been taken from the ranks of a scattered resistance movement which, up till now, without our knowledge, had been fighting to the last ditch for the right to live.

If they seemed wearier than those who had gone before them along the same road that led between darkly gleaming slagheaps and through engine-sheds to Calvary, it was because they had suffered a twofold defeat. They had been surrounded in the forest, they had been arrested at night on the roads or among the brambles in the ravines, where for so long they had been wandering round and round in dazed despair. Now, in the evenings near the graveyard, we often caught sight of nonchalant armed soldiers making their way in extended line into the forest, and bending down from time to time to pick a strawberry. Brodno was encircled with a military cordon, and the whole region was being combed step by step.

This state of siege, of which we shortly felt the oppressive effects, brought back a certain animation around the camp and around our graveyard. The inhabitants—Poles, Ukrainians, and Ruthenians—realizing that for the moment the Germans had no designs on theft, suddenly felt the need to move around in all directions within the circle that hemmed them in. They came to look at the graveyard, the fame of which had reached them. They stood still at some distance from it, motionless, communicating with one another by gestures. One evening two girls came forward as far as the verge of the forest, close to the spot where we had discovered the charnel.

One of them was plain and awkward; the other was slender and seemed younger. The brightness of her blue-green eyes disturbed me. They shouted to the soldiers that they were Polish. The setting, the gathering dusk and my own troubled heart made the younger girl's smile seem like that of a vision. To the German who, with one foot on a grave, asked them their names and ages, she called out "Maria!" and there was still joy in her voice. I had gone up to the sentry; the girl looked at me and waved to me as she went off. Next day as we made our way to the graveyard I caught sight of her at the door of the new canteen and we made signs of greeting to each other.

From that time on I clung to her image. The first rains of autumn had begun; the graveyard had ceased to be a garden and was once more a burial-ground. The earth sank under one's feet; it was deep again, and heavy, like a morass. Autumn promised to be a season rich in deaths. More trains came through from the further end of the plain, with white faces framed in the narrow windows, trains full of condemned creatures who, this time, uttered no cries of thirst but stood motionless, clutching their despair between their hands like a twisted handkerchief. My mind was fixed on her image.

I turned to it again when new processions appeared on the road leading to the station or when, towards evening, groups of soldiers made their way into the forest with more speed than usual. Three or four times a day, whether we were going to the graveyard or coming away from it, Maria, standing at the door of the Polish canteen, would watch me thoughtfully and smile at me. My friends nudged one another but let fall no word. From their dealings with the dead they had learnt to respect mysteries. And this was undoubtedly a mystery—my devotion to the image of this girl about whom I knew nothing to suggest that she was worthy of it surprised me more than it surprised them. I pushed back my hair from my forehead—it was damp from the drizzling rain—and stood upright; there were still many things to which I should have to bear witness later, many sufferings to be shared, many hopes to be nurtured, many steps to be taken which would add up to something some day. But as soon as

I had reached the graveyard and was standing under the branches at the verge of the forest, where raindrops rustled, the image recurred to me again.

One morning I was sunk in this sort of reverie when Cordonat called me. He led me to the end of the last row of graves where, covered with planks and with an old tarpaulin to keep off the rainwater, the spare grave lay empty, awaiting its corpse. He had just been inspecting it and had found there, besides more subtle traces which, as an expert poacher, he had picked out, a cigarette end of unfamiliar origin. It was rolled in a scrap of paper from a child's exercise book and made of coarse unripe tobacco, presumably taken from one of the plants which, in those penurious times, the peasants used to grow outside their houses.

"It wasn't there last night," Cordonat told me. "For several days I'd noticed that somebody had been taking up and putting back the planks and the tarpaulin during the night. So I began to keep an eye on the grave. The other proofs are more tricky, you might not believe them. But this one! There's no possible doubt about it: a man comes to sleep in our grave at night."

"Well, what then?" I asked.

"Well, so much the better," he cried. "It must be a hunted man. For once, let this graveyard be some use to a living man!" (Cordonat had never been really enthusiastic about the graveyard.) "Only we ought to help him. This evening, for instance, we might leave him some provisions."

I did not doubt Cordonat's charitable intentions, but I also suspected that he was anxious to secure a further proof by this method. We had lately been receiving a little food from France and we were able, without too great a sacrifice, to deposit in the grave for the benefit of the stranger who inhabited it a handful of sugar, a piece of chocolate or a few army biscuits deducted from our store of provisions, which were meticulously arranged and counted, dry and crumbly as rats' provender. When evening came, before leaving the graveyard we slipped a parcel between the planks and then replaced them as before. Next day the parcel had disappeared. Cordonat found at the bottom of the grave a scrap of paper on which a message of thanks was pencilled, in English. The two words had been written with a trembling hand, no doubt by the first light that filtered through the parted planks as dawn brought back panic.

That evening our gift was made up merely of a few cigarettes. I added a message: "Who are you?" Although the answer consisted only of two initials, it was clear and it did not surprise me. It was written on a piece of packing paper: I. L. An arrow invited me to turn over the page: "You know me Peter = (the arithmetical sign *equals*) I know you. Keep quiet, both of you, keep quiet. Thank you." I had recognized Lebovitch. But how could he know that it was I who had put the cigarettes there and that only one other knew the secret?

"During the day he must stay hidden inside the verge of the forest and watch us," said Cordonat.

It would have been madly imprudent, and the Germans would have discovered him long ago; Cordonat admitted it. These communications through the trap-door of a grave, these notes with their anguished laconicity, the condition of "semi-survival" in which Lebovitch existed and the second-sight with which he seemed to be endowed, all these things concurred to give me the impression that our continual contact with death was beginning to open for us a sort of wicket-gate into its domain. I almost forgot Maria. Sometimes, in the evening, she would walk a little way along the road below the graveyard just as we had slipped a few provisions into the grave and were replacing the planks, the tarpaulin and the stones that held it down with furtive care, as though we were laying snares. Cordonat rediscovered the pleasures of his poaching days. I would stand up and wave to Maria. The sentries were amused by my performance and it distracted their attention from the mysterious tasks which we were performing over the empty grave.

"How do you live?" I wrote to Lebovitch, leaving him a few sheets of blank paper. His answers grew longer but also more obscure. He lived with difficulty. During the day he remained hidden, no doubt, in the high branches of a tree, for he wrote: "I am very high up. Do not look for me. A glance might betray me. I see them come to and fro. Please tell me what is happening about the dogs" (these last words were underlined). "How soon will autumn be here? Have I the right to try and escape from God's will? Anyhow all this is unendurable and I shall not hold out much longer! If only they would let me speak! I should be exempted. Yes, they should let me speak! Have you heard tell in the village of anyone being exempted? Keep quiet! Thank you."

During the days that followed I had difficulty in preventing Cordonat from staring up at the tree-tops on the forest border; he would have attracted the guards' attention. Instinctively, as one accustomed to roaming the woods and starting animals from their lair, he found it an exciting game to hunt for Lebovitch's aerial shelter. One morning I surprised him sitting down with his back turned to the forest and staring into a pocket mirror concealed in his hand which he was slowly turning in all directions.

"I tell you he's not found a perch in any of these trees," he told me, putting back his little mirror into his pocket. "Even if he'd been well camouflaged I'd have discovered him. There's no foliage thick enough to conceal a man. He'd have been obliged to surround himself with other branches, cut off from other parts of the tree, and believe me, I know from experience that the color of leaves changes as soon as they're cut. Ask him about it, once and for all. . . ."

I wrote a note to Lebovitch to this effect, accompanying it with a handful of army biscuits.

"I can't tell you where I am," replied Lebovitch. "You haven't told me anything about the dogs. And the exemptions? Do they ever exempt anybody? Yesterday three more trains went past. During the night there were luminous things drawn on the carriages! You can have no idea of it." (The last words were underlined.) "This morning I vomited because of all the raw mushrooms I'd eaten. God rises early just now. So does the wind! Couldn't they have pity on me? Tell me if it's humanly possible?"

"We shan't learn anything more," said Cordonat when I had read him this letter.

The incoherence of these notes depressed him. We were too close to the world beyond death not to be aware of its dank breath when speech became so sparing and sibylline, when a human being's presence proved so elusive, while these brief messages expressed a tortured silence pierced by a thousand exclamation marks, like nails. We continued to offer food to this Egyptian tomb, which a couple of days later had to remove further off; death provided Lebovitch with a new neighbour.

Cordonat offered to dig the spare grave into which, that same evening, Lebovitch would creep to rest, and at the bottom of the grave he arranged a little pile of earth for the sleeper to lay his head on. I helped him in this task which, as we soon admitted to one another, filled us with a strange uneasiness; we had the feeling that we were preparing to bury an unseen friend. The present that we left in the grave that evening was more generous than usual. I avoided putting any message with it, however. The tone of the answers distressed me.

Lebovitch only broke silence on the second morning (he must have written his notes during the day, up in his tree or inside some unknown retreat). He had been deeply touched by Cordonat's thoughtfulness in providing the earthen pillow. Perhaps, also, by the nearness of a newly dead Frenchman, whose burial he must have watched, since he never took his eyes off the graveyard. He wrote: "I know that one day there will be no more morning. Last night I went on knocking for an hour against the earth, on the side where all the others are lying. I say an hour, but my watch has stopped. I wanted to go on knocking all night. As long as I'm knocking I'm alive. Even here, where I am now, at this moment, I'm knocking. And I keep saying: have mercy, have mercy! They've killed them all, Peter, killed them all! What is loneliness?"

I could no longer keep up this dialogue, and I could hardly bear the abstract presence that now filled my narrow universe. I could no longer look with confidence at the forest trees or into the hollow grave, nor gaze out over the plain where one of those trains was always dawdling. Like those tireless birds that drop to the ground like stones and as soon as they have touched it dart back to perch on one of a hundred quivering branches, then dizzily gravitate to the ground once more and once more rebound upward, as though in avid quest nor of earthly or aerial prey but of pure trajectories, of secretly deliberate flights, of prophetic tangents, or as though irrevocably doomed to this endless to-and-fro, Lebovitch moved between the grave and the tree-tops every day; he was only fit for shooting down.

Yet I would have liked to save him. His talk of exemptions, although I had at first put it down to insanity (and I was beginning to find out how rich and full was insanity's account compared with the meager bankbooks of reason), had made an impression on my mind. I felt I must sound the Germans, or Maria, who doubtless knew what was happening in the village now.

The Germans told me that the fate of the Jews of Brodno (and elsewhere too) was old history now. "Let's talk of Maria instead," they said to me. "You're keen on her, aren't you, you rascal?"

I endured their mockery. As it happened I was anxious to speak to Maria. If she passed along the road tomorrow, might I not beckon to her to come? I'd only want a couple of minutes with her. I felt infinitely sorry for myself. Evening with its swift black clouds was falling over Volynia and its crowd of dead, over the distant fires of war, and I was standing there, eager to strike my pitiful bargain—two minutes of that time!—I was standing there with Lebovitch at my back, weighing me down, his hard hands against my shoulders. The Germans made fun of my anxiety. "Maybe," they said, sending me back to my graves. I slipped a note into the pit: "In two days I'll know for sure about the exemptions."

Next evening Maria appeared on the road with her friend. "You can call her," cried the sentries, laughing. I called her. She saw me. I beckoned to her to meet me at the graveyard gate. But she shook her head with a smile. She walked away. I had turned white with vexation to which, in the depths of my heart, I gave a bitter name. On the new message that I found in the grave Lebovitch wrote: "I'm knocking harder than ever, Peter. It's the only thing to do: knock, knock, knock!" He said nothing more about exemptions.

A few trains full of condemned victims still passed through the plain. When the sound of them had faded away I still seemed to hear behind me the dull persistent rhythm of blows hammered against the earth, against a tree-trunk, mingled with the throbbing of my temples, the tapping of summer's last woodpecker, a far-off woodcutter's blows and the rumble of a passing cart, in a soothing confusion.

◆ XI

Summer drew to a close. In the darkened countryside all life was slowed down; even the great convoys of death became more infrequent—those harvests too had been gathered in. But the dawn of a new season was less like the morning after a bad dream or the lucid astonishment of life than the final draining away of all blood, the last stage of a slow haemorrhage behind which a few tears of lymph trickle, like mourners at life's funeral. Autumn brought a prospect of exhausted silence, of a world pruned of living sounds, of the reign of total death. What had I left to delay this consummation, when every gust of wind in the branches of the trees, every leaf blown away, every corner of the naked sky, reminded me of its imminence?

It was from that moment that the life of Lebovitch, his dwindled, precarious existence, became for me the last remaining symbol of a denial of death—of that death which was so visibly being consummated all around me. I renewed our dialogue. I sent him urgent messages: "Where were the rest? What had happened to him? and indeed, who was he?" I urged him to tell me about his own past and that of all the others.

For nothing makes you feel so impoverished as the death of strangers; dying, they testify to death without yielding anything of their lives that might compensate for the enhanced importance of darkness. Thus what did he know of Lidia's fate? He must tell me; the survival of all my hopes depended on it.

These questions remained unanswered. Lidia sank in her turn, with all the others, like them consecrated to death, behind those distant horizons of memory where, even after we have forgotten everything, there lingers a pale light, an endless comforting twilight, a thin streak of radiance which will perhaps serve us for eyes when our eyes are closed in death. Lebovitch soon caught up with Lidia on that dark slope where never, not in all eternity, should I be able to reach them.

One morning on arriving at the graveyard we found that the planks covering the empty grave had been thrown to one side. At the bottom of the grave there lay a black jacket without an armlet. One of its pockets was full of acorns. I knew then that Lebovitch would never come back. Had he been surprised in his sleep or, in a fit of madness, had he suddenly rushed out into the forest to meet his murderers? I raised my head. Clouds were rising towards the west. The wind had got up. My companions were taking away the dead leaves that fell on the graves. In the flowerbeds the summer flowers had turned black. Soon no more convoys passed along the railway over the plain, which in the mornings was drowned in mist. There were no more soldiers to be seen patrolling the woods, where the trees were growing bare. Autumn was really there now.

Maria chose this time to visit the burial-ground. I had been waiting for her there for a long time, secretly convinced that she would come. One evening she came along the ill-paved road, her thin summer dress clinging to her in the wind. She walked slowly, her face uplifted, quietly resolute, and her fair hair was fluttering over her brow. A violent fit of trembling possessed me. I turned towards the single sentry who now guarded us. He was a prematurely old man, full of melancholy resignation. He knew about my romance, and nodded his head.

I darted towards Maria like a dog let off the leash. Seeing me come, she hurried forward without taking her eyes off me and, passing the gate of the graveyard, quickly made for the verge of the forest. The sky had grown dark and the wind was blowing stronger. I only caught up with her under the trees.

I seized hold of her arm, and she drew me on involuntarily while I spoke to her in breathless tones. I did not know what I was saying; I was in a sort of ecstasy. Suddenly I drew her to me and pressed her closely. My face groped feverishly for the hollow of her shoulder. For so long I had been waiting for this moment of blindness, of oblivion, this ultimate salvation! It was the only refuge within which to break the heavy, clipped wings that thought had set growing on one's temples, the only place where the mind, like a heavy-furred moth dazzled by the great light of death, could for an instant assuage its longing to return to the warm, original darkness of its chrysalis.... Frightened by the desperate wildness of my movement, Maria sharply withdrew from my arms, kissed me on the lips and fled. For a moment I tried to follow her. Then I leaned against a tree. Within me and about me a great silence had fallen. After a moment I wiped away my tears and went back to my dead.

## Chaim Grade 1910–1982

Grade was born in Vilna, Lithuania. His father was an "enlightened" Hebrew teacher, committed to both the observance of traditional Judaism and the acquisition of secular knowledge. Although Grade personally rejected the former, after fifteen years of study in yeshivas in Vilna, Valkenik, and Bialystok and ordination as a rabbi in 1932, the vanished culture and world of Talmudic Judaism in Eastern Europe remained his literary preoccupation.

Grade had left Vilna and the "Young Vilna" group of Yiddish writers in his search to infuse European modernism into Yiddish literature, but he had returned to Vilna from the Soviet Union when the Nazis invaded the city in 1941. He escaped with the withdrawing Soviet army, leaving behind his wife and widowed mother. His mother was murdered in Vilna in 1941; his wife was killed when the ghetto was liquidated in September 1943.

Grade spent most of the war years in Soviet Central Asia where he survived on payments (per line of poetry) from the Soviet Writers Union. When the war had ended, he went first to Paris and then to the United States. In 1980 he was the only Yiddish poet invited to read at a literary festival held at the White House.

His "Elegy for the Soviet Yiddish Writers" (Yiddish 1962; English 1969) and his 1939 epic poem *Musarnikes* ("the ethical ones") have become Yiddish classics. He also wrote numerous powerful Holocaust poems, including the "Chariot in Auschwitz" and "Ezekiel in Auschwitz."

At the age of forty, he began to write prose, but his first volume of stories, *Di mames shabeysim* (*My Mother's Sabbath Days*), did not appear until 1955 (English 1986). With the translation of his novels into English in the 1970s (*Seven Little Lanes,* 1972), many about Jewish refugees who escaped the advancing

German armies—*The Agunah,* 1974 and *The Yeshiva,*
2 volumes, 1976–1977—Grade gained international
acclaim. His was a unique perspective: a secular Yiddish writer thoroughly trained in rabbinic literature who wrote poetry and fiction with a primarily
religious content.

# MY QUARREL WITH HERSH RASSEYNER

◆ *1*

In 1937 I returned to Bialystok, seven years after I had been a student in
the Novaredok Yeshiva of the Mussarists, a movement that gives special importance to ethical and ascetic elements in Judaism. When I came back I found
many of my old schoolmates still there. A few even came to my lecture one
evening. Others visited me secretly; they did not want the head of the yeshiva
to find out. I could see that their poverty had brought them suffering and that
the fire of their youthful zeal had slowly burned itself out. They continued to
observe all the laws and usages meticulously, but the weariness of spiritual
wrestlings lay upon them. For years they had tried to tear the desire for pleasure out of their hearts, and now they realized they had lost the war with themselves. They had not overcome the evil urge.

There was one I kept looking for and could not find, my former school-
mate Hersh Rasseyner. He was a dark young man with bright, downcast
eyes. I did not meet him, but heard that he kept to his garret in solitude and
did not even come to the yeshiva.

Then we met unexpectedly in the street. He was walking with his eyes
lowered, as is the custom with the Mussarists; they do not wish to be "eye to
eye" with the world. But he saw me anyway. He put his arms behind him, thrust-
ing his hands into his sleeves, so that he would not have to shake hands. The
closer he came, the higher rose his head. When we finally stood face to face,
he looked at me intently. He was so moved his nostrils seemed to quiver—but
he kept silent.

Among the Mussarists, when you ask, "How are you?" the question
means, What is the state of your religious life? Have you risen in spirituality?
But I had forgotten and asked quite simply, "Hersh Rasseyner, how are you?"

Hersh moved back a little, looked me over from head to toe, saw that I
was modishly dressed, and shrugged. "And how are you, Chaim Vilner? My question, you see, is more important."

My lips trembled and I answered hotly, "Your question, Hersh Rasseyner,
is no question at all. I do what I have to."

Right there, in the middle of the street, he cried out, "Do you think, Chaim Vilner, that by running away from the yeshiva you have saved yourself? You know the saying among us: Whoever has learned Mussar can have no enjoyment in his life. You will always be deformed, Chaim Vilner. You will remain a cripple the rest of your life. You write godless verses and they reward you by patting you on the cheek. Now they're stuffing you with applause as they stuff a goose with grain. But later you'll see, when you've begun to go to their school, oh, won't the worldly ones beat you! Which of you isn't hurt by criticism? Is there one of you really so self-confident that he doesn't go around begging for some authority's approval? Is there one of you who's prepared to publish his book anonymously? The big thing with you people is that your name should be seen and known. You have given up our tranquillity of spirit for what? For passions you will never be able to satisfy and for doubts you will never be able to answer, no matter how much you suffer."

When he had spoken his fill, Hersh Rasseyner began to walk away with a quick, energetic stride. But I had once been a Mussarist too, so I ran after him.

"Hersh, listen to me now. No one knows better than I how torn you are. You're proud of yourself because you don't care if the whole street laughs at you for wearing a prayer vest down to your ankles. You've talked yourself into believing that the cloth with the woolen fringes is a partition between you and the world. You despise yourself because you're afraid you may find favor in the eyes of the world, the world that is to you like Potiphar's wife. You fear you won't have the strength to tear yourself away as the righteous Joseph did. So you flee from temptation and think the world will run after you. But when you see that the world doesn't run after you, you become angry and cry out: Nobody enjoys life. You want to console yourself with that idea. You live in solitude in your garret because you would rather have nothing at all than take the crumb that life throws you. Your modesty is pride, not self-denial.

"And who told you that I seek pleasure? I seek a truth you don't have. For that matter, I didn't run away, I simply returned to my own street—to Yatkev Street in Vilna. I love the porters with their backs broken from carrying their burdens; the artisans sweating at their workbenches; the market women who would cut off a finger to give a poor man a crust of bread. But you scold the hungry for being sinners, and all you can tell them is to repent. You laugh at people who work because you say they don't trust in God. But you live on what others have made. Women exhausted with work bring you something to eat, and in return you promise them the world to come. Hersh Rasseyner, you have long since sold your share of the world to come to those poor women."

Hersh Rasseyner gave a start and disappeared. I returned to Vilna with a burden removed from my conscience. In the disputation with the Mussarist I myself began to understand why I had left them. If at the time, I said to myself, I didn't know why and where I was going, someone else thought it out for me, someone stronger than I. That someone else was—my generation and my environment.

◆ *2*

Two years passed. War broke out between Germany and Poland. The western Ukraine and western White Russia were taken over by the Red Army. After they had been in Vilna a few weeks, the Russians announced that they were giving the city back to the Lithuanians. To Vilna there began to come refugees who did not want to remain under Soviet rule. The Novaredok Yeshiva came also. Meanwhile the Soviets remained. Hunger raged in the city. Every face was clouded with fear of the arrests carried out at night by NKVD agents. My heart was heavy. Once, standing in line for a ration of bread, I suddenly saw Hersh Rasseyner.

I had heard that he had married. His face was framed by a little black beard, his gait was more restrained, his clothing more presentable. I was so glad to see him that I left my place in the line, pushed through the crowd, and came up to him.

He said little and was very cautious. I understood why. He did not trust me and was afraid of trouble. I could see that he was trying to make up his mind whether to speak to me. But when he saw how despondent I was, he hid his mouth with his hand, as though to conceal his twisted smile, and a gleam of derision came into his eyes. With his head he motioned toward the bridge, on which were parked a few tanks with Red Army soldiers.

"Well, Chaim," Hersh said to me quietly, "are you satisfied now? Is this what you wanted?"

I tried to smile and answered just as quietly, "Hersh, I bear no more responsibility for all that than you do for me."

He shook himself and pronounced a few sharp, cutting words, seeming to forget his fear. "You're wrong, Chaim. I do bear responsibility for you." He retreated a few steps and motioned with his eyes to the Red Army soldiers, as though to say, "And you for them."

◆ *3*

Nine more years passed, years of war and destruction, during which I wandered across Russia, Poland, and Western Europe. In 1948, on a summer afternoon, I was riding in the Paris Métro. Couples stood close together. Short Frenchwomen, as though fainting, hung by the sides of their black-haired lovers.

I saw a familiar face. Until then it had been concealed by someone's shoulder, and only when the couples had to move a little did that corner of the car open up. My heart began to pound. Could he really be alive? Hadn't he been in Vilna under the German occupation? When I returned to the ruins of my home in 1945, I did not see him or hear of him. Still, those were the same eyes, the same obstinately upturned nose; only the broad black beard had begun to turn gray. It was astonishing to me that he could look at the couples so calmly, and that a good-natured smile lit up his melancholy glance. That was not like him. But after a moment I noticed that there was a faraway look in his eyes. He really did not see the people on the train. He was dressed neatly, in a long cloak and a clean white shirt buttoned at the throat, without a necktie. I thought to myself, he never wore ties. This more than anything else convinced me that it was he.

I pushed my way to him through the passengers and blurted out, "Excuse me, aren't you Reb Hersh Rasseyner?"

He looked at me, wrinkled his forehead, and smiled. "Ah, Chaim, Chaim, is that you? *Sholom aleichem!* How are you?"

I could tell that this time when Hersh Rasseyner asked, "How are you?" he did not mean what he had meant eleven years before. Then his question was angry and derisive. Now he asked the question quietly, simply. It came from his heart and it showed concern, as for an old friend.

We got into a corner and he told me briefly that he had been in a camp in Latvia. Now he was in Germany, at the head of a yeshiva in Salzheim.

"The head of a yeshiva in Germany? And who are your students, Reb Hersh?"

He smiled. "Do you think that the Holy One is an orphan? We still have lads, praise be to the Almighty, who study Torah."

He told me that he had been in the camp with about ten pupils. He had drawn them close to him and taught them Jewishness. Because they were still only children and very weak, he helped them in their work. At night they used to gather about his cot and all would recite Psalms together. There was a doctor in the camp who used to say that he would give half his life to be able to recite Psalms too. But he couldn't. He lacked faith, poor man.

I was happy to meet my old friend and I preferred to avoid a debate, so I merely asked, "And what brings you here so often? Are you in business?"

"Of course we're in business." He stroked his beard with satisfaction. "Big business. We bring yeshiva people here and send them off to Israel and America. We take books back from here. With the help of the Almighty, I have even flown twice to Morocco."

"Morocco? What did you do there, Reb Hersh?"

"Brought back students from among the Moroccan Jews, spoke in their synagogue."

"And how did you talk to them? You don't know Arabic or French."

"The Almighty helps. What difference does it make how you speak? The main thing is *what* you speak."

Unexpectedly he began to talk about me. "How will it be with you, Chaim? It's time for you to start thinking about repentance. We're nearer rather than farther."

"What do you mean?"

"I mean," he said, drawing out his words in a chant, "that we have both lived out more than half our lives. What will become of Reb Chaim?" He strongly accented the word Reb. "Where are you voyaging? Together with them, perhaps?" His eyes laughed at the young couples. "Will you get off where they do? Or do you still believe in this merciless world?"

"And you, Reb Hersh," I asked in sudden irritation, "do you still believe in particular providence? You say that the Holy One is not, as it were, an orphan. But we are orphans. A miracle happened to you, Reb Hersh, and you were saved. But how about the rest? Can you still believe?"

"Of course I believe," said Hersh Rasseyner, separating his hands in innocent wonder. "You can touch particular providence, it's so palpable. But perhaps you're thinking of the kind of man who has faith that the Almighty is to be found only in the pleasant places of this world but is not to be found, God forbid, in the desert and wasteland? You know the rule: Just as a man must make a blessing over the good, so must he make a blessing over evil. We must fall before the greatness—"

"What do you want, Reb Hersh?" I interrupted. "Shall I see the greatness of God in the thought that only He could cause such destruction, not flesh and blood? You're outdoing the Psalms you recited on your bed in the concentration camp. The Psalmist sees the greatness of God in the fact that the sun comes out every day, but you see miracles in catastrophes."

"Without any doubt," Hersh Rasseyner answered calmly, "I see everywhere, in everything, at every moment, particular providence. I couldn't remain on earth for one minute without the thought of God. How could I stand it without Him in this murderous world?"

"But I won't say that His judgment is right. I can't!"

"You can," said Hersh Rasseyner, putting a friendly hand on my shoulder, "you can—gradually. First the repentant understands that the world can't be without a Guide. Then he understands that the Guide is the God of Israel and that there is no other power besides Him to help Him lead the world. At last he recognizes that the world is in Him, as we read: 'There is no place void of Him.' And if you understood that, Chaim, you would also understand how the Almighty reveals Himself in misfortune as well as in salvation."

Hersh Rasseyner spoke in a warm voice. He did not once take his hand off my shoulder. I felt a great love for him and saw that he had become more pious than ever.

◆ *4*

We left the Métro near the Jewish quarter, at the rue de Rivoli, and we passed the old city hall, the Hôtel de Ville. In the niches of the walls of the Hôtel de Ville, between the windows, in three rows, stand stone figures, some with a sword, some with a book, some with brush and palette, and some with geometric instruments. Hersh Rasseyner saw me looking at the monuments. He glanced at them out of the corners of his eyes and asked, "Who are those idols?"

I explained to him that they were famous Frenchmen: statesmen, heroes, scholars, and artists.

"Reb Hersh," I pleaded with him, "look at those statues. Come closer and see the light streaming from their marble eyes. See how much goodness lies hidden in their stone faces. You call it idolatry, but I tell you that, quite literally, I could weep when I walk about Paris and see these sculptures. It's a miracle, after all. How could a human being breathe the breath of life into stone? When you see a living man, you see only one man. But when you see a man poured out in bronze, you see mankind itself. Do you understand me? That one there, for instance, is a poet famous all over the world. The great writer broadens our understanding and stirs our pity for our fellow men. He shows us the nature of the man who can't overcome his desires. He doesn't punish even the wicked man, but sees him according to his afflictions in the war he wages with himself and the rest of the world. You don't say he's right, but you understand that he can't help it. Why are you pulling at your beard so angrily, Reb Hersh?"

He stared at me with burning eyes and cried out, "For shame! How can you say such foolish things? So you could weep when you look at those painted lumps of matter? Why don't you weep over the charred remains of the Gaon of Vilna's synagogue? Those artists of yours, those monument-choppers, those poets who sang about their emperors, those tumblers who danced and played before the rulers—did those masters of yours even bother to think that their patron would massacre a whole city and steal all it had, to buy them, your masters, with the gold? Did the prophets flatter kings? Did they take gifts of harlots' wages? And how merciful you are! The writer shows how the wicked man is the victim of his own bad qualities. I think that's what you said. It's really a pity about the arrogant rebel! He destroys others, and of course he's destroyed too. What a pity! Do you think it's easier to be a good man than an adulterer? But you particularly like to describe the lustful man. You know him better, there's something of him in you artists. If you make excuses for the man who exults in his wickedness, then as far as I'm concerned all your scribbling is unclean and unfit. Condemn the wicked man! Condemn the glutton and drunkard! Do you say he can't help it? He has to help it! You've sung a fine song of praise to the putrid idols, Chaim Vilner."

Hersh Rasseyner looked into my eyes with the sharp, threatening expression I had seen eleven years earlier, when we met in that Bialystok street. His voice had become hard and resounding. Passers-by stopped and stared at the bearded Jew who shook his finger at the sculptures of the Hôtel de Ville. Hersh did not so much as notice the passers-by. I felt embarrassed in the face of these Frenchmen, smiling and looking at us curiously.

"Don't shout so," I told him irritably. "You really think you have a monopoly on mercy and truth. You're starting where we left off eleven years ago. In Novaredok you always kept the windows closed, but it was still too light for you in the House of Study, so you ran off to your garret. From the garret you went down into a cellar. And from the cellar you burrowed down into a hole under the earth. That's where you could keep your commandment of solitude and that's where you persuaded yourself that a man's thoughts and feelings are like his hair; if he wants to, he can trim his hair and leave nothing but a beard and earlocks—holy thought and pious conduct. You think the world is what you imagine it, and you won't have anything to do with it. You think men are what you imagine them, but you tell them to be the opposite. But even the concentration camps couldn't make men different from what they are. Those who were evil became worse in the camps. They might have lived out their lives and not known themselves for what they were, but in the crisis men saw themselves and others undisguised. And when we were all freed, even the better ones among us weren't freed of the poison we had to drink behind the barbed wire. Now, if the concentration camp couldn't change men from top to bottom, how can you expect to change them?"

Hersh Rasseyner looked at me with astonishment. The anger that had flared in his eyes died down, though a last flicker seemed to remain.

"You don't know what you're talking about, Chaim," he said quietly and reluctantly. "Who ever told you that afflictions as such make people better? Take the day of a man's death, for instance. When a God-fearing man is reminded of death, he becomes even more God-fearing, as we read in Scripture: 'It is better to go to the house of mourning than to the house of feasting.' But when a free thinker is reminded of death he becomes even wilder, as the prophet says about the thoughts of the wicked: 'Let us eat and drink, for tomorrow we shall die.' It's quite clear that external causes can't drag people back to a Jewish life. A man's heart and mind have to be ready.

"If a man didn't come to the concentration camp with a thirst for a higher life, he certainly didn't elevate himself there. But the spiritual man knows that always and everywhere he must keep mounting higher or else he will fall lower. And as for the claim that a man can't change—that is a complete lie. 'In my flesh shall I see God!' The case of Hersh Rasseyner proves that a man can change. I won't tell you a long story about how many lusts I suffered from; how often the very veins in my head almost burst from the boiling of the blood; how many obstinacies I had to tear out of myself. But I knew that whoever denies himself affirms the Master of the World. I knew that the worst sentence that can be passed on a man is that he shall not be able to renounce his old nature. And because I truly wanted to conquer myself, the Almighty helped me."

"You are severe in your judgments," I answered. "You always were, Reb Hersh, if you'll pardon my saying so. You call these wise men putrid idols, but you refuse to see that they lifted mankind out of its bestial state. They weren't butchers of the soul and they didn't talk themselves into believing that human beings can tear their lower urges out of themselves and lop them off. They were very well aware of the hidden root of the human race. They wanted to illuminate men's minds with wisdom, so that men would be able to grow away from their untamed desires. You can't banish shadows with a broom, only with a lighted lamp. These great men—"

Hersh began to laugh so loud that I had to interrupt myself. He immediately stopped laughing and sighed. "I am very tired," he said. "I have been traveling the whole night. But somehow I don't want to leave you. After all, you were once a student at Novaredok; perhaps there is still a spark of the spirit left in you somewhere."

We walked to a bench in silence. On first meeting him I had thought that he had become milder. Now I realized regretfully that his demands upon me and his negation of the whole world had grown greater. I hoped, though, that the pause would ease the tension that had arisen between us, and I was in no hurry to be the first to talk again. Hersh, however, wrinkled his forehead as though he were collecting his thoughts, and when we were seated on the bench he returned to my last words.

◆ 5

"Did you say they were great men? The Germans insist they produced all the great men. I don't know whether they produced the very greatest, but I don't suppose that you worldly people would deny that they did produce learned men. Well, did those philosophers influence their own nation to become better? And the real question is, were the philosophers themselves good men? I don't want you to think that I underestimate their knowledge. During my years in the concentration camp I heard a good deal. There were exceptionally learned men among us, because the Germans mixed us all together, and in our moments of leisure we used to talk. Later, when with the help of the Almighty I was saved, I myself looked into the books of you worldly people, because I was no longer afraid they would hurt me. And I was really very much impressed by their ideas. Occasionally I found in their writings as much talent and depth as in our own Holy Books, if the two may be mentioned in one breath. But they are satisfied with talk! And I want you to believe me when I say that I concede that their poets and scientists wanted to be good. Only—only they weren't able to. And if some did have good qualities, they were exceptions. The masses and even their wise men didn't go any farther than fine talk. As far as talking is concerned, they talk more beautifully than we do.

"Do you know why they weren't able to become better? Because they were consumed with a passion to enjoy life. And since pleasure is not something that can be had by itself, murder arose among them—the pleasure of murder. And that's why they talk such fine talk, because they want to use it for fooling themselves into doing fine deeds. Only it doesn't help. They're satisfied with rhetoric, and the reason is that they care most of all for systems. The nations of the world inherited from the Greeks the desire for order and for pretty systems.

"First of all, they do what they do in public. They have no pleasure from their lusts if they can't sin openly, publicly, so that the whole world will know. They say of us that we're only hypocrites, whereas they do what they want to do publicly. But they like to wage war, not only with others, but with themselves as well, argue with themselves (of course, not too vigorously), even suffer and repent. And when they come to do repentance, the whole world knows about that too. That is the kind of repentance that gives them an intense pleasure; their self-love is so extreme it borders on sickness. They even like their victims, because their victims afford them the pleasure of sinning and the sweet afflictions of regret."

Hersh Rasseyner had moved away from me to the other end of the bench and had begun to look at me as though it had occurred to him that by mistake he might be talking to a stranger. Then he lowered his head and muttered as though to himself, "Do you remember that time in Bialystok?" He was silent for a moment and pulled a hair out of his beard as though he were pulling memories with it. "Do you remember, Chaim, how you told me on that Bialystok street that we were running away from the world because we were afraid we wouldn't be able to resist temptation? A Mussarist can labor for a lifetime on improving his qualities, yet a single word of criticism will stick in him like a knife. Yes, it's true! All the days of my youth I kept my eyes on the earth, without looking at the world. Then came the German. He took me by my Jewish beard, yanked my head up, and told me to look him straight in the eyes. So I had to look into his evil eyes, and into the eyes of the whole world as well. And I saw, Chaim, I saw—you know what I saw. Now I can look at all the idols and read all the forbidden impurities and contemplate all the pleasures of life, and it won't tempt me any more because now I know the true face of the world. Oh, Reb Chaim, turn and repent! It's not too late. Remember what the prophet Isaiah said: 'For my people have committed two evils: they have forsaken me, the fountain of living waters, and hewed them out cisterns, broken cisterns, that can hold no water.'"

Hersh had spoken like a broken man. Tears were dropping on his beard. He rubbed his eyes to hold the tears back, but they continued to flow down his cheeks.

I took his hand and said to him with emotion, "Reb Hersh, you say that I have forsaken a fountain of living waters for a broken cistern. I must tell you that you're wrong. I draw water from the same pure fountain as you, only I use a different vessel. But calm yourself, Reb Hersh.

"You yourself said that you believe that the nations of the world had men of wisdom and men of action who wanted to be good, but couldn't. I think I'm quoting you accurately. What I don't understand is this. It's a basic principle of Judaism that man has free will. The Novaredok people actually maintain that it's possible to attain such a state of perfection that we can do good deeds without the intervention of our physical bodies. Well then, if a man can actually peel the evil husks from himself, as he would peel an onion, how do you answer this question: Since the wise men among the gentiles wanted to be good, why couldn't they?"

I was unable to keep a mocking note of triumph out of my question. It stirred Hersh Rasseyner out of his mournful abstraction. With deliberation he straightened himself and answered gently, "Chaim, you seem to have forgotten what you learned at Novaredok, so I'll remind you. In His great love for mankind, the Almighty has endowed us with reason. If our sages of blessed memory tell us that we can learn from the animals, surely we can learn from reason as well. And we know that the elders of Athens erected systems of morality according to pure reason. They had many disciples, each with his own school.

"But the question hasn't changed. Did they really live as they taught, or did their system remain only a system? You must understand once and for all that when his reason is calm and pure, a man doesn't know what he's likely to do when his dark desire overtakes him. A man admires his own wisdom and is proud of his knowledge, but as soon as a little desire begins to stir in him he forgets everything else. Reason is like a dog on a leash who follows sedately in his master's footsteps—until he sees a bitch. With us it's a basic principle that false ideas come from bad qualities. Any man can rationalize whatever he wants to do. Is it true that only a little while ago he was saying the opposite of what he is now saying? He'll tell you he was wrong then. And if he lets you prove to him that he wasn't wrong then, he'll shrug and say, 'When I want to do something, I can't be an Aristotle.' As soon as his desire is sated, his reason revives and he's sorry for what he did. As soon as he feels desire beginning to stir once more, he forgets his reason again. It's as though he were in a swamp; when he pulls one foot out, the other sinks in. There is delicacy in his character, he has a feeling for beauty, he expresses his exalted thoughts in measured words, and there is no flaw in him; then he sees a female ankle and his reason is swallowed up. If a man has no God, why should he listen to the philosopher who tells him to be good? The philosopher himself is cold and gloomy and empty. He is like a man who wants to celebrate a marriage with himself.

"The one way out is this. A man should choose between good and evil only as the Law chooses for him. The Law wants him to be happy. The Law is the only reality in life. Everything else is a dream. Even when a man understands rationally what he should do, he must never forget that before all else he should do it because the Law tells him to do it. That is how he can guard against the time when his reason will have no power to command him.

"Wait a moment, I'm not through yet. A man may tell himself, 'I don't live according to reason but according to the Law.' And he may feel certain that when temptation comes he'll look into the appropriate book to see what he should do, and he'll do it. He tells himself that he is free. Actually, the freedom of his choice goes no farther than his wish. Even a man who has a Law won't be able to withstand his temptation if he doesn't watch over himself day and night. He who knows all secrets knew that our father Abraham would stand ready to sacrifice Isaac; but only after the Binding did the angel say to Abraham, 'Now I know.' Hence we learn that until a man has accomplished what he should, the Law does not trust him. A child has the capacity to grow, but we don't know how tall he'll grow. His father and mother may be as high as the trees, but he may favor a dwarf grandfather. Only by good deeds can we drive out bad deeds. Therefore the Jews cried out at Sinai, 'We will do'— only do, always do; 'and we will obey'—and now we want to know what the Law tells us to do. Without deeds all inquiry is vain.

"That is the outlook and the moral way of the old one, Reb Joseph Yoizl, may his merit be a shield for us, and thousands of students at Novaredok steeped themselves in it day and night. We labored to make ourselves better, each of us polished and filed his own soul, with examiners gathering evidence of improvement like pearls. But you laughed at us. Then came the German, may his name be blotted out, and murdered our sainted students. And now we're both face to face with the destruction of the Community of Israel. But you are faced with another destruction as well—the destruction of your faith in the world. That's what hurts you and torments you, so you ask me: Why weren't the wise men of the gentiles able to be good if they wanted to be good? And you find contradictions in what I said. But the real contradiction you find is not in what I said but in yourself. You thought the world was striving to become better, and you discovered it was striving for our blood.

"Even if they wanted to, the wise men of the gentiles couldn't have become good to the very roots of their being because they didn't have a Law and because they didn't labor to perfect their qualities all their lives long. Their ethics were worked out by human minds. They trusted their reasoned assumptions as men trust the ice of a frozen river in winter. Then came Hitler and put his weight on the wisdom of the wise men of the nations. The ice of their slippery reasoning burst, and all their goodness was drowned.

"And together with their goodness to others their own self-respect was drowned. Think of it! For a word they didn't like they used to fight with swords or shoot one another. To keep public opinion from sneering or a fool from calling them coward, though they trembled at the thought of dying, they went to their death. Generation after generation, their arrogance grew like a cancer, until it ended by eating their flesh and sucking their marrow. For centuries they speculated, they talked, and they wrote. Does duty to nation and family come first, or does the freedom of the individual come before his obligations to parents, wife, and children—or even to one's self? They considered the matter solemnly and concluded that there are no bonds that a nation is not free to break; that truth and reason are like the sun, which must rise; can the sun be covered by throwing clods of earth at it? So there came in the West a booted ruler with a little mustache, and in the East a booted ruler with a big mustache, and both of them together struck the wise man to the ground, and he sank into the mud. I suppose you'll say that the wise men wanted to save their lives. I can understand that. But didn't they insist that freedom, truth, and reason were more precious to the philosopher than his life? Take that wise man whose statue is standing there, with his instruments for measuring the stars and planets. When everyone else argued, 'The sun revolves about the earth,' he said, 'Not so; do what you will to me, break me, draw and quarter me, the earth revolves about the sun!' What would he have said to his grandchildren today? If the spirit of life could return to him, he would crawl down from his niche in the wall, strike his stone head against the stone bridge, and recite Lamentations."

### ◆ 6

Hersh Rasseyner had begun by speaking slowly, like the head of a yeshiva trying to explain a difficult passage to his pupil for the hundredth time, pausing briefly every now and then so that I could follow what he was saying. Gradually he grew animated. I was reminded of the discussions we used to have at Novaredok during the evenings after the Sabbath in the weeks before the Days of Awe. He began to speak more quickly, there was more excitement in his voice, and he ended his sentences like a man hammering nails into a wall. He shouted at me as though I were a dark cellar and he was calling to someone hiding in me.

The square and the neighboring streets had grown quieter and the flow of people had thinned out. On the benches in the little park passersby sat mutely, exhausted by the intense heat of the day and trying to get some relief from the cool evening breeze that had begun to blow in the blue twilight of Paris.

"Hear me out, Chaim," Hersh resumed. "I'll tell you a secret. I have to talk to you. I talked to you during all those years when I was in the ghetto and later in the camps. Don't wonder at it, because you were always dear to me, from the time you were a student in Bialystok. Even then I had the feeling that you stood with one foot outside our camp. I prayed for you. I prayed that you would remain Jewish. But my prayers didn't help. You yourself didn't want to be pious. You left us, but I never forgot you. They used to talk about you in the yeshiva; your reputation reached us even there. And I suppose you remember the time we met in Bialystok. Later our yeshiva was in Vilna, under the Bolsheviks, and we met again, only then you were very downhearted. In the ghetto they said you had been killed while trying to escape. Afterward we heard from partisans in the forest that you were living in Russia. I used to imagine that if we were both saved, a miracle might happen. We would meet and I could talk to you. That's why you mustn't be surprised if I talk to you as fluently as though I were reciting the daily prayers. Believe me, I have had so many imaginary debates with you that I know my arguments as well as the first prayer of the morning."

"Reb Hersh," I said, "it's getting late. The time for afternoon prayers will be over soon."

"Don't worry about my afternoon prayers, Chaim!" He laughed. "I said them just after twelve o'clock. In the camp it became a habit with me not to delay carrying out any commandment. I reasoned that if any hour was to be my last, I didn't want to come to heaven naked.

"Do you have time and strength to go on listening to me? You do? Good. So far I've talked to you about the gentile wise men. But first we ought to be clear in our own minds about our relation to them and to the whole world. And one thing more: if anything I say strikes you as too harsh, don't take it amiss. Even though I'm talking to you, I don't mean you personally; I really mean secular Jews in general. So don't be angry."

◆ 7

"Your Enlighteners used to sing this tune: 'Be a Jew at home and a man in public.' So you took off our traditional coat and shaved your beard and ear-locks. Still, when you went out into the street, the Jew pursued you in your language, in your gestures, in every part of you. So you tried to get rid of the incubus. And the result was that the Jew left you, like an old father whose children don't treat him with respect; first he goes to the synagogue and, then, because he has no choice, to the home for the aged. Now that you've seen what has happened to us, you've turned your slogan around. Now it's be a man at home and a Jew in public. You can't be pious at home because you're lacking in faith. Out of anger against the gentile and nostalgia for the father you abandoned, you want to parade your Jewishness in public. Only the man you try to be at home—I'm using your language—follows you out of your house. The parable of the Prince and the Nazirite applies to you. A dog was invited to two weddings, one near and one far. He thought, I won't be too late for the nearer one. So he ran first to the farther wedding—and missed it. Out of breath he ran to the one nearer home, and came after the feast. When he tried to push through the door, all he got was the stick. The upshot was that he missed both. The moral may be coarse, but you remember from your Novaredok days that it was applied to those who wanted to have both the pleasures of this world and the Law.

"You cried in the public square, 'The nations of the world dislike us because we're different. Let us be like them!' And you were like them. Not only that, but you stood at the head of their civilization. Where there was a famous scientist, thinker, writer—there you found a Jew. And precisely for that reason they hated us all the more. They won't tolerate the idea of our being like them. In the Middle Ages the priests wanted to baptize us. They used to delight in the torments of a Jew who tried to separate himself from the Community of Israel—with his family mourning him as though he were dead and the entire congregation lamenting as though it were the fast of *Tishe b'Av*. In our day, though, when they saw how easy it had become for a Jew to leap over into their camp, they stationed themselves at the outposts with axes in their hands, as though to fend off wild beasts. But you were hungry and blind, so you leaped—onto their axes.

"When you ran away from being Jewish, you disguised your flight with high-sounding names. An enlightened man would talk in the most elevated rhetoric about Enlightenment; but what he really had in mind was to become a druggist. He yearned for the fleshpots of Egypt. His ambition was to dig his hands into the pot with no one to look him in the eyes, like the miser who doesn't like anyone near him when he's eating. With the nations of the earth the great thing is the individual—his sovereignty, his pleasure, and his repose. But they understand that if they acted on the principle that might is right, one man would devour the other; so they have a government of individuals, and the rule is: Let me alone and I'll let you alone. With us Jews the individual doesn't exist; it's the community that counts. What's good for all must be good for each. Till your rebellion Jews lived as one—in prayer and in study, in joy and in sorrow. But you incited the tribes: 'Every man to your tents, O Israel!' Let each of us follow his own law, like the nations of the world. What's more, not only did you want to live as individuals, you wanted to die as individuals too. To avoid being confused with the other dead on the day of your death, you spent your lives erecting monuments for yourselves—one by great deeds; another by imposing his dominion; a third by a great business enterprise; and you by writing books. You didn't violate the commandment against idolatry. Of course not! You were your own gods. You prophesied, 'Man will be a god.' So naturally he became a devil.

"Why are you uneasy, Reb Chaim? Didn't we agree you wouldn't be angry? I don't mean you personally; I'm only speaking figuratively. But if you really feel I mean you, then I do! The wicked are as the unquiet sea. Every wave thinks it will leap over the shore, though it sees millions of others shattered before its eyes. Every man who lives for this world alone thinks that he will succeed in doing what no one else has ever been able to do. Well, you know now how far you got! But instead of looking for solace in the Master of the World and in the Community of Israel, you're still looking for the glass splinters of your shattered dreams. And little as you'll have the world to come, you have this world even less.

"Still, not all of you secularists wanted to overthrow the yoke of the Law altogether. Some grumbled that Judaism kept on getting heavier all the time: *Mishnah* on Bible; *Gemarah* on *Mishnah*; commentaries on *Gemarah*; codes; commentaries on the codes; commentaries on the commentaries, and commentaries on them. Lighten the weight a little, they said, so what is left can be borne more easily. But the more they lightened the burden, the heavier the remainder seemed to them. I fast twice a week without difficulty, and they can hardly do it once a year. Furthermore, what the father rejected in part, the son rejected in its entirety. And the son was right! Rather nothing than so little. A half-truth is no truth at all. Every man, and particularly every young man, needs a faith that will command all of his intellect and ardor. The devout cover a boy's head with a cap when he's a year old, to accustom him to commandments; but when a worldly father suddenly asks his grown son to cover his head with a paper cap and say the prayer over the wine on a Friday evening, the young man rightly thinks the whole thing is absurd. If he doesn't believe in Creation, and if the Exodus from Egypt is not much of a miracle, and if the Song of Songs is to him only the song of a shepherd and a shepherdess—God forbid!—and not the song of love between the Assembly of Israel and the Holy One, blessed be He, or between the supernal soul and the Almighty, why should he bless the Sabbath wine? Anyone who thinks he can hold on to basic principles and give up what he considers secondary is like a man who chops down the trunk of a tree and expects the roots not to rot.

"I've already told you, Chaim, that we of the Mussar school are very mindful of criticism. Do you remember telling me, on a street in Bialystok, that we try to escape by withdrawal because we would rather have nothing in this world than only a little? That's true. We want a more onerous code, more commandments, more laws, more prohibitions. We know that all the pleasures of life are like salt water: the more a man drinks of it, the thirstier he becomes. That's why we want a Torah that will leave no room in us for anything else.

"Suppose the Master of the World were to come to me and say, 'Hersh, you're only flesh and blood. Six hundred and thirteen commandments are too many for you, I will lighten your burden. You don't need to observe all of them.

Don't be afraid, you won't be deprived of the resurrection of the dead!' Do you understand, Chaim, what it means to be at the resurrection of the dead and see life given again to all the Jews who fell before my eyes? If the Father of Mercy should ask less sacrifice of me, it would be very bitter for me. I would pray, 'Father of Mercy, I don't want my burden to be lightened, I want it to be made heavier.' As things are now, my burden is still too light. What point is there to the life of a fugitive, of a Jew saved from the crematorium, if he isn't always ready to sacrifice his bit of a rescued life for the Torah? But you, Chaim, are you as daring in your demands upon the world as I am in my demands upon the Master of the World? When you were studying with us, you were so strong and proud that you could be satisfied only by getting to the very bottom of the truth. And now do you think it right to crawl under the table of life, hoping for a bone from the feast of unclean pleasures, or a dry crumb of the joys of this world? Is that what's left to you of your pride and confidence in the warfare of life? I look at you and think, I'm still very far from being what I ought to be. If I had reached a higher stage, my heart would be torn with pity for you.

"The rebellious seducer rejected everything, while the one who halted between two opinions left something; but both of them, when they wanted to show their unfaltering good sense, first denounced the Community of Israel for allowing itself to be bound in the cobwebs of a profitless dialectic, living in a cemetery and listening to ghost stories, concerning itself with unrealities and thinking that the world ends at the ruined mill on the hilltop. The clever writer described it with great artistry, and the vulgar laughed. And the secularist reformers with their enlightened little beards justified themselves with a verse: 'Whom the Lord loveth He correcteth.' In other words, only because they really loved us did they attack us. But they groveled before everything they saw elsewhere. They called us fawning lickspittles—but with their own souls, like rags, they wiped the gentry's boots. The overt rebel and the man who prayed secretly and sinned secretly—why antagonize either side?—were at one in this, that the thing they mocked us for most enthusiastically was our belief in being chosen. What's so special about us? they asked, laughing. And I say, you may not feel very special—but you have to be! You may not want it, but the Almighty does! Thousands of years ago the God of Israel said through Ezekiel His prophet: 'And that which cometh into your mind shall not be at all; in that ye say: We will be as the nations, as the families of the countries, to serve wood and stone. As I live, saith the Lord God'—do you hear, Chaim? the Almighty swears by His own life—'As I live, saith the Lord God, surely with a mighty hand, and with an outstretched arm, and with fury poured out, will I be king over you.' You're a writer; write it on your forehead. You don't seem very impressed. You don't consider a verse to be proof. But the German is a proof, isn't he? Today, because so many Jews have been cut down, you don't want to remember how you used to laugh at them. But tomorrow, when the destruction will be forgotten, you'll laugh again at the notion that God has chosen us. That's why I want to tell you something.

"You know that I was in a camp. I lay on the earth and was trampled by the German in his hobnailed boots. Well, suppose that an angel of God had come to me then, that he had bent down and whispered into my ear, 'Hersh, in the twinkling of an eye I will turn you into the German. I will put his coat on you and give you his murderous face; and he will be you. Say the word and the miracle will come to pass.' If the angel had asked me—do you hear, Chaim?—I would not have agreed at all. Not for one minute would I have consented to be the other, the German, my torturer. I want the justice of law! I want vengeance, not robbery! But I want it as a Jew. With the Almighty's help I could stand the German's boots on my throat, but if I had had to put on his mask, his murderous face, I would have been smothered as though I had been gassed. And when the German shouted at me, 'You are a slave of slaves,' I answered through my wounded lips, 'Thou hast chosen me.'

"I want to ask you only one question, no more. What happened is known to all Jews. 'Let the whole House of Israel bewail the burning which the Lord hath kindled.' All Jews mourn the third of our people who died a martyr's death. But anyone with true feeling knows that it was not a third of the House of Israel that was destroyed, but a third of himself, of his body, his soul. And so we must make a reckoning—you as well as I. Anyone who doesn't make the reckoning must be as bestial as the beasts of the wood. Let's make the reckoning together. In justice and in mercy, may we forgive the murderers? No, we may not! To the end of all generations we may not forgive them. Forgiving the murderer is a fresh murder, only this time of brother by brother.

"Neither you nor I has the right to sleep at night. We have no right to flee the laments, the eyes, and the outstretched arms of the murdered; though we break under the anguish and affliction, we have no right to flee their outcry. What then? I know that the reckoning is not yet over; far from it. And I have never thought for one moment that anyone in the world besides the jealous and vengeful God would avenge the helpless little ones that the Gestapo stuffed into the trains for Treblinka, treading on their delicate little bodies to get as many children as possible into the cars. That is why I don't have the slightest shadow of a doubt that the great and terrible day, behold it comes! When I hear people quibbling about politics and calculating the position of the powers, I know that there is another set of books, kept in fire and blood. There's no use asking me whether I want it that way or not; that's the way it has to be! And that's what sustains me as I try to go in tranquillity about the work of the Creator.

"But you, Chaim, how can you eat and sleep and laugh and dress so elegantly? Don't you have to make your reckoning too? How can you thrust yourself into the world when you know it consorts with the murderers of the members of your own house? And you thought the world was becoming better! Your world has fallen! As for me, I have greater faith than ever. If I had only as much faith as in the past, that would be an offense against the martyred saints. My answer is, more and more self-sacrifice for the Master of the World; to cry out until the spirit is exhausted: 'For Thy sake are we killed all the day'; to go about, until the soul departs, with a shattered heart and hands raised to heaven: 'Father, Father, only You are left to us!' But what has changed with you, Chaim? What is your answer?"

◆ 8

Hersh Rasseyner's speech was like a dry flame, progressively taking fire from itself. I realized he was unburdening himself of much accumulated anger. Finally he grew quiet. His lips were pinched with the effort he had to make to obey himself and speak no more.

The blue of the evening sky was growing darker. The stone figures around the Hôtel de Ville had shrunk, as though frightened by what Hersh Rasseyner had said, and quietly burrowed deeper into the walls. The old building was now half in darkness. The street lamps brought out the flat green color of our surroundings. Black shining autos slid quietly over the asphalt. A thin little rain began to come down. Windows were lighting up. The people walking along on the other side of the street seemed to be moving with a silent, secret pace behind a thick silken curtain, woven of the summer rain.

From our little empty corner I glanced across the street. In the light of the electric lamps the raindrops looked like millions of fireflies joyously hastening down from the sky. I had an impulse to merge myself with the human stream flowing down the surrounding lighted streets. I stirred, and I felt little pricks of pain in my stiffened limbs. The light rain came to an end. Hersh sat near me, motionless and as though deaf, his shoulders sharp and angular and his head bowed and sunk in darkness. He was waiting for me to answer.

"Reb Hersh," I finally said, "as I sat here listening to you, I sometimes thought I was listening to myself. And since it's harder to lie to yourself than to someone else, I will answer you as though you were my own conscience, with no thought either of merely being polite or of trying to win a debate. I am under no greater obligation than you to know everything. I don't consider it a special virtue not to have doubts. I must tell you that just as the greatness of the faithful consists in their innocence and wholeness, so the heroism of thinkers consists in their being able to tolerate doubt and make their peace with it. You didn't discover your truth; you received it ready-made. If anyone should ask you about something in your practice of which you yourself don't know the meaning, you answer, 'The work of my fathers is in my hands.' As a rule, a man is a rebel in his youth; in age he seeks tranquillity. You had tranquillity in your youth, while I don't have it even now; you once predicted it would be so with me. But is your tranquillity of soul a proof that the truth is with you? For all your readiness to suffer and make sacrifices, there is an element of self-satisfaction in you. You say of yourself that you were born in a coat of many colors.

"They used to call 'the old one,' the founder of Novaredok, the master of the holes. It was said that Reb Joseph Yoizl lived apart for many years in the woods in a hut that had two holes in the wall; through one they would hand him dairy foods and through the other meat foods. When he put his withdrawal behind him and came back into the world, his philosophy was either milk or meat, one extreme or the other, but nothing in between. His disciples, including you, took this teaching from him. His disciples want what they call wholeness too, and they have no use for compromises. What you said about our wanting a small Torah so that it would be easier for us was simply idle talk. On the contrary, we make it harder for ourselves, because we acknowledge a double responsibility—toward Jewish tradition and toward secular culture.

"You said that among Jews the important thing was always the community and not the individual, until we came along and spoiled it; we wanted to be like the gentiles, for whom the 'I' is more important than anything else. And in order to hurt me you tried to persuade me that what I want to do is to climb up the Hôtel de Ville and put myself there as a living monument to myself. You allow yourself to mock, because, after all, what you do is for the sake of heaven, isn't that so? I won't start now to tell you historical facts about leaders and rulers who made the community their footstool. As for what you say, that the principle among Jews was always the community until we came, I agree. We secularists want to free the individual. You say a man should tear his individual desires out of himself. But for hundreds of years men have gone to torture and death so that the commonwealth shall consist of free and happy individuals. I could read you an all but endless list of our own boys and girls whose youth was spent in black dungeons because they would not be deterred from trying to make the world better. You yourself know about Jewish workers who fought against all oppressors and tyrants. The only thing is that you won't concede that free thinkers can sacrifice themselves too, so you complain that they left Jewish tradition only to enjoy forbidden pleasures. That is untrue. In my own quarter I knew as many 'seekers' as in Novaredok—and more. Because you denied the world, Reb Hersh, you withdrew into an attic. But these young people dearly loved the world, and they sacrificed themselves—to better it.

"What right then do you have to complain to us about the world? You yourself said that we dreamed about another, a better world—which nullifies your accusation. We carried into the world our own vision of what the world should be, as the Jews in the wilderness carried the Ark with the tablets of the

Covenant, so that they could enter the land of Canaan with their own Torah. You laugh; you say that we deceived ourselves. I'll ask you: Do you renounce Judaism because the Samaritans and the Karaites distorted the Law of Moses?

"But I don't have to apologize to you. You lump me together with the murderers and demand an accounting of me for the world. I can be as harsh an accuser as you. I can cry out against you and demand an accounting of you. If we have abandoned Jewish tradition, it's your fault! You barricaded yourself, shut the gates, and let no one out into the open. If anyone put his head out, you tried to pull him back by his feet; and if you couldn't, you threw him out bodily and shut the doors behind him with a curse. Because he had no place to go back to he had to go farther away than he himself would have wished. From generation to generation you became more fanatical. Your hearts are cold and your ears deaf to all the sciences of the world. You laugh at them and say they are futile things. If you could, you would put people in the pillory again, as the Gaon of Vilna did to a follower of the Enlightenment who dared say that the old exegetes didn't know Hebrew grammar too well. Even today, for the smallest transgression you would impose the gravest punishment, if you could. But because you can't, you shorten your memories. You pretend not to remember how you used to persecute anyone who was bold enough to say anything different from you without basing himself on the authority of the ancient sages of blessed memory, or even with their authority. All your life you studied *The Path of the Upright*. Do you know how much its author was suspected and persecuted, how much anguish they caused him, how they hunted for heresy in his writings? Do you know that, at least? And you yourself, didn't you examine the contents of your students' trunks, looking for forbidden books? Even now, doesn't your voice have in it something of the trumpet of excommunication? Doesn't your eye burn like the black candle of excommunication? And do you really think that, with all your protestations, you love Jews more than the writers for whom it was so painful to write critically of the Jewish community? Didn't you bury them outside the wall, when you could, with no stones to mark their graves? Incidentally, Reb Hersh, I want you to know that this neighborhood we're in is old Paris. Here by the Hôtel de Ville, where we're sitting, is the Place de Grève—that is, Execution Square, where they used to torture and execute those who were condemned to death. It was right here, more than seven hundred years ago, that Maimonides's *Guide to the Perplexed* was burned, on a denunciation by eminent and zealous rabbis. Rabbi Jonah Gerondi had a hand in it. Later, when the priests began to burn the Talmud too, Rabbi Jonah felt that it was a punishment from heaven for his warfare against Maimonides, and he repented. That was when he wrote his *Gates of Repentance*. In Novaredok they used to read the *Gates of Repentance* with such outcries that their lungs were almost torn to shreds; but they never thought to learn its moral, which is not to be fanatical.

"How estranged you feel from all secular Jews can be seen in your constant repetition of 'we' and 'you.' You laugh at us poor secularists. You say that our suffering is pointless: we don't want to be Jews, but we can't help it. It would follow that the German made a mistake in taking us for Jews. But it's you who make that mistake. The enemies of Israel know very well that we're the same; they say it openly. And we're the same not only for the enemies of Israel, but for the Master of the World as well! In the other world your soul won't be wearing a cap or a beard or earlocks. Your soul will come there as naked as mine. You would have it that the real Community of Israel is a handful of Hersh Rasseyners. The others are quarter-Jews, tenth-Jews—or not even that. You say that being Jewish is indivisible, all or nothing. So you make us Jews a thousand times fewer than we already are.

"You were right when you said that it was not a third of our people who were murdered, but rather that a third was cut out of the flesh and soul of every Jew who survived. As far as you're concerned though, Reb Hersh, was it really a third of our people who perished? The gist of what you say—again the same thing!—is that anyone who isn't your kind of Jew is not a Jew at all. Doesn't that mean that there were more bodies burned than Jews murdered? You see to what cruelty your religious fanaticism must lead.

"I want you to consider this and settle it with yourself. Those Jews who didn't worry night and day about the high destiny of man, who weren't among the thirty-six hidden righteous men who sustain the world, but who lived a life of poverty for themselves, their wives, and their children; those Jews who got up in the morning without saying the proper morning prayers and ate their black bread without saying the blessing for bread; those Jews who labored on the Sabbath and didn't observe the last detail of the Law on Holy Days; those Jews who waited submissively and patiently at the table of this world for a crumb to fall their way—that's what you, Reb Hersh, the hermit of Novaredok, the man who lives apart, taunted them with; those Jews who lived together in neighborliness, in small quarrels and small reconciliations, and perished together in the same way—do you admit them to your Paradise or not? And where will they sit? At the east wall, together with the Mussarists, or at the door, with their feet outside? You will tell me that the simple man is saintly and pure, because he perished as a Jew. But if he survived, is he wicked and evil, because he doesn't follow in your way? Is that your mercy and love for the Community of Israel? And you dare to speak in their name and say you're the spokesman of the sainted dead! Why are you getting up? Do you want to run away? But you assured me you used to dream of meeting me and talking it out with me. Can you only talk and not listen? Novaredok Mussarist, sit down and hear me out!

"If secular Jews are so alien to you, why should I be surprised at the blackness of your hatred against the whole non-Jewish world? But let's not quarrel any more, Reb Hersh; let's reckon our accounts quietly. May we hate the whole non-Jewish world? You know as well as I do that there were some who saved the lives of Jews. I won't enter into a discussion with you about the exact number of such people. It's enough for me that you know there were some.

"In 1946, in Poland, I once attended a small gathering in honor of a Pole, a Christian, who had hidden ten Jews. At that little party we all sat around a table. We didn't praise the doctor, we didn't talk about noble and exalted things, about humanity and heroism, or even about Jews and Poles. We simply asked him how it was that he wasn't afraid to hide ten Jews behind the wall of his office. The doctor was a small, gray-haired man. He kept on smiling, almost childishly, and he thanked us in embarrassment for the honor—a great honor!—that we were doing him. He answered our question in a low voice, almost tongue-tied: when he hid the Jews he felt sure that, since it was a good deed, nothing bad would happen to him.

"Here in Paris there's an old lady, a Lithuanian. I know her well. Everybody knows that in the Vilna ghetto she saved the lives of Jews, and also hid books. The Germans sentenced her to death, but she was spared by a miracle. She's an old revolutionist, an atheist; that is to say, she doesn't believe in God.

"Imagine that both of them, the old lady and the old man, the Lithuanian and the Pole, the revolutionist and the Christian, were sitting here listening to us! They don't say anything, they only listen. They are frightened by your accusations, but not angry, because they understand that your hatred grows out of sorrow. Neither do they regret having saved the lives of Jews; they feel only an ache in their hearts, a great pain. Why do you think they saved the lives of Jews? The devout Christian didn't try to convert anyone. The old revolutionist didn't try to make anyone an atheist; on the contrary, she hid our sacred books. They saved the lives of Jews not from pity alone, but for their own sakes as well. They wanted to prove to themselves—no one else could possibly have known—that the whole world does not consist only of criminals and those who are indifferent to the misfortunes of others. They wanted to save their own faith in human beings and the lives of Jews as well. Now you come along and repudiate everything in the world that isn't piously Jewish. I ask you: Is there room in your world for these two old people? Don't you see that you would drive them out into the night? Will you take them, the righteous of the nations of the world, out of the category of gentile and put them in a special category? They didn't risk their lives so that Reb Hersh Rasseyner, who hates everyone, everyone, could make an exception of them.

"But you ask me what has changed for me since the destruction. And what has changed for you, Reb Hersh? You answer that your faith has been strengthened. I tell you openly that your answer is a paltry, whining answer. I don't accept it at all. You must ask God the old question about the righteous man who fares ill and the evil man who fares well—only multiplied for a million murdered children. The fact that you know in advance that there will be no explanation from heaven doesn't relieve you of the responsibility of asking, Reb Hersh! If your faith is as strong as Job's, then you must have his courage to cry out to heaven: 'Though He slay me, yet will I trust in Him; but I will argue my ways before Him!' If a man hasn't sinned, he isn't allowed to declare himself guilty. As for us, even if we were devils, we couldn't have sinned enough for our just punishment to be a million murdered children. That's why your answer that your faith has been strengthened is no answer at all, as long as you don't demand an accounting of heaven.

"Reb Hersh, we're both tired and burned out from a whole day of arguing. You ask what has changed for me. The change is that I want to make peace with you, because I love you deeply. I never hated you and I never searched for flaws in your character, but what I did see I didn't leave unsaid. When you became angry with me before I left, I became angry with you, but now I'm filled with love for you. I say to you as the Almighty said to the Jews assembled in Jerusalem on the feast days: I want to be with you one day more, it is hard for me to part from you. That's what has changed for me, and for all Jewish writers. Our love for Jews has become deeper and more sensitive. I don't renounce the world, but in all honesty I must tell you we want to incorporate into ourselves the hidden inheritance of our people's strength, so that we can continue to live. I plead with you, do not deny us a share in the inheritance. However loudly we call out to heaven and demand an accounting, our outcry conceals a quiet prayer for the Divine Presence, or for the countenance of those destroyed in the flames, to rest on the alienated Jews. The Jewish countenance of the burned still hangs in clouds of gas in the void. And our cry of impotent anger against heaven has a deeper meaning as well: because we absolutely refuse our assent to the infamous and enormous evil that has been visited on us, because we categorically deny its justice, no slavish or perverse acquiescence can take root in our hearts, no despairing belief that the world has no sense or meaning.

"Reb Hersh, we have been friends since the old days in the yeshiva. I remember that I once lost the little velvet bag in which I kept my phylacteries. You didn't eat breakfast and you spent half a day looking for it, but you couldn't find it. I got another bag to hold my phylacteries, but you're still looking for the old one.

"Remember, Reb Hersh, that the texts inscribed in my phylacteries are about the Community of Israel. Don't think that it's easy for us Jewish writers. It's hard, very hard. The same misfortune befell us all, but you have a ready answer, while we have not silenced our doubts, and perhaps we never will be able to silence them. The only joy that's left to us is the joy of creation, and in all the travail of creation we try to draw near to our people.

"Reb Hersh, it's late, let us take leave of each other. Our paths are different, spiritually and practically. We are the remnant of those who were driven out. The wind that uprooted us is dispersing us to all the corners of the earth. Who knows whether we shall ever meet again? May we both have the merit of meeting again in the future and seeing how it is with us. And may I then be as Jewish as I am now. Reb Hersh, let us embrace each other."

*Henryk Grynberg 1936–*  Grynberg was born in the hamlet of Radoszyna near Minsk Mazowiecki (Warsaw province) as the son of a dairy merchant. He graduated from the University of Warsaw School of Journalism in 1959 and worked as an actor and translator in Warsaw. In the late 1960s anti-Jewish riots, fostered by the communist government in Poland, prompted him to emigrate to the United States. He did graduate work in Slavic languages and literature at the University of California at Los Angeles.

One of a few child survivors of the Holocaust, Grynberg published his first collection of short stories in Warsaw in 1963 (*The Antigone Gang*). A volume of poems followed a year later. He also published a thinly veiled autobiographical novella (translated as *Child of the Shadows,* 1969). He continues to write Holocaust fiction and poetry in Polish, and his work is increasingly translated into Hebrew and English (*California Kaddish,* 1991; *The Victory,* 1993; *The Children of Zion,* 1997).

## UNCLE ARON                    *"Memory is the secret of redemption"*

They owned some land in Wygledowek but couldn't make a living off it, so after he was discharged from the army, Aron used to buy produce and take it to Warsaw. His wedding with Feyga, my father's oldest sister, took place in Rembertow, in the big house of Yides from Makowiec who was a sister of my grandmother from Nowa Wies. My grandmother's second sister lived in Kaluszyn. Aron doesn't remember her first name but her married name was Guzik and they owned a tannery. Her sons had already wives and children and worked in the tannery. The third sister of my grandmother, Sura, lived in Czarnoglow. Aron doesn't remember her married name. Some children and grandchildren of my grandmother's three sisters lived in Minsk Mazowiecki, Jadow, Wegrow, Radzymin and Wolomin. That was our homeland—literally. And one should add my grandfather's brothers and sisters whom Aron doesn't remember. And brothers and sisters of my other grandparents, those from Dobre. And their children and grandchildren. They all lived around there too.

Aron's and Feyga's wedding was attended by my father and mother and my father's whole family. It was their last family gathering. Soon afterwards big Nutek wanted to marry Rywka but my grandfather didn't give her to him, as before he hadn't given Feyga to Nutek's brother Biumek. My grandfather helped Aron to open a grocery in Rembertow, on Kosciuszko Street. Feyga used to mind the shop and Aron would take goods to Warsaw. Their son was born in August. One day when Aron came back from Warsaw, Feyga showed him a draft card. "We didn't know anything," says Aron. At the *pidion ha-ben* he wore a uniform and right after the ceremony went to Modlin to join the 71st regiment. There are twelve of them in the photograph in neat dress-uniforms carefully buttoned up and tall four-cornered caps resembling *shakos*. All of them in the light artillery, resembling one another, not like Jews but like brothers—it is really difficult to guess which of them is Aron. And they are serious, no smiles, not even one. Modlin defended itself for a long time.

Big Nutek served in the army in Praga, the right bank part of Warsaw, and it was there that he met Esterka who sold rolls on Brzeska Street. In September he was taken prisoner by the Russians, but a year later he crossed the Bug river and came back. He got Esterka out of the Warsaw ghetto with help from a Pole, married her at Aron's and Feyga's in Rembertow and took her to Solki. When Esterka became pregnant, Nutek wanted her to have an abortion, but she refused. Aron was also against it. Aron's and Feyga's little son stayed with our grandparents in Nowa Wies because there was no food in the Rembertow ghetto. Aron insisted that Feyga move to Nowa Wies too but she didn't want to leave her shop. She stayed in the shop when Aron went with Nutek to the country to slaughter sheep and cows. She was taken while he was away, together with the Rembertow ghetto; only the shop remained. Our grandparents from Nowa Wies were first deported to Dobre and then to Stanislawow, as all of us were. So Feyga wasn't killed with her little son as I had thought before. And Rywka didn't go with grandfather and grandmother but tried to run away with Feyga's child in her arms. Alone, she could have managed—her sister Itka did—or perhaps she would have gone voluntarily, not wanting to leave her old mother and father. Big Nutek and Esterka escaped with their baby. Esterka got Aryan papers and a Pole found her a place in Miloena; she became a caretaker there.

Aron had to take off his boots while running from the policemen who found him and Itka in Gryz's barn. He waited in the woods till dark and went, barefoot, to Milosna. When somebody passed him, he would walk into the snow to hide his bare feet and whistled merrily pretending he liked to trek through the snow. Not wanting to be seen without footwear by a watchman, he could only go to Miloena where Esterka was a caretaker. Esterka gave him a basin full of snow and he warmed his feet up in that snow; otherwise he would have lost his toes.

He had strong legs and could depend on them. He would wake up in the woods, look at his legs and ask, where will you take me today? Because his legs by themselves would take him. He felt he had to go and he would go even when there was no place to go. He would take a can of milk on his shoulder, a pat of butter in his rucksack and go to the railway. He would come to the Wschodni Station in Praga with pieces of straw in his clothes so people couldn't doubt he was a smuggler from the country. He would walk all day and wouldn't sell anything to anybody. He would pop into stores, get acquainted with shopkeepers, take orders which he had no intention of filling. At the end of the day he would go to homes from which nobody was turned away before curfew. Just to spend a night at a home, to be among people for a day. He always wore a clean shirt and fancifully pushed his thick light curls—maybe too thick and too curly—out from under his cap to show what a light blonde he was. And he didn't look down, so that everyone would see his bright blue eyes and not his big, hooked nose. There were many very lonely women in Praga who willingly made him a place at the table and engaged him in conversation so he would miss his train. And he gladly let them do it and was grateful to them for putting him up, but he never moved any closer. They were surprised and invited him to stay all the more.

Esterka went to church, talked with people, was seen everywhere. Nutek, by contrast, didn't like to be seen. Aron says that the Volksdeutsch who had brought the Germans suspected something and that was why Nutek wasn't told that they only wanted him to bury a body. He was only told to take a spade and go with them. And that was why Nutek tried to run. When they led Nutek away, Esterka grabbed the baby and ran out through the back gate which she left wide open. It was a sign for Aron. When Aron came, he saw the open gate from a distance and went straight to Praga, to Wilenska Street where Esterka's brother and sister-in-law were staying. There he found Esterka in tears. Soon after they had to run from Wilenska Street as well. Aron came with his can on his shoulder and a neighbor told him that his friends no longer lived there. Ay-ay, Aron worried, they owe me money for milk. And who gives things on credit today?—wondered the lady.

Roundups were getting more and more frequent. Once they stopped the train for a whole hour. Fortunately they caught enough people before they got to Aron's carriage. After that he traveled by train only if he had to. Like when he had to bring me over. We walked through Pustelnik with a very pretty, Nordic looking young lady. I had a new overcoat with a sealskin collar and a cap with the same kind of fur. Nobody was to know that I had been brought out of the woods. But I didn't look like a child from that vicinity either, and we had to walk about twenty kilometers to the station. We had to cross a bridge where a gendarme was standing. At the bridge there was a mill. An apprentice came out of the mill and recognized Aron at once, but Aron told us nothing so we crossed the bridge quietly and didn't know that the bridge was shaking under Aron's feet all that time. He told us nothing even after we got off at Wschodni Station. He came several more times to see my mother at the confectioner's on Wilenska Street and give her money or jewelry from my father.

Aron wanted to join the partisans but they didn't want Jews. He joined some young people who got out of the burning Warsaw ghetto and had guns. Their leader was Olek, a fellow who feared nothing. A tall man with a mop of black hair, he left the ghetto wearing a German officer's uniform. With this uniform on, he stood in the middle of the road and stopped a German truck. They took the Germans' guns and pushed them into the woods and took their clothes and shoes. During the day they slept or played cards, at night they would sneak out in search of prey. Aron showed the way. They took only from those who had Jewish things. Two gamekeepers lived between Jadow and Malkinia. They were brothers-in-law. One of them used to hunt Jews who escaped from the trains headed for Treblinka. They went to him and shot him; they did nothing to the other. Those men from the Warsaw ghetto were just, but they didn't quite understand what a gamekeeper is and what a brother-in-law means to a gamekeeper. That day Olek didn't draw the right cards. When they heard the snapping of branches, Aron stood up to see what was going on, but Olek pushed him back to the ground. "Sit!" he said angrily and went with his revolver in one hand and a fan of cards in the other. He had taken only a few steps when from behind a tree came "Halt!" He turned around and was astonished to see a handsome German officer with an automatic in front of him. He was even more surprised when Olek lodged a bullet in him, but then an automatic from behind another tree quilted Olek's back. They threw all the grenades they had and broke through. Besides Olek, Antek and Genek were also killed. Aron got away with a slight wound in his knee.

They were having supper at Sobotko's when suddenly two Germans walked in and told them to raise their hands. They did so obediently. They were surprised, because Germans had never come to a village at night before. And if they had, they would come in a squad or by truck and then everybody knew. Aron had his parabellum in the back of his trousers, under his shirt. Old Mrs. Sobotko started to plead with the Germans to leave the young men alone because they were her sons, decent fellows, everybody knew them. One German stood at the door and the other searched their bellies and thighs. When they finished, they both sat down and told Mrs. Sobotko to give them vodka. She eagerly pulled out two bottles of moonshine and a piece of bacon from the cellar. After the Germans drank the first glass, they demanded that the others drink with them. Aron was the first to reach for a glass.

On a bright day in May, Germans arrived along the highway from Lochow. Again somebody denounced them. In the woods they heard the German trucks coming but didn't think they were coming for them. Surrounded on all sides, they lost their last leader, Ignac. Among those killed were also Rywka and Mechel, sisters from Dobre and their brother Shlomo, who were my mother's first cousins. And also Eli, the youngest brother of Biumek and Nutek. Aron got a severe shot in his hip and he wouldn't have gotten away this time if it hadn't been for Slon who lugged him across the water to Piwki. That was on May 5, 1944.

◆

Each time I visit with Aron, I think that he has already told me everything and then I learn some new details. I come every few years and then we talk from morning till evening. Rutie wonders about it. She doesn't understand our language but she knows what we are talking about. Her family comes from Cairo and Bukhara. Rutie has a son from her first husband who was killed in 1948 but she was unable to have a child by Aron. Her son has two sons and a daughter who will have their own children soon. Their homeland is here. We drink two glasses of mild Carmel vodka and Rutie loyally serves us turkey sausage, turkey cutlets, turkey "ham" and pickles with dill because she knows that we like such things. Though she says she is afraid Aron exhausts me with these conversations, what she really thinks is, it's I who exhausts Aron. She can't understand that no other subject is more important to us and that we have to talk about it.

On the Shabbat, after breakfast there is hardly anybody in the streets, just as it once used to be over there. We walk to the Yarkon, a village stream that has followed us here and lost its way with us. It's early spring; the Yarkon, full of water, looks like a real river and its banks are overgrown with clean moist grass. From a distance, a dinghy looks like a fisherman's boat, the sky is cloudy at this time of the year, like over there, and Aron is wearing a peaked cap, a shirt without a tie and a jacket that doesn't match his trousers. He looks as if he had never left Wygledowek and Rembertow. His curls haven't thinned at all and seem now even blonder, though his bright eyes have become a bit smaller and his nose seems larger. We take snapshots of each other and the river to record that we are here, that we managed to get all the way here. Only wires in the sky and dead, lonely posts disturb our view.

Then we walk along elegant streets, among handsome modern buildings with colored balconies, neatly trimmed hedges and lawns. Aron holds himself well and he walks well, but he complains that it is hard for him to stand at the butcher's stall, even for half a day as he does. Suddenly around the corner of two elegant streets, we see old cottages and ramshackle houses which we know from somewhere else, weeds and wild bushes, potholes and hoofprint. We turn into a bushy backyard where a horse is feeding on a bundle of hay. It is as if the shtetl has come here after us. "Who lives here?" I ask. "Eh, people who do not want to move," answers Aron. "They don't want to move?" I wonder. "They were offered a lot of money but they wouldn't take it. They say they like it this way and nothing can be done."

We are walking toward the beach where highrise hotels shoot into the sky. Every year there are more of them on the shore. They grow like monuments of the years. They cut the horizon of water, earth and sky with their vertical flight. Like hotels on the way to heaven. And souls from all over the world fly in—to rest and reflect on the edge of the void. We stop at the shore, we breathe the cool wind. There is nobody on the beach except us and this pale void which we have managed to traverse. It has already taken back my mother, and Esterka who died of cancer in Canada. Only two of us are here, as if in the next world.

As if we were in the next world and not they. As if we had left, not they. They who stayed—in our homeland. But we're not in the next world. In the next world we could stay and conduct our talk—to infinity. In the other world we wouldn't have to—after all that's happened—part forever. And we wouldn't be counting highrises. A few more highrises, and another few, and I will have to talk to myself.

Suddenly Aron reminds me that Esterka's son Kalman lives in Canada. I must find him. He hardly remembers anything. All the more reason for me to find him.

## Rachel Haring Korn 1898–1982

Rachel (Rokhl) Haring was born in a Galician town near Pikliski, Poland, among farmers and peasants. She wrote poetry in Polish before switching to Yiddish, which she learned from her husband, and published several volumes in Poland before World War II. Her postwar Yiddish poems rank with the finest produced in that language. English translations include *Generations* (1982), *Paper Roses* (1985), and *Rachel Korn: Selected Poems* (1986). Her first collection of Yiddish short stories appeared in Montreal in 1957, where she had settled in 1949.

When the Nazis invaded Poland, she managed to flee to Uzbekistan (Soviet Union) with her youngest daughter. Her husband and most of her family were killed. After the war, she returned to Poland and resumed her literary career in Lodz, but eventually moved to Montreal (via Sweden) where she continued to write and publish poetry and stories. The State of Israel honored her with the Itzig Manger Prize of Yiddish Literature in 1974.

## THE ROAD OF NO RETURN

By morning the whole city had heard about the new edict, but in Hersh-Lazar Sokol's household everyone pretended they knew nothing. And just like on any other day, Beyle lit the stove and began to cook the family's ghetto portion of grits and half-rotten potatoes. And just like on any other day, she set the table with seven plates and seven spoons laid out in a double row. The double row was to ward off the evil spirits lurking outside.

Every few minutes she ran to the door, and with a corner of her apron wiped the steam from its glass windowpane and looked down to the street. On that autumn day of 1942 there wasn't a Jew to be seen in that Galician village, except for a Jewish policeman with a bundle of documents under his arm who would pass by and disappear in the street that led to the office of the *Yudenrat*.

"Father hasn't come back yet," Beyle muttered, more to herself than to the others. Her aged mother-in-law, who was sitting near the kitchen sorting plucked feathers into a patched bag, turned and asked, "What's that you're saying Beyle?"

"Nothing, *Shviger.*"

All at once there was a commotion in the corner where the two youngest children were playing. Dovidl was pulling a doll out of Sorke's hands and waving a stick at her. "When I order you to hand over the baby you must obey! Otherwise, I'll take you away too, and you'll be beaten into the bargain."

Beyle ran over to the children. "What's all this uproar about—what's going on here?"

"Mother, he's hitting me!" Sorke burst out.

"Let go of her this minute!" Beyle ordered. But eight year old Dovidl wouldn't let go, and kept on tugging at his sister's doll.

"We're playing the game of cursing, and in cursing, there's no mother around. In this game you must obey the police! If she won't hand over her baby then both she and the baby will have to go! See, here's my rifle," and he pointed to the stick.

"Tfu, may your game moulder and smoulder in some wretched wilderness! Throw away the stick this instant! And come here! Some game you've invented for yourselves!"

"But Mother, you saw what happened to our neighbour Malke, and to Shmerke-Yoysef's son? The police took her away along with her child—don't you remember?"

"In my house I won't allow such games, you hear? Such a big boy and he understands nothing! Go, go to your brother Lipe."

Whenever Beyle couldn't handle Dovidl she would turn him over to her oldest son. Lipe was the only one Dovidl would listen to.

Lipe was sitting at the table in the next room, writing. He neither fumed around nor uttered a single word. His mother came in and stood at his back waiting for him to help her rein in her unruly young one. Dovidl too was waiting. He had become suddenly quiet and was staring eagerly at his older brother. The pen in Lipe's hand moved quickly across the blank paper as if it were hurrying towards some inevitable goal where Lipe was only an accessory and the instrument of someone else's will.

Beyle's ears, always alert to the smallest sound, now heard an odd rustling like the swish of silk. Turning towards the sound she saw the open wardrobe, and between its doors her daughter Mirl taking out her dresses and trying them on one by one in front of the mirror.

"What bleak holiday are you celebrating today?"

"Oh Mother, I just felt like trying on my dresses."

Beyle gave her a searching glance as if she were some newly arrived stranger. For the last two years, living with constant anxiety and fear, she had begun to think of her children as a precious charge she must protect from all outside threat and danger. And in that same instant she recognized that Mirl, her fourteen-year-old daughter, had suddenly grown up and ripened into a young woman. Mirl's thin childish shoulders were now softly curved as if waiting to take on the burden of new and mysterious longings. Her brown gazelle's eyes were filled with a womanly acceptance of fate.

And as if she owed this burgeoning daughter something she could never repay, Beyle, like a bankrupt debtor, sat down and gave herself up to a wail of grief. Her bottled-up fear and dread of the unavoidable future now found its way through some obscure channel inside her, releasing a storm of tears. Beyle began to rock to and fro, her head in her arms, sobbing all the while as if her breast were being torn to pieces inside her.

The two children tiptoed into the kitchen and began to nose around like two kittens among the pots and pans. Sorke returned and pulled Mirl away from the clothes cupboard, "Come, let's stick a fork into the potatoes and see if they're done."

Dovidl ran to the door. "I'm going outside to find out what's taking Father so long."

Beyle was startled out of her trance. "Don't dare step out of this house! Do you want to cause, God forbid, a catastrophe?"

The dragging sound of feet was now heard on the stairs, climbing each stair slowly one at a time. Lipe folded his writing in his breast pocket and ran to open the outside door, which had been kept locked and bolted since the arrival of the Germans.

Father and son confronted each other. The son's eyes were full of questions, demanding to know what the father had learned and what, for the time being, would have to be kept hidden from the others.

The father bowed his head as if he himself were guilty for what was now happening, guilty for having taken a wife and for having brought children into the world—a wife and children he could no longer protect.

It took only one look at her husband for Beyle to realize there was no point in asking him anything.

The lines in Hersh-Lazar's face had grown deeper. They were etched in greyness, as if they had absorbed all the dust and debris of the street. His nose seemed to have grown longer and was as sharp as that of a corpse, while his usually neat and tidy dark beard was unkempt and dishevelled.

"Will you wash your hands now, Hersh-Lazar?"

"Yes, at once, and we'll sit down to eat."

They ate in silence. No-one paid attention to what and how much each spoonful held. They swallowed their food half-chewed. Even the children, already used to uncertainty and fear, felt a disaster was about to happen but dared not ask what. Something ominous was in the air.

Whenever a spoon accidentally struck the edge of a plate and made it ring, they were all startled and looked reproachfully away. Of them all, only the grandmother concentrated on her food as she brought each spoonful to her toothless gums.

The first to rise from the table was Hersh-Lazar. Wiping his moustache with the back of his hand, he began to pace back and forth with maddening regularity. When Beyle started to clear the table he signalled her—"Don't bother, Beyle."

She let her hands fall; they had suddenly become too heavy and she stood in front of her husband blocking his way and trying to stop him pacing the room.

"Have you heard anything more? Is it true what people are saying?"

"True, all true, Beyle." Her husband's voice sounded hoarse and muffled as if a thorn were stuck in his throat.

"Placards are posted everywhere—on all the buildings and fences. Every family must send one of its members within two hours. Do you realize what that means? Each family must choose its own victim. One of us must go, otherwise all of us will be taken. All of us, without exception! And," he added ironically, "the Germans are allowing us free choice!"

They were all stunned but no-one was surprised. You could expect anything from the Germans. Each one studied the others. Who, who would go? Go to the place from which there is no return?

Abruptly a wave of estrangement overwhelmed them. Each one could already see the victim in the other. Each one felt the enmity of the others. Who would be chosen and who would do the choosing? With what measure should they be measured, on what scales should they be weighed in order to decide who must die now, and who deserved to stay alive, at least for now?

"In that case," Lipe spoke with unusual calm without looking at the bowed heads. "In that case . . .", and he stopped in mid-sentence as if the weight of his just-now-uttered words were too heavy for their quaking limbs to bear.

"In that case . . .", all of them sat down. They all tried to find the lowest, most insignificant chair as if they intended to sit *shive* for their own inner selves.

Beyle seized the two youngest as if she could hide them in her own two hands, or build walls around them which no enemy could breach.

The grown-ups had begun to calculate the years each had already lived and the years still promised. They added up the lines in every face and counted the gnarled veins on the back of every hand.

The father mustn't go, that was clear. He was the provider, the breadwinner. And the mother, definitely not. What would become of the children without her? As for Lipe, what had he tasted of life in his four-and-twenty years, the last two darkened by the German occupation? Let him consider carefully. Maybe he should quickly steal away and be done with it. His mother would wail and tear her hair, his father would agonize while saying *kadesh*, and Dovidl would miss him day and night without understanding why his Lipe had disappeared.

But at first they would all breathe easier because he would have released them from the need to mourn their own lost souls.

In his mind Lipe was already bidding them all adieu. Tomorrow he would be gone. Everything would remain just as it was except that he would no longer be among them. He would no longer see the sun, the sky, or the old clock on the bureau. He touched his breast pocket and removed his watch and the money he kept there, and unobserved, pushed them underneath the big clock, folding a few bank notes into the pages he had been writing. It was a letter to Elke; his last letter. He would have to find a Polish messenger since it was forbidden to receive letters from the ghetto. Elke was living on the other side as a Pole with false aryan papers, and she had recently let him know that she was preparing similar papers for him, complete with seals and signatures. Together they would go to one of the big cities where it would be easier to hide and lose themselves in the Polish crowds.

Was there anyone who should go in his place? What about the grandmother, his old *bobe*? As Lipe's glance searched for the grandmother it met his parents' eyes. They had already added up her years, years that had fallen as gradually as leaves from a tree in autumn, leaving its trunk naked and vulnerable. But no-one dared utter such thoughts aloud, no-one dared to say "go" or to become the judge of her last few ragged years. As their eyes ate into her, the old lady began to droop and hunker down into her chair, as if she would have liked to dissolve and become part of the chair. She wanted to become so rooted in the bit of ground under her that no-one would ever be able to dig her out. In that moment the senses of the others became suddenly keener, and more sensitive. Each one's thoughts lay open to the others in these moments of heightened perception. Only the grandmother's thoughts remained closed to them, as closed as her half-blind extinguished eyes. She had sealed all the avenues to her inmost self in order to ward off this prelude to death. She suddenly felt isolated in the circle of her family—beside the son she had given birth to and cared for, beside her own flesh and blood. Even her son's eyes sought her out, and pointed to her. And because of it she would resist with all the strength of her being. There was no-one to take her part, no-one to give her a loving look across the wall of separation. When you know you will be missed, it is easier to die.

They imagine it's less difficult for old people to die. Maybe so. But only if death comes in its proper time and place, in your own bed. But to go forth and meet death willingly, carrying your bundle of worn-out bones! Quiet, hold everything, she's not ready yet—she still has to go back over her life, she still has to remember it once more from the beginning, starting with the time she was a child in her mother's house. She too had been a child just like her son and grandchildren. She too had sat on her mother's lap just like Sorke on Beyle's; "Mother, Mother," she murmured through blue lips as if she would call her back from the world of the dead. "Mother," she called, just as she used to do in her childhood when she was afraid of being spanked. She had almost forgotten what her mother looked like—her features had faded, and were rusted with time. Two big tears rolled from her closed eyes and fell into the net of wrinkles covering her face.

And later—she pictured herself as a bride. She had only seen her bridegroom David once, at the time of the betrothal. Even then, all her dreams were centred on him. When they began preparing her wedding clothes she had insisted on the best of everything, on the most costly materials. She chose an iridescent blue silk shot through with roses woven into the cloth. She had wanted to please her bridegroom. Her wedding dress had hung in the cupboard until recently. She hadn't let anyone touch it. It was only during the last few months that she had let them make it over for Mirl, because Mirl looks like her. When she looks at Mirl she sees herself as a girl.

The clock struck once and then twice. Everyone suddenly came to life. Soon, soon. Until now they had all been waiting for something to happen. Some miracle. And now there was less than an hour left.

Mirl drew herself up to her full height. She whipped her coat off its hanger and stood in the middle of the room.

"I'm leaving."

All heads turned.

She stood there in the made-over iridescent silk dress she had forgotten to take off when her mother scolded her for trying it on. Or perhaps she just enjoyed wearing it. Whether the dress made her look older and more grown-up, or whether it was the stubborn expression on her face, it seemed to everyone that Mirl had grown taller in the past few hours.

"Where—what kind of going?" This from her father with his red-rimmed bloodshot eyes.

"You know very well where. . . . Goodbye everybody." And she was at the door.

With a single leap her father was beside her, holding her sleeve.

"Get back this minute. If you don't there'll be trouble! Do you hear?"

As Mirl struggled with her father there was a sharp whistling noise as the ancient silk of her sleeve split and tore.

Everyone looked on but no-one moved, neither to stop the father, nor to help Mirl. With one hand Hersh-Lazar was holding Mirl, and with the other he was undoing his belt.

No-one understood what was happening. Was their father intending to beat Mirl now of all times? His favourite child against whom he had never before raised a hand? The one for whom he always bought special gifts—for her rather than for the two youngest? It could only be due to the confusion and turmoil they all felt, the kind they had suppressed with all their might. Now it had grown and festered in their father like a boil that ripens and finally bursts.

At last he had the belt in his hand and was twirling it above Mirl's head like a lasso. He lowered it over her shoulders then slid it down to her waist and tightened it as if she were a stook of wheat in a field. He tested the belt several times to see if it was tight enough. Only then did he grasp the loose end, and, dragging Mirl like a trussed-up calf, he led her to the table and fastened the belt to the table's leg post. Tying a knot at the other end he pulled the belt through the buckle with his teeth, then he wiped his forehead and sat down with his hands on his knees and drew a few harsh choppy breaths.

Mirl was on her knees leaning against the table leg where her father had left her. She was motionless, completely drained by the scene of the last few minutes. For the first time in her young life she had aspired to something brave—let it be death—so what? She had gone forth to meet it like a bride her bridegroom. From early morning she had been preparing for this gesture. And now she had been shamed and humiliated. And her father, her darling father, who knew her better than anyone else, including her mother—was the one who had shamed her. He wouldn't let her make her sacrifice. It was all very well, it seems, for Isaac to be sacrificed, but not for her. And his father, Abraham was himself the one who brought him—he had taken him by the hand knowing full well what God demanded. And here, all of them—yes, she saw it, she knew, all of them wanted the grandmother to go. Did grandmother have the strength to drag herself to faraway places? And what was the sacrifice of an old person worth, since the old person would have to die soon anyway?

For the first time in her life Mirl felt a deep hatred for her father. She tried angrily to free herself so she could at least stand up, but she had forgotten about the belt which now cut more and more into her body. She fell back and lay stretched out across the threshold, her head buried in her arms.

A band of light from the window came to rest at her feet. As the light fell on her the iridescent blue silk interwoven with rose-coloured flowers shone with new life. The room had grown silent again, except for the buzzing of a single fly as it searched for a quiet spot to have its last wintry sleep.

All heads were bowed. Let whatever was to happen, happen. Let the parting be dictated by some external force, by fate. And if all of them had to go instead of just one, then so be it. If God above willed it, if he could let it happen, they would accept it gladly.

Only the ticking of the clock divided the silence as its hands moved inexorably towards the appointed hour.

Abruptly the father turned; all eyes followed the direction of his glance. The grandmother's chair was empty. Everyone was so absorbed in his own thoughts that no-one had noticed her going. Where had she gone? How did she leave the house so quietly that no-one had heard her? Not one of them had heard her. It must have happened only a few minutes ago.

Everyone's eyes now searched the corners of the room. Suddenly a shadow appeared on the glass pane of the door that led to the vestibule. As the shadow came closer it gradually filled the entire window. All eyes followed it—yes it was the grandmother in her old black cape, the one she wore on holidays. Under one arm she carried a small pouch with her prayer book, while with the other arm she slowly unfastened the chain on the outer door. Soon the door closed and swung back on its hinges.

None of them left their places. Not one of them called her back. All remained seated, frozen into place. Only their heads moved and bowed lower and lower as if their rightful place lay there at their feet with the dirt and dust of the threshold.

*Arnošt Lustig 1926–*     Born and educated in Prague, Lustig has been
a tailor's apprentice, decorator, radio correspondent
(1948–1968), and screenwriter (1960–1968). In
1968, when the Soviet army invaded his homeland, he left and arrived in the United States in 1970.
He taught literature at American University in
Washington D.C. for many years. A bestselling author
in Czech, many of his books are well-known in English as well, including two short story collections,
*Night and Hope* (Czech, 1958; English, 1962 and
1985) and *Diamonds of the Night* (Czech, 1958; English, 1962 and 1986), and *A Prayer for Katarina
Horovitzova* (Czech, 1964; English, 1973 and 1985).
All three won numerous prizes and became the
basis for Czech films for which Lustig wrote the
screenplays in the 1960s.

Lustig had spent most of his adolescent years in
Nazi camps. In 1942 he was sent to Terezin (Theresienstadt) and from there to Auschwitz in 1944,
where both of his parents perished. Early in 1945 he
escaped from a prisoner transport en route from
Buchenwald to Dachau. He went into hiding in
Prague until the Czech uprising two months later.

In 1980 and 1986 he received the National
Jewish Book Award for fiction, and in 1986 an
Emmy from the National Academy of Television
Arts and Sciences. His stories and novels are available in some twenty languages. *A Prayer,* his most
widely translated story, combines two actual events:
the blackmailing of twenty Jewish prisoners, own-
ers of large accounts in foreign banks, by the Nazis
and a revolt staged at the gas chamber door by a
beautiful Polish actress.

# THE LEMON

Ervin was scowling. His feline eyes, set in a narrow skull, shifted nervously and his lips were pressed angrily into a thin blue arch. He hardly answered Chicky's greeting. Under his arm he was clutching a pair of pants rolled into a bundle.

"What'll you give me for these?" he demanded, unrolling the trousers, which were made of a thin nut-brown cloth. The seat and knees were shiny.

Chicky grinned, "Ye gods, where did you pick those up?" He inspected the cuffs and seams. "Jesus Christ himself wouldn't be caught dead in such a low-class shroud."

Ervin ignored the sneer. "I'm only interested in one thing, Chicky, and that's what I can get for them." He spoke fast.

"Listen, not even a resurrected Jesus Christ on the crummiest street in Lodz would wear a pair of pants like that," Chicky went on with the air of an expert.

He noticed the twitching in Ervin's jaw. "Well, the knees still look pretty good, though," he reconsidered. "Where did you get them?"

It was cloudy and the sun was like a big translucent ball. The barn swallows were flying low. Ervin looked up at the sky and at the swallows swooping toward unseen nests. He'd been expecting Chicky to ask that and he'd prepared himself on the way.

He displayed his rather unimpressive wares again. He knew he had to go through with it now, even if the pants were full of holes. The skin on Chicky's face was thin, almost transparent; he had a small chin and rheumy eyes.

A member of the local security force came around the corner.

"Hey, you little brats," he snapped, casting a quick glance at their skinny bodies, "go on, get out of here!"

They turned around. Fortunately, a battered yellow Jewish streetcar came along just then and diverted the security guard's attention.

"Don't tell me it's a big secret," Chicky said. "Anybody can easily see those pants belonged to some grown-up. What're you so scared of?"

"What should I be scared of?" Ervin retorted, clutching the trousers close. "I've got to cash in on them, that's all."

"They're rags."

"They're English material, they're no rags."

"Well, I might see what I can do for you," Chicky relented. "But on a fifty-fifty basis."

Ervin handed over the bundle, and Chicky took a piece of twine from his pocket and tied up the trousers to suit himself, making a fancy knot. He looked up and down the street.

The security guard was at the other end of the street with his back to the boys. They were on the corner of an alley which hadn't had a name for a long time. It was intermittently paved with cobblestones. People hurried on; Ervin and Chicky moved closer to the wall. The streetcar now took a different route. The next stop was out of sight.

Chicky, the smaller of the two, the one with the shaved head, was clutching the brown checkered pants under his arm as Ervin had done.

"But don't you go having second thoughts, Ervin. Don't let me go ahead and work my ass off and then . . ."

"My dad died," Ervin said.

"Hm . . . well," Chicky remarked. "It's taken a lot of people these last few weeks," he observed.

"Now there's only one important thing, and that's how you're going to cash in on those pants."

It occurred to Chicky that Ervin might want a bigger share of the take because the pants had been his father's.

"Who's your customer, Chicky?"

"Old Moses," Chicky lied.

"Do I know him?"

"Little short guy."

"First time I've heard of him."

"He just comes up as high as my waist. He's absolutely the biggest bastard in town. But he kind of likes me. Maybe it's because I remind him of somebody."

"He's interested in pants?"

"He's interested in absolutely everything, Ervin."

"Funny I never heard of him."

"Well, I guess I'd better be going," Chicky said.

"What do you suppose your friend would give me for these pants?" Ervin asked.

"Give *us*, you mean," Chicky corrected.

"Anyway, go on and see what you can do," said Ervin, dodging a direct answer.

"He might cough up some bread in exchange for these pants. Or a couple ounces of flour." He unrolled the trousers again. "Like I told you, the knees are still pretty good and the lining's passable. The fly isn't stained yellow like it is in old men's pants. In that respect, these trousers are in good shape and that tells you something about the person who wore them. I'll try to get as much as I can for them, Ervin." He bared his teeth in a tiger grin.

"I need a lemon, Chicky."

"What about a big hunk of nothing?"

"I'm not joking," Ervin said curtly. "All right, then half a lemon, if you can't get a whole one." The expression on Chicky's face changed.

"You know what *I* need, Ervin?" he began. "I need an uncle in Florida where the sun shines all year long and trained fish dance in the water. I need an uncle who would send me an affidavit and money for my boat ticket so I could go over there and see those fish and talk to them." He paused. "A *lemon*! Listen, Ervin, where do you get those ideas, huh, tell me, will you?"

Chicky gazed up into the sky and imagined a blue and white ocean liner and elegant fish poking their noses up out of the silver water, smiling at him, wishing him bon voyage.

Swallows, white-breasted and sharp-winged, darted across the sullen sky. Chicky whistled at them, noticing that Ervin didn't smile.

"That lemon's not for me," said Ervin.

"Where do you think you are? Where do you think Old Moses'd get a lemon? It's harder to find a lemon in this place than . . ."

But he couldn't think of a good comparison.

Chicky's expression changed to one of mute refusal. He thought to himself, Ervin is something better than I am. His father died, Ervin took his trousers, so now he can talk big about lemons. Chicky's mouth dropped sourly.

"It's for Miriam," Ervin said flatly. "If she doesn't get a lemon, she's finished."

"What's wrong with her?"

"I'm not sure . . ."

"Just in general. I know you're no doctor."

"Some kind of vitamin deficiency, but it's real bad."

"Are her teeth falling out?"

"The doctor examined her this morning when he came to see my mother. The old man was already out in the hall. There's no point talking about it."

"It's better to be healthy, I grant you that," Chicky agreed. He rolled up the pants again. "At best, I may be able to get you a piece of bread." He tied the twine into a bow again. "If there were four of us getting a share of this rag, Ervin—your mom, your sister, and you and me, nobody would get anything out of it in the end."

"If I didn't need it, I'd keep my mouth shut," Ervin repeated.

"I can tell we won't see eye to eye, even on Judgment Day."

A Polish streetcar rattled and wheezed along behind them. The town was divided into Polish and Jewish sectors. The streetcar line always reminded Ervin that there were still people who could move around and take a streetcar ride through the ghetto, even if it was just along a corridor of barbed wire with sentries in German uniforms so nobody would get any ideas about jumping off—or on.

"It's got to be something more than that. Everybody's got a vitamin deficiency here. What if it's something contagious, Ervin, and here I am fussing around with these pants of yours?" He gulped back his words. "And I've already caught whatever it is?"

"Nobody knows *what* it is," said Ervin.

"Well, I'm going, Ervin . . ."

"When are you coming back?"

"What if we both went to see what we could do?"

"No," said Ervin quietly.

"Why not?"

Ervin knew what it was he had been carrying around inside him on his way to meet Chicky. *It was everything that had happened when he'd stripped off those trousers. His father's body had begun to stiffen and it felt strange. He kept telling himself it was all right, that it didn't matter.* Instead, he kept reciting the alphabet and jingles.

*This was your father a living person. And now he's dead.* Chicky was the only one he could have talked to.

"I haven't got a dad or a mother even," Chicky said suddenly. A grin flickered. "That's my tough luck. They went up the chimney long ago."

The sky above the low rooftops was like a shallow, stagnant sea.

Chicky lingered, uncertain.

*It was just his body,* Ervin told himself. *Maybe memory is like the earth and sky and ocean like all the seashores and the mountains like a fish swimming up out of the water to some island poking out its big glassy eyes just to see how things look. Like that fish Chicky had been talking about. Nobody knows, not even the smartest rabbi in the world. And not the bad rabbis either. But while he was taking his father's trousers off he knew what he was doing. He wasn't thinking about his father, but about an old Italian tune he used to sing and which Miriam loved. Father sang off key but it sounded pretty. Prettier than a lot of other things. It was about love and flowers and his father had learned it during the war when he fought in the Piave campaign.*

*He already had the trousers halfway off. And he knew the reasons he loved his father would never go away.*

The swallows flew quietly in low, skidding arches. Ervin looked around to see how the weather was, and finally his gaze dropped. The rounded cobblestones melted away.

"All right then, I'll bring it around to your place later," Chicky said.

"By when do you think you can do it?"

"In two or three hours."

"But, Chicky . . ."

Chicky turned and disappeared around the corner as another streetcar came clanging along.

Now Ervin could think ahead, instead of going back to what had been on his mind before. He set off down the alley in the opposite direction, toward the house where he and his family had been living for two years.

The tiny shops upstairs and in the basement had been hardly more than market stalls which had been converted into apartments for several families.

*He remembered how he discovered that his father no longer wore underpants. The stringy thighs. The darkened penis, the reddish pubic hair. Rigid legs. Scars on the shin bone. His father had gotten those scars when he was wounded fighting in Italy.*

*Then that old tune came back to him, sung off key again, the song from somewhere around Trieste that he and Miriam had liked so much.*

*Hell, who needed those pants more than they did? Father had probably traded in his underpants long ago. Who knows for what?*

*So Father died, he is no more,* Ervin thought to himself.

He reached home, one of the dwarfish shops where he and his mother and sister lived.

The corrugated iron shutter over the entry had broken a spring, so it wouldn't go all the way up or down. He could see a mouse.

He squeezed through a crack in the wall. Mother was scared of mice, so he'd repaired the wall boards through which the mice came in and out. Pressing against the wall, Ervin was suddenly aware of his body and that reminded him of his father again.

"It's me," he called out.

It had occurred to him that there was nothing to be proud of, being unable to cash in on the trousers *himself.* (Even so, his mother must have known what he had done.) He had to take a deep breath and adjust to the musty smell in the room. It was easier to get used to the difference between the light outside and the darkness inside.

Mother greeted him with a snore. She had long since lost any resemblance to the woman who had come here with him. He peered around him. He had been almost proud of having such a pretty mother. On top of everything else, her legs had swollen. She hadn't been able to get out of bed for the past eight weeks. She'd waited on everything for Father, and now for him.

"Where've you been?" his mother asked.

"Out," he answered.

He crawled into his corner where he could turn his back on everything, including his father who lay out in the hall wrapped in a blanket. Miriam, too, was curled up next to the wall, so he couldn't see her face. He heard her coughing.

He bundled his legs into the tattered rug that used to be his father's. *He'd always had the worst covers. He didn't want to admit he was a loser, and as long as he was able to give up something for them, maybe it wasn't so obvious. The dim light made its way through the thin fabric of dust and dampness and the breath of all three of them. When he lost, he put on the smile of a beautiful woman. He was making a point of being a graceful loser. As if it made any difference to anybody except himself.*

"Did you find anything?" his mother asked.

"No . . ."

"What are we going to do?"

"Maybe this afternoon," he said, his face to the wall.

"Miriam," his mother called out to his sister. "Don't cough. It wears you out."

"Mirrie," Ervin said, "Miriam." She didn't answer.

"Can't she speak?" he asked his mother.

"It wears her out," she repeated. "You really ought to look around and see if you can't scrape up something."

"There's no point so early in the afternoon."

"You ought to try at least," his mother insisted.

*That's how it used to be with Father, Ervin recalled. She always kept sending him somewhere. But Father had gone out just as he'd done now, and like him, he almost felt better outside; he also may have believed that just by going out he was getting back in shape, that he'd be able to do what he used to do in the beginning. Then Mother started saying things couldn't get any worse. She never went wrong about that. That's because there is no limit to what's "worse." The limit was in his father. And now Ervin had to find it, just like his father.*

"I already told you, I can't find anything just now," he said.

"You ought to go out and try, dear," his mother went on. *This was what Father had had to put up with.* "You see how Miriam looks, don't you?" his mother persisted.

"I can see her," he answered. "But I can't find anything now."

"This can't help but finish badly."

"Oh, cut it out. I'm not going anywhere," Ervin declared flatly. "I've already tried. There's nothing to be had."

"For God's sake, listen to me," his mother cried sharply. "Go on out and *try.* Miriam hasn't had a thing to eat today."

The stains on the plaster were close to his eyes. The room was damp, and it almost swallowed up the sound of his mother's voice and his own. The dampness didn't bother him, though. He could hear faint scratching noises in the walls.

The boards he'd put up didn't help much. He almost envied mice. Just as he'd felt envy for trees when he was outside. Ervin suddenly wished he could catch one of those little animals. Pet it, then kill it. Father had told them about the time they were besieged during the First World War and the soldiers ate mice.

To kill and caress. Or simply kill, so you're not always bothered by something or somebody. So it is—to be killed or to kill.

But if Chicky was right, a trained mouse should get along great.

"I wonder if I shouldn't air out the room a bit," he said into the silence.

"Have they been here already?" he asked after a while.

"No."

"They're taking their time about it."

Now, in her turn, his mother was silent. "Who knows how many calls they have to make today?"

"Why don't you want to go out, child?"

"I will. In a while," he answered. "It doesn't make any sense now, though."

"Ervin, child . . ."

The room was quiet, the silence broken only by Miriam's coughing.

Ervin put his head between his knees, trying to guess where the mouse was and what it was doing. He stuck his fingers in his ears. The scratching continued. *So Father's still lying out there in the hall. He doesn't have any pants and Mother doesn't even know it. He's naked but that doesn't bother his old Piave scars. Mother could use that extra blanket now,* he thought to himself. *But he left it around his father for some reason which he didn't know himself. So I don't have the feeling that I've stolen everything from him, including our second tattered blanket,* he thought to himself. *It was lucky she couldn't get out of bed now, even if she wanted to. Her legs couldn't support her. She'd see that Father had no pants. They'll probably take him along with the blanket. What the hell? They were certainly taking their time. They should have been here an hour ago. It was a regulation of the Commanding officer and the self-government committee that corpses must be removed promptly. Everybody was scared of infection. The corpse collectors were kept busy. They probably didn't miss a chance to take anything they could get. Everybody knew they stole like bluejays.*

Miriam would probably have been afraid to sleep with a dead person in the same room, even if it was Father, Ervin decided.

"There's some rabbi here who works miracles, I heard," his mother said. "Why don't you go and see him?"

"What would I say to him?"

"Tell him that I'm your mother."

"I don't have any idea where he lives. And even if he could perform a miracle, he certainly won't put himself out to come over here. He waits for people to come to him."

"I feel so weak," his mother told him.

*Suddenly it occurred to him that maybe his mother would have been better off lying out in the hall beside his father. It would be better for Miriam too.* Mother's gestures and the things she told him were getting more and more indecisive.

"Why don't you want to go anywhere?" Mother said.

"Because there's no point," he replied, "I'd be wearing myself out in vain. I'll find something, but not until this afternoon."

"Miriam won't last long. She can hardly talk anymore."

"Miriam?" Ervin called out.

Miriam was silent and his mother added: "You know how it was with Daddy."

"He'd been sick for a long time."

And when her son said nothing, she tried again. "Ervin . . ."

"It doesn't make any sense," he growled. "I'm not going anywhere now. Not till later."

He sat quite still for a while, staring at the blotches and shadows moving on the wall. Rabbis say your soul is in your blood, but some kids and old people say it's in your shadow. There are a lot of lies around. Who cares where your soul is. Maybe under your dirty fingernails? Maybe when you have diarrhea? He could hear mice scampering across the floor toward the mattress where Mother and Miriam were lying. Mother screeched, then Miriam.

Ervin was bored.

It might be more comfortable and pleasant to wait outside. But there was something in here that made him stay. He remembered how he and Chicky used to play poker. They always pretended there was some stake. That made it more interesting. You could bluff and pretend to have a full house when you didn't even have a pair. But there was always the chance—which they'd invented—that you might win something.

He remembered how he and Miriam used to go ice-skating. She was little and her knees were wobbly. He'd drag her around the rink for a while, then take her into the restaurant where you could have a cup of tea for ten hellers. Miriam's nose would be running, and she'd stay there for an hour with her tea so he could have a good time out on the ice. Once his mother had given them money to buy two ham sandwiches. His arches always ached when he'd been skating. So did Miriam's.

*If they'd come for Father—and he wished it were over with—he wouldn't have to worry that the body would start to decay or that his mother would find out he didn't have any pants on.*

"Why don't you go out and see that miracle rabbi?"

"Because it doesn't make any sense."

At first, Mother only had trouble with her legs. And Miriam hadn't coughed *quite* as much.

The sentries along the streetcar line always looked comfortably well-fed, with nice round bellies, as though they had everything they needed. When these sentries passed through the ghetto, they acted as though victory was already theirs, even if they might lose this little skirmish with the Jews. *Daddy once said that this was their world, whether they won or lost.*

Ervin's stomach growled. It was like the noise the mice made. He stretched and waited for his mother to start nagging him again. But she didn't, and it was almost as though something were missing. *He didn't want to think about his father's body wrapped in that blanket out in the hall. Daddy had been sick long enough. He was certainly better off this way.*

After a while, he wasn't sure whether his stomach was making the noise or the mice. His mother groaned. He thought about a nap. Just then he heard someone banging on the iron shutter. He got up.

"Well, I'll be on my way," he said.

"Come back soon," his mother replied. "Come back safe and sound."

"Sure," he answered. As he approached the shutter, he asked, "Is that you, Chicky?"

"No," a voice replied. "It's the miracle-working rabbi with a pitcher of milk."

Ervin pushed the broken shutter and slipped through. It was easy. His body was nothing but skin and bones now. He had a long narrow skull, with bulging greenish blue eyes. He could feel his mother's eyes on him as he squeezed out. Outside in the courtyard he pulled down his shirt and his bones cracked. Chicky was waiting on the sidewalk.

"So?" asked Ervin.

"Even with those stains on the seat," Chicky started.

"What're you trying to tell me?"

"He gave me more than I expected." He smiled slyly and happily.

Chicky produced a piece of bread, carefully wrapped in a dirty scarf. He handed it to Ervin. "This is for you. I already ate my share on the way, like we agreed."

"Just this measly piece?"

"Maybe you forgot those stains on the seat of those pants."

"Such a little hunk?"

"What else did you expect, hm? Or maybe you think I ought to come back with a whole moving van full of stuff for one pair of pants?"

Chicky wiped his nose, offended.

"You just better not forget about those stains on the seat. Besides, almost everybody's selling off clothes now."

Ervin took the bread. Neither one mentioned the lemon. Ervin hesitated before crawling back into the room, half-hoping Chicky was going to surprise him. Chicky liked to show off.

"Wait here for me," he blurted. "I'll be right back."

Ervin squinted through the dimness to where his mother lay on the mattress.

"Here, catch," he said maliciously. He threw the bread at her. It struck her face, bounced, and slid away. He could hear her groping anxiously over the blanket and across the floor. As soon as she had grabbed it, she began to wheeze loudly.

She broke the bread into three pieces in the dark.

"Here, this is for you," she said.

"I don't want it."

"Why not?" she asked. He heard something else in her voice. "Ervin?"

He stared at the cracks in the wall where the mice crawled through. He was afraid his mother was going to ask him again.

"My God, Ervin, don't you hear me?"

"I've already had mine," he said.

"How much did you take?"

"Don't worry, just my share." He felt mice paws pattering across the tops of his shoes. Again, he had the urge to catch one and throw it on the bed.

"Miriam," his mother called.

Ervin left before he could hear his sister's reply. He knew what his mother was thinking.

Chicky was waiting, his hands in his pockets, leaning against the wall. He was picking his teeth. He was looking up at the sky trying to guess which way the clouds were going. There must be wind currents that kept changing.

For a while the two boys strolled along in silence. Then just for something to say, Chicky remarked: "You know what that little crook told me? He says you can't take everything away from everybody."

*Everything melted together: father, bread, mother, sister, the moment he was imagining what Chicky might bring back for them. Mice.*

"He says we can *hope* without *believing*." Chicky laughed, remembering something else.

"Do you feel like bragging all day?"

"If you could see into me the way I can see into you, you could afford to talk. When my dad went up the chimney, I told myself I was still lucky to have my mother. And when I lost Mother, I told myself that at least I was lucky to have a brother left. He was weaker than a fly. And I said to myself, it's great to have your health at least."

Ervin was silent, so Chicky continued: "Still, we're pretty lucky, Ervin. Even if that's what my little businessman says too. Don't get the idea the world's going to stop turning just because one person in it is feeling miserable at this particular moment. You'd be exaggerating."

They didn't talk about it anymore. They could walk along like this together, so close their elbows or shoulders almost touched, and sometimes as they took a step together, their hips. The mice and the chameleon were gone; Chicky was really more like a barn swallow. Chicky was just slightly crooked. The thought suddenly put him in a better mood. Like when the sun came out or when he looked at a tree or the blue sky.

"He's full of wise sayings," Chicky resumed. "According to him, we have to pay for everything. And money and *things* aren't the worst way to pay."

"Aw, forget it. You're sticking as close to me as a fag."

"What about you?" Chicky's little face stretched.

"They haven't come to get him yet, the bastards."

"I can probably tell you why," Chicky declared. "Would you believe it, my dad's beard grew for two days after he was already dead?"

"Do you ever think you might have been a swallow?"

"Say, you're really outdoing yourself today," Chicky remarked. "But if you want to know something, I *have* thought about it."

Ervin looked up into the sky again. He might have known Chicky would have ideas like that. Ervin himself sometimes had the feeling that he was up there being blown around among the raindrops when there was a thunderstorm. The sky looked like an iron shutter. Sometimes he could also imagine himself jumping through the sky, using his arms and legs to steer with.

"Ervin . . .", Chicky interrupted.

"What?"

"That old guy gave me a tremendous piece of advice."

"So be glad."

"No, Ervin, I mean it."

"Who's arguing?"

"Aren't you interested? He asked me if your old man had anything else."

"What else could he have?"

"He was just hinting."

"These have been hungry days for us. That crooked second-hand man of yours, his brains are going soft. I hope he can tell the difference between dogs and cats."

"Considering we're not their people, Ervin, what he told me wasn't just talk."

"My dad was the cleanest person in this whole dump," said Ervin.

"He didn't mean that and neither did I, Ervin."

"What's with all this suspense?"

"Just say you're not interested and we'll drop it," Chicky said.

"Come on, spill it, will you? What *did* he mean then?"

"Maybe there was a ring or something?"

"Do you really think he'd have let Mother and Miriam die right in front of his eyes if he'd had anything like a *ring*?"

"He wasn't talking only about a ring. He meant gold."

"Dad had to turn over everything he had that was even gilded."

"He hinted at it only after I tried to explain to him about the lemon."

"You know how it was. Mother doesn't have anything either."

"He only hinted at it when I told him how important it was for you to have that lemon, Ervin."

"Well, what was it he hinted, then?" Ervin noticed the expectant look on Chicky's face.

"He hinted that it wasn't impossible, but only in exchange for something made of pure gold. And that he didn't care what it was."

"Don't be a bastard," said Ervin slowly, "Forget it. My dad didn't have anything like that. Go on, get lost."

"He even indicated exactly *what* and *how*."

"Look, come on—kindly spill it," Ervin said with irritation. *Once again he saw his father lying there wrapped in the blanket. It flooded through him in a dark tide like when his mother didn't believe that he hadn't taken more than his share of the bread. He'd known right from the start what Chicky was talking about.*

Ervin didn't say anything.

"Gold teeth, for instance. It's simply something in the mouth he doesn't need anymore, something nobody needs except maybe you and me."

Ervin remained silent.

"Well, I wasn't the one who said anything about a lemon," he concluded.

Ervin stopped and so did Chicky. Then Ervin turned and looked him up and down, eyes bulging.

"Aw, cut it out," Chicky said wearily. "Don't look at me as though I killed your dad."

Suddenly Ervin slapped him. Chicky's face was small and triangular, tapering off crookedly at the top. It was very obvious because his head was shaved. Then Ervin slapped him again and began to punch his face and chest. When his fist struck Chicky's Adam's apple, Ervin could feel how fragile everything about him was.

*Again he saw himself stripping those brown checkered trousers off his father's body. The undertakers would be coming along any minute. [They should have been here long ago.] He thought of how he'd managed to do that before they came and how he'd probably manage to do even this if he wanted to. And he knew that he couldn't have swallowed that piece of bread even if his mother had given it to him without those second thoughts of hers.* He kept pounding his fists into Chicky, and it was as if he were striking at himself and his mother. *He kept telling himself that his father was dead anyway and that it didn't matter much and that it didn't have any bearing on the future either.*

Then he felt everything slowing down. Chicky began to fight back. Ervin got in two fast punches, one on the chin, the other in the belly. Chicky hit Ervin twice before people gathered and tried to break it up, threatening to call the security guards.

Ervin picked himself up off the sidewalk as fast as he could. He shook himself like a dog and went home through the courtyard.

"Ervin?" his mother called out. "Is that you?"

"Yeah," he answered.

"Did you find anything else?"

He was shivering as he sometimes did when he was cold because he'd loaned his blanket to his mother or Miriam.

"Mirrie . . . ," he tried.

He bundled himself up into the rug. He was glad Chicky had hit him back. It was hard to explain why. It was different from wanting to catch a mouse and kill it. He touched his cheek and chin, fingering the swollen places. Again he waited for his mother to say something. But she didn't. Mother only knows as much as I tell her, he said to himself. Mother's quite innocent, Ervin decided. Despite everything she's still innocent. Would she have been able to do what she had criticized him for? He wished she'd say something, give at least an echo. He thought of Miriam. For a moment he could see her, tall and slender, her breasts and blond hair.

The twilight began to melt into the dampness of the cellar. The spider webs disappeared in the darkness. He wished they'd muffle the edge of his mother's voice. He waited for Miriam's cough. The silence was like a muddy path where nobody wants to walk. *And his father was still lying out there in the hall.*

*When someone dies,* Ervin thought to himself, *it means not expecting, not worrying about anything, not hoping for something that turns out to be futile. It means not forcing yourself into something you don't really want, while you go on behaving as though you did. It means not being dependent on anybody or anything. It means being rid of what's bothering you. It's like when you close your eyes and see things and people in your own way.*

*That idea of a path leading from the dead to the living and back again is just a lot of foolishness I thought up by myself. To be dead means to expect nothing, not to expect somebody to say something, not to wait for someone's voice. Not to stare enviously after a streetcar going somewhere from somewhere else.*

He looked around. Miriam had begun to cough again. She's coughing almost gently, he thought to himself. She probably doesn't have enough strength left to cough anymore.

*My God, that lying, thieving, sly old man, that bastard who's fed for six thousand years on Jewish wisdom and maybe would for another half an hour—but maybe not even that long. That dirty louse, full of phony maxims and dreams as complicated as clockwork, lofty as a rose, rank as an onion, who perhaps wasn't quite as imaginary as I wanted to think he was, judging from Chicky's descriptions which made him sound as though he'd swallowed all the holy books. That slimy crook with his miserable messages, that you have to pay for everything and that money and things aren't the most precious currency. But he also said you can't take everything away from everybody, as though he wanted to confuse you by contradicting himself in the same breath. Where did he get those ideas?*

"No, I don't have anything," he said suddenly, as if he knew his mother was still waiting for an answer.

He heard her sigh. From his sister's bed he heard a stifled cough. (She's probably ashamed of coughing by now.)

*Nothing's plaguing Father anymore either. Not even the craving for a bowl of soup. He wasn't looking forward anymore to seeing Ervin dash out onto the field in a freshly laundered uniform and shiny football boots, which he took care of, in front of crowds of people waiting for entertainment and thrills and a chance to yell their lungs out. If they come for Father now, they'll do just what Chicky said they would. Anyway, the undertakers themselves do it to the old people. He remembered his father's smile which got on his mother's nerves.*

He stared into the darkness. His mother was bandaging her swollen legs. Her eyes were very bright. She's probably feverish, he thought. She made a few inexplicable gestures. *What if the rabbis are right and there is some afterwards? Then his father must be able to see him. Where do you suppose he really is,* Ervin wondered, *and where am I? Does anybody know? Inwardly he tried to smile at his father. It would be nice if I could really smile at him. To be on the safe side, Ervin tried smiling at his father again.*

"I'm going out and take another look around," he said.

Mother ceased her strange movements. "Where do you want to go in the dark?"

"I want to have a look at something."

"Be careful, child."

He went out into the hall and the place he had avoided before, so he wouldn't have to look at the wall beside which his father's body was still lying. He was squeezing through the crack in the wall. For a short while an insurance agent had lived in the corner shop. *But this isn't your father anymore,* he told himself; *he was only until yesterday. Now there is nothing but a weight and the task of carrying it away,* he reminded himself immediately. *But I'll think of him only in good ways. And Mother and Miriam will think about him as if nothing's happened.*

He threw off the old blanket. He closed his eyes for a second. I won't be able to eat very much, he realized, as though he wanted to convince himself that this was the only difference it would make. Everything moved stiffly. He had to turn the head and open its mouth. He grabbed it by the chin and hair and that was how he managed. He couldn't remember exactly which tooth it was. He tried one after another. He was hurrying. He didn't want Chicky and the men with the coffins to catch him at it. Instead, he tried to imagine that lemon. It was like a yellow sphere at the end of the hall. Suddenly he couldn't remember where lemons came from, except that it was somewhere in the south, and whether they grew on trees or bushes. He'd never really known anyway.

He picked up a sharp stone. He had a sticky feeling as though he were robbing somebody. He tried to decide which was the best way to knock it out.

He tried several times without success. Then he stopped trying to get at just that one tooth. There is no other way, he kept repeating to himself. Do it. Do it fast. The faster the better.

Finally something in the jaw loosened. Ervin could smell his own breath. He tossed the stone away. He was glad nobody had seen him. Into the palm of his hand he scooped what he'd been seeking. (He was squatting and the head dropped back to the floor.)

Ervin stood up slowly. He felt as though his body and thoughts were flowing into a dark river, and he didn't know where it came from and where it was going. He wiped his hands on his pants. The cellar was dark, like the last place a person can retreat to. For a moment he closed his eyes. He had to take it out into the light. He headed for the other end of the corridor.

He'd hardly stepped out into the street when he saw Chicky's face in the twilight. There, you see, Ervin said to himself. He was keeping watch after all. Chicky would have done what he'd just done if he'd had the chance.

"Hello, kid," Chicky began. "Hello, you Jew bastard." Then Chicky exploded: "You lousy hyena. You son of a bitch. I suppose you've come to apologize. At least I hope so."

Ervin was clutching the thing tightly in his fist. He stared at Chicky for a long time.

"But I got in two good punches, didn't I? Like Max Schmeling." Chicky sounded pleased with himself. His eyes shone.

But then he noticed that the skin under Ervin's eyes was bluer than any bruise could have made it. He noticed, too, the pale blotches on Ervin's face. And how he kept his hand in his pocket.

"No hard feelings," Chicky said.

"I have it."

"I was sure you'd manage . . ."

Ervin pulled his hand out of his pocket and Chicky's glance shifted swiftly.

"Bring me that lemon, Chicky, but the whole thing." He unclenched his fist. It lay there cupped in his palm, a rather unattractive shell of gold the color of old copper, and very dirty.

"You won't take the tiniest slice for yourself?"

"If it's pure, Ervin, you're in luck," Chicky said.

When Ervin did not respond, he continued: "Sometimes it's just iron or some ersatz. Then it's worn through on top. The old man warned me about that in advance. But if it isn't, then you're damned lucky, Ervin, honest."

"When will you bring me that lemon?" Ervin asked, getting to the point.

"First hand it over and let me take a look."

Impatiently, Chicky inspected the crown, acting as though he hadn't heard Ervin. He scraped away the blood that had dried around the root and removed bits of cement. He blew on it and rubbed the dull gold between his fingers, then let it rest in his palm again.

"For this, the old runt will jump like a toad."

"I hope so."

"But first, Ervin, it's fifty-fifty."

"The hell it is," he answered firmly.

"I'll only do it for half."

"If Miriam doesn't get that lemon, she won't even last out till evening."

"Why shouldn't she last out? I'm keeping half."

"You're not keeping anything," repeated Ervin. "Now get going before it's too late."

Ervin glared at him, but there was a question in his eyes. Chicky acted calm. None of his self-satisfaction had filtered through to Ervin. His throat tightened. He began to shiver. He could feel the goose pimples on his neck and arms. It wasn't the way he wanted to think it was, *that his father had died and otherwise everything was just the same as before.* And when Chicky looked at him, Ervin could read in his eyes that instead of bringing a lemon or some kind of pills that have the same effect as lemons, Chicky would probably bring another piece of bread.

Ervin heard a quiet gurgle rising in his throat. He tried thinking about that runty second-hand dealer.

"I'd be crazy to do it for nothing," said Chicky slowly. He squinted warily and his nostrils flared. He bared his teeth. There were big gaps between them.

"Either we go halves or I tell your mom how you're treating me."

"You're not such a bastard, Chicky, are you?"

"Well, I'd have to be," replied Chicky.

"Get going," Ervin said.

"That sounds more like it."

"I'll wait at home."

"All right."

"And hurry up. Honestly, it's very important."

"Fast as a dog can do you know what," grinned Chicky.

Small and nimble, he dodged among the pedestrians. In the meantime, two men with tubs had appeared. Chicky must have passed them. The tubs were covered with tattered sheets and something bulged underneath. Everybody stepped aside as the porters passed. They knew what they were carrying.

Ervin didn't feel like going back home. He crawled into the opening of a cement culvert pipe. His long skinny head stuck out as he sat there watching the sun set behind the clouds. It dropped slowly. The barn swallows were flying lower now than they had been earlier that afternoon, flying in flocks, suddenly soaring up, then back toward earth.

He kept looking up and down the alley so he wouldn't miss Chicky when he came back.

It all began to melt together before his eyes: the silhouettes of the buildings and the cobblestones that had been pounded into the earth and then washed loose by long-gone rains. He watched the sky which was full of barn swallows and the sun disappeared. Rain was gathering in the clouds as their colors changed.

I ought to be like a rock, he told himself. Even harder than a rock. He forced his eyes up to the sky where the swallows were wheeling. Maybe swallows are happy, free, without guilt. He tried to swallow the distance, the wet air and the disappearing light, the flowing wind.

And he wept, quietly and without tears, in some little crevice which was inside.

# STEPHEN AND ANNE

He lay there quietly.

The beam he was gazing at had a dark, nut-brown color. On it someone had scribbled the word *quarantine*. It struck him as funny that the walls here inside should be the same red color as the outside walls. He already had his bed—a narrow strip of the paving-stone floor. In the semidarkness he could make out the rounded shapes of the women, who were getting ready to lie down in the uncertain, flickering light of the candles. He had been lying here in this way for many seconds, in the grip of a fever he was not even aware of, and full of tantalizing thoughts.

Then he fell asleep. He would wake up, wild with desperation, thinking that it was almost dawn, would close his eyes again, desiring to protract the delicious darkness in which he dropped, rose and dropped anew.

He awoke early in the morning. Astonished, he looked around to find out where he was. Next to him slept a girl, covered by knapsacks and a dark blanket, on his other side an old man who snored with the exertion of sleep.

He narrowed his eyes and saw her clearly like the white summit of some snow-capped mountain. Her brow was smooth and her skin well-nigh transparent, she had loosely flowing golden hair and an equally fair nape. The violence with which her image kept returning to him frightened him.

He waited for her to wake. Her hair was like autumn leaves, her lips were pale and half-open. He felt a current pass through him, a current in which there was the light of dawn and the quiet of night.

She sat up, slightly startled. She covered her face with her long fingers.

"Good morning," he said.

"Good morning."

"Please don't be angry that I am lying here," he said. "I didn't see properly last night."

"It doesn't matter," she replied.

She looked across him to where the old man was lying.

"Are you getting up?" he asked.

"Yes, I am," she said.

"Have you been here long?"

"A week," she replied.

And then: "I was already asleep when you arrived."

"We came in the night," he said.

"Some transports do come at night," she replied.

"We don't even know each other," he said.

She smiled, and he could see both bitterness and embarrassment on her lips.

"My name is Stephen," he said.

"Mine is Anne," she replied. And she repeated it: "Anne."

An official appeared on the threshold of the wooden staircase.

"It's one of ours," she said. "He has a star."

A wave of silence swamped the attic.

"What's he want?"

"He is going to read out the names," she said.

"Our names?"

"Yes, perhaps our names, too," she replied.

The official stopped a few paces away from them. He spread out his papers like huge bank notes. Then he said that those whom he was going to read out had been selected by the Council of Elders—entrusted with this task by the German HQ—and would go and live in the ghetto.

"And the others?"

"Elsewhere," she said.

"Where?"

"Nobody knows," she replied.

And then: "In the east," she said.

The old man next to them was awake now. He was holding a wrinkled, sallow hand to his ear, so as to hear better. "My name is Adam," he said. "Adam," he mumbled.

"Haven't you been read yet?" Stephen asked her.

"No," she said.

Suddenly she felt ashamed that they had not read her yet.

"My name is Adam," murmured the old man.

Then Stephen's name was read out.

"That's you," she said. "Stephen."

"Perhaps he'll read you, too," he said.

He did not.

"Be glad," she said.

He was silent, frightened suddenly by the infinitude of leave-taking that clung to him.

"Don't cry," he said.

"I'm not crying," she replied.

The official announced that those whose names had been called were to go downstairs into the courtyard within ten minutes.

"Just those I've read out—neither more nor fewer," he said curtly.

Then he added: "I'm not making this up—it's orders from HQ."

"Adam," the old man repeated.

The official left.

"Are you thinking about it?"

"No," she answered.

"They'll read you tomorrow," he said. "Or some other time."

He could not make himself stand up, yet he knew he would have to.

He took her hand.

"Come and see me, won't you?" she said.

"I'll come," he replied.

"We have known each other so short a time," she said.

"I'll come for sure," he said again. "I'm alone here. We can be friends."

"If they leave us here," she said.

"Why?"

"I've heard things."

"What things?"

"That we are to be sent on," she said. "Maybe within a week."

He helped her with the knapsacks.

"You're lucky," she said.

He was looking at her, unable to reply.

The current rose up in him from somewhere deep inside, right to the top and back again to his finger tips with which he was touching the palm of her hand.

"Perhaps," she said quietly, "I will still be here."

"You will," he muttered.

And then he added: "Certainly you will."

"Go on, then," she said.

He looked at her, and he again felt the current, being drowned in it. Then he got up, letting her hand slip out of his, and something stopped inside him; he felt it in the contraction of his chest and the smarting of his eyes that increased with each step he drew farther away from her.

"Adam," mumbled the old man.

Then he ran along L Avenue; everything that had enveloped him like a spider's web and that alternately burned and went out inside him, driving him forward and drawing him back to the attic of the *quarantine*, turned over inside him and reverberated like the echo of those words.

He put down his knapsack on the bed assigned to him.

Then he ran back the way he had come, not caring what would become of him and his things.

He dashed inside. He saw her, so slim, on the grey pallet.

"Stephen," she said.

Then: "It's you."

And finally: "So you've come." She lowered her eyes.

"Annie," he said.

"I didn't really expect . . . ," she said.

He ignored the old man, whose snoring disturbed everyone near him. He sat down at her side on the mattress, out of which the straw projected like so many arrows. He did not feel any need to say more than that one word he had said already.

"Annie," he repeated.

He embraced her shoulders and felt the current surging up from inside. The feeling that he was protecting her with the hand that touched her stifled him.

He sat silently next to her, in front of the barrier of stone that was the old man, whose glassy eyes did not take them in and whose sallow neck, resembling a human tree trunk, shielded them from view.

Suddenly his eyes met those of the old man.

"What is it?" she asked.

"Nothing," he replied.

He could feel that she was afraid. She pressed herself closer to him.

Then she saw the old man's gaze and she was frightened by what she read in it—a wild, imploring insolence and an inquisitive envy.

"My name is Adam," the old man muttered.

He kept holding his hand up to his face to catch the sound of words that did not reach him.

"Let's get away from here," said Stephen.

"Yes, let's," she said.

Then she added: "What if the official comes?"

"Why should he?"

Her eyes fell and she looked at the floor.

"Let's go, then," she said.

She did not dare to look again into the dark pools of the old man's eyes. She rose. She had on a coat of some warm, blue material.

Looking at her, the coat and everything else seemed to him to be as clear and clean as the sky.

He had to step across the old man's mattress.

He knew he would speak to him.

"Look after Anne's things," he said.

And to Anne it seemed as if only these words really woke the old man. He dropped the hand that had acted as a hearing aid. His almost-brown eyes grew wide and soft.

"Adam," he said.

Then he added: "Right! You run along, children!"

She had to lower her eyes once more.

"Is that your brother?" the old man asked.

They looked at each other. He felt the current again running through him.

"Yes," he replied for her.

They went out, and it seemed to them that everything they looked at was without shadow.

And Stephen wished that the current should pass through the tips of his fingers to Anne, that she might feel in that touch the sun, and hope, and the rosy rays of day and its light.

"Brother and sister," he said.

And then: "More than that."

They walked round the blacksmith's shop. On the other side of the slope that towered above the town they saw the rambling building of the Council of Elders.

"If only I had an uncle here," she said.

"Has he gone?" he asked.

She turned her face to his and, with her finger quite close to him, tapped her forehead.

"Silly," she said, "I was thinking of an uncle who does not exist."

"Are you alone?"

"Completely," she replied.

"Are you hungry?"

"What could you do about it?"

"Do you know where I live?"

"No," she said.

"Here," he said. "Wait a second."

He ran upstairs and pulled a piece of cake out of his knapsack; this he broke in two, leaving one of the halves to the boys who were watching him.

"For your hunger," he said when he was downstairs again.

"Thanks," she said

Suddenly they both laughed.

"Let's go back there," she said then.

"There?" he asked.

"Yes," she said.

"Yes," he repeated.

When they were sitting down again, he said: "They'll read you tomorrow."

"Oh, I'm not thinking about it," she said.

"There are other things apart from that," he said.

"What things?"

"Other things," he repeated.

Then they went out, but they only had time to walk once round the town.

The darkened trees began to merge with their own shadows, the twilight toying with the leaves.

"Come," she said. "I'll accompany you."

He gazed into her eyes, so close to his. He put his arm around her shoulders, which were frail and gentle, making him think it was up to him to protect her. The strong feeling that seemed to have a life of its own inside him and rose in waves up to his throat and farther, both the light and the dark curve of her silhouette, that which at once constricted him and released him from the shadows, holding out the promise of a sensation of freedom—all this flowed into the single word which he now uttered:

"Anne!"

"Stephen!"

He kissed her on the mouth.

"I've never . . . been like this before," she said.

It was his first kiss as well as hers. And he again felt those waves returning, clean and fragrant, and he kissed her lips and eyes, which were now filled with tears, and felt a desperate longing to never, even at the price of death, live otherwise than at this moment.

They walked a little way from the door, to the spot where a yellow, wooden fence divided off the ghetto from the HQ. They shivered with the chill of evening.

"It's not so late yet," she said.

"Annie," he said.

"Where shall we go?" she asked.

"Annie," he repeated.

"We'll have to be going," she said, and stood still. He felt the irrevocability of the hour that closes the day like a thin blade having the power to cut even the invisible current somewhere deep inside where no one can see.

He led her wordlessly round the block of houses next to Q 710. He was aware that some outside influence was disturbing that current inside him, and yet he was glad he was walking by her side and feeling her warmth, and at the same time unhappy because he knew what was coming; his throat was constricted by the same huge hoop that was encircling his chest and pressing against his eyes.

"Annie," he said.

"Yes?" she replied.

And then, after a long silence: "If you want, Stephen," she said, "come and see me in the night."

"I will," he whispered. He felt as though she had cut through ropes which had until now bound him.

"Yes, I will," he said again. "I'll come for sure."

"You can go across the courtyards," she said.

Then she added: "That's how they do it here."

"Yes," he said.

"We'll be moved soon," she said. "I feel it."

"I'll come," he repeated.

"I feel it somehow," she said.

And then, "I'm terribly afraid. It's even worse now."

"Don't worry," he said. "I'll come for sure."

"It's not far across the courtyards," she said.

"Yes," he said.

He took off his coat and threw it over her. She returned it to him.

Then, all at once, she ran off, suddenly and unexpectedly. She tore herself away from his hands, regretting that she had said what she did. She had known the laws of the ghetto a week longer than he. He heard only her steps, receding into the darkness.

A fraction of that moment was before his eyes every second that passed by, deepening the darkness, these fractional parts of the picture composing a huge mosaic which contained the current and her half-open lips and her tears.

Then the boys became quiet and went to sleep.

He knew he would stay awake. He pieced together the fragments of the night, and only when it seemed to him that the stillness was going to overwhelm him with its immense, unbearable weight did he steal from his bed.

He jumped over the knapsacks and shoes lying in the middle of the room and stood by the door. He reached out for the handle. In the instant when the cool contact poured a whole ocean into his brain, the shining brass growing dull under the imperceptible shadow of his palm, he was again conscious of the warm waves and heard the creaking of the wooden stairs that led up to the attic. At that moment he heard his heart beating, a bronze bell tolling inside him. He pressed down the handle, cautiously but firmly.

The ocean poured itself out into emptiness. The room was locked. He felt the soft blow. The earth fell away beneath him. He swallowed his tears. Now he could see the emptiness, and in it a small face and the transparent skin of her forehead, that indescribably fragile something that filled him with a feeling that there was a reason for his existence, those frightened eyes and that breath bitter like almonds.

He crept back to his bed, and then again to the door. The white square, full of an overpowering silence, gave back a mute echo of the brotherhood he felt for her, a brotherhood that from that moment elevated him above this world and at the same time flung him down to its very bottom.

He rattled the handle.

"Be quiet!" someone shouted. And added something else.

He tried to make himself believe that she could see him all the way from where she was, through the silken web of the night, that it was all one great window, and that behind it was she.

Then he lay on his back, his eyes fixed on the grey ceiling, upon which was her image, indistinct and hazy, but clear in all details—her eyes and lips. Her hair fell loosely down in the shadows and her voice sounded in the stillness.

His eyes smarted. He was aware of this only every now and again, in the intervals of his imaginings in which he heard every word a thousand times and once, as a single word, and then as one great silence.

She penetrated everything: the white door and the stillness of the night. She returned to him in his feverish visions, and he walked with her, his hand on her shoulder, and the waves rose and fell in him and filled both of them.

In the morning he ran, breathless, through the town. He flew upstairs. All he found was an empty attic. The transport to the east had left in the night.

## Sara Nomberg-Przytyk 1915–

Born in Lublin into a chassidic family, Sara Nomberg attended the gymnasium in Lublin and the University of Warsaw. She was imprisoned for five years for political activities. In 1939, she fled east as the Nazis invaded Poland. From 1941 to 1943 she lived in the Bialystok ghetto. When the ghetto was liquidated, she was sent to Stutthof and then to Auschwitz. When the war ended she returned to Poland, married Andrzei Przytyk, and worked as a journalist in Lublin for more than twenty years. Forced to leave in 1968 in the wake of the outbreak of anti-Semitic riots, she subsequently lived in Israel and then in Canada.

Sara's memoir of the Bialystok ghetto, *Pillars of Samson* (Lublin), appeared in 1964, two years after the memoir *Transport Was My Home,* describing her life in Poland from 1933–1938. *Auschwitz: True Tales from a Grotesque Land* (Polish 1966; English 1985) covers her time in Stutthof and Auschwitz.

## OLD WORDS—NEW MEANINGS

For some people, Auschwitz was an ordinary term, but now the word had taken on a completely new set of meanings. An unusually interesting psychological study might result if someone could demonstrate the way in which meanings passed beyond the accepted boundaries of conventional significance. Why a psychological study? Because the new set of meanings provided the best evidence of the devastation that Auschwitz created in the psyche of every human being. No one was able to resist totally the criminal, amoral logic of everyday life in the concentration camp. To some extent all of us were drawn into a bizarre transformation of reality. We knew what those innocent words meant, such words as "gas," "selection," but we uttered them, nevertheless, as though there was nothing hidden behind them.

Take the word "organize." Usually it is associated with such positive values as political, social, and cultural order and well-being. When we say of someone that he is a good organizer we usually mean that he is a constructive leader who brings sanity and tranquility to the whole community. In Auschwitz, however, "to organize" meant to improve your own situation, very often at someone else's expense by taking advantage of that person's ignorance or inexperience. "To organize" meant to procure for yourself, by any means, better clothing, lodging, or food. The person who knew how "to organize" slept under a silk comforter, wore silk underwear, and had not only enough bread and soup but even meat. How did she do it? I thought about it after I saw how she had prospered. When I first met her she was in tattered rags. Now she wore warm boots and an elegant sweater. She had a full belly and a smile on her face. When I asked the other prisoners about her I kept getting the same answer: "Apparently she knows how to organize." I managed to observe the workings of this kind of "organizing" in the young lady from Cracow named Fela.

In January 1944 we were both inmates in the new arrivals block. Eighteen years old at the time, she had been sent to Auschwitz when she was caught smuggling food into the ghetto for her family. She was a tall, slim girl with very light blond hair. She was not a beauty, but she had a quality that was impossible to describe. Something forced you to look at her. She was alone, without family or friends, but in spite of that, she did not give the impression of being helpless. She looked around attentively as though looking for some way to put her past experience to use. She did not cry, and she was not dismayed by the things that were taking place around her. She analyzed the situation carefully as if she were calculating how to establish herself most comfortably. An aura of self-assurance radiated from her whole being. This self-assurance allowed her to move freely without cramping her style in any way.

Fela did not talk to anyone. She was always alone. That girl interested me very much. I tried to get closer to her but she would not even stop for me. It was only after one of the selections, when she saw that I had protectors, that she reconsidered, deciding, apparently, that my acquaintance could be useful. One evening she came to talk to me.

"Taking everything into account," she said, "is it really that bad for everybody in Auschwitz? *Blokowe*, wardens, and many other people who are hangers-on are living very well. They will certainly live through Auschwitz. I am trying to figure out how to get myself into that group. I have to think of something to avoid being a victim who is always hungry and who is always being beaten by everybody. I have to find a way out, and I'm sure I will."

The girl amazed me. She spoke about the weak, persecuted, and hungry women with such contempt. Such a lack of all scruples in a girl barely eighteen years old was something unusual.

"I have to organize something. I have to see to it," she ended.

That was the first time I heard the term "to organize" in the new Auschwitz sense. After that talk I did not see Fela for a long time. We had been working in different areas, but one evening we met by chance. I had almost forgotten about her when I met her that evening on the hospital block. She was carrying a sack full of bread. Our chance encounter took her aback a little, but only for one short moment.

"What are you doing here," I yelled angrily. "Is this what your 'organizing' looks like? Is it part of your 'organizing' to steal bread from the sick? Get out of here quickly, before I call the head of the block!"

But Fela did not run away. She stood there, waiting for my anger to disappear.

"Now I will tell you where I got the bread," she said after a minute. "It is a long and not so simple story. 'You steal the bread,' you said. I didn't steal it, I earned it."

There was a pause, but I did not question her. I waited for further explanation.

"There was a woman from my *kommando* lying on this block. One evening I came to see her and brought her a cup of potato soup cooked with one measly potato. You should have seen how she ate it, and how the other women who were lying next to her begged me to cook some soup for them. The next day, after the evening assembly, I went to the back of the kitchen with my portion of bread, which I had not eaten. I was looking for the woman who was working at the potatoes, in the hope that she would trade some potatoes for my bread. I found the woman, who gave me seven potatoes and a small onion for one portion of bread. I went into the block, and in a big tin can that I had brought with me from work, I cooked a potato soup with the seven potatoes. I fried the onion in my portion of margarine and put it into the soup. The soup smelled good. It was hot and fresh. I went to the hospital and sold the soup to the sick. I got a portion of bread for a cup of soup. They couldn't eat that dry bread, and the rats wound up taking it right from under their pillows. That very first evening I took in five portions of bread. You yourself must admit that I didn't steal the bread but earned it. The next time I earned four portions, and today I got fourteen portions of bread for the soup."

I stood there facing her, not knowing what to say to her or how to act toward her. It was certainly an ugly way of "earning" bread, taking it from unfortunate, very sick women, tearing the very last bite out of their mouths. But that is what they wanted. They preferred this cup of watery soup smelling of home to the portion of stale bread. To throw Fela out of the hospital would be to deprive the women of the soup for which they had been waiting all day. Nobody else would "organize" the soup.

"Ask the sick," she said, as though reading my mind. "Ask them whether they want the soup or not. See what they say."

I already knew for certain that I was not going to tell the head of the block and that Fela would continue to sell her soup to the sick.

"What are you doing with the bread?" I looked at the sack full of bread. "Don't tell me that you're going to eat fourteen portions of bread all by yourself."

"I don't eat it all. I exchange some of it for cigarettes. There is somebody I meet at work who gives me cigarettes for bread. You know, for cigarettes you can buy anything in the camp: clothes, good food, even good work. I have to give some cigarettes to the *blokowa* and, what is more important, some to the *sztubowe* so they won't interfere. But there are still enough left for me. I can get good food and good clothes. I can even bring something for you. I am collecting cigarettes now because I want to get good work. I have something particular in mind."

Fela left. That night I pondered our encounter and the moral problems that Fela had set before me. How could I evaluate her behavior? In Auschwitz she would have earned an A+. But what grade would Fela have earned if her behavior were viewed within a larger perspective?

A few weeks went by. It was lunch time when, from the main road, there came the sound of a German song pounded out to the rhythm of bootsteps. I went out in front of the infirmary. It was the marching of the *kommando* who worked in the *effektenkammer*, commonly known as *kanada*. In *kanada* things brought to Auschwitz by Jews from all over Europe were sorted out. All of them thought that they were going to work, that they would work and live. People took all of their best things with them. The Germans allowed them to take only one valise and one knapsack. People packed gold and jewelry, furs and their best clothes. Now, the girls from the *effektenkammer* worked at unpacking the valises, sorting and shipping the goods to Germany. Only the young and pretty girls were chosen for this *kommando*. They wore red kerchiefs on their heads and belts that were made especially to each girl's measurements. They had it good. A fortune passed through their hands. No wonder they lived in comfort.

They paraded to lunch in fours to the accompaniment of a marching song. I looked at them from afar and thought that, if I were to see their picture in a newspaper, I would have had a hard time believing that they were prisoners in the death camp of Auschwitz. Those singing prisoners were part of the system of the death factory. Suddenly, one of the marching girls caught my eye. It was Fela. She noticed me from afar. She tore the red kerchief from her head and waved happily to me. This was the good work she was dreaming about when she had collected the bread for the cups of hot soup that reminded the dying women of the taste of home. With that bread, which she had then

exchanged for cigarettes, Fela got the job in *kanada*. Now she no longer carried soup to the hospital block. She was too busy with other higher-paying
transactions.

A few more weeks went by. One evening Fela came to the infirmary. She
walked in very quietly, without her usual self-assurance. Was it possible that she
was not working in *kanada*? She had brought me a present, a beautiful nightgown. I knew that she wanted to tell me something, but she did not know where
to start. We were quiet for a long time.

"Don't you work in *kanada* anymore?" I threw the first line from the shore.

She was still working there, but terrible things were happening. Even for
her they were terrible.

"Imagine. I unpack a valise, and I find a dead girl in it. She must have been
about two years old when she died. I was terribly disturbed. The girls told me
that they often find dead children in the valises. The mothers hid the children
in the hope that once they got them into the camp they and the children would
remain together. Later, the valises were taken from them and brought to us,
but by that time the children were no longer alive. I can't forget about it. I can't
help thinking that all those beautiful clothes belonged to people who are no
longer living. The girls say that this feeling will pass, that I will get used to things
and forget about it. I don't know whether I'll be able to stand it there. It's worse
than the business with the soup," she said at the end.

A few weeks went by again. Fall had arrived. A cold rain was falling outside. The mud was so thick and clinging that it was difficult to walk between
the blocks. That evening, in addition to the regular staff, we had a visitor,
Kwieta, a good friend of Marusia's, who worked in the *leichenkommando*. She
was waiting for the car that was to pick up the dead bodies that were
heaped in a huge pile. Suddenly we heard the roar of the car, and Kwieta
jumped up from her seat in order to get to the pile of corpses. The entire
*kommando* was supposed to help load the car. Kwieta did not have a chance
to leave the infirmary. The door opened with a crash, and in staggered a peculiar figure covered with soot and wrapped in a blanket. Behind her appeared
an SS man. "The driver of the dead," Kwieta whispered.

"Do something with her," he said. "She will tell you everything."

He came in. The peculiar figure tumbled to the floor. It was Fela. Except
for the blanket she had nothing on. She was naked and covered with ashes.
Mancy and Marusia revived her. Later, we washed her up, dressed her, and fed
her. Then Fela started her unusual story.

"Two weeks ago I fell sick with pneumonia. I was in the hospital and
was recovering. The day before I was supposed to go back to *kanada* to work,
Mengele wrote down my number for the gas. I found myself on the death ward.
Yesterday the car came to take us to the crematorium. I didn't want to die. I
was looking for a way out. All of a sudden, I saw something like a chimney

jutting out of one side of the car, and I got into it. 'Maybe they won't see me,' I thought. Later, I figured out that the car ran not only on gasoline but also on wood.

"The car went to the crematorium. The women were chased into the gas chambers. I remained in the chimney unnoticed. The empty car returned to the garage. I was in the garage alone. Covered with soot and without any clothes, I got out of the car. That's how I spent the night. I didn't know what I would say when the SS man returned. In the morning he came and was terribly frightened when he saw me. He probably believed in devils and thought that I was a creature not of this earth. After I told him the whole story, he brought me a blanket and food and told me to sit there till evening, when he would be going for the dead. Then he would take me back to the women's camp."

The next day we did not report the death of a woman who had died that day, and Fela took her place on the register of the area.

She left Auschwitz with the next transport. I do not know whether she "organized" further. I never saw her again.

*Hans Peter Richter 1925–*     Born in Cologne, Richter joined
the Hitler Youth and, despite having lost an arm
before the war, he served in the German army
from 1942–1945. He became a lieutenant, was
wounded in action, and received many decorations, including the Iron Cross. After the war, he
studied at the universities of Cologne, Bonn, Mainz
and Tübingen, receiving a doctorate in 1968. He was
a professor, independent social psychologist, and
radio and television broadcaster and wrote many
television and radio scripts. He also is the author of
adult nonfiction, scholarly monographs, novels, and
award-winning children's books. Many of the latter
are set in the Third Reich and have been translated
into other languages, including English (e.g., *I Was
There,* 1962; *The Time of the Young Soldiers,* 1975). In
*Friedrich* (German 1961; English 1970), an "autobiographical documentary," read in school by nearly
every sixth or seventh grade German child, a young
boy describes his early childhood and his family's
friendship with a Jewish family, the Schneiders, who
fall victim to Hitler and the Nazis. The fortieth edition appeared in 1993 and over four million copies
have been sold.

## THE TEACHER

The school bell rang. At the last tone, Teacher Neudorf closed the book and
stood up. Slowly, in thought, he walked toward us. He cleared his throat and
said: "The lesson is over—but please stay a little longer; I want to tell you a
story. Anyone who wants to can go home, though."

We looked at each other quizzically.

Herr Neudorf stepped to the window, turning his back to us. From his
jacket pocket he drew a pipe and began to fill it, looking at the trees in the
schoolyard all the while.

Noisily we collected our things. We prepared our briefcases and satchels. But no one left the classroom. We all waited.

Awkwardly, Herr Neudorf lit his pipe. With obvious enjoyment he blew a few puffs against the windows. Only then did he turn to face us. He surveyed the rows of seats.

When he saw that all were still filled, he nodded to us with a smile.

All eyes focused on Herr Neudorf. We didn't talk. From the hall came the sounds of the other classes. In one of the back benches someone shuffled his feet.

Herr Neudorf walked to the front row. He sat on one of the desks. His pipe glowing, he looked at each of us in turn and blew the smoke over our heads to the window.

We stared at our teacher, tense and expectant.

At last he began to speak in a calm, soft voice. "Lately, you've heard a lot about Jews, haven't you?" We nodded. "Well, today I also have a reason to talk to you about Jews."

We leaned forward to hear better. A few propped their chins on their schoolbags. There wasn't a sound.

Herr Neudorf directed a blue cloud of sweet-smelling smoke up to the ceiling. After a pause, he continued, "Two thousand years ago all Jews lived in the land which is now called Palestine; the Jews call it Israel.

"The Romans governed the country through their governors and prefects. But the Jews did not want to submit to foreign rule and they rebelled against the Romans. The Romans smashed the uprising and in the year 70 after the birth of Christ destroyed the Second Temple in Jerusalem. The leaders of the revolt were banished to Spain or the Rhineland. A generation later, the Jews dared to rise again. This time the Romans razed Jerusalem to the ground. The Jews fled or were banished. They scattered over the whole earth.

"Years passed. Many gained wealth and standing. Then came the Crusades.

"Heathens had conquered the Holy Land and kept Christians from the holy places. Eloquent priests demanded the liberation of the Holy Grave; inflamed by their words, thousands of people assembled.

"But some declared, 'What is the use of marching against the infidels in the Holy Land while there are infidels living in our midst?'

"Thus began the persecution of the Jews. In many places they were herded together; they were murdered and burned. They were dragged by force to be baptized; those who refused were tortured.

"Hundreds of Jews took their own lives to escape massacre. Those who could escape did so.

"When the Crusades were over, impoverished sovereigns who had taken part in them had their Jewish subjects imprisoned and executed without trials and claimed their possessions.

"Again, many Jews fled, this time to the East. They found refuge in Poland and Russia. But in the last century, there, too, they began to be persecuted.

"The Jews were forced to live in ghettos, in isolated sections of towns. They were not allowed to take up so-called 'honest' professions: they could not become craftsmen nor were they allowed to own houses or land. They were only allowed to work in trade and at moneylending."

The teacher paused, his pipe had gone out. He placed it in the groove for pens and pencils. He got off the desk and wandered about the classroom. He polished his glasses and continued:

"The Old Testament of the Christians is also the Holy Scripture of the Jews; they call it Torah, which means 'instruction.' In the Torah is written down what God commanded Moses. The Jews have thought a great deal about the Torah and its commandments. How the laws of the Torah are to be interpreted they have put down in another very great work—the Talmud, which means 'study.'

"Orthodox Jews still live by the law of the Torah. And that is not easy. The Torah, for instance, forbids the Jew to light a fire on the Sabbath or to eat the meat of unclean animals such as pigs.

"The Torah prophesies the Jews' fate. If they break the holy laws, they will be persecuted and must flee, until the Messiah leads them back to their Promised Land, there to create His Kingdom among them. Because Jews did not believe Jesus to be the true Messiah, because they regarded him as an impostor like many before him, they crucified him. And to this day many people have not forgiven them for this. They believe the most absurd things about Jews; some only wait for the day when they can persecute them again.

"There are many people who do not like Jews. Jews strike them as strange and sinister; they believe them capable of everything bad just because they don't know them well enough!"

Attentively we followed the account. It was so quiet that we could hear the soles of Herr Neudorf's shoes creak. Everyone looked at him; only Friedrich looked down at his hands.

"Jews are accused of being crafty and sly. How could they be anything else? Someone who must always live in fear of being tormented and hunted must be very strong in his soul to remain an upright human being.

"It is claimed that the Jews are avaricious and deceitful. Must they not be both? Again and again, they have been robbed and dispossessed; again and again, they had to leave everything they owned behind. They have discovered that in case of need money is the only way to secure life and safety.

"But one thing even the worst Jew-haters have to concede—the Jews are a very capable people! Only able people can survive two thousand years of persecution.

"By always accomplishing more and doing it better than the people they lived among, the Jews gained esteem and importance again and again. Many great scholars and artists were and are Jews.

"If today, or tomorrow, you should see Jews being mistreated, reflect on one thing—Jews are human beings, human beings like us!"

Without glancing at us, Herr Neudorf took up his pipe. He scraped the ashes out of the bowl and lit the remaining tobacco. After a few puffs, he said, "Now I am sure you will want to know why I have told you all this, eh?"

He walked to Friedrich's seat and put a hand on his shoulder.

"One of us will leave our school today. It appears that Friedrich Schneider may no longer come to our school; he must change to a Jewish school because he is of the Jewish faith.

"That Friedrich has to attend a Jewish school is no punishment, but only a change. I hope you will understand that and remain Friedrich's friends, just as I will remain his friend even though he will no longer be in my class. Friedrich may need good friends."

Herr Neudorf turned Friedrich around by his shoulder. "I wish you all the best, Friedrich!" the teacher said, "and *Auf Wiedersehen!*"

Friedrich bent his head. In a low voice he replied, "*Auf Wiedersehen!*"

With quick steps Herr Neudorf hurried to the front of the class. He jerked up his right arm, the hand straight out at eye level, and said: "Heil Hitler!"

We jumped up and returned the greeting in the same way.

*Isaiah Spiegel 1904 (1906?)—1990*  Born and raised in the Balut, a poor Jewish quarter of Lodz, Spiegel received a traditional Jewish and general education. He taught Yiddish and Yiddish literature in Bund schools between the world wars. While living in the Lodz ghetto from 1940 to 1944, where he worked for the Jewish Council (*Judenrat*) in various positions, he wrote many stories and poems about the Jews in the ghetto, especially the Balut. In August 1944, he was among those sent to Auschwitz and other labor camps. After the war, he lived for a few years in Poland (Lodz, 1945–1948 and Warsaw, 1948–1950), before emigrating to Israel.

His first Yiddish poems appeared in 1922 and his first book of Yiddish poetry in 1930. His first published collection of ghetto stories (*Light from the Depths—Ghetto Novellas*) appeared in Yiddish in 1952, and the second (*Stars Shine in the Abyss— Collected Stories, 1940–1944*), also in Yiddish, in 1976.

# A GHETTO DOG

Anna Nikolaievna, widow of Jacob Simon Temkin, the fur dealer, had only time enough to snatch up a small framed photograph of her husband, for the German was already standing in the open doorway shouting, *"R-raus-s!"*

There were no more Jews in the house by now, and if she had failed to hear the noise they made as they fled it was because with age she had grown hard of hearing and because that very morning, before the light had seeped through the heavy portieres, a desire had come over her to open her piano— a grand piano, black—and let her old parchment-like fingers glide over its yellowed keys. One could scarcely call what she was playing music, since her fingers, which were as gnarled as old fallen bark, had been tremulous with age for years. The echoes of several tunes had been sounding in her deaf ears the whole morning, so that she had failed to hear the German when he appeared shouting on the threshold.

All the while Nicky, the widow's dog, had been lying near one of the heavy portieres, dozing and dreaming an old dog's dream, his pointed muzzle resting on his outstretched paws. He was well along in years; his coat was shedding and light patches showed in its sandy hue. His legs were weak, but his big eyes—brownish with a blue glint—reminded one that he too had once been a puppy.

The widow and her dog led a lonely life. Nicky wandered through the rooms on his weak stumpy legs, his head drooping, and swayed mournfully, his whining quieted by weary thoughts. The Temkins had got him from a farm a long time ago. After his master's death the widow used to listen all day to Nicky moving through the stillness of the house. Whenever she sat by the table and Nicky was in the bedroom opposite (he had refused for several days to leave the bed where his master had died), it seemed to her as though her late husband were again walking through the bedroom in his house slippers. She used to listen to the least noise from the bedroom, pricking up her deaf ears, and as a sudden pallor spread over her wrinkled forehead she seemed actually to hear Jacob Simon's soft slow tread. Any moment now he would appear on the threshold of the bedroom, seat himself in the plush *fauteuil*, reach out for a plaid rug, and throw it over his knees, which had been rheumatic for so many years.

Between the widow and her dog there had formed a mesh of otherworldly thoughts and dreams. She saw in his drooping old head, in his worn-out fur and his pupils with their blue glints, a shadow of her husband. Perhaps this was because Nicky had been close to his master for so many years and had been ready to lay down his life for him, or perhaps because with time he had taken on his master's soft tread over the rugs, his master's lax mouth and watery eyes—whichever it was, the widow had never clasped the dog's head without feeling some inner disquiet. Between them there was that bond which sometimes springs up between two lonely creatures, one human and the other brute.

While the German was still in the open doorway, and before the widow had time to snatch up the photograph, Nicky had already taken his stand at the threshold. He raised his old head against the German, opened his mouth wide to reveal his few remaining teeth, let out three wild howls, and was set to leap straight for the German's throat. One could see Nicky's hackles rise and hear his old paws scrape as he dashed about, ready to leap at the stranger in the outlandish green uniform. Suddenly the dog had shed his years; his legs straightened and hot saliva drooled from his muzzle as if he would say, "I know you're our enemy, I know! But you just wait—wait!"

The German at the door became confused for a moment. Taken aback by the fire glinting in the old dog's eyes, he clutched at his pistol holster.

"Have pity!" the old woman quavered. "It's only a poor animal—"

With her old body she shielded Nicky from the German and at the same time began patting the dog. In a moment he lay quiet and trembling in the old woman's arms. At last the widow tugged at his leash, and the two of them made their way through the dark hallway and into the street. As she hurried through the hallway she seized a small black cane with a silver knob; without this cane, a memento of her husband, she could hardly take a step.

She found herself in the street, leaning on the black cane with the silver knob, the rescued photograph safe in her bosom, and tugging the dog on his leash. Her eyes could scarcely be said to perceive what was going on around her. The day was frosty, blue; a blue silvery web of mist, spun by the early Polish winter, was spreading over the houses, the street, the sidewalks. The faces of the fleeing Jews were yellow, pallid. Nicky was still restless and was drawing back all the time; he did not know where his mistress was leading him. From time to time he fixed his eyes on the widow's face, while she, as she trudged along, felt a sudden icy fear grip her heart. From the dog's eyes raised to hers there peered the watery, lifeless gaze of her late husband. And here were the two of them, linked together in the web of frosty mist that was swirling under a lowering dark sky. The two of them were now plodding close to each other, their heads downcast. Cold, angry thoughts kindled in her drowsy old mind. She actually felt a chill breath swishing about her ears and she caught words—far-off words, cold and dead.

The widow who had for so long lived a life apart from Jews and Jewishness had suddenly come to herself, as if awaking from a state of unconsciousness. She had been driven out of her house, of course, as a Jew like any other, although for many years her house had been like any Christian's. Her only son had become an apostate, had married a Christian girl and gone off to Galicia, long before the war, where he was living on his father-in-law's estate. During the Christian holidays various gifts would arrive from him. She knew beforehand what he would send: a big, well-fattened turkey and half a dozen dyed Easter eggs. The turkey she could use, but when it came to the colored eggs the old woman had a strange oppressive feeling. They would lie around for months, gathering dust on their shells, until some evening she peeled them in the bright light of the girandole and then left them on the window sill for the hungry sparrows.

She herself had been estranged from Jewishness since her very childhood. For years on end no Jewish face appeared at her threshold. The war, which had come so suddenly to the town, had during the first few days failed to reach her comfortable home. The catastrophe that had befallen the Jews had not touched her, and the angry prophecy of the storm that was raging in the streets had not beaten upon her door.

When the German had opened it that morning, he had aroused the little old woman from her torpor and had reminded her that she was a Jew and that heavy days had come for her and all other Jews. And though the old woman had during so many years been cut off from Jewishness and Jews, she had accepted the sudden misfortune with courage and resignation, as if an invisible thread had connected her to her people all through the years.

Now she was trudging through the streets with so many others whose faces were strange and distracted. She recognized these faces from her remote youth, faces framed in black unkempt Jewish beards and surmounted by small round skullcaps, which Jacob Simon used to ridicule so in his lifetime. Jews in gabardines, Jewish women wearing headkerchiefs and marriage wigs were dragging their children by the hand. Anna's heart was filled with a friendly feeling as, leaning on her black, silver-knobbed cane, she led Nicky with her left hand. The fleeing Jews cast surly sidelong looks at her and the dog. Nicky plodded on without once lifting up his head; the light had gone out of his eyes. A small spotted dog suddenly emerged from the crowd, ran up to Nicky, and placed a paw on the old dog's neck as if seeking consolation; thereafter both dogs walked side by side.

Nicky sensed the strange atmosphere as they turned into the next street. It was poorly paved, with gaping pits; the press was greater here. He could barely make his way among the thousands of unfriendly feet. They kept stepping on his paws, and once his mistress almost fell. Anna held her head higher and was pulled along by the crowd of Jews. She drew the leash closer to her, every so often saving Nicky from being trampled. By now he kept closer to her, mournful, and with his head still lower.

Fine, wet snowflakes swirled in the air, unwilling to fall to the ground, and settled on Nicky's grizzled, closely curled coat.

The widow found herself in a narrow squalid street in the Balut district of Lodz, where all the hack-drivers, porters, and emaciated Jewish street-walkers lived. She had come here with a host of strangers who quickly made themselves at home in a huge empty barn. The Jewish streetwalkers brought them all sorts of good things baked of white flour. The widow sat in the barn, her gray disheveled head propped on the silver knob of her cane, while Nicky sprawled at her feet and took in the angry din made by the strange people.

It was late at night before everyone in the barn was assigned quarters in the district. The widow found herself in the room of a tart known as Big Rose— a very much disgruntled tart, who did not want a dog in the house.

"It's enough that I have to take in a female apostate!" she kept yelling. "What do I need a sick old hound for?"

Anna stood on the threshold before the tart, the dog close to her on his unsteady legs; his body emanated a forlornness that was both animal and human.

"Quiet, quiet!" The widow's hand fell shakily on Nicky's drooping head and patted it.

The room where Big Rose lived lay under a gabled roof. It held a small shabby sofa, strewn with yellow and red cushions. A low ceiling made the place dreary and depressing. Outside the window was the hostile night, spattered with the silver of the first frost. This night-silver interlaced with the reflections of light from the room and fell on the windowpanes like dancing stars.

The nook that sheltered the widow and her dog was very dark; the warmth lingered there as if in a closed warm cellar. Throughout the room there hovered a sour odor of sin and lust. The old woman did not realize where she had come to; nothing mattered any longer. She and her dog huddled in their nook and for a long while squatted there like two huge rigid shadows. From time to time Nicky put his head in her lap, and a soft, long-drawn-out whine issued from the dark nook, like the moan of a hopelessly sick man.

Later that night, when the old woman and the dog had stretched out in their nook on some rags, Big Rose closed the red hangings which screened the shabby sofa from the rest of the room. The little red flame of the small night-lamp hanging on the wall wavered slowly and angrily, licking at the musty darkness around it.

Only now, when everything had become utterly quiet, did certain huge shadows appear in the darkness of the threshold. The shadows entered one by one; each hovered for a moment on the threshold, looked about, then disappeared within the hangings. In the dark little hallway on the other side of the door other shadows gathered and waited for the door to open. They did not have to wait long: each shadow, after darting out from behind the hangings, rushed through the door and disappeared down the dark stairs.

The widow was dozing by now. From time to time she awoke and put her arms around Nicky's warm neck. The dog continued snoring with a low, canine snore. Each time the door opened and a shadow darted within the hangings, from which there immediately issued Big Rose's witchlike snicker, Nicky would emit a low growl.

This suddenly angered Big Rose. She sprang up naked by the drawn-back hangings and, brandishing her arms, shouted at the widow in the nook, "My grand madam! May a curse light on you! Maybe madam would like to step out for a little while on the balcony with the hound? He's driving everybody away, may the devil overtake him! I'll poison that hound!"

The widow, startled from her sleep, was frightened by Big Rose's stark nakedness and its pungent reek.

"Sh, sh, sh!" she at last managed to whisper to the dog.

She stood up in her nook, took Nicky's head, and started for the door. Through the small dark hallway the two of them, the widow and the dog, reached the deserted balcony. Below them lay a tangle of dark Balut streets. The wind drove nearer and scattered the grayish, tenuous whiteness of the still swirling night snow. From the south side of the city the dusty glow of electric lights was borne through the night. The widow watched these lights blinking on and off, like inflamed eyes.

"See there, Nicky? Over there—there. That's our house, our street—"

The dog lifted his head, stood up on his hind legs, and peered into the darkness. For a while he stood thus, with the widow's arms around him, then suddenly let out a howl. It rent the sky like lightning, beat against the clouds, and then died away in the cold darkness of the earth.

◆

In the morning, when the chilled widow awoke in her nook, the dog was no longer by her side. Nobody had any idea where he had vanished to. Big Rose kept saying that this was no dog but a werewolf and that she hadn't even heard the dog leaving the house.

He was gone the whole day, and only toward evening did they hear him scraping at the door. He fell into the nook in great excitement, with foam on his hanging tongue, and threw himself on the frightened widow's lap.

Nicky lay on her knees, quivering with an ardent, old-dog sob. The widow took his shivering head and for some time gazed into his watery pupils, as if into the small openings of two wells. She could not understand what had happened to the dog. He barked in a subdued way, as if some words were struggling to escape him, as if he were straining to tell everything to the old woman bending over him. His whole body quivered, and his narrow face seemed to wear the twisted grimace of a dog in lament. Yet this was not whining; rather a noisy outburst of joy and consolation. He kept lifting his paws and putting them on the old woman's knees. The widow took the paws and brought them to her aged, withered lips, bent over, and for a long, long time, with her eyes closed, rested her head upon them.

For a long time the widow sat in the darkness embracing the dog, while the night-lamp, which had been turned low and had been burning all day near the red hangings, now cast a mysterious reddish reflection on the wall. The sharp silhouette of the dog's pointed head and the widow's arms swayed on the ceiling in a network of dancing shadows.

The next morning Nicky again disappeared and did not come back until nightfall. This was repeated day after day.

These disappearances coincided with the time the Germans built a wall around the ghetto, barbed wires dividing the Balut from the rest of the city. Nobody was allowed to leave or enter the Jewish district. But just the same Nicky used to disappear every day and come back only at night.

Once, when Nicky returned as excited as always, the old woman put her hands on his head and drew them back: they were sticky with blood. His fur was split and torn with open wounds. He was holding his paws on her knees, as always, but this time his pupils were reddish, glowing, and little green fires kept dancing across his watery eyes.

The widow applied rag after rag soaked in cold water to the dog's open wounds. Only now did she realize that Nicky had been crawling through the barbed wire, that each morning he had run off to the city and each evening he had come running home. The widow kept on washing the warm blood and applying the cold wet rags, while Big Rose ran to fetch basins of water. The bitterness she had felt in her heart for the dog had quickly vanished. She took a white blouse from her closet and tore it into narrow bandages; she also procured from somewhere a salve that was good even for human wounds. She smeared torn strips with the salve and then, kneeling by the door, started to bind the dog's wounds.

A sudden fright came over Big Rose; an other-wordly expression appeared on her face, as if she felt a cold breath upon her. She could have sworn by all that was holy that, as she had been binding the dog's wounds, he had given her a mournful human look.

◆

From the day Big Rose had bound the open wounds the dog had got by crawling through the barbed wire strung around the ghetto—from that day her attitude toward the widow had undergone a complete change. She took down the red hangings that had divided the room in two and asked the old woman to leave her dark nook and share the room with her. All three of them, the two women and the dog, now used the sofa. Nicky lay propped up by the colored cushions, lost in an old dog's dream.

This happened just about the time when the Germans issued an order that all animals—horses, cows, goats, and dogs—must be turned over to them. Only two broken-down horses were allowed to remain in the whole ghetto. For generations the old Jewish residents of the Balut had made their meager living as animal-breeders. The hack-drivers and cabbies, the milk dealers, small middlemen, organ-grinders, and innkeepers had to give up the horses and cows they had tended in the crowded dark stables and stalls. They unharnessed their horses for the last time and embraced the warm necks of their cows; they led out the mournful Jewish cows and the frightened Jewish goats. The draymen led their beautiful, glossy chestnut draft horses through the streets, the whole family marching in step with them, wringing their hands as if they were following the dead to a yawning grave. The women dragged the cows and goats along—the animals became stubborn and refused to budge. At the tail end of the procession, on ropes and leashes, other Jews were leading watchdogs, Dalmatians, poodles with mournful eyes, and common household pets with bobbed tails. The Jews hoped that their dumb creatures would be better fed than they had been in the ghetto. The horses and cows were taken into the city, but the dogs were immediately shot in a field close to the market place.

At daybreak Big Rose had thrown a torn black shawl with long fringes over her, and the widow, without uttering a word, had taken Nicky on his leash with one hand and her small silver-knobbed cane in the other. Both women were going to take the dog to the market place. Big Rose kept mauling her cheeks and softly weeping. The widow's disheveled hair, gray and lifeless, hung over her ashen face.

The compulsory surrender of her dog had come as such a shock to the widow that at first, when Big Rose had shouted the news into her face, she had clutched her head with her withered fingers and had remained still for several minutes. Big Rose thought the old woman had died, standing with her fingers in her hair, and her eyes not even blinking. She just stood there, stunned and stone-cold.

The dog let them do with him whatever they liked. He dropped at their feet and held his pointed head up to them, then yawned and let his muzzle sink to the cold floor.

The two women started out through the small courtyard, Nicky on his long leash between them. The snow was coming down in flakes as slender and chill as needles and stabbed their hands, their faces, and the dog's fur. It was bitter cold. Although dawn had broken a comparatively short while ago, the ghetto seemed already to be in twilight—night can fall abruptly in that region.

Big Rose bit her lips as she walked along. She peered out from the black shawl in which she was wrapped and could see nothing but the widow's half-dead face. Nicky still had his back bound in rags.

As they neared the market place they saw Jewish children emerging from the surrounding little streets, leading gaunt, emaciated dogs on ropes and leashes. There was a pound in the market place where the Germans collected the dogs. The horses and cows had already been transferred to German civilians to bring into the city proper. The dogs within the pound were looking out on the ghetto through barbed wire, their eyes watering. A shadowy terror was frozen upon their frightened, pointed muzzles.

A German stationed near the wicket leading into the pound relieved each owner of his or her dog, pushed the wicket open, kicked the dog with the point of his boot—and the animal found itself in the pound. Rarely or ever did any dog snarl at the German. Sudden shock paralyzed the dogs, depriving them of their strength and numbing their rage. Perhaps this was due to the reek that now came to them from the field where the dogs were being killed.

By the time the widow and Big Rose approached the pound with Nicky it was full of Jewish dogs. They were jammed together, huddled in twos and threes, their heads resting on one another's shoulders. Perhaps they did this because of the cold, which beat down upon them from the sky. A few of them were close to the barbed wire, prodding it with their paws in an attempt to get free. But they had to fall back with a childlike whimper when they felt their paws become sticky with blood. The barbs of the wire were sharp and rusty and stuck out like little knife points.

The widow and Big Rose halted before the German. He was waiting for the old woman to let go of the leash. But, instead of letting go, she wound the leash still tighter about her wrist and even her forearm. She did this with her eyes closed, the way a Jew winds the straps of a phylactery on his forearm. The German snatched at the leash. The widow staggered on her old legs, since Nicky was by now pulling her into the pound. She let herself be dragged along. In the meantime the German kicked the wicket shut. His loud, tinny laughter ran along the barbed wire.

Big Rose saw the widow standing inside the enclosure ringed by a pack of dogs and still holding Nicky on the leash. In her left hand she had the small cane with the silver knob and was keeping it high over the heads of the dogs. She stood there with her cane raised, her hair disheveled, the dogs circling at her feet. Some of the dogs lifted up their mournful heads and looked into the old woman's face. Nicky alone remained unperturbed. His back was still bound up in the white rags torn from Big Rose's blouse. From time to time he lifted his head toward the wicket where Big Rose was standing, petrified.

Exhausted, the widow sank to her knees in the snow. By now one could barely make out her body. The snow was falling more heavily, in bright shimmering stars. The widow's head stood out in the whiteness like a dazzling aureole.

Big Rose saw another wicket fly open on the other side and someone begin driving the dogs out into an open field. The widow stood up, leaned on her small silver-knobbed cane, and, with Nicky leading, started toward the field. . . .

Big Rose wrapped the small black shawl more tightly about her head. She did not want to hear the dull, tinny sounds that came from the sharp-edged shovels scooping up the frozen ground of the Balut. It was only the wind, playing upon the shovels that delved the narrow black pits—only the wind, chanting its chill night song.

*Leonard Tushnet 1908–1973*  Born in Newark, New Jersey, of a poor Jewish family, Tushnet received his B.S. (1927) from Washington Square College ( New York University) and his medical degree from Bellevue Hospital Medical College. He started a practice in Irvington, New Jersey, in 1932 and earned enough by 1939 to marry Fannie Brandchaft, whom he met at a county meeting of the Communist Party. They were arrested during their honeymoon on a picket line for striking waiters and busboys. He was a general practitioner in New Jersey until his retirement in 1966, except for service in the US Army Medical Corps during World War II (1st lieutenant). Tushnet retired early in order to devote himself full-time to writing. He published dozens of science fiction tales in addition to award-winning stories (e.g., "The Klausners," *The Best American Short Stories 1971*), monographs, and studies of the Holocaust. The latter included *To Die With Honor: The Uprising of the Jews in the Warsaw Ghetto* (1965), *The Uses of Adversity* (1966), about Jewish doctors in the Warsaw Ghetto who scientifically studied the process of starvation forced on the Jews by the Nazis, and *The Pavement of Hell* (1973), about three *Judenrat* leaders. Like Bryks, he wrote extensively about Rumkowsky and the Lodz Ghetto.

## THE BAN

In that confused period after the Liberation, the brothers' paths must have crossed a dozen times in their wanderings across Poland. Like hundreds of others, they searched, with little hope. With little hope, and yet with hope. Miracles had occurred. Had not Lazar Katz's wife and children, hidden in an attic, been found by a friendly Gentile, and been kept safe for four years? Had not Abrasha Veingold's two girls run away from the trains and been taken into the Convent of

St. Anthony? And had not Moritz Praszkower's son been found in the Assumptionist Fathers' Home for Orphans? And had not Israel Hamburger's wife returned from Ravensbrück? Indeed, was not their own continued existence a miracle? Who knows?—perhaps one had escaped the gas chambers, or two, or maybe even three.

For the Wolf brothers the search was fruitless. In one last despairing effort they each made their way to Oswiecim. There, in the accursed Auschwitz, perchance someone knew something, had a bit of reassuring news. And it was there that they met, in the dark barren shack for wayfarers outside the now-barred gates.

They wept. Shmarye, the oldest, the scholar-turned-blacksmith, choked on his tears. "We ran from them all the way from Lodz to Warsaw. At the end I was sent to Trawniki, and from there—." He waved his hands. No further words were needed. The others had had the same experience—from one labor camp to the next. "Sarah and the two boys—Treblinka. And you?"

Jacob, the youngest, who bad been called The Terrible by his fellow students in the House of Study because of the way he had single-handedly thrown out two drunken peasants who had wandered into the synagogue one Friday night to have fun with the Jews, rocked back and forth on the low box he used as a seat. He started to speak but could not for the racking cough that brought blood to his lips and left him trembling. Another decrepit scarecrow standing near him explained to his brothers, "We were in camp together. He's always like this. The medical commission wanted him to go to the hospital but he didn't trust them. Neither did I. Who would?" He finished with a shrug.

"His wife? They were in Vilna. They fled early. And where is she?" asked Shmarye.

Scarecrow answered, "Dead—taken to Belszyc."

Meir, the middle one, was sobbing silently and steadily, leaning against the doorpost and beating his breast as at the recitation of the *Al-Het*. His clothes were ragged, his boots torn. His beard, half-grown again, was straggly as a goat's. Through his cracked lips, frosted with dried rheum, came the hoarse cry, "All gone! None left! My Yamele, my pride—my Dovidel, my treasure—my sparkling Rochele—disappeared! Vanished! All, all, in Chelmno!" He howled like an animal and beat his head on the wall.

Here and there a head came up in the crowded little hut, then dropped again. Who was this Jew who cried so loudly? Who was he, that he thought himself different from the others? Who had not lost his Yamele, his Dovid, his Rochele?

Shmarye and Jacob put their arms around their brother and wept with him. How had the mighty fallen! The light of the province, the sage sought after before the bloom of youth had left his cheeks, Meir, before whom the richest merchants had stepped aside in honor when he walked proudly in the streets,

Meir was a broken old man with a bent back. They drew him away from the wall and sat with him through the night on the cold packed earth, like mourners.

◆

At the first streak of dawn, some of the other Jews got up, put on their praying shawls and wound their phylacteries, and started to pray. Shmarye rose to join them, but Meir angrily pulled him down again. Jacob looked at him in inquiry.

Meir's voice was hot with rage. "For what shall we pray? And to Whom? To the One Who cast the infants into the belly of Moloch? To the One Who dashed out the children's heads against the wall ? To the One Who watched while Amalek rejoiced in our afflictions?"

Jacob's eyes opened wide. He tried to speak but his cough prevented him. Shmarye glared at his brother. "Have your sufferings made you insane? Are you become a blasphemer? Have the wicked ones converted you to their bestiality?"

The other Jews crowded around, attracted by the loud voices. "Brothers, do not quarrel!" one called out. "In our misery we are all one. Let us console each other."

Meir sprang to his feet. "How long, you pious Jews, how long will you yet believe you are the Chosen? It is finished! We are less than the Gentiles! How the nations jeer at us! Look around you! More bones than Ezekiel saw! And more destruction than Jeremiah!" As though to strengthen his argument, a light breeze blew in some ashes from the huge mound outside.

"He is mad!" one cried out.

"Mad!" others agreed.

"Watch for your lives!" another shrieked, making for the door. Pushing and shoving, the Jews scrambled from the hut, leaving the three brothers alone.

Shmarye looked in his brother's face. No, he was not mad. He asked him, "Why do you speak so? Are not the troubles we have undergone enough?"

Jacob painfully rose from the ground to stand by Meir. Leaning on his shoulder, he said, with great effort, his speech broken again and again by the rattling cough, "Meir is right. We have been dealt with unjustly. We have been shamed before the nations. We have been stricken, root and branch. Shall we then give thanks that we see the light of a new day?"

Meir shook Shmarye by the arms. "Brother, brother mine, you were the upright man, the scholar who would not use the Torah as a spade, you tell us— can we pray?"

Shmarye shuddered and closed his eyes. "No, we cannot pray, not for the sun, nor for a long journey, or the washing of the hands, nor for the fruit of the vine. We are helpless and doomed. We are cut off."

Meir's eyes glittered as he said, "Let us sit down, my brothers, and discuss a point of the Law." Shmarye thought, perhaps he is indeed insane? The brothers sat again on the low boxes.

Meir held up his hand and, as though he were again in the House of Study, ticked off the points of his reasoning on his fingers. "We are cut off. And unjustly. And who cuts off one of the children of Israel unjustly must come under the ban. In the commentary, the Rambam says, 'for twenty-four causes may the excommunication be pronounced,' and the twenty-fourth is cutting off unjustly the children of Israel. Further, it is also written, in the same commentary if a private insult is given, one need pay no attention to it, but when the insult is public, it is an insult to the Law and it must be avenged by excommunication until the offender apologizes.' And further, the children of Israel have been made a mock of, and derided, and beaten and slain, and their teachers destroyed, and the Holy Arks desecrated, and filth thrown on the Scrolls of the Law, and all this in public. Further, the insult cannot be answered by wiping off the spittle from the face, nor by petition, but only by excommunication until the offense is acknowledged and recompense made therefor. Further—."

At this point, Jacob wailed and threw himself on the ground, beating his head on the earth. Shmarye's eyes widened in terror; his hands quivered as he stretched them out to stop his brother. "Who is guilty? Who?"

"Who, then, but He Who is the Master of the Universe?" thundered Meir. Now Shmarye, too, wailed loudly and, seizing a corner of his tattered coat, ripped it down its length.

The breeze made a fog of ashes over the Jews peering through the door and the two square holes that served as windows for the hut. Open-mouthed they stood, the gray film settling on their furrowed cheeks as they heard Meir say, "For the crimes, for the selling into slavery, for the neglect, for the indifference, for the casting away, by virtue of my authority as a teacher in Israel, I place a ban on You, and cut You off from the children of Israel from now and evermore!"

## S. L. Wisenberg 1955–

Born in Houston, Texas, Sandi Wisenberg was named after her grandfather, Solomon Louis Wisenberg, who was born in Kishinev, Moldavia, and lived his adult life in Georgia, Mississippi, and Texas, after coming to the United States. Wisenberg's stories have appeared in numerous literary magazines and journals, including *The New Yorker, Tikkun, Ploughshares,* and *Lilith,* as well as several anthologies. She has received fellowships from the Illinois Arts Council, the National Endowment for the Humanities, Ragdale Foundation, and the Millay Colony for the Arts.

Wisenberg has a journalism degree from Northwestern University's Medill School of Journalism and a Master of Fine Arts degree from the University of Iowa Writers' Workshop. She was a feature writer with the *Miami Herald* and is currently the creative nonfiction editor of the literary journal *Another Chicago Magazine.* She lives in Chicago and is working on a novel, teaching creative nonfiction, and studying Yiddish.

## LIBERATOR

My father was a liberator. I don't know when I first knew that. It's one of those things you know before you know what it means: My father was a liberator.

When he was a young man, a son, before he became a husband, father, owner of a Texas delicatessen, before his hair turned gray and thin, he was a member of a platoon that opened the gates of Mauthausen, the gates that his country would not bomb. Opened life back up, offered it to the prisoners, the ones who waited at the gates and the ones who did not wait.

He wore a dull uniform pinned with shiny badges, and shoes that glistened with mud. He was a liberator. Like a gladiator. Like a knight, his mail glinting in the sunshine, silvery as fish scales. I imagine him strong, sword upraised, a shield in the other hand. The frail grateful, kneeling at his feet. Like certain engravings of Lincoln with the slaves. Chains broken, rendered harmless, like beheaded snakes.

He loved Lincoln. Abraham, patriarch of a divided nation. Abraham, dark-bearded like a Jew.

My father talks about Lincoln. He talks more about Lincoln than he talks about the war. A little bronze bust of Lincoln sits on the piano. As if he were a bringer of music. On the shelf, as far back as I can remember: Sandburg's biography. My father refused to read Gore Vidal's. He said, "Let an old man keep his illusions, Ceci."

But he is not an old man. He is a gray-haired, clean-shaven man who admires Lincoln. Some of the time he can remember who he was.

My father never signed up for an army reunion. He didn't tell war stories. He left Europe with the rest of the U.S. troops and went back to Houston, to work in his father's bubble-bath factory downtown. He stayed there for a year. Then he bought a delicatessen nearby. Named it Ruben Rubin's Rubens. He thought about making it kosher, decided that his clientele wouldn't care.

He was right. He patented his special five-course meal: peanuts in the shell, Lone Star Beer, kosher-style ruben sandwich, scoop of Borden's Butter Brickle, a Lovera cigar. His logo, on napkins, giveaway pens, plastic cups: a map of Texas, a corned beef sandwich instead of a dot for Houston.

"A five-course meal," he says now. "I used to charge only a buck fifty. Can you believe it? In 1950s dollars. The things you could buy for a dollar then. When a cup of coffee was really only a dime, just like in the songs."

I am here only for a visit, but he speaks as if I have always been here. Then other times, other times—I wait for those times, am relieved when they finally arrive: the worst, the mind like a naked wall, awaiting the family movies. "Who is it? Ruthie? Ellen? Miriam?"

◆

Every time he looked out the window of the deli he could see the family bubble-bath factory, just down Main Street. On top of the factory was the kewpie doll he'd designed as the symbol of Barnston's Bubblers just before the war. Dolly, the Barnston bubble-girl. (My grandfather Chaim was the one who'd invented the name Barnston. Thought it sounded American, New England-y. Instead, it sounded like an Ellis Island name. Suppliers would call the factory, demanding to speak with Bernstein, the owner.) Every day from the deli window, my father would watch Dolly twirling in neon and every Friday he would take my mother to his parents' house for Shabbat dinner. And every Shabbat my grandfather would wink at them and say, "You know what they say, Ruben, Ruthie—the Sabbath is the time to be fruitful and multiply."

That part I do not know for certain. I am spinning here. I know that for six years my parents were not fruitful; they were fruitless, non-multipliers. They did not divide, add, or subtract. I imagine my grandfather, for whom I am named (Chaim becoming Charles, becoming Chaya, my Hebrew name, turning into Cecilia, Ceci), leaning over my grandmother's white tablecloth, the one she would give to the dry cleaning man when he came to the door each week; I see my not-yet-dead grandfather leaning his arm over the crumbs from the challah, and asking, every Friday night, without fail: "When will you kids give us a grandchild? You know what the rabbis say about creating on the Sabbath—"

I stop here, with the yellow crumbs making indentations on Chaim's lower arm, his fingers (long and sure, like my father's? Like mine?) clasping my mother's, and my mother, circumspect, looking down, wanting to get up to help her mother-in-law in the kitchen, where she can hear water running over the china and silver. I stop with my mother's embarrassment, my father's slight dip into anger, wearying of his father's joke that never varies. I stop—it doesn't pay to delve too deeply into the lives of your parents. This is what I do know: My mother and father wanted children so badly that they consulted a specialist. He advised them to keep track of my mother's temperature every day. My older sister Ellen was a wanted child. This is what they told me once. Faces aglow. They didn't mean to tell, as if they felt a taboo against discussing someone else's wantedness.

In their sixth year of marriage, this is what did or did not happen. My father tells me this story on this visit. As if it is a parting gift. His speech is clear, like a polished window. I see the images perfectly, the way I see the entrance of the camps, the big iron gates, the dark, squalid barracks.

This is what he, Ruben, ex-liberator, ex-owner of a Texas delicatessen, tells his daughter in English, his mother tongue: that one afternoon, after the press of the lunch crowd had ended in the deli, a man walked in. Quietly. "He had a scrunched-in face—like a crumpled piece of paper," says my father, scrunching up his face. The man was carrying a rolled-up Yiddish newspaper in his coat pocket. He must be visiting from New York, my father thought, must be in for Passover; nobody in Houston read Yiddish newspapers. My father was intrigued by this man. He wanted to ask him how he came to be carrying a Yiddish paper, how he had happened upon Ruben Rubin's Rubens non-kosher deli in the heart of downtown Houston. It was the afternoon of the first night of Passover. Without thinking it through, my father asked him to the seder. It was going to be a small one—just my father, my mother, an engineering student from Rice and his wife and three-year-old daughter. My grandparents had gone to Corpus Christi to be with elderly cousins. The real reason they left: My father felt the need to make his own table, away from pointed comments about where was a young child who could ask the Four Questions.

He called my mother to set another place. She was worried about having enough food. My father told her, "He's just a little old man. Very little." My mother laughed into the telephone. "I'll put more water in the soup," she said. I have heard her say this. She would say it when I brought friends home for dinner in junior high, and I would say, "What soup? Are we having soup?" My father said, "I'll bring him home with me." The man seemed content with the invitation, but not so grateful once he arrived at the house. He seemed to be a scholar. He knew much Hebrew and extemporized from the little Haggadahs that each person had, the booklets that came free from Maxwell House Coffee. He complained about the thinness of the service. Everyone grew tired, impatient, but he was from Europe, it was clear, and was therefore somewhat exalted.

Toward the end of the meal, my father asked the daughter of the engineering student if she would walk to the front door to open it for Elijah the prophet. "A cute kid," says my father now. "All red hair and freckles. They called her Howdy Doody for a nickname." The mother and daughter opened the door. The mother came right back to the table. The little girl dawdled. "I figured it's because her legs were shorter," says my father. As soon as she resumed to the table, she started to cry.

Blood streamed from her eyes. My father repeats this. Blood. He raises his eyebrows, impressed with the simplicity of this extraordinary sentence. "Real blood, Ceci," he says, looking me in the eye. "I was thinking at the time, 'as if from a gunshot wound.' " Everyone saw this, her cheeks as if washed with dark red watercolor. But when they went to wipe it, the tears became transparent again, plain salt water, no stain on the napkin. He shakes his head: "The darndest thing," he says. "It seems impossible. All we could do was stare."

And then the man, the strange little man, like a Yiddische Rumpelstiltskin, carefully removed his shoes and climbed up onto his chair. Then he pointed his finger at my father and began to speak. His words were clumsy, dense, the words of a foreigner struggling for elevation: "You, Ruben of the double name, you Ruben, born of American soil, you looked at death in the eyeballs, you, you—" and then the rest of his words were in Yiddish, but a Yiddish no one could understand. Says my father, "A *meshuggenah* kind of Yiddish, garbled, half-words, pieces of words stuck on other words that didn't make any kind of sense. And I know my Yiddish, Ceci. I used to speak it like a native." He laughs, his old joke, because Yiddish is from no country, every country. "Your mother thought we should call the cops. I said, 'For what? Speaking a foreign language in America? Relax,' I told her. 'Have a good time. Bring on the dessert.' It was that coconut cake that she made every Passover, a recipe she got from Mother. I told her I'd make sure the old man didn't break anything." My father's eyes look to the side, as if seeing the same younger self that the old man saw. I have disappeared. I am not yet born.

My father continues: "And then the man kissed the little red-haired girl, who was now sleeping, and walked out the door that they had opened for Elijah. His kiss made a red mark right on her cheek. And that mark," says my father, pausing for drama, "this red mark, has confounded dermatologists to this day."

Where did the girl go? What is her name?

How, I wonder, do her parents explain the mark to her?

She would be six years older than I am. I imagine myself searching the city for women with this mark, women with the Howdy Doody grin and freckles. I will not be distracted by marks on arms, legs, fingers. I will not imagine that her father left town as soon as he was awarded his engineering degree, that she has moved, had cosmetic surgery, or died.

That Passover night was the night they conceived my sister Ellen. (I feel their tiredness, after the guests have gone. I see them washing and wiping the dishes, sweeping the floor. Or did my father say, "Ruthie, let the dishes go hang, we'll make a child and if we like her, we'll make another." I see them clutching, clinging, into the night.) He puts it delicately: "That night we created your sister Ellen." He looks down shyly. I count the months: April, May, June, July, August, September, October, November, November 20.

"Every day in life is a miracle, Ceci," he says, as if this is the logical end of the story, the story of The Mysterious Little Old Man Who Came to the Seder and Removed the Curse of Sterility. The story blossoms out of what is known as a lucid moment. Or more precisely, lucid passages of time. Lucid—a word no one uses except in cases like this.

When he is not lucid, I learn formulas for bubble baths, old marketing approaches abandoned, names of scented flowers, suppliers of corned beef. Shelf lives of fragrances. I hear what I think are Zionist labor songs in Yiddish, which he must have learned from his father.

Sometimes he falls asleep in the middle. Drops off, head drooping on a pillow. In sleep he appears scholarly.

I ask my mother about the old man and she says, "Yes, there was a man—"

My father walks into the room, drowsily, "Like one of those Saint Patrick's Day, Saint Pat's—leprechauns."

He retrieves the word himself.

"—a funny little man," says my mother. (It hurts her to look at my father, to remember, actually hurts the most when he is silent, because then she forgets, forgets he has changed.) "I think he stole something," she says, "some little knickknack. Where did he come from? We never saw him again, did we? I think that couple brought him. What was their name? They both taught French, didn't they, at a high school in Clear Lake?"

"No, no," says my father, angry, and his face crumples up like paper.

I look for tears in the edges of his eyes.

"They had a daughter," I say. "With red hair. Maybe freckles."

My mother shakes her head. "No. There wasn't a child at either of the seders that year. Those were the smallest seders we've ever had. That was the year that Chaim and Miriam went to Corpus. There was only that couple and the old man. I remember that I had to ask the Four Questions. I sang it with that French woman. She was French or Belgian. I think she was Belgian, yes, she was Belgian, I remember thinking I'd never met anybody from Belgium before. I kept thinking about lace. She'd met her husband in Europe, during the war. He was American, and he spoke French, and she spoke beautiful English. I remember the tunes were the same. I couldn't get over that, that she'd learned the same tunes for all the prayers in Belgium. It gave me the shivers." Goose bumps rise on her arms, now. "The next year, that was the year Ellen was a baby, and Chaim took pictures all during dinner."

What about the little man?

"He just up and left in the middle of everything," she says. "Why—?" She is going to say—why bring it up now? Then she remembers again that she is grateful for any link he can give her, any bridge to the past life they had, because it makes him closer, but then she remembers the closer he is, the more painful it all seems. She sighs, turns away.

Then, in a minute, two, the scrim drops and he asks, "What man? What man? What little man?"

He does not look different. He does not, for example, drool. He has his teeth. He does not gum. He looks the same.

They still sleep in the same bed, together; he's on the left, she's on the right. Which gates, once opened, remain open?

◆

My father was a liberator. This is undeniable. There are records that declare it. They are in books, microfilm, microfiche, in government depositories, archives. You can look up ranks, platoons, serial numbers. Combat Command B of the 11th Armored Division of the Third Army. You can watch documentaries, read diaries and memoirs of survivors and soldiers and workers from the Red Cross. You can examine maps, store up details, memorize the lexicon. *Kapos. Badeanstalten. Musselmen. Musselmen* were the slaves who lost all hope, who moved like zombies. Became as foreign and unknowable as Moslems. Named for the hollow-eyed people seen in newsreels, before the war, starving in foreign lands.

My father and his buddies in Combat Command B opened the doors of Mauthausen, eighty miles from Vienna, and liberated the people who might have been us, the people we used to be. They were emaciated, diseased. Some were too frightened to come out of their shacks. Some gathered a *minyan* and prayed. Some stooped down to kiss American hands and feet.

◆

My father was a liberator. He roams the neighborhood. He talks about Lincoln. He takes bubble baths. He eats corned beef sandwiches. There are times he remembers how much he has forgotten. And times he remembers only that he's forgotten. And times that he says, "What little old man? What delicatessen? I was never a soldier boy, soldier boy. I was killed in the war. A bullet pierced my skull. All men are created equal. God sails the open seas."

The books about liberators say that most of them are silent about the experience. Even the ones who are Jewish. An alloy of pride, impotence, fragility. I get this idea and I fight it: that a shrapnel of the past is lodged in his brain, damming up the currents of now, of this life, and if he could remove it—if I could remove it—his life would come flooding back to him.

Or this: If he could somehow retrieve the crazy, garbled Yiddish words of the old man, unravel the riddle of the Rumpelstiltskin, and get them translated—find some combination scholar-psychiatrist, a healer, who could tell us what the message was that the old man was trying to impart—

◆

When my father arrived at Mauthausen on May 6, 1945, I imagine he felt mingled pity, grief, shame: They did this to his people. But they were not his. His people were the men in the division, men who were dressed like he was, in drab, helmeted to protect themselves. They shared coffee, cigarettes, they joked. The ones from the South had familiar accents. They passed around pictures of their girls, of Betty Grable. They were fighting for those legs. For Veronica Lake's curtain of hair.

The story is: We always arrive too late, never knowing what the other has seen. We open gates that others have locked. Scraping the earth as we pull. Rooting out grasses tethered, clinging.

He did or did not tell the prisoners he was Jewish. Is it too much to say that he saw his own death there?

Probably.

Did you try to use Yiddish? Did you look for those who could understand English? Did you ask them, as the doctor asks you, "What is your name? What is your family name? Where are you from? How old are you? Are you in pain? Do you know what is wrong?" Did you ask them in Yiddish, the language of your early lullabies and curses: "Brothers, sisters, where did your lives go? At what point did you feel it fly from you? Did you strain to catch it? Did you shrug, did you turn away?"

# My Mother's War

My mother was an artist. When I was ten, she entered her bone and glass period. I would eat pastrami sandwiches in the utility room, the thick smell of boiling beef fat in the kitchen permeating each bite. I held pickles to my nose like ether. Rings of white grease lined the double stainless steel sinks. She would stand, her French twist unraveling as she blew into the hollow end of a leg bone to free the marrow. The marrow was long and slimy inside the splintering bones, sharp as shards of brown, clear and green glass she collected from the street. (You won't believe how much glass there is outside, she said. You better quit going around barefoot.) In the oven they were supposed to melt together into the kind of threads that glassblowers make. But it never got hot enough. She couldn't understand this. Why then, she asked, do people spend their money on Pyrex if any old glass in the oven doesn't break or melt?

She glued the glass to the bones. She filled their cavities with ground-up glass, the way other mothers filled turkeys with homemade dressing. She always bought chicken Kiev pre-stuffed. At other people's houses I would see mothers wrist-deep inside chickens as if they were caught, momentarily, in their own private patches of quicksand.

◆

The reviewers came to the opening of her show. It was in a rented loft above a weaving factory. The man from the Post called it brilliant. The woman from the Chronicle said it was a sham. That her seven-year-old son working with her three-year-old spaniel could do better, except that they both had more sense than to play with broken glass.

A loudmouth TV anchor ridiculed her for three minutes on the five o'clock news and everyone I met after that said my name sounded familiar.

At her next show she strung baling wire through the bones. Black lights hung from fishnets. Everywhere was the smell of jasmine. The people who attended the opening were long-haired and bearded, wore muted flowing clothes and passed around hash pipes. The Post critic shared his Acapulco Gold.

Someone called the police.

The Post carried the story on the Arts page. The Chronicle put it on Page One. It was an open invitation, my mother said into the phone. We didn't station guard dogs at the door. Middle-class morality, she hissed after she slammed the receiver.

After that she always had to have two opening nights to accommodate the crowds.

◆

Her hippies came to my Bat Mitzvah. My speech was about Jonah and the Whale. That was a violation. I knew it at the time. The story about Jonah is part of Yom Kippur. I was supposed to stick to the Torah portion. But that was about punishment for sorceresses and people who coveted. That's not something a child can relate to, my mother said.

I described the blubber inside the whale. Jonah almost drowned in the fat. This was more frightening than darkness. He felt like he was walking through slimy white mud, through melted chocolate, whipped cream cheese, cakes of softened soap. This was not manna. He could not eat any of it. He was looking for a righteous man. He struck a match and burned the top of the whale's insides. The whale blew him out his blowhole.

This proves, I told the congregation, that the search will save you.

Her hippies told her I was a deep thinker.

At the reception, I rested on a chair along the folding partition that separated the social hall from the sanctuary. A boy sat on my lap and fed me stale sponge cake. When he pinched my nipples and said, Milk Duds, I stood up.

He scampered away.

◆

By the time I was fifteen, she was famous. She flew to New York every two weeks. I lived on Sara Lee cheesecake and Mrs. Paul's fish sticks. In the afternoons I skipped algebra and sat on the sloping cement along the bayou and watched the overflow of the storm sewer. There was much green glass.

◆

Senior year I worked in a pet store. I changed straw every day and caught fish in my bare hands. The goldfish beat against my cupped palm like a heart pressed flat. I would take a deep gulp as I tossed it into a plastic bag. I exhaled as I tied the twist-em.

Don't overfeed her, I warned the earnest little kids.

◆

She bought me a Nikon for graduation. She said, Do you want to take a year off? Not everybody goes to college.

I took one year and it grew to three, four, six.

We count what we call life-credits, the dough-faced lady at the community college said, like she was explaining the rules for hopscotch. You could get an AA degree in three months. What would you say your specialty is? Philosophy?

◆

Two years later I became an artist in the schools. My fingernails turned yellow and my hands always smelled acrid. I concentrated on portraiture. Look what you can do, I told the kids. Preserve what you see. Paint with light. Capture someone and make copies forever.

I would fill in the pictures true-to-life with crayon and copy them on a color Xerox machine. They looked realistic, only somehow rougher. That became my trademark. Post-modern realism, they called it.

◆

Her fame deserted her like a bored lover. She shaved her head and glued her hair to the wall in the living room. She separated the white strands from the black, burning the ends. This took an entire month. If you didn't look closely, it seemed like a small patch of zebra skin was attached to the wall over the couch.

She walked on glass-covered bones, barefoot, like an Indian brave.

I am trying to strengthen myself, she said.

◆

I moved to the next state. I became active in community life. I worked my ten hours a month at the food co-op. I joined the artists' collective gallery. I took an "i" out of my last name. On Sundays I tutored migrant workers' kids. I taught them the game, rock-scissors-paper. Sometimes there was a waiting list for me in the artists-in-the-schools program. The students often sent thank-you notes.

◆

When my mother died, her hippies came to the funeral in black suits. At home, they passed around joints and 'ludes. They brought homemade wine and Hershey bars. Chocolate, someone named Lydia said, has a chemical that uplifts you. That is the reason women eat it after breakups. It's therapeutic. Body wisdom.

You could have brought Toblerone, someone said, instead of some corporate product.

Aren't we supposed to boycott them? a man, someone's new lover, asked.

That's Nestlé, a skinny girl said.

The European bars are the best, said the man. I like Cherry Screams.

I think of chocolate-covered cherries. Inside the chocolate is a sugar crust, which holds in the sweet runny syrup and real fruit, round and still red. It is a house inside a house, a bunker, Jonah in his whale.

And what will you do? Cleo asked me, her smile a withered purple between tissue-thin wrinkles.

What I always do, I said.

She's been on her own for years, said someone I didn't recognize.

◆

This is what she left: scrapbooks of clippings. Invitations to openings. Diploma from Pratt. The certificate of the get, the Jewish divorce.

And instructions for a new show. An environmental piece about the Holocaust. Posthumous. Something that would say, Conceived by Celeste Meyeroff, when it opened.

It needed a builder, someone to execute it. A general contractor sort of artist. I advertised in Art News, American Artist, Present Tense, The Chronicle of Higher Education, small newsletters. It could be set up and shown anywhere. It was that kind of thing.

The best person lived two states north in a college town. I moved there; all places are the same. I became again an artist-in-the-schools. I located a color copying machine at the print shop downtown. I built another darkroom. On weekends I took pictures of traffic accidents and fires for the newspaper.

I helped the artist write the NEA for a grant application form. When she got the money I stopped returning her calls. I said I wanted to be surprised.

The artist invited me on the Sunday before the opening. She left the key to the gallery under the welcome mat. The door opened easily.

I was alone in a large dark room. I stripped, like the sign said. The walls were cementblock. A yellow lightbulb shone from the ceiling in a black cage. I felt it on my back like a sunlamp.

Metal claws snatched at my clothes. I was not given a claimcheck.

I waited for a voice over a loudspeaker. Instead I heard a xylophone, the melody from All Things Considered, cut short.

The light went out. I waited to sense bodies around me.

So what did you expect? I asked myself. This is the artist's conception of the Holocaust. Did you think she would manufacture crematoria? German kapos, shaved heads, lice—those are cliché. You expect these things. Your aunts and uncles, they didn't know what to expect. Didn't know about the showers. Or work camps.

They weren't really my aunts and uncles.

Someone's aunts and uncles. They could have been my relatives, if my great-grandfather had not left Vilna. There had been a family dispute. Something about land. He was disowned.

So there will be no cattlecars. No stench. My mother made her Hell antiseptic.

◆

What will the critics say?

Banal? Passé? The arts critic on the newspaper also covers drama, dance, photography, music (rock and classical), visiting authors and beauty pageant winners. I imagine her sitting at her desk, shuffling press releases with her long fingers that end in narrow slices of red. She smokes. Ashes sprinkle themselves on the white papers, filter into the crevices of the computer keyboard. One day the machine will refuse to mark on its screen and the repair man will be dispatched. He will find ash damage. The newspaper will be presented with an ethical problem: Was it her fault?

Yes. But the editor points out that the paper's medical insurance will cover the stop-smoking sessions at Mercy Hospital.

◆

Walk five paces.

No wall.

Five more.

Run, hands out, like floating on my back, always having an arm extended to rasp against the concrete edge, saving my head. No wall. Counting to 1,000 I run to the left.

No wall.

Blessed art Thou, O Lord our God, King of the World, who has created the never-ending universe, extending far beyond our ken.

I begin in Hebrew. Baruch ata Adonai—but can remember only the blessings over Sabbath candles, wine and bread. And the generic, Thank you for enabling us to reach this season.

◆

This is not our Sabbath. It is the Christian sabbath. The day that nothing is open but 7-Elevens. On Mondays, museums and beauty salons are closed. On Thursdays, retail outlets stay open till nine. Every night except Sunday, the downtown shopping mall is open till nine. White letters proclaim this on the glass doors in front of Penney's: These doors are to remain open at all times during business hours.

What happens to the employee who locks up early? A scolding. He is tired of traffic, of bag-laden shoplifters who graze from department to department, slipping in lacy Hanes and earrings that grow in sharp angles. The girls behind the counter promote these in their many-pierced ears. Pink enamel triangles dancing on turquoise. Hoops. Gold balls.

The Nazis yanked out the Jewish teeth for gold.

The Jews at the foot of Sinai built a calf of gold.

What did Moses do with the calf?

What did the Nazis do with the gold?

Gold, we are told, is precious because it is fragile. Other elements must be added to bolster it. The human being holds trace elements of everything.

Zinc. Uranium. Gold. Silver. Copper. Rubber. Paper, ink. Glass. Inside me is the universe. I am inside a microcosm.

My eyes are the color of a Seven-Up bottle, fragments shining in the sun. I loved my mother.

Her whispers coming from loudspeakers: The exhibit is dedicated to my daughter, because she has been inside whales without a lantern. Behind her lids it is as dark as any Nazi midnight.

The Holocaust is a state of mind, the voice says.

It is wrong. I stand in her limitless night. No stars glitter like broken glass. Dear Lise, says the voice. This is what my world was like, except for the 10 years when my arrangement of the discards of life and death brought me into the circus. I made something new and I was rewarded. But the audience went home.

She is attaching her loneliness to the 6-millionfold horror of burning. My mother did not wear a tattoo, bore no more distinguishing a characteristic than the pain of abandonment. But even if the Holocaust was the human condition writ large, if she attached her wagon to that black star, she refused a chance at happiness.

I do not refuse mine. I do not rejoice at the mutilated: singed hair and broken bits of bone. I do not twist and fray what should be left to rest. I photograph what is. I keep the laws of kosher; I do not cook the lamb in its mother's milk. I do not attach like to unlike. I always focus before shooting.

Lise, you do not create, the voice says. You absorb. Now, I am blinding you with my sorrow.

The Holocaust, says the voice, is my story. It is your story. It is Jonah's story inside the whale.

I remember from my Bat Mitzvah speech: Seek, seek a way out. In the seeking is the answer.

The child's riddle comes back to me: What would you do if you were inside a brick house with scissors and a piece of paper?

Answer: Cut the paper in half. Two halves make a whole. Crawl out through the hole.

That is art.

*Jerzy Zawieyski 1902–1969*  Born in Radogoszcz and raised in Lodz, Poland, Zawieyski studied art history and philosophy at universities in Warsaw, Vilna, and Paris. He acted in the Reduta drama for three years and traveled throughout Europe and Africa in the 1930s.

He made his literary debut in 1932 with a novel; his first play was produced in 1934. He spent the war years in Warsaw, active in the literary, theatrical, and educational activities in the anti-Nazi underground. In the years after World War II, he gained prominence, especially in Catholic intellectual circles, though forced from print and stage during the Stalinist repression. Zawieyski was elected deputy to the Polish parliament by the Catholic group Znak (1957) and became a member of the Council of State. He championed Judaism and attacked Gomulka's anti-Zionist campaign, and finally resigned in protest in 1968 over the repressive measures against the student riots.

He was widely read in western literature and wrote six novels, including *Where Are You, Friend?* (1930) and *The Way Back Home* (1942), nine volumes of essays, stories, journals (e.g., *Pages from a Diary, 1955–1969* [1983]), poetic prose, and twenty-seven plays. Some of his plays are biblical and classical dramas (*Reprieve of Jacob*; *Socrates*); others deal with themes of the Stalinist bureaucracy, the Algerian war of independence, the Canadian Rockies, and wartime Poland.

## CONRAD IN THE GHETTO

I went unwillingly to open the door; I felt sure that it was a mistake, as often happens here, and that it would again be someone asking for my neighbor, Mr. Konieczny, who is never at home. When the bell rang again, I opened the door hastily, pen in hand, mentally concluding the second part of the sentence which I had begun.

It was dark in the passage (it was an afternoon in autumn). I put on the lamp in the hall and by its light saw an elegantly dressed woman, still young, waiting with a flirtatious smile on her face for me to greet her.

"Don't you recognize me?"

"No. Please refresh my memory."

"I'm Dora Rosenblum. Henry's wife."

That's how it began, just as it used to in the stories of olden days—"One fine day in autumn . . ."

I had not seen Dora for almost twenty years, not since the days when I used to visit her and her husband (the poet Henry P., now deceased) in the Warsaw ghetto. So how could I have recognized her immediately? It was only when she mentioned her second husband's surname—and her late husband's first name—that it all came back to me.

No sooner had Dora come in than she burst into a flood of complaints. First of all, she said that she had been looking for me for a long time and only by chance had discovered my purposely concealed address. Then, when she had finally tracked me down, it turned out that she was told that I had gone away, which, according to her, was untrue. She complained, too, about the city. Complained? No. She cursed those who had so designed the reconstruction of the city: nothing was in its place, whole districts were new, and you got lost at every turn because the streets had changed their direction.

"So how can one say that it is the same city? Why has it the same name? It's a lie!" she said, flying into a rage. "Invent whatever you like, but don't parody the old city! Where has it gone? Where?"

It was a long, slow business before her anger subsided and she came to the real purpose of her visit. Dora had come from Tel Aviv to find Henry's grave, and to see to the publication of his poetry. But she had not discovered his grave, and in the matter of having his poetry published, she had also encountered difficulties. On the site of his grave, in the courtyard of a house in the former ghetto, there stood now a block of flats containing thirty-eight apartments.

"Thirty-eight!" she exclaimed excitedly. "What is this—America? How do people here find the way to their flats?"

As she had not succeeded in finding Henry's grave, she no longer wished to wait for a decision about the publication of his poetry, which was not properly appreciated by the publishers here.

She spent the whole evening with me. From the years of our youth she slowly came back to me as she sat opposite me talking about her life in Tel Aviv, about her husband, whom I knew of old, and about her children, now growing up. She and her husband were running a small textile factory, as they had formerly done here. They were doing quite well.

"But what of that?" Dora threw out her arms in a gesture of despair.

I did not understand. Was she referring to the grave which she had failed to find? To Henry?

During this conversation it was not Dora I was thinking about. It was Henry—and, because of him, I was thinking of Daniel.

"Daniel, Dan, Danny." In my thoughts I repeated the name of the six-year-old boy who had died in the ghetto and for whose death Henry was no less to blame than I, but my guilt was the greater. Perhaps, indeed, I am completely weighed down with it. For had it not been for those letters, those ridiculous, idiotic letters!

And this is the story—a story that gives me no peace—which came to life with the arrival of Dora Rosenblum.

Daniel appeared on the scene in the final stage of my friendship with Henry, when it was at its climax, as it were, a few weeks before his death.

I got to know Henry quite by chance, in the army, during our training. Fate ordained that we should occupy bunks in the same barracks. Only Henry had the top bunk and I the one below. I had already read his poems in the literary magazines; consequently, when I heard the familiar name, I eagerly held out my hand to the poet.

Afterwards—many years later—we would often, when we talked, go back to our time in the army, which seemed much more interesting in retrospect than it had been in reality. Our chief recollection was of how we both used to go about exhausted all the time and half-asleep, and how we made use of every free period to have a nap—no matter where, no matter how. Henry, for example, could sleep, or rather doze, even during roll calls, when anything could happen. Once, in a moment of regained consciousness, after taking a nap while at ease during a drill period, Henry, as though pronouncing a metaphysical truth, declared that everything is Sleep and Yawns, "and a monstrous Kip," he added after a moment's thought.

Such then were the impressions which we took away with us from our army service, a trifle ghostlike, a trifle nightmarish, but not so much so that we could not still, years later, discuss them feelingly. The one and only occasion when Henry roused up was when he heard our corporal bawling at the soldiers. This corporal came from Silesia, and his father had played the trombone in a circus. He had at his command an NCO's vocabulary of the highest order. It was not, however, the individual words that set the stamp of originality on his speech: it was the combinations of words, the unexpected, amazing magnificent juxtapositions. The man's speech aroused in Henry, the poet, disingenuous admiration. He exaggerated, of course; but then exaggeration, of good and ill alike, was a trait of his personality.

Henry, then, loved Corporal Przyciasny's extra-subtle turn of phrase, while I, for my part, loved the ceremonial marches to the city. Not a bad

city—Torun. Copernicus's old city. From the barracks you went by a cir-
cuitous route over the bridge on the Vistula before you got to the market-
place. That was where parades and inspections were held. The band used to
march before us, while the section was under the immediate eye of its squat,
swarthy corporal.

"He *is* the army!" I would say in admiration as I studied him on our marches,
during training exercises or even in the barracks.

But it was later on, after we had left the army, that Henry and I went over
all this, when I went to see him at his home.

Henry's home!

His mother had died when he was born: that he might live, his mother
had to die. This was the bitter comment which Henry's father used to make.
Henry's father was a short, thickset, gray-haired man. He had been for many
years a confidential clerk in the Commercial Bank. Nowadays not many
know the meaning of this title, but in those days, in that far-off world before
the Second World War, the post of confidential clerk was quite an important
one. Old Mr. P. had his own favorite pursuits, which had nothing to do with
the bank or banking. He liked philosophy, and of all the philosophers he was
keenest on Friedrich Nietzsche.

It may be that he did not read Nietzsche carefully and failed to perceive
in his philosophy all the somber, suspicious aspects which were aimed at his
race and thereby directly at him. Henry, too, was fond of Nietzsche. Did he,
too, not read him carefully? But who at that time was aware that a criminal
police-state system might derive support from a few sentences torn from their
context, from a few fragmentary theses? On Henry's desk stood a bust of
Nietzsche, which, for my sins, I had once taken for a bust of Pilsudski. Henry
for a long time teased me about this mistake, while old Mr. P. never again spoke
with me about serious matters. The remaining member of this "Nietzschean"
household was Miss Roza, Henry's aunt. She took the place of a mother to
him and brought him up from infancy.

My recollection of Henry's home is made up of the sadness and loneliness of two old people, together with an atmosphere of refined intellectual pleasures. If I called on him before midday, I always found him in bed surrounded
by books. His health was poor, and he had to spend much time in bed, always
anxious lest his temperature might go up. His illnesses were invented by Aunt
Roza; she treated, with remedies of her own contriving, not only Henry and
old Mr. P., but also acquaintances near and far. Despite her special and, one might
call it, hermetic medical knowledge and superior intuition, Miss Roza died
suddenly of aneurysm of the heart, as it used to be called. By that time, Henry
had completed his law studies and was just finishing his bar practice in
preparation for entry into the legal profession. One year after Miss Roza, Henry's
father died, in consequence of what had seemed a trifling complaint. A spot

had formed on his tongue. Mr. P. ignored it. Meanwhile it turned out that
the spot was a cancer.

Thus Henry was left alone in the world. I lost touch with him for several years, and when I again located him, Dora was already on the scene.

Henry had moved and was living in a five-room flat on one of the main
streets. He was a practicing lawyer, but it was obvious that he had not abandoned poetry. In his study, which was furnished with easy chairs and settees,
as befitted a lawyer dealing with important cases, there stood a row of bookcases filled with works entirely unrelated to his profession. On a high pedestal
the bust of Nietzsche stood in the middle of a wall, between the bookcases.
Henry was lost amid the cumbersome, ugly furniture—the atmosphere of solid
affluence which Dora had created. How had the marriage come about? Probably through Henry's poetry, for Dora had long been among the admirers of
his gift. She had come to him once with a slim volume of poems, asking if she
might dedicate them to him. She found him in a deep depression, sick and unable
to cope with life. She made up her mind that she was needed. And so she stayed.
She had recently inherited a textile factory and a large sum of money. She was
an enterprising and courageous woman and managed the factory herself, and
this probably influenced Henry's decision to entrust himself to her care. He
did not need to worry now about his legal practice; he could occupy himself
with writing and his intellectual life. Nietzsche continued to be his favored
thinker, while among writers his only rival was Conrad.

Conrad! It was thanks to him, among others, that little Daniel met his death.
For if Henry had not reread Conrad there, in the ghetto, would Daniel have
come to knock on my door? But I do not wish to anticipate events before concluding the story of Henry.

What, then, do I know about Henry? In truth, so little that despite the bond
of friendship which united us, perhaps I ought not to write about him. But
he will lead me to Daniel and that is why I want to divulge that fragment of
truth about him, as known to me, which will justify events still to be told.

It must be remembered that Henry was a poet and that, because of this,
perhaps, he failed to come to grips with the world and did not understand other
people's affairs. Sometimes I managed to watch him unobserved, during peri-
ods when he was engaged in writing. He reminded me of an unleashed
spaniel, vigilantly and eagerly following the scent of game. If he happened to
be out of doors, he would stop and note down the word which he hunted; if
indoors at home, it would seem to me that he was ill, in a fever, or else that
he had not yet awakened after sleep. He derived his literary pabulum from every
quarter. From every quarter? No, only from dreams, from his own visions, or
from the mystery which resides in recording the world in the first person.

This tendency to see nothing outside oneself and to be incapable of
understanding people, necessary no doubt for writing poetry, was gradually

becoming a facet of his nature, an inhuman facet, I make so bold as to call it. Henry passed people by and failed to comprehend the world, although he was neither bitter against it nor in revolt. Is it any wonder that he failed to understand the history of his own times, or, to be exact, regarded the world as unworthy of notice?

Let us not hold that against him. He was like other poets of his time. Let us remember only that it was poetry that gave his life its purpose; thus we will better understand his behavior in the period of the war and the ghetto. During the time which I am now describing, Daniel was not yet in the world, and I am writing about Henry in order to come to Daniel. Thus, although Daniel did not yet exist, events had begun which were later to destroy the little boy— events which can be expressed by the names Nietzsche and Conrad. It might seem that these are symbols, existing only in the realm of literary tastes.

So it might seem. Yet Nietzsche provided the inspiration for a system which built—if it built anything at all—the crematoriums in the concentration camps. And Conrad? Little Daniel knew nothing of either Nietzsche or Conrad.

Conrad then. Besides Nietzsche, Henry read Conrad with pleasure and delight. And, probably, reading him, he did not interpret his meaning aright, since later . . . But there is time enough for this "later," and, by Heaven, there is no call for haste.

In order to raise her social standing in the circle of small-scale manufacturers, Dora used to put on frequent and sumptuous receptions. To these I would sometimes be invited. Henry, of course, was the chief and sole attraction at these occasions. It was touching to see the adoration accorded the poet by people occupied solely with swelling their bank accounts, solely with that unclean, if not positively dirty, business. If he so much as deigned to speak, silence and rapt attention ensued. The program at Dora's receptions was always the same: as soon as everyone was assembled in the ugly green drawing room, Henry would read his latest poems aloud. And Henry, as I observed, enjoyed the most lavish flatteries paid him, even—oh horrors!—the comparison of his poetry with that of Goethe! Why with Goethe's it was impossible to discover. (Nor did Henry know why this company should have thought of Goethe.)

After a few glasses of vodka had been downed, in the interval between courses, Henry would give a second piece. This was by way of being an act of rebellion against Dora's friends, so he explained it to me. But nobody took it in this way—on the contrary. His second reading was considered a splendid joke. Henry, slightly tight, would bang on his plate, take a slip of paper out of his pocket, and read out neither more nor less (only skillfully arranged in sequence) than a catalogue of the barracks phrases used by our corporal. "There's poetry for you! There's real poetry!" He would

shout this in ecstasy, amid general laughter and the plaudits of the assembled
company.

But how else could Dora's guests react to the corporal's "poetry"? And
could they realize that Henry was expressing his rebellion? I always had the
impression that, contrary to his intention, he sustained a painful defeat by
reciting from the corporal. Possibly Henry sensed this too, since more often
than not, he would vanish immediately from the dining room and shut himself up in his own room, on the pretext of having a headache. Dora's friends
continued to amuse themselves, probably feeling relief at being freed from
the burden of this fantastical poet, the supposed new Goethe.

Of the guests only one abstained from applauding Henry when he recited
the corporal's poetry. This was Samuel Rosenblum, who had recently become
a partner in Dora's firm. Did he perhaps understand the significance of the recital?
Or did he think that Henry had exceeded the bounds of decency?

When I asked him why he was not amused by what Henry read at the
table, he replied simply, "It bores me."

Mr. Rosenblum was always silent and preoccupied, his brows knitted on
his low forehead. But one time I heard the sort of confidences which he
addressed to Henry's wife. It was at the end of one of these showy parties,
already getting on toward morning. I was sitting in an easy chair, listening to
a technical discourse from the director of a chemical factory, when there reached
me the words which poor (as he struck me)—poor, tormented Mr. Rosenblum was uttering.

"They're all rotten to the core. Rotten, did I say? In plain terms, it's like
a lot of swine wallowing in the mire. I'm not talking about that filth that Henry
read out. All around. Look at that Mrs. Goldberg and that Zimmer of hers,
Dora! Perhaps I'm supposed just to look at you and be content, Dora, while
they can do what they like? I shan't be stealing you from him—he hasn't got
you as it is. Tomorrow—tomorrow week perhaps—we'll make a business trip
to Vienna. We must! No? Why not? Do let's go! Dora, Dora . . ."

Henry's relations with Dora's partner were on a correct footing and,
knowing Henry, I can risk the assertion that it never occurred to him that Mr.
Rosenblum might be Dora's lover. It was not until they were all three together
in the ghetto that Henry's eyes were opened.

Again I lost track of him for a while, and the occasion of our being reunited
was associated with Conrad. It was in a well-known café patronized by writers. Henry had matured; he had put on weight and become bald, but, although
he had aged, he had lost none of the charm of his poetic nature, somehow so
childlike and impulsive. He was just telling me excitedly how he was working on a film script, when suddenly in the middle of a word he stopped, seized
me by the arm, and, looking in the direction of a man who was coming into
the room, whispered:

"Conrad!"

And so it was. Just as if a well-known photograph of Conrad had come to life—wearing a black overcoat, with a hat, and carrying a stick. The supposed Conrad walked slowly, with dignity, as befitted one of his small stature. We thought that we could see the Malay isles, or that any moment the unhappy Lord Jim would appear, or Heyst perhaps, or Lingard.

"Conrad" looked around the room for a minute, then sat down near us, where there was a table free. We watched him in silence, our hearts standing still. But then up came rushing a stoutish individual and shouted to him from across the room:

"Mr. W., will you go at once to the warehouse. A fresh load has arrived from Lodz."

Our reverie was cut short. It was a sad moment.

I began to see a lot of Henry again. Not at his home, in the study with the easy chairs, but more often than not in that same well-known café. This was now the period when Nietzsche, brought out into the light of day by the new politicians, uttered a threat only later to be recognized.

During that time I had been in Nietzsche's native land. I returned from it with the feeling that I had been on a journey to hell. Henry listened unenthusiastically to my impressions; some of the things which I had seen there he took jokingly as manifesting stupidity not unmixed with a certain piquancy. I think now that Henry, who had failed to comprehend Nietzsche and Conrad, failed still more dismally to comprehend his own time. But did others comprehend it any better? I too succumbed to the collective unconcern, although the recollection of what I had seen in Nietzsche's native land oppressed me like an incubus's importunities. To all outward appearances things could not have been better. There were visits by ministers and marshals and diplomats, and there were diplomatic hunting parties, at which toasts of friendship were exchanged.

"Look! Our president, Moscicki, and that fat German slob Field Marshal Goering." Henry would wave the paper in front of my face. "Do you see? This means something, doesn't it?"

"My dear fellow, let's talk about serious matters. There's a new book by Lesmian out. Have you seen it?"

It was at about this time that Daniel was born. Yes. He was already alive and kicking, growing up to meet his fate. His place in the world was a mean and humble one, in a shed in a yard, in one of those suburban holes which it is a pitiful irony to call a town. One Sunday toward the end of the last years, or months perhaps, of that era in which the world was walking upon a precipice, not seeing it or wishing to see it, it was possible to read in the papers that in the land of Nietzsche Jews had been forbidden to enter public places, such as theaters, cinemas, and concert halls. A decree was also issued which obliged Jews to wear the Star of David on their arm.

I was sure that anyone reading this must feel shame that anywhere in the world such a thing could be thinkable, above all in Europe! And that this was being done by the compatriots of Goethe! Of Thomas Mann! Of Bach! I hurried to town, thinking, of course, about Henry and imagining his dismay.

The café was packed, and I managed with difficulty to get to Henry's table. On all sides I heard the laughter of lively, cheerful people. Henry, like the rest, was enjoying himself hugely, Dora was laughing her high-pitched laugh, and even Mr. Rosenblum had succumbed to the general atmosphere of gaiety.

I showed Henry the paper.

"Rubbish! Nonsense!" he cried, with a loud guffaw.

I went out of the café quickly; then I ran through the streets, as if I were running away. For I was running away. I was running away.

Carnival time came around; again there were repeated visits by ministers, again toasts and speeches. And certain speeches, of course, were taken seriously by nobody.

In his yard, beside the gutter. Daniel was growing. He was four, then five, then six. Then came what had to come.

A few weeks after the outbreak of war, one cold, rainy day, following my return from travels in the East, I saw Henry in the distance down the street. On his left sleeve was an arm band with the Star of David.

◆

I visited Henry in the ghetto a few days after our encounter in the street. The heat of the fires in the city had not yet died. Streetlamps, bowed toward the ground, still swayed in the breeze. The rubble had not yet been cleared. Those who had stayed on in the first days of the war, those who had not marched off to the East, remembered with horror the siege of the city, especially a certain Monday, a few hours before the capitulation, when it seemed that the sky had been transformed into a hell, as fire and iron rained down from the silvery airplanes overhead. In the rare intervals of quiet the Lord Mayor's voice could be heard—a hoarse, rasping voice which appealed for calm, offered counsel, but above all gave an assurance that someone was keeping watch and that someone existed. That someone existed, just that. From time to time the radio emitted a tragic tune, the same that the French sent the city in the time of the 1831 November Uprising—the "Warszawianka."★ The song wreathed itself about the deserted, empty, dead-looking city, calling now only to the paving stones, to the ruins, to go and fight at bayonet point. Fight whom? A fiery abyss?

Now, after the disaster, an amazed human silence filled the streets. It was the end of November, frosty already and presaging an early, hard winter.

---

★ "The Warsaw Song."

Henry was living in the heart of the Jewish quarter in a gloomy house, the stone courtyard of which was filled with lofty outbuildings. When I knocked on the door on the third floor, he drew me into a dark passage, cluttered with cupboards, then led me through another, somewhat lighter passage to his apartment. In the first large room, I came upon Dora and Samuel, who were sitting at a table playing patience. We greeted one another more effusively than usual, like people who have survived a common disaster. A second room, which was small and narrow, was occupied by Henry. I noticed at once a great change in him. He was slimmer and seemed younger. The arm band with the Star of David hung on the door handle. I looked around the room: a bed, a small table, chairs, and around the walls large cupboards, on top of which there were boxes reaching up to the ceiling. There was little room to move, and the room was dirty. From time to time we punctuated our labored silence with exchanges of information about everyday matters. After a while Dora brought in tea, a strong, fresh brew, made from a supply laid in long before. Contrary to her wont, she did not try to disturb us but retired quickly to her own room.

"They live in there; I live in here," said Henry, with a bitter smile.

I had not raised the subject, in order to avoid giving away what I had known all about long before. Henry's fate since the war began had been quite simple: the house in which he lived had been bombed, so he and Dora had gone straight from the shelter to relatives of Samuel's. And so they had come to stay here as a threesome, not knowing what would happen next.

I expressed the generally accepted conviction that it would last only till spring. Henry smiled and shook his head in disagreement.

"The war will last for years," he said.

I made light of this, as if it were a specimen of the perversity which is understandable in high-strung people.

So we sat in silence till dusk, which fell early. Henry lit a candle, since there was no electric light now in that quarter, and at my request he read his latest poem aloud. It was a poem about his father. At the end Henry said that the spot on old Mr. P.'s tongue had come at the right time. That, I think, was the only allusion to the times through which we had been living.

At that period one often saw people with arm bands doing manual labor or being conveyed—or, rather, unceremoniously driven—to work. So Henry seldom went out of the house. What did he do? What did he think about? His poem about old Mr. P. suggested to me that Henry was now at last coming to terms with the past. Probably he had been roused from his dreams with a greater sense of alienation than others, with a greater sense of dread. At that time everyone was busy looking for scapegoats, raking through recent history. Whom did Henry blame? Did he remember that day when I brought him the news about the Star of David? When I visited him in his crowded, dark, dirty room I had no wish to go back to the past. The subjects of our conversation were political news and news from the front, and banalities. Politics consisted of the frequent lengthy speeches churned out by those conducting the war. The news from the front irritated us more, because there was no sign of any offensive getting under way. We lived in daily expectation of this. Happenings in the city and the country were the only reality. The prisons were permanently filled, and the camps, prepared beforehand in the land of Nietzsche, were engulfing great numbers of innocent people. The whole country had impressed upon it the existence of the camp at Oranienburg, to which forty professors from the Krakow Jagellonian University had been sent. A still greater impression was made by the news that these men, while on muster parade in the frosty weather waiting for they knew not what, would exchange talk about their latest scholarly researches. Thus hope came to the whole country, and a model of unshakable resolve was established: notions abandoned in the days of unconcern and license returned. The appeals of poets, humanists and preachers for man to rise above his limited humanity again became alive. Henry acknowledged that a moral rebirth of mankind was being achieved, although unhappily through a bloody harvest of misfortune.

Even then, when our misfortunes had scarcely begun, we devised various systems of consolation, having no inkling of the gradual pressure exerted by evil. So also today, years later, we do not know if the measure of evil has been fulfilled without residue. From that bloody seed time has there come forth that of which Henry and I used to talk? Today there exists no longer either the quarter where Henry lived or the narrow, crowded room in which we comforted each other with visions of the future. Today bright, spacious new blocks of dwellings, erected by the faith and hope of those who came through, rise up on the very spot where he once lived; but would it be going too far to express a fear that misfortune is still lying in wait to descend on us, this time without any hope for the future? And, by Heaven, have we learned any more than that evil is infinite and that it exists not beyond but within the human kind? Henry happily was spared confirmation of the full extent of mankind's capabilities. His death, like old Mr. P.'s spot, came just in time.

Meanwhile, on the threshold of a new epoch, we both lived on illusions, believing, for example, in the power of the type of culture expressed by the professors imprisoned in Oranienburg. But could there be any other symbol for us? If the authority of statesmen had been overthrown, if military heroism had yielded, if on the streets of our capital only a tragic foreign song about our way of dying remained—what other choice had we?

After a while Henry began to occupy himself with translating Rilke; he had always liked and admired the poet, and he had known German well since childhood.

We were seeing less of each other now that life provided us both with so many day-to-day cares. I was incomparably worse off materially than he, and I had difficulty in getting through the first terrible winter of the war. I availed myself of an invitation from friends, and I was to go away to the country from mid-December until the end of March. Henry regarded this as a fortunate solution of my problem.

I went away. I returned, however, not in March but in October.

A few days afterwards I went to visit Henry. Alas! It was too late. The ghetto was now walled off and surrounded by barbed wire. I could not get through to him. But he reached me—through Daniel.

◆

A trifling thing happened: I lost my food ration cards. I searched for them at home, in the street, in the shop; I searched the staircase; I ransacked the papers on my desk. I went outside several times, in case someone had found them and might be looking for me. I had just come home after a vain search, when by the door, in the dark passage, something moved. In the corner a child was sitting, a little boy, staring at me.

"What are you doing here?" I asked in amazement.

The child pulled out a battered envelope, on which I made out my name. I took him by the hand and led him into my apartment. I was in a bad mood and, with the letter in my hand, I continued to search for the lost food cards. When finally I gave up and came back to the room, the little boy, slumped against the stove, seemed to be asleep. But he woke up at once. He had a bold, inquiring look.

The first sentences of Henry's letter informed me that the boy was from the ghetto, that his name was Daniel, and that from now on he would act as courier between us. For, wrote Henry, only a nimble and crafty six-year-old shrimp such as he could get past the wire and through a hole in the walls without attracting the notice of the guards.

It was a long letter. I deferred reading it until later, intrigued by this singular courier.

"Your name's Daniel, then?"

The little boy nodded.

"And what do they call you at home?"

"Where?"

"At home," I repeated.

"I haven't got a home," replied Daniel, looking me in the eye.

I noticed that his voice sounded harsh, as if he were hoarse.

"What about your mummy and daddy?"

Daniel hung his head and fingered a hole in his stocking. Feeling that I must have hurt him with my questions, to make up for it, I started telling him about a certain Wladek, with whom I used to go fishing.

But Daniel displayed no interest in my story. I suggested, therefore, that we should have something to eat, and I began making tea. After a while Daniel followed me into the kitchen. Again I talked to him, as if to a grownup, about my stay in the country and about the children whom I had met there. This time he listened.

Tea was now ready and the bread cut, and there was also some gingerbread. Daniel, to my astonishment, asked of his own accord where he could wash his hands. He returned presently with hands clean and face washed. He was grinning contentedly. Now at last I had a good look at him for the first time. He had large black eyes with an expression of touching seriousness. His hair, long uncut, fell about his head in curls and ringlets. His most surprising feature was his voice, which contrasted with his childish good looks. I remember how difficult it was that first day to start up a friendship between us. Only when we were in the kitchen did he begin to talk about himself. I learned that he had three elder sisters, Leah, Sarah and Manya, and that his father had been killed by the Germans because he would not leave his workshop in a small place near Warsaw and go to the ghetto. It happened before the eyes of the entire family. His mother went to work somewhere different every day and only came back now and then, once or twice a week, to the apartment of a washerwoman, who lived in the basement of the house where Henry lived. His sisters were also working, but where, Daniel did not know. He himself stayed here, there and everywhere, but most often with Mr. Samuel Rosenblum's relatives.

Daniel talked about all these matters with quiet dignity, not at all like a six-year-old child. When we went back to the room, he announced that he had to go now.

"What about the letter?" I said, pointing at the reams of paper from Henry lying spread out. "I must read it and send a reply."

"I'll come tomorrow at midday. I have to go somewhere else now," he said.

He was going two streets farther, as it turned out, to run another errand. But he would not say to whom he was going or what he had to deliver there. He had nothing on him. He added that he would stay the night at the place he was going to. When I bent down to kiss Daniel good-bye, I could feel papers rustling beneath my fingers down his back. He had them under his pullover and jacket.

"Aren't you afraid of the Germans?" I asked seriously.

"I can always give them the slip!" Daniel boasted. "I've given them the slip once already. I hollered and made off."

We parted until the next day.

After Daniel had left I continued to watch him out of the window; I saw him quickly running past pedestrians. I wanted to start reading Henry's letter, but I kept thinking about this unusual courier from the ghetto, who, with illegal papers concealed down his back, was running through the streets to meet someone and execute the commission entrusted to him.

I took up Henry's letter. I read it. I read, not believing what I was reading. I reread this letter of Henry's written from behind the walls. It was an impassioned, though distant, letter, and in it I found something of the attitude of the Oranienburg academicians, something of the perversity of the poet defending the honor of a humanist down in the ghetto. The letter was about Conrad.

Henry was rereading his favorite writer and this time, according to him, reading him properly, apparently for the first time. Behind the walls, cut off from the world, he understood better the meaning of Lord Jim's Patusan—Patusan, the ghetto of loneliness. The whole letter was the result of his reading.

He and Lord Jim were united by similarity of experience, although Henry, as he admitted, had not run away from any *Patna* in order to save himself. But at the same time he posed the dramatic question: had he not run away? Had not both he and others? Had we not deserted the ship when the storm drew nigh?

Henry directed these questions not only at himself but also at me, making me, too, responsible for our ship.

He devoted a large portion of his letter to the great dialogue, as he called it, between the criminal Brown and Lord Jim. Henry asserted, like Marlow, that this dialogue was one of the cruelest duels that had ever been fought on earth. The dialogue was watched by Fate, cold and indifferent, for only it knew how the struggle would end.

He reported that during one of the numerous checkups he had had a conversation at his place with a Gestapo officer, an educated Bavarian, who was an admirer of Rilke. It was precisely the dialogue described many years earlier by Conrad, which that great writer, unaware of what might happen on earth in time to come, had placed in a tropical land with the attractive name of Patusan. In his letter Henry continually stressed the analogy, saying "here in Patusan" or "in our Patusan." He promised to write about his talks with the Gestapo man in his next letter.

What did Henry want? Seemingly—so I understood his letters then—he wanted to perish, holding converse with the criminal Brown, to die with honor and a clear consciousness of his own death, since he saw no deliverance after death.

It was just this that aroused my opposition. How could Henry want this? Terror was spreading ever wider; executions were being carried out in the streets, and camps were being set up, not somewhere in the land of Nietzsche, but here, in our own country. People were being picked up everywhere, from their homes, in trams, in cafés. The ghetto, Henry's Patusan, was walled up, and only someone like little Daniel could get through a hole to the city. We were all living on the thirst for revenge. We impatiently awaited an offensive in the West. We knew that the ghetto's walls of shame would crack.

It was from these realistic premises that my letter to Henry stemmed. It began with the words: "Ruler of Patusan, dear Lord Jim!" I wrote this partly in irony because of his absorption with Patusan, and partly in acknowledgment of his inventive interpretation of Conrad; but I also described quite forcefully the reality in which we outside the walls were living. I defined the attitude common now to many in these words:

"The one really worthy answer to the barbarians is a gun in one's hand!"

Again at the end I banged out the word "gun"; then I put this anti-Conradian letter into the envelope which I was to hand to Daniel the next day.

But Daniel did not come at midday, as he had promised. He did not come until nightfall was far advanced. He was different, gayer than the previous day, relaxed and talkative. But, despite this, he would not say why he was late or where he had been or what he had been doing. He ran all around the apartment, then washed his hands and face in the bathroom, delighted to be able to do so. He would not eat anything, however, as he was in a great hurry to get to Henry before the curfew hour.

I put my letter into the inner pocket of Daniel's jacket and again down his back I could feel a packet containing papers.

I, too, began to read Conrad, following the same lines as Henry in his Patusan. But I read him differently, with resistance, polemically. More than once—why I cannot now understand—I threw the book from me almost with hatred. But I went back to it again when my antagonism had died down. At that time, in 1940, nobody was reading Conrad; probably nobody in our wounded city thought of reading him over again. Was it otherwise behind the walls? Was Henry alone in his passion for penetrating to the nerve of history?

In Henry's courtyard (this is connected with Daniel) not a blade of grass would grow. Only later—oh God, that courtyard!—but let us not anticipate events. We are waiting then for Daniel, and whatever we say about the poet concerns also this child. Especially that barren stone courtyard as severe and harsh to the eye as only prison courtyards are.

Daniel came a few days later, just before the curfew. He did not knock, did not ring, but scratched on the door.

"Well, here I am!" he said as he came in.

This time he was distracted and restless. He had to touch every single thing on my desk and on the shelves and look it over, asking all the while, "What's this? What's this for?" Then he did not listen to my explanations and at first would not answer when I asked him something. Later, when he finally sat down in an arm chair, I could see that he was bored as I told him about a journey I had made to Africa some years ago. Perhaps it was too difficult, because he showed no interest either in the monkeys which had removed my helmet and scampered off up a palm tree or in the Negroes whom I had visited in their village and who might have eaten me.

Suddenly Daniel interrupted my story and said, "And I've been in Pyry. There the cabbages grow as big as . . . oh, as big as that table."

I seized upon this visit to Pyry, but Daniel changed the subject to practical matters. "I'd like some cabbage," he announced. "Is there any?"

Fortunately there was cabbage. There were also various delicacies which I had saved for him.

In the kitchen Daniel felt more comfortable than in the other room, where apart from the books, desk and settee there was nothing of interest to a child. Here, however, the sideboard and its contents sent him into raptures. I let him do whatever he liked, because his very presence gave me pleasure. Was this because it was Daniel in particular, or because there was a child around me? Perhaps both. Probably even then I loved my little courier. That evening I became conscious of the fact that I could take him to myself and thus save him from an evil fate. For what might be in store for him down there outside the walls? Lately news had been going around that the Germans were removing people from the ghetto to the camps. They might take Daniel too. They might catch him carrying some secret literature, or they might intercept my letter to Henry, or one from him to me. I knew inevitably that Daniel faced death, since these criminal "Browns" did not spare even children.

I resolved to save Daniel.

"Do you like it here?"

He shrugged his shoulders and after a while said yes, he did.

"Perhaps you'd like to stay?"

"For good?"

"Yes, for good."

"No! I don't want to!" cried Daniel, stamping his feet. Then he burst into tears. For a long time I tried to calm him, and of course I withdrew my proposal. He sat down under the stove, with his back turned to me, and sobbed quietly. He refused to undress for bed and would not lie on the sofa, preferring to sleep where he was, under the stove. I spread rugs on the floor, brought cushions, then went back to my work at the desk. Presently he wriggled under the blankets fully clothed, except for his little shoes, which he placed beside him.

I did not give up, however. I decided to ask Henry for help.

I began reading the letter which Daniel had brought.

Once more it was about Conrad. But this time Henry described his conversations with the Gestapo man; he had taken a fancy to Henry and visited him, invariably drunk, at various times of night and day, but more often than not in the night or at daybreak. The Gestapo man was called Rudolf Stein, but Henry saw in him the criminal Brown, coming to destroy Jim—that is, himself, Henry P., in Patusan, the land of loneliness. So at unexpected hours, their interviews continued—a savage duel between Henry and Stein, Lord Jim and Brown, perhaps even between Faust and Mephistopheles. Henry wrote that his life now consisted of waiting for his Brown, a waiting equivalent to waiting for death. On the table, at which their great dialogues took place, there was always vodka and beer, and a gun.

A gun! The word which I had used carelessly had come back in Henry's letter.

So, with vodka and a gun in front of him, Stein told Henry all about the great crimes committed by Jews in history. He told him that he, Henry P., the poet who translated Rilke, had poisoned men's souls with his poetry. He was guilty of a crime—deeply serious because it was a spiritual crime and infinite in its consequences. Stein hoped his pupil understood this and the duty Providence had laid upon Nietzsche's noble people to exterminate a race so criminal and perfidious. Stein, who loved Rilke, who loved poets in general, who loved music and everything of the spirit, everything beautiful—Stein, a worshiper of Bach, was obliged to be here, in this Philistine, louse-ridden, half-savage country and had to be here in the ghetto to carry on apostolic conversations (were they not apostolic?) with a poet criminal!

More than once Stein burst into tears over his lot, poured himself more vodka, and took up his gun, aiming it at Henry.

The worst of all, according to Henry, was Stein's lyrical-*cum*-emotional outbursts. He had a wife called Else and a daughter named Luise. Stein suspected Else of being unfaithful to him with Erik, who worked in the military administration. When Stein talked about this, he trembled with indignant rage; here he was having to talk to Henry, when at that very moment Erik was probably lying serene and happy in the embrace of his Else. What had the poet to say to that? Could he give him any advice? Henry tried to assure Stein that it was inconceivable that Else could prefer anyone else to such a splendid officer and subtle connoisseur of the arts as he, Stein. Stein genuinely seized upon this apparently, for he clapped Henry on the back, put away his gun, and took his leave.

Dora and Samuel Rosenblum, closeted in their relatives' overcrowded room, used to wait for Stein's departure, and then put Henry to bed, for after these visits he always looked as if he were on the point of death.

At the end of his letter he again touched on Lord Jim's sufferings and his sense of guilt, which seemed so much the greater since the *Patna* did not sink. But our *Patna*? Our *Patna*? he beseeched. I decided to write about this too. In my letter I wanted also to raise the separate question of Daniel.

I spent a long time writing to Henry. The quiet of the house and city contrasted with the horrors of the second year of war. Next morning about noon our little courier set out to take my letter to the ghetto. This time he carried no illicit literature; this I had discovered by making a thorough search the previous evening.

He was in a better mood. He had slept well and was washed and fed. I wanted to see him off when he left, but he objected. However, I accompanied him down the stairs to the gate, then watched for a long time, until the droll, enchanting little figure disappeared from view.

The house seemed empty after he had gone.

I cannot now reckon up the number of visits from Daniel; neither can I reproduce from memory all of Henry's letters. I do know that on occasion, Daniel dropped in for just a moment and that he did not always bring news from my friend. But this happened probably not more than three times, if that. Daniel would scratch on the door, then come in with his little triumphant cry, "Well, here I am!"

He would roam about the apartment for a while, always making a visit to the bathroom, then he would have something to eat and make a speedy departure, indifferent to my appeals to him to stay longer.

One of Henry's letters concerned only Daniel. It was a reply to my plea for the little boy to stay with me permanently, or with my relatives who lived nearby. Henry did not regard my proposal with enthusiasm. He said I should realize that we needed Daniel—"we" meaning he and I. The boy was irreplaceable as a means of communication with the outside world and indispensable to many others in the ghetto. Above all, however, Henry went on, this little shrimp was able to produce a soothing effect on him during the fits of depression which came after Stein's visits—the child knew when to come, what to say, how to behave; he knew how to chase away the ever-present specter of death.

"I sometimes think of him as my own son," Henry wrote.

His son! I guessed immediately that this was the real reason why he did not want me to take Daniel. Afterwards I often reproached myself for not being able to muster up the strength to carry out my resolve. But how could I deprive Henry of his one solace? The one solace of his nightmarish existence, taken up with waiting for visits from Stein.

So I let things stand. Daniel was becoming attached to me and probably enjoyed dropping in, just as the fancy took him, without warning, if only for a brief visit. I discovered, moreover, a mutual pastime which Daniel liked— drawing. Who could draw the best duck? Or airplane? Or soldier? Or tree? We both drew with enthusiasm and of course Daniel's drawings were always much better than mine. They really were better. They were bold, unusual and had a tendency for exaggeration which bordered on the grotesque. I genuinely admired his wit and shrewd observations. Daniel might have become a real artist, for his drawings expressed something more than the drawings of the ordinary child. I often wondered what Daniel would grow up to be, if he survived— if he survived.

Fear for his life never left me. At the same time I did nothing to guard him from danger. And danger threatened him continually, every day, every hour.

One day before my very eyes I witnessed what might have been the death of Daniel.

I was riding in a tram along the main street of our city when suddenly through a windowpane I saw a group of people watching two gendarmes, armed with rifles and grenades, escorting or, rather, leading by the arm a little boy who was weeping and shouting, stamping his feet, and crying for help. I recognized Daniel. The tram was packed, but despite that I managed to jump off fairly quickly while it was moving. When I succeeded in getting near the group of people, Daniel was no longer there. The gendarmes were proceeding down the street, looking solemn and haughty, doubtless somewhat ashamed that the victim of their rough treatment was so incongruous to the physical and armed might which they were flaunting. I did not need to ask what had become of Daniel, for everyone was remarking upon the little boy's courageous escape. Why and in what circumstances had the Germans taken him? Where had he escaped to? Nobody knew.

Although he had got away, I continued to worry about him. I resolved this time not to give in to Henry. I would keep Daniel with me the next time he came. Therefore, I began to think of the details of life needed for a child in a house not prepared for a child; I arranged for a teacher to come, so that the boy should have lessons, and I came to an agreement with my relatives by which we would jointly take care of him. And I waited daily for Daniel.

At last he came. He arrived at nightfall, just before curfew time, making his special scratching noise on the door. He walked in with his triumphant "Well, here I am!" bringing a long letter from Henry, which I immediately put away on my desk for nighttime reading. I reproached Daniel for not coming sooner and also questioned him about the gendarmes. He burst out laughing, waving his hand deprecatingly, making light of the affair. A very ordinary incident, he said; there had been many like that. He knew how to shout and cry so they always let him go.

"But what did they pick you up for?" I insisted.

"Oh, because I spat at them!"

"Daniel!" I cried severely.

He threw his arms around my neck and pulled me over to the desk to do some drawing with him. After that we had supper, and after that Daniel had a good wash in the bathroom and went to bed. This time he agreed to sleep on the divan.

I decided to say nothing about keeping him with me until next day at breakfast time.

After Daniel had gone to sleep, I began reading Henry's letter. First of all he reported that Stein had gone on ten-day's leave to be with his Else; that was why Daniel had not been coming to me. They had been spending the time together playing and he had had a wonderful feeling of freedom, at least for these ten days, which would be up today. Doubtless, tonight or in the early morning Stein would arrive with his gun and vodka bottle.

I looked at the date. The letter was dated the previous day, so Daniel must have left the ghetto then and had doubtless spent the night at the place with the people two streets away to whom he took the secret messages. I was disturbed by news that Henry was ill; he had a high fever, but only Daniel knew this.

"It must be kept a secret from Dora," Henry stated. I did not know why. However, at the time I did not attempt to solve the mystery, being concerned with whether Stein might now be at Henry's with the inevitable gun and vodka bottle.

His letter was once again mostly about Conrad. To be exact, the first part, which referred to *The Rescue*, contained comments about love, skillfully concealed beneath a description of the conversations of people threatened with disaster, stranded on sand banks in a shallow sea, cut off from the world. Once again a discovery on Henry's part, full of allusions to his conditions in the ghetto—the selfsame shoals, the vast expanse of waters, the condemnation to loneliness and banishment from the world.

The people in *The Rescue* were threatened with a death which hourly drew nearer. Yet their souls were filled, not with fear, but with love—in other words, filled with something diametrically opposed to that other extreme which is death. Lingard, the splendid, valiant sea wolf, experiences the birth of love, its growth, the insane passion and agony of it, to all of which he was ever faithful. Poor Miss Travers, beautiful and lonely, is only able to say to herself, "So be it," as if this sentence contained a summary and balance sheet of her entire life. The conversation between Lingard and Miss Travers, which occurs on a reef washed round by the boundless sea, on a tiny hunk of sandy soil, moist beneath their feet, is a hopeless dialogue embracing only the themes of love and death. This dialogue, according to Henry, was a tremendous testimony to the greatness and weakness of man.

"Only we who are confined to the ghetto can understand this," he wrote. "For this is, as it were, a ballad or folk tale about us, about people dishonored, to whom there remains yet one resource—to be transported by love."

I broke off reading and put the letter aside. Daniel was asleep. I could not look enough.

So this conclusion too, I thought sadly as I paced my room in the middle of this wartime night, had to occur to Henry, and release with it hopeless yearnings, truly inconceivable in his position. Henry described Miss Travers, not as Conrad described her, but as if he were describing his dreams of a unique woman created in his imagination to the specifications of his own longing. What could this be if not that which he called "a tremendous testimony to the greatness and weakness of man"?

In the next section of his letter there were a few sentences about Dora and Samuel, who were now—and perhaps for the first and last time—experiencing after their fashion a "transport of love." Isolated, like everyone down there in Patusan, they had only themselves, the solace of their bodies, and fear and despair in the face of death. But they did have themselves. Henry acknowledged that they were good to him, kind and solicitous. And Miss Travers? Conrad had given him her to mock and deride, especially now that right before his eyes he observed Dora and Samuel every day.

Henry ended this truly heart-rending part of his letter with the remark that he lived continually stretched out between the two great, cruel dialogues which Conrad had created for him. These were the dialogue between Brown and Lord Jim, and the dialogue between Lingard and Miss Travers. On the one hand, Patusan, the land of loneliness—on the other, the reefs, the sandy islets, surrounded by the waters which cut men off from the world.

"And I know that no rescue will come my way," he wrote in conclusion.

The second part of his letter began with the words:

"I've got it! I've got it!" This section was a confused, intricate discourse, full of triumphant cries of discovery, about "Heart of Darkness."

Henry had buried himself in the gloomy recesses of something which he called the soul of criminals, hence also the soul of Stein.

"At last"—Henry stressed the words with exclamation marks—"I know why it is that Stein gets drunk, why he comes to me at night, recites Rilke, and pulls out his gun! At last I know whence he derives his vision of the extermination of the Jews, of the extermination of those who are lower than his race! I have discovered the heart of darkness of Stein and the Steins. It was they who produced Bach and Goethe, they who created the science and subtle cognitive tools of man, but this is only appearance! Only appearance!! Kurtz's heart of darkness is within them, tragic and insane! This is why they know dialectics so well, and every contradiction and every abyss of the soul, these people who have been expelled from Paradise, fettered by a mission, brimming over with contempt, sensitive and subtle, sentimental, endowed with the gift of tears."

"I've got Stein!" cried Henry. "I've got him firmly in my grasp!"

And in the same vein he continued writing with passionate satisfaction about the complexities of the soul of Stein and the Steins.

For Henry, Lord Jim, the discovery of knowledge about the Steins had come, seemingly, too late, and it had now become for him a source of inexhaustible grief.

I spent almost the entire night writing to him. I began the letter several times, and kept tearing it up, starting my reply afresh. But no, it was not a "reply," for how could one make an answer to the ravings of a soul thirsting for the "transport of love," or for the discovery of the heart of darkness in the intricacies of the Steins? I wrote a letter about hope. I sent him news from the front and a bit of political news, assuring him that the coming spring would be the last spring of the war. Once again it was an anti-Conradian letter, a letter about hard realities, but, my God, didn't it, too, cling to myths? If only the myth of this spring being the last, because it was unthinkable that things could go on any longer. In those days nobody, unfortunately, thought otherwise.

The morning brought a disappointment to Daniel and me. It was drizzling and spotting with rain; the wind was whistling, and there was a soughing in the trees, not at all like December. Daniel's good spirits departed as soon as he looked out of the window. I recognized the uselessness of discussing my proposal about staying. Once more I postponed the matter till his next visit.

At breakfast Daniel made faces, and spilled the milk; nothing suited him, and he hardly touched his food. He took my letter and, as usual, set off in great haste. Despite his protests, I wound a woolen scarf around his neck against the cold. Off he went. This time he consented to be seen to the tram.

Thus quickly—perhaps too quickly?—we have completed our journey to the end of the lives of Daniel and Henry. I never saw Daniel again, although I waited for him impatiently, almost desperately.

One evening, on returning home, I found a letter stuffed in the door handle. It was from Dora. Henry had died a week ago of typhus. Daniel was also dead, she wrote, and his death had been witnessed by all of them from the window. Daniel died by the hand of Stein. Having returned from leave, Stein had come to see Henry that rainy day when Daniel went back with my letter. On the door of Henry's apartment there hung a notice, terrible to all Steins, saying: "Typhus." Stein retreated in fury; he was drunk already and staggered on the stairs. In the courtyard he encountered Daniel, who, at the sight of Stein, began to run away. Stein chased him and, when he caught him, drew out his revolver and fired. He took the letter, which was protruding from Daniel's pocket; then he unfolded a large sheet of the *Völkische Beobachter*, covered the body with it, and went off, reeling and swearing.

I have said already that when Dora visited me for the first time after the war, I had a lot of work on my desk. I was, in fact, in the process of putting together a piece about those days, and Daniel and Henry had kept recurring in my thoughts. Could I now, after Dora's visit, not bear witness to their lives? I am always with Henry and always with Daniel, who were crushed beneath the wheels of history.

What more can I do for them today? May they, I beg, accept from a Christian a fervent Requiem for them both.

# Glossary

[Only words not in *Webster's Collegiate Dictionary* are italicized; e.g., Hallel is in the dictionary, *challah* (braided Sabbath and holiday bread) is not.]

**1831 November Uprising** a Polish insurrection in Warsaw against the Russian rule.

**"248 limbs of his body"** of the 613 commandments in the Torah, 248 are positive; there is a positive commandment for each of the 248 bones that Aristotle identified in the human body.

**"613 commandments"** the number of divinely ordained laws (*mitzvot*) contained in the Torah (first five books of the Hebrew Bible).

**Adoration** conclusion of the Jewish worship service beginning with "It is our duty to praise the Lord."

*Aktion* code name for the Nazi extermination program. These "actions" began in June 1942 with the incineration of the corpses in the Chelmno death camp, continued through 1942 and 1943 with the burning of bodies in Belzec, Sobibor, Treblinka, and (until the crematoria were in place) Auschwitz, and included liquidating mass graves (e.g., Janowska) in Poland and Russia in 1943 and 1944.

*Al-Het* one of two public, confessional prayers in the Yom Kippur liturgy. It is commonly known by its first two Hebrew words, "For the sin. . ."

*alef-bet* the first two letters of the Hebrew alphabet and short for the entire alphabet.

*Appelplatz* German for place where roll call was held in the concentration camps.

*Arier! kauft nicht beim Juden* (**"Aryans! Don't buy from Jews"**) Nazi slogan initially used during the one-day boycott of Jewish stores on April 1, 1933.

**Aristotle** Greek philosopher, logician, moralist, political thinker, and literary critic who lived from 384–322 BCE.

*Auf Wiedersehen* German for "goodbye."

**Auschwitz (Polish, Oswiecim)** the largest Nazi labor and extermination camp, 37 miles west of Cracow. It included Auschwitz I (the main camp), Auschwitz II or Birkenau (gas chambers, crematoria), and Auschwitz III (labor camp) where roughly 2 million Jews were murdered.

*Ausweis* German for "identification card."

**Baal Shem Tov (Israel ben Eliezer also BeShT)** founder of modern Chassidism, who lived in the eighteenth century in the Carpathian Mountain area of Poland and whose name means Good Possessor of the Divine Name.

**Bach, Johann Sebastian (1685–1750)** German composer and organist who served as cantor and music director of St. Thomas Church in Leipzig from 1723 until his death. His religious compositions, preludes, and fugues have steadily increased in popularity and stature.

*Badeanstalten* German for public baths or swim clubs.

**Balut district of Lodz** slum quarter of Lodz where the Nazis established the ghetto in 1940.

**bar mitzvah ("liable for the commandments")** religious status of a Jewish male beyond the age of thirteen. The attainment of this status is recognized by calling the child to the pulpit for the public reading of passages from Holy Scripture.

*Baruch Atah Adonai* **("Blessed art Thou, Lord")** these Hebrew words occur twice in the Bible and form the standard opening phrase of most blessings.

**bat mitzvah ("liable for the commandments")** religious status of a Jewish woman beyond the age of thirteen (Reform and Conservative) or twelve (Orthodox). The attainment of this status is recognized in some congregations by calling the child to the pulpit for the public reading of passages from Holy Scripture.

**Bayreuth** town in northern Bavaria. Its Jewish population dated to the thirteenth century. Since the nineteenth century the town has been closely associated with the notoriously anti-Semitic composer Richard Wagner.

**Belszyc (Belzec)** small Polish town in the Lublin district on the Lublin-Lvov rail line where the Nazis established an extermination camp in February 1942 to kill the Jews of the Lublin and Cracow districts as well as of eastern Galicia. Between February 1942 and December 1942 the Nazis gassed about 600,000 Jews at Belzec.

**Bialik, Chaim Nachman (1873–1934)** Hebrew poet, essayist, translator, and editor, born in Zhitomir, Russia. His poem "The Slaughter Town," written in Hebrew, vigorously condemns the Jews' meek submission during the 1903 Kishinev pogroms and the lack of justice afterwards.

**Bialystok** industrial city and vital center of Jewish life in northeastern Poland, which was part of Russia between 1807 and 1921 and again occupied by the Soviet Union in 1939. Under German occupation from June 1941 to July 1944, its Jews were herded into a ghetto; most were deported to Treblinka in 1943.

*bitte* German for "please."

**Black Brigade (*Brigate Nere*)** Italian Fascist brigade organized in 1944 to conduct antipartisan operations.

*Blokowe (Blokowa,* **sing.)** female prisoners in charge of a block; block leaders.

*bobe* Yiddish for "grandmother."

**Bolsheviks** name assumed by the radical left-wing of the Russian Social Democratic Labor Party in 1903 under Lenin; the party that gained power in Russia in October 1917.

**Brodno** Nazi concentration camp in Volynia, Ukraine.

**"Broken slivers of glass"** Jewish wedding ceremonies end with the groom shattering a glass, symbolic of the destruction of the temple in Jerusalem.

**Brunswick** town and former duchy in northern Germany where Jews were living as early as the twelfth century.

**Buchenwald** concentration camp in Germany, five miles south of Weimar, established by the Nazis in 1937 to house political prisoners, Poles, "asocial" elements, and Jews.

**Bundist** member of the General Jewish Workers' Union (a Jewish socialist party founded in Russia in 1897) in Lithuania, Poland and Russia.

*challah (challot,* **plur.)** a type of bread mentioned in the Hebrew Bible (2 Samuel 6:19); now a term for special Sabbath and holiday loaves.

**chassid** Hebrew for a pious person; a follower of Chassidism.

**Chassidism** popular Jewish religious movement marked by mysticism, ecstasy, mass enthusiasm, group cohesion, and strict observance; originated in southeastern Poland in the eighteenth century. See Baal Shem Tov.

*cheder* Jewish elementary school. In traditional society Jewish boys went to *cheder* from age five to ten, approximately, to study the Hebrew Bible.

**Chelmno (German, Kulmhof)** first Nazi death camp (December 1941), 37 miles from Lodz on the Ner River. Jews were murdered by carbon monoxide poisoning in sealed trucks.

**"City of Slaughter"** see Chaim Nachman Bialik.

*Code of Jewish Law* **(Hebrew, *Shulchan Aruch*)** authoritative code of Jewish law for Orthodox Jews, composed by Joseph Caro (1564–1565).

**Conrad, Joseph (1857–1924)** Polish-born, English novelist whose many celebrated novels include *Lord Jim* (1900).

*corvée* French for forced labor.

**Council of Elders** select group of men in ancient Israel. Leaders of the Jewish communities in Germany were called *Judenälteste* (Elders of the Jews); the Nazis used that term for the functionaries they put in charge of the ghettos.

**Cracow** city in southern Poland; an important center of Jewish life in the sixteenth and seventeenth centuries. Under the Nazis, the first shootings took place there in 1939. In 1941 a ghetto was established and in 1942 most Cracow Jews were sent to the death camp at Belzec.

*cuadrilla* a matador's team.

**Dachau** first concentration camp, located 10 miles northwest of Munich, opened in March 1933. More than 200,000 prisoners—among them communists, social democrats, Jehovah's Witnesses, Roma and Sinti (gypsies), homosexuals, and Jews—were registered at Dachau in the twelve years (1933–1945) of its existence. The camp also served as a training ground for the SS.

**Days of Awe** ten days of penitence in the Jewish calendar, starting with Rosh Hashanah and ending with Yom Kippur.

**Days of the *Omer*** the forty-nine days between Passover and Shavuoth, marked by counting the *omer* (grain) each day.

*Donnerwetter* German expletive, which roughly translates to "Oh, damn!"

**Dresden** capital of Saxony, Germany. The Jewish community went back six hundred years when the Nazis deported most of its Jews to Theresienstadt in 1942. It was heavily bombed by the Allies during World War II.

*Effeketenkammer* German term for warehouse in the death camps where confiscated goods were stored; also known as Kanada.

**Elders of the Jews** see Council of Elders.

**Ellis Island** island in Upper New York Bay between New Jersey and New York and chief entry station for immigrants to the United States between 1892 and 1943.

*entre deux guerres* French for "between two wars," meaning world wars I and II.

**Fascist Social Republic** Mussolini's government in northern Italy between September 1943 and April 1945.

**Faust, Johann** sixteenth-century German metaphysician whose life has been the subject of plays and operas; most notable is the drama *Faust* by Goethe.

*fauteuil* French for "easy chair."

*Feldgendarmerie* German for "field police."

**Göring, Hermann (1893–1946)** one of Hitler's earliest followers and founder of the Gestapo (secret police); commanded the German air force during World War II.

**Four Questions** part of the Passover Seder when the youngest child present asks a set of four questions of the leader concerning the meaning of the ritual.

***Führer* of the Lodzer Jews** refers to Mordechai Chaim Rumkowsky, the leader of the Lodz ghetto.

**Galicia** an area of southeastern Poland, formerly part of the Austro-Hungarian Empire; for centuries an area of vibrant Jewish life.

**Gaon of Vilna or Vilner Gaon (Elijah ben Solomon Zalman, 1720–1791)** the most prominent rabbinic scholar in eighteenth-century Poland. Vilna under the Gaon became a center of the Haskalah (Jewish enlightenment) and opposition to Chassidism.

***Gates of Repentance*** title of a work by Jonah ben Abraham Gerondi (c. 1200–1263), Spanish rabbi and mystic.

**Gemorah (also Gemara)** Amoraic (post–200 CE) rabbinic discussions of the Mishnah which, together with the Mishnah, forms the Talmud.

**Gerondi, Jonah** thirteenth-century Spanish Jewish mystic who wrote *Gates of Repentance.*

**Gestapo** Nazi secret police under Heinrich Himmler and Reinhard Heydrich which rounded up Jews, stole their property, and deported them.

***get*** Jewish divorce decree, written in the presence of witnesses and presented by the husband to the wife.

**Goethe, Johann Wolfgang (1749–1832)** German poet, dramatist, novelist, and scientist whose dramatic poem *Faust* is one of the great works in world literature.

***goyim* (goy, sing.)** Hebrew for "nations"; has come to mean all non-Jews.

***Guten Abend*** German greeting meaning "good evening."

**Hallel** prayers in Jewish liturgy consisting of thanksgiving Psalms 113–118; recited on all biblical festivals except Rosh Hashanah and Yom Kippur.

**"Heil Hitler"** Nazi salute to their leader Adolf Hitler.

**Hercynian period** in geology third phase of mountain building in Europe; origin of the mountains that extend into southern Poland.

***homme de confiance*** French for "right-hand man."

**Horst Wessel Lied** Nazi party song; Horst Wessel was a Nazi thug killed by a communist in a brawl in 1930.

**Ibn Gabirol, Solomon** eleventh-century Spanish Jewish poet (lyric and religious) and philosopher.

**Judah Maccabee** one of the five sons of Mattathias of Modin, who led the guerilla war against the Syrian Greeks upon his father's death (165 BCE), occupied Jerusalem, and rededicated (Chanukkah) the Temple in 165 BCE.

***Judah, verrecke!*** German for "Croak, you Jew!" Usually juxtaposed in Nazi propaganda with slogans such as "Deutschland, erwache!" ("Germany, awake!").

**Judenrat (Judenräte, pl.)** Jewish councils established in Jewish communities of Nazi-occupied Europe, first in Poland (1939) and then throughout Europe. The council received and implemented German orders, including providing labor and quotas for deportation to death camps. Among the most prominent *Judenrat* leaders were Efraim Barash (Bialystok), Mordechai Chaim Rumkovsky (Lodz), and Jacob Gens (Vilna).

*kadesh* **(Hebrew,** *kaddish***)** the mourners' prayer in Jewish liturgy.

**"Keyser" (German, Kaiser) Rumkovsky** refers to Mordechai Chaim Rumkovsky, head of the Jewish council in the Lodz ghetto.

**Kanada** name for storage areas in the death camps.

**Kapos** inmates of labor and concentration camps appointed by the SS as "bosses" or "chiefs" of a Kommando (work gang) unit of prisoners.

**Karaites** Jewish sect which emerged in the eighth century; rejected the oral or rabbinic tradition and adhered exclusively to the Hebrew Bible, especially with regard to calendar, Sabbath observance, and marriage laws.

*Kommando* Nazi usage for work detail in a labor or concentration camp.

**Krakow Jagellonian University** one of the oldest Polish universities.

**Kurtz** protagonist in Joseph Conrad's novel *Heart of Darkness* (1902). Eloquent, hypnotic, and mysterious, he rules over native Africans.

*Lager* German for "camp."

*Leichenkommando* German for work battalion assigned to bury the dead.

**Lemberg (Polish, Lwow)** city in Galicia with the third largest Jewish community in Poland in 1939 (110,000). Lemberg was first annexed by the Soviet Union at the beginning of World War II and occupied by the Germans on June 30, 1941; the killing of Lemberg's Jews began almost immediately.

**Lessing, Gotthold Ephraim (1729–1781)** German dramatist, aestheticist, and leader of the eighteenth-century Englightenment and friend of Moses Mendelssohn.

**Lodz** second largest city of Poland, 80 miles southwest of Warsaw. The Nazis established one of the largest ghettos there. Its Jews were among the first to be deported to the death camps in early 1942.

*Louis Lambert* novel by the nineteenth-century French writer Honoré de Balzac (1832).

*ma'ariv* evening prayers in Jewish liturgy.

*Machzor* Jewish prayer book for the High Holy Days, containing special prayers for these days.

**Maimonides (Moses Ben Maimon, 1135–1205)** Spanish Jewish scholar and physician; his work *Guide for the Perplexed* attempts to harmonize religion and philosophy (1185 or 1190). See also Rambam.

**Mann, Thomas** German novelist (1875–1955) and recipient of the Nobel Prize for literature in 1929; he wrote vigorous denunciations of fascism after leaving Germany in 1933.

**Marlow** Joseph Conrad's mouthpiece in his novel *Lord Jim*.

**Marseillaise** French national anthem.

**Mauthausen** concentration camp near Vienna, created in 1938 after the *Anschluss* (incorporation) of Austria. It housed prisoners from all over Europe (especially Poland) under especially brutal conditions.

*Meister* German for "master."

**Mephistopheles** name of the devil to whom, according to legend, the sixteenth-century German doctor Johann Faust sold his soul in exchange for youth, knowledge, and magic powers.

*mère de famille* French for "mother/housewife."

*meshuggenah* Yiddish for "crazy" or "mad."

*minchah* Jewish afternoon prayers, before sunset.

**Minsk Mazowiecki** town in the Warsaw district in Poland. After setting up a *Judenrat* and a ghetto, the Nazis murdered most of its Jews in August 1942.

**Mishnah** Rabbi Judah's encyclopedia or code of rabbinic law, composed ca. 200 CE; the basic text of the Oral Torah.

**Mizrachi women** the women's branch of the international, religious Zionist organization.

*mussar* Jewish school or movement of religious/ethical practice in Eastern Europe which emphasized rigorous, unremitting self-examination as the means to attaining the highest standards of moral purity and righteousness.

*Mussulman* concentration/labor camp term for an inmate on the verge of death; someone who has lost all will to live.

**National Committee of Liberation** political arm of the Italian resistance movement which operated in northern Italy after Mussolini established the Fascist Social Republic in 1943.

**NCO** noncommissioned officer.

**New Moon (Heb., Rosh Chodesh)** minor Jewish festival at the beginning of each month.

**Nietzsche, Friedrich** German moral philosopher (1844–1900) whose writings (especially *Thus Spake Zarathustra,* 1888–1891 and *Beyond Good and Evil,* 1886) were distorted by the Nazis to support their ideology of racial superiority.

**NKVD agents** People's Commissariat for Internal Affairs, successor (1934) to Cheka, which served as the Soviet state security service, including the secret police.

**Novaredok Yeshiva** *mussar* yeshiva in Belorussia about 70 miles southwest of Minsk. See also *mussar.*

**Nowa Wies** name for more than a hundred cities in Poland.

**Oranienburg** one of the original concentration camps, established near Berlin in 1933; closed in 1935.

**Oswiecim** Polish name for the town of Auschwitz.

*panie* Polish for "lord" or "master"; common courtesy address.

**Partisans Association** a group of irregular forces operating in enemy-occupied territory, primarily in eastern Europe and the Balkans.

**Passion** Gospel narrative of the torture and crucifixion of Jesus Christ.

**Passover** Jewish spring festival of freedom, first celebrated following the exodus of the Israelites from Egypt.

**patois of Languedoc** dialect of the southern region of France.

*pidion ha-ben* **(Heb., redemption of the first-born son)** Jewish ceremony on the thirty-first day of a boy's life to "redeem" him from the priesthood, fulfilling laws contained in Exodus, Deuteronomy, and especially Leviticus 27:1–8.

**Pilsudski, Joseph (1867–1935)** Polish general and politician; proclaimed an independent Poland in 1918 with himself as head of state. He retired in 1922 but returned via a coup in 1926 and established a military dictatorship which kept Polish anti-semites at bay.

*piyyutim* prayer-poems composed in late antiquity or in the Middle Ages as an addition to or commentary on the liturgy.

**Potiphar's wife** character in the book of Genesis who tried to seduce Joseph.

*pro temporum calamitatibus* Latin "for the misfortunes of the time."

**Rabbi Nachman of Bratslav** Chassidic leader (1772–1811) in Podolia and the Ukraine.

**Rambam** acronym for Rabbi Moses ben Maimon. See Maimonides.

*Raus!* German for "get out!"

**Ravensbrück** concentration camp for women, located 56 miles north of Berlin. Opened in 1939, it had 11,000 prisoners at the end of 1942 and 26,700 in 1944.

**Reb** Yiddish address before a name of a male, equivalent of "Mister."

**Red Army** Army of the Soviet Union established during the Bolshevik Revolution of 1917. The Nazis captured about 5.7 million Red Army soldiers during World War II and murdered more than 3,000,000.

**Requiem** Catholic mass for the souls of the dead, performed on All Souls Day, at funerals, and on request. Requiem music has a traditional Gregorian setting.

**resettlement** Nazi euphemism for deportation of Jews to death camps.

**Rilke, Rainer Maria (1875–1926)** renowned German lyrical poet.

*Rollkommando* German for roving mobile firing squads that carried out murder sweeps against Jews in eastern Europe.

**Rosh Hashanah** Jewish New Year, inaugurates the most sacred period of the Jewish year.

**Rumkowsky, "King of the Ghetto" Mordechai Chaim (1877–1944)** leader of the *Judenrat* in Lodz from October 1939 until the liquidation of the ghetto in August 1944. He has been portrayed by some as a traitor and collaborator, and by others as a savior enabling five to seven thousand Jews to survive the Lodz ghetto deportations.

**Rumpelstiltskin** passionate deformed dwarf; figure in German folklore.

**Ruthenians** Slavic population settled primarily in the Carpathian mountains.

**Samaritans** a Jewish sect that recognizes only the first five books of the Hebrew Bible.

**Sandburg, Carl (1878–1967)** Pulitzer Prize–winning American poet and biographer of Abraham Lincoln.

**Schiller, Friedrich (1759–1805)** German lyrical poet, translator, historian, and essayist.

**Shavuot (Weeks)** Jewish festival which occurs seven weeks after the beginning of Passover. Originally, Shavuot was a celebration of the harvesting of the first fruits; after the destruction of the Temple, tradition added to it the commemoration of the giving of the Law on Mount Sinai.

*Shevet Yehudah* summary of the persecutions of the Jews from the destruction of the Second Temple by the Romans (70 CE) to the fifteenth century, compiled by the Spanish Jewish historiographer Samuel ibn Verga in 1554.

*shive (shivah)* the seven-day period of mourning following a Jewish burial.

**Sholom aleichem!** Hebrew and Yiddish greeting.

*shul* Yiddish for "synagogue."

**Silesia**  region of east central Europe, located partly in Germany and partly in Poland (all Polish since 1945); Upper Silesia has extensive coal and lignite deposits. Germany annexed most of Polish Silesia in 1939.

**Sivan**  third month in the Jewish calendar year. It is thirty days long and begins no earlier than May and ends no later than July.

**SS man**  member of the Nazi elite guard (*Schutzstaffel*).

**Stanislawow**  name for more than ten Polish towns.

**Star of David**  a Jewish symbol in the shape of a six-pointed star. Beginning September 19, 1941, the Nazis forced the Jews in Germany and occupied Europe to wear a yellow patch of this star, in public at all times.

**Succos/*Sukkot***  Jewish Feast of Tabernacles, festival of eight days commencing five days after Yom Kippur. Sukkot originated as a harvest festival, but later came to serve as a commemoration of the Israelites' wandering in the desert, when, according to tradition, they lived in booths, or sukkot.

*Sztubowe*  "room elders" or "room overseers," assistants to the *blokowa*, whose job it was to maintain order among the prisoners in labor/concentration camps.

*t'fillin*  phylacteries containing words of Holy Scripture which are tied onto the arm and forehead with leather tongs during the recitation of the morning prayers.

**tallith**  prayer shawl worn by adult males (in Orthodox congregations often after marriage), pulled over the head during the more important sections of the service.

**tarantass**  four-wheel, jeeplike vehicle.

**Temple Mount**  area above the Western Wall in the Old City of Jerusalem, site where the Second Temple of the Jews once stood; now site of two mosques.

***The Path of the Upright***  influential work in ethics by the mystic, poet and ethicist Moses Chaim Luzzato, an Italian Jew (1707–1746).

**Tisha b'Av**  Ninth of Av (Hebrew month around July–August); the anniversary of the destruction of both the First and Second temples, a day of fasting and deep mourning. The Book of Lamentations (traditionally ascribed to Jeremiah) is given a special reading on this day.

**Treblinka**  Nazi death camp in the northeastern part of the Polish General Government (near Malkinia) on the rail line from Warsaw to Bialystok. Opened in July 1942 to hasten the killing of Jews from Warsaw, Radom, Lublin, and Bialystok; nearly 900,000 Jews were gassed from July 1942 to July 1943.

**Tuscan-Emilian Apennines**  part of the Apennines, a mountain range in Italy running the length of the peninsula. Mussolini proposed reforesting the Tuscan-Emilian Apennines to make the climate more severe in the hope that it would kill off the weaklings and make the race more robust.

**tzaddik** Hebrew for a "holy man," a "saintly person." Chassidim regard their rebbe as a *tzaddik* and believe in the sublime power of his will and the blessings he bestows upon them.

**vigneron** French for "winegrower."

**Vilna** capital of Lithuania, under Polish rule from 1920–1939, incorporated into the Soviet Union in July 1940, and occupied by the Germans on June 24, 1941. The Nazis murdered thousands of Vilna Jews at Ponary on the outskirts of the city.

**Völkischer Beobachter** Nazi newspaper, infamous for its virulent anti-Semitism.

**volksdeutsch** refers to ethnic Germans living in eastern Europe, especially Poland and Ukraine. Hundreds of thousands joined the Waffen-SS when the Germans invaded.

**wadi** a dry river bed.

**War of Independence** Israel's defensive war against five invading Arab armies after the United Nations voted for partition of Palestine and the State of Israel was declared in 1948.

**Warsaw** capital of Poland and chief city of the Warsaw district, located on the Vistula (Wisla) River.

**Warsaw Ghetto** restricted area in Warsaw established in 1940 by the Nazis where Jews lived in abject conditions. In April 1943 the Jews of the Warsaw ghetto revolted against the Nazis. The uprising was crushed only after three weeks of bitter fighting.

**Wolliner Synagogue** synagogue in the northwestern Polish town of Wolin.

**Y.K./Yom Kippur** the Day of Atonement, ten days after Rosh Hashanah; the holiest day in the Jewish calendar.

**Yudenrat** see *Judenrat*.

# Further Reading

For further readings on almost any Holocaust topic, the editors recommend David M. Szonyi, *The Holocaust: An Annotated Bibliography and Resource Guide* (Hoboken, N. J.: Ktav, 1985); Abraham J. and Hershel Edelheit, editors, *Bibliography on Holocaust Literature* (Boulder, Col.: Westview Press, 1986); Idem., *Bibliography on Holocaust Literature: Supplement* (Boulder, Col.: Westview Press, 1990); Idem., *Bibliography on Holocaust Literature; Supplement, Volume 2* (Boulder, Col.: Westview Press, 1993).

## ◆ General Histories, Criticism

Abramson, Glenda. *The Writing of Yehuda Amichai: A Thematic Approach*. Albany: State University of New York Press, 1989.

Adelson, Alan and Robert Lapides. *Lodz Ghetto: Inside a Community Under Siege*. New York: Viking, 1989.

Améry, Jean. *At the Mind's Limit: Contemplations by a Survivor on Auschwitz and Its Realities*. Bloomington: Indiana University Press, 1980.

Appelfeld, Aharon. "Buried Homeland," *New Yorker* (November 23, 1998): 48–61.

Band, Arnold J. *Nostalgia and Nightmare: A Study in the Fiction of S. Y. Agnon*. Berkeley: University of California Press, 1968.

Bartov, Omer. *Murder in Our Midst: The Holocaust, Industrial Killing, and Representation*. New York: Oxford University Press, 1996.

Berger, Alan L., ed. *Judaism in the Modern World*. New York: New York University Press, 1994.

Bryks, Rachmil. "How to Write Churban Literature." In *Hebrew Literature in the Wake of the Holocaust*. Leon I. Yudkin, ed. Rutherford, N. J.: Fairleigh Dickinson University Press, 1993.

*Dimensions*, Volumes 1– (1985 to current).

Dobroszycki, Lucjan, ed. *The Chronicle of the Lodz Ghetto, 1941–1944*. New Haven, Conn.: Yale University Press, 1984.

Ezrahi, Sidra DeKoven. *By Words Alone: The Holocaust in Literature*. Chicago: University of Chicago Press, 1980.

Friedlander, Henry. *The Origins of Nazi Genocide: From Euthanasia to the Final Solution*. Chapel Hill: University of North Carolina Press, 1995.

Friedländer, Saul, ed. *Memory, History and the Extermination of the Jews of Europe*. Bloomington: Indiana University Press, 1993.

————, ed. *Probing the Limits of Representation: Nazism and the "Final Solution."* Cambridge, Mass.: Harvard University Press, 1992.

Fuchs, Esther. *Encounters with Israeli Authors.* Marblehead, Mass.: Micah Publications, 1982.

Hartman, Geoffrey, ed. *Holocaust Remembrance: The Shapes of Memory.* Cambridge, Mass.: Blackwell, 1994.

Hayes, Peter, ed. *Lessons and Legacies: The Meaning of the Holocaust in a Changing World.* Evanston, Ill.: Northwestern University Press, 1991.

*Holocaust and Genocide Studies,* volumes 1– (1986– to current).

*Holocaust Studies Annual,* volumes 1–3 (1983–85).

Horowitz, Sara R. *Voicing the Void: Muteness and Memory in Holocaust Fiction.* Albany: State University of New York Press, 1997.

Kahn, Yitzhak. *Portraits of Yiddish Writers.* New York: Vantage Press, 1979.

Lang, Berel, ed. *Writing After the Holocaust.* New York: Holmes & Meier, 1988.

Langer, Lawrence L. *Admitting the Holocaust: Collected Essays.* New York: Oxford University Press, 1995.

————. *Art From the Ashes: A Holocaust Anthology.* New York: Oxford University Press, 1995.

————. *The Holocaust and the Literary Imagination.* New Haven, Conn.: Yale University Press, 1975.

————. *Holocaust Testimonies: The Ruins of Memory.* New Haven, Conn.: Yale University Press, 1991.

Patterson, David and Glenda Abramson, eds. *Tradition and Trauma: Studies in the Fiction of S. Y. Agnon.* Boulder, Col.: Westview Press, 1994.

Ramras-Rauch, Gilah. *Aharon Appelfeld: The Holocaust and Beyond.* Bloomington: Indiana University Press, 1994.

Rosenfeld, Alvin H. *A Double Dying: Reflections on Holocaust Literature.* Bloomington: Indiana University Press, 1980.

————. *Thinking About the Holocaust: After Half a Century.* Bloomington: Indiana University Press, 1997.

———— and Irving Greenberg, eds. *Confronting the Holocaust: The Impact of Elie Wiesel.* Bloomington: Indiana University Press, 1978.

Schneider, Marilyn. *Vengeance of the Victims: History and Symbol in Giorgio Bassani's Fiction.* Minneapolis: University of Minnesota Press, 1986.

Schulman, Elias. *The Holocaust in Yiddish Literature.* New York: Education Department of the Workmen's Circle, 1983.

Siegel, Ben. *The Controversial Sholem Asch: An Introduction to His Fiction.* Bowling Green, Ohio: Bowling Green University Press, 1976.

*Simon Wiesenthal Center Annual,* volumes 1–6 (1984–1989).

Tushnet, Leonard. *To Die With Honor: The Uprising of the Jews in the Warsaw Ghetto.* New York: Citadel Press, 1965.

White, Hayden V. "The Fictions of Factual Representation." In Idem., *Tropics of Discourse: Essays in Cultural Criticism.* Baltimore, Md.: Johns Hopkins University Press, 1978, 121–134.

*Yad Vashem Studies,* volumes I–XX (1957–1990).

Young, James E. *The Texture of Memory: Holocaust Memorials and Meaning.* New Haven, Conn.: Yale University Press, 1993.

————. *Writing and Rewriting the Holocaust: Narrative and the Consequences of Interpretation.* Bloomington: Indiana University Press, 1988.


◆ *Fiction and Poetry*

Agnon, Samuel. "The Sign." In *Response* 7,19 (fall 1973): 378–409.

Appelfeld, Aharon. *Badenheim 1939.* Boston: David R. Godine, 1980.

Bryks, Rachmil. *A Cat in the Ghetto: Four Novelettes.* New York: Bloch Publishing Company, 1959.

————. *Kiddush ha-Shem.* New York: Behrman House, 1977.

Bukiet, Melvin Judes. *After.* New York: St. Martin's Press, 1996.

————. *Stories of an Imaginary Childhood.* Evanston, Ill.: Northwestern University Press, 1992.

————. *While the Messiah Tarries.* New York: Harcourt Brace and Company, 1995.

Fink, Ida. *The Journey.* New York: Farrar Straus and Giroux, 1992.

————. *A Scrap of Time and Other Stories.* New York: Pantheon Books, 1987.

Gascar, Pierre. *Beasts and Men and The Seed.* New York: Meridian Books, 1960.

————. *The Fugitive.* Boston: Little, Brown, 1964.

Grossinger, Harvey. *The Quarry: Stories.* Athens: University of Georgia Press, 1997.

Grynberg, Henryk. *Child of the Shadows.* London: Vallentine, Mitchell, 1969.

Korn, Rachel H. *Generations: Selected Poems.* Oakville, Ontario, Canada: Mosaic Press, 1982.

Lustig, Arnošt. *Children of the Holocaust.* Evanston, Ill.: Northwestern University Press, 1995.

————. *A Prayer for Katerina Horovitzova.* Woodstock, New York: Overlook Press, 1985.

Nomberg-Przytyk, Sara. *Auschwitz: True Tales From a Grotesque Land.* Eli Pfefferkorn and David H. Hirsch, eds. Chapel Hill: University of North Carolina Press, 1985.

Ozick, Cynthia. *The Shawl.* New York: Knopf, 1989, 1983.

Ramras-Rauch, Gila and Joseph Michman-Melkman, eds. *Facing the Holocaust: Selected Israeli Fiction.* Philadelphia: Jewish Publication Society, 1985.

Richter, Hans Peter. *Friedrich.* New York: Puffin Books, 1987, 1970.

————. *I Was There.* New York: Holt, Rinehart and Winston, 1972.

Rosenbaum, Thane. *Elijah Visible: Stories.* New York: St. Martin's Press, 1996.

Rosenfeld, Morris, ed. *Pushcarts and Dreamers: Stories of Jewish Life in America.* Philadelphia: Sholom Aleichem Club Press, 1967.

Schiff, Hilda, ed. *Holocaust Poetry.* London: Fount, 1995.

Szeintuch, Yehiel, ed. *Isaiah Spiegel—Yiddish Narrative Prose from the Lodz Ghetto.* Jerusalem: Magnes Press, 1995 (Yiddish).

Thomas, D. M. *The White Hotel.* New York: Viking Press, 1981.

# Copyrights and Permissions

## About the Editors

**LINDA SCHERMER RAPHAEL** teaches literature at George Washington University in Washington, D. C. She received her Ph.D. degree in literature from Ohio State University. Her writings have focused on nineteenth- and twentieth-century literature, narrative theory, and moral skepticism in fiction.

**MARC LEE RAPHAEL** is Nathan and Sophia Gumenick Professor of Judaic Studies and Professor of Religion at The College of William and Mary in Williamsburg, Virginia. He received his Ph.D. degree in history from the University of California, Los Angeles. He has served as cochair of the Teaching Training Committee of the Ohio Council on Holocaust Education and has taught university courses on the subject since 1976.